A Good Hard Look

Also by Ann Napolitano

Within Arm's Reach

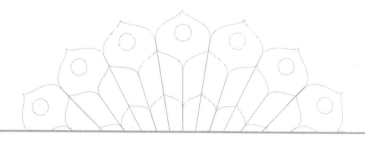

A Good Hard Look

· · ·

Ann Napolitano

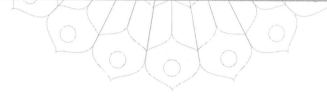

The Penguin Press

New York

2011

THE PENGUIN PRESS
Published by the Penguin Group
Penguin Group (USA) Inc., 375 Hudson Street, New York, New York 10014, U.S.A •
Penguin Group (Canada), 90 Eglinton Avenue East, Suite 700, Toronto, Ontario, Canada M4P2Y3
(a division of Pearson Penguin Canada Inc.) • Penguin Books Ltd, 80 Strand, London WC2R 0RL,
England • Penguin Ireland, 25 St Stephen's Green, Dublin 2, Ireland (a division of Penguin Books
Ltd) • Penguin Books Australia Ltd, 250 Camberwell Road, Camberwell, Victoria 3124, Australia
(a division of Pearson Australia Group Pty Ltd) • Penguin Books India Pvt Ltd, 11 Community Centre,
Panchsheel Park, New Delhi - 110 017, India • Penguin Group (NZ), 67 Apollo Drive, Rosedale,
Auckland 0632, New Zealand (a division of Pearson New Zealand Ltd) • Penguin Books
(South Africa) (Pty) Ltd, 24 Sturdee Avenue, Rosebank, Johannesburg 2196, South Africa

Penguin Books Ltd, Registered Offices: 80 Strand, London WC2R 0RL, England

First published in 2011 by The Penguin Press, a member of Penguin Group (USA) Inc.

Excerpt from *The Habit of Being*: *The Letters of Flannery O'Connor*, edited by Sally
Fitzgerald, Farrar, Straus & Giroux, 1979.

Publisher's Note
This is a work of fiction. Apart from the well-known actual people, events, and locales that
figure in the narrative, all names, characters, places, and incidents either are the products of
the author's imagination or are used fictitiously. Any resemblance to current events or locales,
or to living persons, is entirely coincidental.

Library of Congress Cataloging-in-Publication Data

Napolitano, Ann.
A good hard look : a novel/Ann Napolitano.
p. cm.
ISBN 978-1-59420-292-6
1. O'Connor, Flannery—Fiction.   2. Women authors—Fiction.   3. Milledgeville (Ga.)—Fiction.
I. Title.
PS3614.A66G66 2011   2010051241
813'.6—dc22

Printed in the United States of America
10 9 8 7 6 5 4 3 2 1

Designed by Susan Walsh

To

HELEN ELLIS AND HANNAH TINTI,

for everything

The truth does not change according to our ability to stomach it.

—Flannery O'Connor

Good

The peacocks tilted their heads back and bellowed and hollered their desires into the night. They snapped their shimmering tails open and shut like fans. Behind each male's pointy head, a green-bronze arch unfurled, covered with a halo of gazing suns. The females brayed and shook their less-attractive tails in return.

The birds didn't care that it was the middle of the night, and they didn't care who they were disturbing. They didn't care that there was a wedding tomorrow, or that the groom, who had just arrived from New York City, was lying beneath a lace canopy at his in-laws' house, paralyzed with fear. They didn't care that his fiancée startled awake in the next room and toppled out of her high bed, and they certainly didn't care that her face hit a stool on the way down. They didn't care that the rest of the small Georgia town was also awake, twitching in their beds like beached fish.

The peacocks were not out to make friends. They were out to do what they liked, when they liked. They chose this particular time on this particular night for the same reason they chose to eat the flowers in the side garden the moment they bloomed. They preferred roses and hyacinths, but deigned to eat tulips as well. They had claimed every inch of the farm, which meant the wide expanse of lawn in front of the farmhouse shimmered under a layer of white refuse.

The peacocks chased the peahens across the crunchy grass, short legs thrusting, three-pronged feet grabbing at the dirt. The females stole glances over their shoulders. Fans were unfolded and then gathered back close. White, yellow, and green eyes stared out from the feathers, ogling the darkness.

The males covered the ground with improbable speed. They trampled grass and hay and hopped onto the white fence that lined the property. The wooden beams objected, leaning beneath the sudden weight. The birds puffed out their chests. They opened their beaks and screamed. They sustained the noise until a lone flower fell from the magnolia tree. The petals drifted, reluctant and aromatic, to the ground.

In the center of town, Melvin and Cookie huddled together on the floor of her room. They spoke in rushed whispers designed to fit between the bouts of noise.

"I hit my eye," she said. "I hit it hard."

Cookie's window was open. Enough moonlight coated the scene for Melvin to see that her right eye had already puffed up; it looked like a knuckled fist ready to throw a punch. A dark pink stain spread across the skin.

"How bad is it?" she asked.

"It's fine. It's nothing."

"I can feel it throbbing. Oh my God, I'll look terrible tomorrow."

"You'll look beautiful. You always do," Melvin said. He meant this. He had met her on a park bench in the city several months earlier, and since that moment had never seen her look anything less than perfect. He almost didn't believe that the bruise existed, even as he watched it grow and deepen.

Cookie didn't hear him. Something occurred to her, and she gazed at him with fresh panic. "Is it after midnight?"

Melvin looked down at his bare wrist. His watch was back in the guest room, lying on the night table. "I think so. It must be."

"You're not supposed to see me until the altar. This is bad luck!"

He wanted to reply, but the noise was unrelenting. It plowed through the walls. It crowded the room.

Cookie sobbed and cupped a hand over her eye. She reached out for Melvin with the other. She was glad she wasn't alone in this dark room, which had become, after an absence of almost three years, strangely unfamiliar. She hoped that returning home had been the right decision. She hoped that asking Melvin to move here had been the right decision. Cookie had never fallen out of bed in her life. Her eye pulsed against her palm. She thought about her wedding dress and she thought about tomorrow, which was also, apparently, today.

The warm air was thick with the smell of magnolia blossoms. Cookie shuddered. A single scream, louder than the others, shot like a firecracker into the sky.

Her body unlatched, like a young girl's diary sprung open by a pin. She leaned closer to Melvin and laid her head against his chest.

He could feel her heart racing beneath her thin nightgown. He couldn't hear anything above the screams. Melvin tried, in vain, to organize his thoughts. Cookie had said that peacocks were making this noise. He believed her, but at the same time he couldn't. This noise—this incredible din—could surely not be made by beaked, feathered *birds*. The entire town must be awake around them; only the deaf or the extremely drunk could sleep through this cacophony, and if that was the case, how could it be allowed to carry on? *Someone needs to shut this down*, he thought. *Where are the police? The peacock wranglers? Who's in charge here?*

Cookie's breath hit Melvin's bare chest in quick, warm puffs. She tilted her head back. She looked like she had something to say.

The cries perforated the air. The ruthless sound fragmented the darkness and splintered Cookie and Melvin's thoughts. They lost coherence, and articulacy. They wished they could escape. They wished they knew what to do. They not only wanted the screams to stop, they wanted to *make* them stop. A force was pushing against them, and their instinct was to push back.

Melvin looked at Cookie and her radiating eye.

"Please," she said.

He knitted his fingers through her hair and kissed her so hard they both slid a few inches across the floor.

When he pulled away, she tugged him closer.

"You should go back to your room," she said.

Another lock was picked, this time within Melvin, and he pushed her white nightgown up her thighs. His breath was thick in his throat. He inhaled flowers and Cookie's skin and the dirt from a farm he had never laid eyes on. The birds seemed to be screaming at him now. They were taunting him, goading him, trying to pick a fight. *Come on*, they yelled. *Do it! What are you made of?*

Melvin's hands swept up and down Cookie's back. He wanted to leave himself and crawl into her. He wanted to block the screams out. He wanted to hurt Cookie with kisses. He felt dizzy, and somehow, somewhere, wounded. He pulled on Cookie, and she pulled back. They scrambled against each other. It seemed conceivable to both of them, in the darkness, that this noise, and this night, might never end.

"My parents," she whispered.

"They won't hear. No one can hear anything."

Cookie's fingertip traced a figure eight against his shoulder. "It is technically our wedding day," she said, as much to herself as anyone.

The skin around her right eye tinted purple, on its way to every color in the rainbow. Melvin tugged her nightgown over her head. She didn't know where to put her hands. The man and the woman, intertwined, shimmied to their feet and fell onto the bed.

"Why won't they just be quiet?" Cookie said, and was surprised by how loud and unattractive her voice sounded.

This had not been her plan, and she was a young woman who lived by plans. If she did this—no, as she did this, because it was happening, his lips were pressing her bruise and she was crying out in a confused medley of pain and pleasure—who would that make her be?

Any evidence of her distress was lost on Melvin. He felt dwarfed, in yet another canopied bed, by the size of his own expectations. There was a grit of shame caught beneath his fingernails as he gripped Cookie's soft, white thigh. He knew he would not sleep again that night; he wouldn't even try. Melvin batted his fiancée around the bed as if she were a firefly he was trying to catch in a bottle, while the birds roared in the distance.

The wedding guests, strung like beads across the church pews, pinned their gazes on Melvin. He reeled slightly on the altar, his own vision bleary with exhaustion. Cookie had prepared him for the attention. *This town is small*, she had said. *Our wedding is the most exciting thing to happen here in years.*

Melvin listened carefully whenever Cookie spoke about Milledgeville. He was curious about her commitment to this place. From the moment they'd met, she had the look of a woman on her way out of town. Every dinner and every date in the city had a ring of finality. It was clear that Cookie was going to leave New York, and it became clear that she hoped Melvin would come with her. She had been relieved, and moved, when he said he would. But when he asked why she wanted to return home so badly, she had steered the conversation to wedding planning.

Melvin understood feeling an allegiance to a particular place; he had rarely left home until now. But he was from New York City. Loyalty to that metropolis made inherent sense to him. People moved *to* the city from all over the world. No matter what a person was looking for—art, business, culture—New York undoubtedly had the best to offer. It had seemed perfectly natural for Melvin to attend college there, and then to return to his parents' large town house. He had worked at his father's bank during school vacations, and after graduation he accepted a full-time position. It was an international bank, founded by his father thirty years earlier. As with the city, it seemed ridiculous to go anywhere else.

Milledgeville, however, was a quiet, decorous place. It had no dominant industry, and hosted a miniature economy. It didn't have a cinema or theater, and the local library was modest in size. It was difficult for Melvin to see how this place stood apart from anywhere else, and therefore his fiancée's hunger to return intrigued him. He knew it would take time to discover the reason, but he didn't mind the wait. He had nothing but time, and nothing was more important than Cookie.

He knew that she wasn't one to explain things. In fact, Cookie was a camera flash, a series of bright lights: bright love when she looked into Melvin's eyes, jealousy when she saw another woman look at him, concentration during her morning crossword puzzle, pleasure while in his arms. She flashed on and off, always alive, always conquering the moment. In the Himmel living room the previous evening, Melvin had watched Cookie's eyes shine as if with fever while she flew around the small space, talking to, and charming, everyone in sight.

The music flared, and the rhythm shifted. People straightened in the pews, and handkerchiefs came out in preparation. The bride appeared at the top of the aisle on her father's arm, dressed in a cloud of white. The crowd gave a stricken gasp, which exhaled into a sea of murmurs.

Cookie was wearing a beautiful dress, her blond hair curled perfectly over her shoulders, and her bouquet of lilies was exquisite. But all anyone could see, and all anyone would remember, was her eye. It was awash with color, despite the formidable coating of concealer her aunts and mother had applied. There was an inch of blue below her eyebrow, then a streak of bright rose. Her thick eyelid was yellowy green, and a swathe of deep purple sat on her cheekbone. The swollen area beat occasionally, like a heart. Several men swiveled their heads to look at Melvin and then back at her, tracing possible explanations in the air.

Melvin took Cookie's hand when she reached him. Her fingers skittered across his palm. "They think *you* did this," she whispered.

"It's okay."

"Those awful birds."

They shared a look, and Melvin knew Cookie was thinking about the night before. She was thinking about how everything had turned on its head. They had consummated their love on the wrong side of this event. This was not how she had planned to feel, and certainly not how she'd planned to look, on her wedding day.

The minister's words sounded so familiar—*to have and to hold, in sickness and in health, in poverty as in wealth*—that Melvin couldn't shake the feeling that this was a rehearsal. *Focus*, he told himself. *This is the real thing and it's going by.*

Cookie's closed eye pulsed gently, and she became his wife.

The moment Melvin exited the church, his mother-in-law, Daisy, commenced an endless stream of introductions. He turned his head obediently, looking from one face to the other. He wondered if everyone was as tired as he was. Cookie had sent him back to his room at dawn, where he had sat in a semi-stupor on the side of the bed until it was time to get dressed. There had been no rest, no chance to seal off yesterday and prepare himself for today. The door between the two days yawned open, combining Melvin's delayed flight from New York with the tight grip of strangers' handshakes with his wedding vows. In between, incredibly, peacocks had screamed.

Cookie reached for her mother's hand. "Mama," she said, "you promised she wouldn't be here."

"Who?" Melvin asked.

"I saw her staring at my eye in church."

"Now, sweetheart," Daisy said. She put her arm around her daughter's shoulders and led her away, talking softly.

Melvin looked after them, but only for a second, because the departure of Daisy ignited the wedding guests. Women descended in a herd, midway through greetings by the time they reached him. He leaned sleepily into the warmth of middle-aged perfume. The men seemed more aggressive and less coordinated than their wives. They hovered behind the women, then lurched forward. They slapped Melvin hard on the back. He quickly finished his drink and gestured for another.

"I was so sorry to hear about your parents," one woman said, with a smile. She was impressively large, easily the width of two people. She wore a blue, capacious dress. "Must be difficult to celebrate such an important moment with a bunch of strangers."

Melvin returned her smile. He had the odd sense that this woman, who was somehow familiar, knew all about him.

"I always say, though, that a roomful of strangers is a roomful of friends I haven't made yet. Isn't that a nice way of looking at it?"

"It is," he said, and it was.

"I'm Mary Treadle," she said, offering her hand. "But everyone around here calls me Miss Mary."

Melvin wrapped his hand around hers. He felt jet-lagged, even though New York and Georgia were in the same time zone. He glanced around the lawn. The men here wore suits that belonged to a different decade. His own lapel was thinner, and his pant leg shorter. They had put on generous amounts of aftershave to mark the occasion, and Melvin wore none. They looked at him through narrowed eyes. He hadn't set out to make a new friend in a long time. It seemed a dubious prospect.

When Miss Mary turned away, Melvin headed in the opposite direction. He walked with a sense of purpose, to keep people from following. He rounded the back of the church and came to a stop. He stood in the cool shade of the building, and breathed in the blurred quiet. He noticed that the sun was beginning to drop over the graveyard across the street, highlighting and then shading the names of the deceased.

The sun poured yellow syrup over the grass and stone slabs. In New

York, the light was thinner, more brothlike. Melvin sighed and rubbed a hand over his eyes. He let himself consider his mother, and how happy she would have been to attend this occasion. He shook the thought away; it was a remnant from a different life. He was a married man now. He and Cookie would eat dinner together every night. They would raise children. They would take each day as it came. Melvin would find a job that was not a birthright, but simply a job, and he would live a quiet, normal existence.

A new smell laced the air. Earthy and dense, the scent reminded him of his college days. It took a moment for him to place it. Melvin glanced around, but didn't see anyone. He took a few steps forward, then looked again. A pale woman with dark hair was sitting on the back steps of the church. He had seen her by the buffet table earlier, accompanied by a stocky policeman. She held a joint to her lips. She inhaled, then released a gray fog. She didn't appear surprised to see the groom standing on his own.

She nodded.

Melvin nodded in return.

He opened his mouth to say hello, then stopped himself. His usual manners weren't necessary. This stranger had no desire to be bothered, and she had no desire to bother him. The moment stretched, and Melvin turned away, toward the sun-dappled graveyard.

He closed his eyes, hoping for rest. But his mind was in motion, picking up threads of past conversations, memories, and intentions and then weaving them into a complex tapestry that hurt his head. He had been convincing Cookie for weeks that he was happy to move here, and he had been telling the truth. But the noise and the unexpectedness of the night before had shaken him. Could a person just pick up and create a new life? Was that a reasonable expectation?

The green grass, left untrimmed at the back of the building, swallowed Melvin's shoes. *You have responsibilities*, he reminded himself, and walked back toward the party. He sought out Cookie, who was surrounded by a group of well-wishers. She looked proud and happy. "You're my wife," he said, into her ear.

"You're my husband," she whispered back.

Guests separated them, gushing about the food and the ceremony.

Melvin thought about how it might be later that night, when he and Cookie were alone in a hotel room, and found that he couldn't imagine touching her without the accompaniment of the peacocks' screams. He and his wife hadn't mentioned what they'd done since he'd crept back to his room at daybreak, and he wondered if they ever would, or if it was the kind of moment that would be silently filed away in a drawer with other disconcerting odds and ends.

Miss Mary said, "Does your eye hurt, darling?"

Melvin watched the large woman consume his bride with a bear hug.

"No," Cookie said, extracting herself. "It's fine. I fell out of bed last night, it was so silly of me."

Miss Mary made a clucking noise with her tongue. "Of course you did, those damn birds threw us all out of whack. Mr. Treadle and I barely slept a wink. Don't worry, I told everyone that your gorgeous new husband had nothing to do with it."

Melvin's chest tightened. He hoped they might mention the birds again. He wanted to hear *how* the noise had thrown Miss Mary out of whack.

He was distracted, though, by a sudden change in the crowd. The group's ebb and flow gathered strength. Men and women near him were bunched up, like water congested near the mouth of a hose. They looked like they were about to explode in different directions.

"Here she comes," he thought he heard Cookie say, under her breath.

There was a final surge of neat haircuts and pastel hats, and the crowd peeled apart like banana skin. Two women walked through the cleared space. The older one, silver-haired with her hat at a jaunty angle, came first. A younger woman on crutches followed.

Loud whispers erupted, a river of words Melvin couldn't separate.

"Child," the older woman said, "you threw a lovely wedding. We've had a grand time."

Cookie offered a tight smile. "I'm so glad you could come, Regina. Have you had a chance to meet my husband?"

They stood in the middle of the lawn: Melvin, Cookie, and what appeared, on closer inspection, to be a mother and daughter. A circle of space surrounded them. On the fringes, people were clearly staring. Their attention seemed to be split between Melvin and the woman on crutches.

"I certainly have." Regina appeared about to continue, but her daughter interrupted her.

"I haven't. Perhaps you can do me the honor?"

Cookie gave a short nod. "Melvin," she said, "this is Flannery O'Connor. She would no doubt like me to introduce her as our town's most famous citizen."

Flannery was already smiling; her smile grew wider. She seemed pleased by this comment. "Cookie means infamous, I think."

Melvin looked from one woman to the other. Having given up his own history, it was jarring to trip over someone else's. Was this woman actually famous? "Pleased to meet you."

Flannery had curly hair and wore cat's-eye glasses. It occurred to Melvin that she looked more comfortable on crutches than most people did on two legs. She turned her attention back to Cookie. "You were a *stunning* bride, as expected. Congratulations."

Cookie's hand floated upward to cover her swollen eye, then stopped. The hand returned to her side.

"Melvin, you've got yourself one of our best specimens," Flannery said. "I'd tell you to take good care of her, but I'm well aware that Cookie can take care of herself."

"You're absolutely right," he said. "In fact, I'm counting on her to take care of me."

This made everyone laugh, except his wife. She gave a small tug on his arm. "If you don't mind, Regina, we have to make the rounds. You understand how it is."

"Of course."

"Just one thing, before you go," Flannery said. "I've been thinking about the perfect gift for you."

There was a pause while everyone worked on their smiles.

"I'd like to give you one of my peacocks."

Melvin stared. *Her* peacocks?

"It didn't seem right," she said, "to bring him to the ceremony, but if you come by the farm after your honeymoon, you can take him home with you. I think you'll enjoy him. The General's a real beauty."

Cookie's fingernails pressed through Melvin's jacket, shirt, and into the skin on his arm. She said, "We don't even have a home yet. I can't exactly move a peacock into my parents' house."

"Oh, pish," Regina said. "Your mother told me you were on the verge of making an offer on the old Johnson house. That's got some lovely grounds. Perfect for a few animals."

Melvin pictured Flannery handing him a leash attached to a huge, menacing bird. He tried to imagine what would happen next.

"Give me a call when you're ready to collect your present," Flannery said. "Or just turn up at the farm if you like. We're always there."

"This is absurd," Cookie said.

Flannery grinned, a show of tall, straight teeth.

"Congratulations again," Regina called, as her daughter led her away.

Melvin watched them go. He felt his wife trembling at his side. He felt his father-in-law's pointed stare, and the pressure of so many perfumed hugs and concrete handshakes. He was sweating now beneath his suit. He was aware of a substantial gap in his understanding, of the woman beside him, and of this place. Why would anyone have a pet that made that kind of noise? And not even one such pet, but an entire flock of them. Enough to wake an entire town.

L ona Waters sat on her back step and smoked. Evening was threatening to fall, grainy with heat. Beads of sweat, too lazy to drop, clung to the nape of her neck. She inhaled, and remembered her husband approaching her in this same spot the night before Cookie Himmel's wedding. He had lifted her hair and licked the sweat away. Lona shuddered. What a strange night that had been. What strange behavior from Bill. They'd had sex, rough and cursory, for the first time in months.

Lona had found a bruise on her thigh the following morning, the shape of her husband's palm. She had traced over the mark for days, her fingers returning to the dark splotch on her skin, testing the soreness. As the bruise began to fade, she had pressed harder, trying to reach the diminishing place, deep down, where the bruise lived. She wanted the pain to still exist, to be accessible. She had used her thumb, then her fist, and then a small rock from the garden, forcing it against her thigh. It was her daughter's voice from the upstairs window that finally stopped her. "Mama, what are you doing?" Lona's hands had gone slack. She was left holding a stone, her skirt hiked up to show a bare leg.

Lona was alone in the house now. This was her favorite time of the day, before she went to pick up her daughter, after she had left her sewing inside. If her husband called on the phone, Lona would claim to be hard at work on a pair of curtains in the back room. She would deliberately sound harried, and he would apologize for interrupting. She would accept his apology, and not feel a speck of guilt. This final hour of the afternoon was all her own. It was the only thing in her day, in her life, that belonged only to her. The rest of the time, she was either working so they would have enough money to pay the bills that her husband's policeman salary couldn't cover, or she was trying to be a satisfactory wife and mother.

She luxuriated in every second of each minute of this one holy hour. Lona allowed her thoughts to taper off. She inhaled and exhaled. She let herself blend in with the porch wood, the jasmine bush near her knee, and the steamy air. She had an aptitude for this, blurring her edges until she merged with her surroundings. She pictured herself as one of the wisps of smoke leaving her mouth. She was able to disappear this way while alone, or in a crowd of people. She'd been doing it since she was a small girl. Flitting in and out of her home, in and out of school, in and out of consciousness.

Very few people in town could recall Lona Waters's story. There was nothing in her past worth repeating and carrying forward. She was the youngest of six children in a poor family. Her mother was a seamstress who supported the family with her small income. Her father was a gentle, ineffectual drunk. By the time Lona was sixteen, her family had begun to disappear. Her mother died of exhaustion in her sleep one night. One of her older brothers drowned while swimming in a nearby lake. Her remaining brothers and sisters began to leave Milledgeville, usually under the dark of night, usually without any warning. They didn't say goodbye, or write when they reached their destination. Lona and her father lived alone in a crumpled house by the railroad track for two months, before he suffered a massive coronary in his favorite seat at his regular bar.

A few months later, Lona met Bill Waters at the local pool. He had just arrived in town, fresh out of the Decatur police academy. She married him quickly. When they settled into a nice neighborhood, and Lona picked up some of her mother's former clients to create a sewing business, she felt like they were both new to the area. It was more than a fresh start; her new life was all there was. Her old life washed away, like footprints after a night of hard rain.

A church bell tolled, and Lona stood up. There was no need to wear a watch in this town. There was always a church within three blocks, letting you know the time. It was five o'clock, which meant she had to pick up Gigi. She ground the joint into the hanging plant by the door— a school friend who had moved to Atlanta sent an envelope filled with them every month, in return for free sewing—and went inside to collect her purse.

Miss Mary had been watching Gigi after school since kindergarten. When Lona tried to remember how the arrangement had started, she couldn't recall the specifics. She had told Bill that she couldn't get her sewing work done with a small child hanging off her skirt, and then, somehow, Miss Mary had offered to babysit. This casual offer, as much as anything, enabled the Waters family to function from one day to the next. Miss Mary claimed that since she already had one child, watching two was no problem. In any case—her argument ran—she had always wanted a daughter, so they were in fact doing her a favor by letting her borrow Gigi every afternoon. Nobody wanted the arrangement to end, even though, at fifteen, the girl was now certainly old enough to look after herself. Gigi and Miss Mary enjoyed their time together. Bill considered a teenager on his or her own to be at risk to limitless juvenile misbehaviors, so he was happy for his daughter to travel out to the Treadle farm. Lona couldn't believe her good luck. She was able to keep her afternoons and her magic hour for herself.

The car needed new shocks, and bounced down the road. The Treadles lived on a farm a few miles north of town. Their nearest neighbor was the O'Connors, and as Lona passed Andalusia's secluded driveway, she heard the cackle of peacocks over her car radio. At this point in the drive, Lona always became more aware of her surroundings, and of herself. When she knocked on the Treadles' door, she needed to successfully present herself as a mother. Miss Mary would invite her in, try to force some kind of baked confection into her hand, and proceed to make small talk.

Lona could do this; she did this every day. She just needed to call herself to order first. She twisted the rearview mirror and looked at her reflection. She thought of Gigi and sighed. The child was growing so fast; the tenth-grader's limbs looked longer and more awkward daily. Gigi's eyes had changed too. They seemed to belong to a young woman Lona hadn't been properly introduced to. Gigi also carried a new, invisible weight; Lona could hear it in her clumping gait. She'd given her daughter the nickname *Old Lady*. *You need to lighten up, Old Lady*, Lona would say. *Just relax*. Gigi would shrug while her mother spoke, but there was alarm in her eyes, as if she suspected these words were true.

Lona pulled up in front of the red farmhouse. She removed the key from the ignition and climbed out of the car. Yellow light flooded from the first-story windows. Pots of geraniums flanked the front door. The sight of the farmhouse always made Lona feel slightly depressed. The lightbulbs in her own home shone a cool light, and there was dust on most surfaces. Her house smelled of something she couldn't identify: a cold, faintly greasy aroma, whereas Miss Mary's invariably smelled of sugar and butter. Lona scrambled all day, trying to achieve something close to the calm happiness of the Treadle house. She knew she was missing some mystery ingredient. She had bought a pot of flowers for her kitchen table, but despite religious watering, the blooms died. Once a month she tried to bake a cake, or a batch of cookies, but the finished product always ended up slightly burnt.

The front door opened before Lona could raise her hand to knock. Miss Mary peered out at her.

"Hello?" Lona said. Miss Mary had never met her at the door before. Usually Lona had to knock for several minutes before anyone heard her over the radio in the kitchen.

"I need to talk to you," the large woman whispered. "Privately."

"Of course. What's happened? Is it Gigi?"

"Oh, no." Miss Mary smiled, and laid her hand on Lona's arm. "She's wonderful. What a sweetheart. Let's sit in your car. No one can hear us there."

Lona led the way back to her beat-up sedan. She got in on the driver's side, and Miss Mary wedged herself into the passenger's seat. They both shut their doors. Lona waited. She felt nervous outside the realm of their shared routine. She listened to a peacock cackle behind the wall of trees in front of her. Night was falling, and with it a blanket of firm heat. School wouldn't end for a few weeks, but summer was already here.

"Heavens," Miss Mary said, and wiped her forehead with her hand. "I should have settled up north. Who can live in this kind of weather?"

Lona gave a small nod, although the heat didn't bother her. She did feel stifled though, inside the car. Miss Mary's girth took up more than just her seat. Her hip extended within an inch of Lona's. Miss Mary was fond of giving hugs and random pats, but here in the enclosed space, it seemed like she was touching Lona even when she wasn't.

Miss Mary wiped her cheeks now, as though pushing away tears. "It's Joe," she said.

Miss Mary's son was finishing his junior year at the local high school. He was one of those boys who didn't excel in school, but never seemed to get in any trouble. Lona rarely saw him, since he was always helping his father on the farm.

"He's such a sweet boy," Miss Mary said. "You know that. Everyone says so. We used to be very close. It wasn't that he told me everything—I don't think any child should tell their parents everything—but he was comfortable with me. He would do his homework in the kitchen while I cooked. He'd tease Gigi about something. He was a happy kid."

Lona considered this. She had never thought to wonder if her own daughter was a happy kid. Lona had never been one herself. She had, she realized, just assumed that no kids were truly happy. They were silly and energetic, but surely not capable of actual joy.

"Did something happen?" she asked.

"Yes, but I don't know what. He's changed. He's dropped out of all his school activities, but he won't say why. He won't talk to me." She looked at Lona. "I need to get him out of his room. I need your help."

Lona pictured herself and Miss Mary, scrawny and gigantic, dragging the boy out of his room by his heels. "I don't see how—"

Miss Mary spoke quickly. "You and Bill have always said you'd like to pay me for looking after Gigi, and I won't hear of it. The girl's a dream and I love our afternoons together. But you *can* do me a favor. Something I'd really appreciate."

Lona's limbs were weighed down by the dark. She wasn't sure where this was headed, but she already knew she was trapped. "Of course," she said. "We'd do anything for you."

"I'd like you to use Joe as your assistant. He could help you hang the curtains and measure them, and carry your supplies. He'd be a huge help to you, I'm sure. He's very organized. You always say you have trouble keeping your calendar straight—he could do that for you. I was thinking maybe three days a week? You could pick him up after school, and then bring him back here when you pick up Gigi. How does that sound?"

While talking, Miss Mary had rotated in her seat. She was squeezed sideways, facing Lona. Her legs were curled under her; her wide lap sat level like a tabletop.

My afternoons, Lona thought. *I'll lose my afternoons.* "I'll have to talk to Bill," she said.

Miss Mary nodded. Her eyes dimmed slightly. "Of course."

"But I'm sure the answer will be yes," Lona said. "How could we say no?"

. . .

When she and Gigi arrived at their house, the girl headed straight for her room. Bill was standing in the kitchen. He was surveying the room—the cabinets, the paint chipping next to the ceiling light, the yellowed linoleum floor—as if he wanted to gut the place and rebuild immediately.

Often when Lona saw her husband at the end of the day, she was startled. He looked middle-aged, and she still thought of herself as young. It felt like weeks had passed since they had met, not years. She remembered the boy who had been new to this town, new to the police department. He had been skinny and solemn, so serious that he found it difficult to make friends. He had strong opinions on how tasks—ranging from how to clean an oven to how to load a rifle—should be done, and he wasn't shy about sharing his opinion. Often upon first meeting someone, Bill would say, *You're doing that wrong. Let me show you a better way.*

Many people found this habit off-putting, but Lona liked it. On their first date, he told her that she would look better with her hair braided, and when she laced her long hair and looked in the mirror, she saw that he was right. He told her that she should stop working at the ten-cent store on the highway and reopen her mother's sewing business, so she did that too. Lona relaxed under his steady stream of direction, and Bill enjoyed having a receptive audience.

After the wedding they purchased a small house, and Bill committed to mastering his career, to growing stronger by lifting weights in the basement, and to giving Lona a child. He woke up every morning prepared to wrestle the day to the ground. His unremitting earnestness was a source of wonder to Lona. She admired him for it. Fifteen years into their union, Bill Waters was a barrel-chested man, with strong, powerful limbs. His uniform fit him like a glove. He rarely sat still, and was always on the lookout for unlawful activity.

"No news today." He stood in the archway that separated the kitchen from the living room, a solid presence in his blue pants and shirt. A dark belt circled his hips, a gun hanging from one side, a billy club from the other.

Lona sidled past him to get to the refrigerator. She kissed his cheek on the way. "No? Well, I'm sure you'll hear something tomorrow."

"You've been saying that for months. I don't know what he's playing at. He can't give the promotion to anyone else." Bill's eyes bulged slightly. "I mean, there's no reasonable alternative."

Lona had recently hung new curtains in Chief Mason's living room. The job had involved two appointments: one to take measurements, and one to install the finished product. The most striking piece of furniture in the room was a burgundy leather armchair. There was an unusually deep impression in the seat cushion, and an impressive selection of bourbon and rye whiskeys set up within easy reach. Lona always pictured the police chief sunk deep into that armchair, whenever Bill complained of bureaucratic delays.

"You're right," she murmured into the crisp air of the refrigerator. "You have no alternative."

"What?"

"Mmm? Oh, I meant, he has no alternative. You're right."

Bill Waters considered the linoleum. Lona could tell that he was trying to stop worrying. This was a regular, fruitless struggle. Her husband didn't want to feel like this, but he couldn't help it. There was an engine inside his chest that turned over and over. His father had been appointed police chief in Decatur when he was forty-two, and Bill wanted to be chief in Milledgeville by the time he was forty. This meant he needed to make lieutenant before his thirty-fifth birthday, which was rapidly approaching.

If Bill couldn't relax—and he couldn't—he could at least shift his focus. Lona's back was turned, but she felt his eyes on her. She listened to him sniff the air, to see if he could smell marijuana. She had promised to quit smoking. Lona had also promised to pay attention when she put together an outfit in the morning and to make polite chitchat with

acquaintances in public. She understood that these details were important to her husband. Bill had to be as careful with her movements as he
was with his own, because he couldn't afford any slipups. He already
had one point against him: he wasn't born and raised in Milledgeville.
Like most small towns, the infrastructure liked to nurture its own. But
that was a challenge Bill was willing to overcome. He was the first man
in the office every morning, the first man to any emergency call, the first
man to cocktail parties where networking with the mayor or other top
officials was key.

"Thank you for not smoking. I appreciate it," Bill said, in his best
approximation of a casual tone. It seemed like he was always approximat-
ing a tone. He was trying to sound respectful, or trying to sound authori-
tative, or trying to sound reasonable. He could never just talk, never just
let the words come out naturally. The stakes were too high for that.

Lona nodded. "Miss Mary asked for a favor today."

"Oh?"

"She wants me to hire Joe as my assistant. Part-time."

Bill raised his eyebrows. "Her boy?"

"We don't have to pay him. It's a kind of exchange. I'll take her son
while she takes Gigi."

"That's a great idea. I should have thought of it myself. You shouldn't
be lugging that heavy bag all over town, or drilling holes into walls." Bill
shook his head. "Yes, that makes real good sense." He rubbed his hands
together. "What's for dinner?"

Lona stared into the refrigerator. She wasn't surprised. She'd known
that her husband would support the plan. Why wouldn't he? This didn't
even look like a sacrifice, to anyone but Lona. She leaned deeper into the
cool air. "There's chicken from the other night?"

Bill sighed. "That sounds great, honey. I'll call Gigi."

The family sat around the square kitchen table chewing stringy
chicken and canned beans. The plates slid on the tabletop, the silverware
clinked, and insects chirped through the open window.

"How was your history test?" Bill asked.

"Fine," Gigi said. "I think I did well."

"I'm sure you did. Let me know when you get the results." Bill looked at his wife. "You're going to the Whitesons' tomorrow?"

Lona blinked. She tried to picture her work calendar. "Next week, I think. We haven't confirmed the starting date because she's waiting on some furniture."

"You should be extra nice while you're there. Really make an effort."

"Why are they so important?" Gigi sat cross-legged on her chair; she pushed food across her plate with a fork.

"Melvin Whiteson has a lot of money." Bill perked up; he clapped his daughter on the shoulder. "He and his wife could make a lot of changes around here, which I think is great. We need some new blood. The people in this town are too stuck in their ways. So just work hard, like always, honey. We'd like to get friendly with them."

"I'll do my best," Lona said.

Bill reached over and squeezed her arm.

His wife gave a small, practiced smile. Lona tried to imagine what Miss Mary would do now, if she were here. This was a trick Lona used regularly, during moments when she felt lost in her own home. She used the answer to propel herself forward, even if it was only one step at a time.

"Who wants ice cream?" she asked, and stood up.

It was birthing season, and Regina had been spending nearly every night in the barn. She napped when she had the chance on a cot set up in the corner, but when the heifers were in labor, she was in the stall. She planted her feet like a linebacker and leaned shoulder-first into the animal's midsection. When she felt life scramble beneath her weight, she leaned in harder. The swollen mother keened and pressed her forehead against the grizzled wall. She shifted her mass from hoof to hoof, causing Regina and the farmhand to jump out of the way. If the birth took place after dawn, Flannery would walk out to the barn to watch the calf fall, a jumble of skinny legs, onto the hay.

"I'm getting too old for this," Regina said. She rocked in her favorite porch chair, her eyes shut.

Flannery was bent over beside her, writing a letter in scrawling cursive. She laid her pen down and looked at the cloud-mottled sky. She tried to recall what day of the week it was. She had recently reached the end of her second novel, but had found no relief in the completion. She was satisfied with the beginning and the end, but something was missing from the middle. She could feel an abyss there, a thumping darkness. She had been working on the book for seven years, but her faith in the story, and in her ability to make it work, had started to crack a few weeks earlier.

Flannery shifted her weight, looking for a comfortable position. "You're not the only one who's tired," she said, and was disappointed to hear the petulance in her voice. She touched her jaw lightly with one finger, even though she knew the gesture would worry her mother. Flannery had recently been in the hospital with an infection in her jawbone. It was fine now, but the doctor had warned them it could recur if she didn't pace herself. *I can't move much slower*, she had joked to the doctor. *Try*, he'd replied.

Regina squinted at Flannery. She was a sixty-year-old widow, as strong as a woman half her age, with gray curls and bright eyes. When Flannery seemed weak, Regina's natural instinct was to attack. She had found that administering blows often made the person on the receiving end find strength they didn't know they had. Regina had done this with her husband, in his final year. When he said he was tired, she told him he wasn't.

She sighed and rubbed the rough back of her hand. Flannery was her only child. Regina was not a sentimental woman, but she was always aware of the relevant facts, and the fact was that Flannery was her heart. As a result, Regina always felt slightly desperate around her. She had the urge to proclaim, over and over at the top of her lungs: *I will not let you go! I won't do it! Don't even think about leaving me!*

She studied the dark spots on the backs of her hands. The stains seemed out of place; they looked like mistakes. Regina felt young, even after so little sleep, even after all the living she had done. *Perhaps*, she thought, *God put the spots there for a reason*. To keep her in check. To keep her from attacking, and shouting. The spots reminded her that she had God-given wisdom she could draw on now. She literally knew better.

"Maybe," she said, "I should schedule another appointment with Dr. Merrill."

"No," Flannery said.

"Well, if you're in pain," Regina said, sharply.

Flannery gripped the pen in her lap like a baseball she wanted to throw. The two main characters in her novel, an uncle and his nephew, stood in the center of her mind. One was made of flesh and blood, the other was two-dimensional. The schoolteacher, Rayber, wouldn't come alive, and no matter how hard Flannery pounded the letters on her typewriter, she couldn't make him so. But his nephew, Tarwater, jittered with energy. He wanted to run, to set fire to something, to kick the life out of someone.

Flannery gave her mother a look. *Leave me alone.*

Regina glared in return. *Don't mess with me, young lady.*

The older woman strode off to the barn, and Flannery walked behind the house to feed the birds. She tried to distract the peacocks that were headed straight for her mother's favorite rosebush by throwing birdseed in their path. Characteristically, they ignored both her and the birdseed, and set about devouring the fat yellow flowers. Flannery watched the birds destroy one row of roses, and then another. She considered stepping in. If her mother had been nearby, Flannery would have made a show of waving her crutches. But the gesture would have been pointless. Even if she succeeded in scaring the peacocks out of the garden, they would strut back as soon as she turned away.

A row of ducks walked between Flannery and the flower bed. A chicken spun in a circle and sat down. Flannery dug a fistful of seed from her pocket and scattered it over the stiff grass. She leaned against the water tower, and a posse of bantam hens, frizzled with electrocuted feathers, skipped up expectantly. They twittered, hopping from foot to foot. Flannery teased them by pretending to toss seeds over their heads. She enjoyed their dumb gullibility, watching them race feverishly in response to every flick and feint of her wrist.

Flannery slowly became aware of a pressure on the back of her neck, which she recognized as guilt. She shouldn't have worried her mother earlier. She actually felt fine—as fine as she ever felt—and her jaw hadn't twinged in days. She looked around at the farm she had been living on for nearly eleven years, since the day she had been put on the train in Connecticut with what she thought was arthritis and had to be carried off in Macon by her uncles, certain she was about to die. The landscape was barely familiar. Stained grass, farm equipment, distant bundles of hay—none of this had been her first choice. Flannery felt tired, standing in the middle of the lawn, birds swirling around her feet. Not sick-tired, but soul-tired.

When the hum of an engine swelled through the birds' chatter, she was irritated at the interruption. She hitched her crutches around to the side of the house. The engine noise stopped, and the birds opened their beaks to compensate. Even the quiet ones joined in, which meant the visitor was unfamiliar. Flannery saw a black car in the driveway, and Melvin Whiteson pressed up against it. He was holding his hat on his head as if it was in danger of being blown off.

Flannery's mouth twisted into a smile. "I didn't expect you to show up," she said. "In fact, I would have put money on it."

Melvin's attention was pointed at the General, the largest of the peacocks. The bird had stepped directly in front of him, like an enemy lining up for a duel. The massive bird's neck and head were dark blue, and reached the middle of Melvin's chest. His feathers were bright orange, yellow, and magenta, fiery as a setting sun. His train extended a full six feet behind him. Muscles rippled from the base of the bird's neck. After a silent moment, his tail began to rise. It hovered for a moment, then shot upward. The feathers separated and fell into a huge, resplendent fan.

"Jesus," Melvin said.

"You've never seen one before?"

He shook his head. "There aren't many of these in New York."

Flannery studied his face. She had bought her first peacock shortly after her first hospital stay, and she estimated that she now owned upwards of forty. She avoided doing a proper head count because if there were more than forty, she didn't want to know about it, and she certainly didn't want Regina, who had declared twenty peacocks to be her god's-honest-I-cannot-stand-these-creatures limit, to know about it.

Flannery had never seen anyone unaffected by his initial encounter with a peacock. Her first exposure had certainly affected her. On the afternoon Flannery uncrated her original peacock, she was in bad shape. Her face was swollen from steroids, her hair was falling out, and she'd said to her mother that she had both the strength and the attention span of a gnat. She had been collecting birds since she was a little girl, and already had a sizeable menagerie of chickens, geese, pheasants, ducks, and swans on the farm, so she wasn't expecting to be fazed by the contents of the box. She had ordered the bird simply for the novelty, as an addition to her collection. But the sight of the bewildered, travel-sick peacock strutting in jagged circles, trying to both absorb and own the ground he covered, wielding his puny tail as if it were covered with all the queen's jewels, had made Flannery sink down on her heels. She had crouched there, amused and fascinated, for hours.

Since that day, she had seen an array of reactions on the faces of her visitors. Some became reverent. Old men took their hats off at the sight of a peacock whose tail was spread like a freckled rainbow. Her editor had followed the birds around the yard with a movie camera attached to his eye, filming their every step and squawk. A few visitors shrugged at the spectacle, and said they didn't see what all the fuss was about. Others turned sullen when confronted with the peacock, convinced that the bird was somehow mocking them. Melvin Whiteson looked scared and disoriented, like a child who had just been woken from a nap.

"Oh, I was going to have a little more fun with this," Flannery said, "but I can see that I need to put your mind at ease. I'm not going to make you take one of my peacocks."

With this announcement, the General stalked away. He disappeared around the back of the house, and Melvin's face relaxed.

"In fact," she said, "even if you wanted one I wouldn't let you. They're my babies. I was just teasing Cookie at the wedding. If I was nicer, I'd apologize, but honestly the joke was too much fun. However, I do have a nicely wrapped silver frame inside for you to take home. It's much more up your wife's alley." She looked Melvin over, not unkindly. "And yours as well, I imagine. Come have a seat and I'll find it."

When she returned to the porch she found Melvin positioned in the corner chair, where he could remain alert to any approaching livestock.

He waved his hand toward the lawn. "They were so loud the night before our wedding, I couldn't believe it. Part of me thought I'd made them up. I told Cookie I was coming out here to be polite, because you'd offered us a gift. But I think I came just to see them for myself."

Flannery gave him a closer look. She hadn't formed much of an impression of Melvin at the wedding. He had seemed well mannered and well educated, with a sheen of money, but that was about as much thought as she had given him. It was the first time she had seen Cookie in years, and the sight of her had darkened Flannery's already pitch-dark mood. Cookie looked luminous, and Flannery found herself wanting to snuff her light out. Daisy Himmel and Regina were old friends, so Cookie and Flannery had been regularly thrown together in the past. It had irritated Flannery that even as a child, even on her worst day, Cookie always looked as if she had been groomed and dressed by a team of elves.

Cookie's swollen eye and some very good punch had brightened the occasion, but Flannery still left the wedding as soon as it was polite to do so. She was too tired to pretend to enjoy herself. She had been awake the whole night prior, sitting by her window, listening to her birds scream louder and longer than they ever had before. Their cries had crashed over Flannery, and with each wave she felt a little more diminished, a little more uncertain. She had found herself remembering the decision she'd made after her diagnosis, on how she would live the remainder of her life. She only had enough energy for one path, one purpose. She would channel what she had left into her writing, and nowhere else. This meant that her novel couldn't just be finished, it had to be great, or she would have let herself down. And she knew, with the birds' screams grazing her skin, the darkness blotting her face, that the book was not great. Therefore, what was she doing with her life?

When day dawned and Regina appeared in the doorway to remind her about the wedding they were to attend—the wedding of a girl who'd always had the things that Flannery lacked: beauty, popularity, boyfriends, health—she wanted to say, *No, I won't go. I can't bear to.* But she lacked the strength for the argument she knew would follow.

She wished she had some of the wedding punch in her hand now, instead of the watery lemonade she had brought from the kitchen. She wanted to swallow something with a kick. The groom had brought back the memory of that hard night and the sand that had seemed to coat her eyes by dawn.

"Regina nearly shot the peacocks after that, if it makes you feel any better," she said. "I had to talk her out of it."

"Why aren't they screaming now?" he asked. "I mean, is the noise restricted to certain times of the day, or how does it work?"

"Peacocks don't suffer restrictions. They do what they want, when they want."

"How often do they spread their tails?"

"Sometimes every hour. Sometimes not for a week. I have no control over them, Mr. Whiteson. I just feed them and watch them."

"Please, call me Melvin. My father was Mr. Whiteson." He cleared his throat. "I hope you don't mind my saying, but they seem like a strange choice for a pet."

Flannery smiled. "They're not pets."

Melvin looked at her, blankly.

"See if you can get them to sit down, or roll over."

He returned her smile. "Point taken. Strange companions, then."

There was a pause while they watched the birds navigate the lawn and hop from one low tree branch to another. Several gathered on the nearby fence, then scattered. They were still agitated from the stranger's arrival.

Flannery turned to look at Melvin.

"Yes?" he asked.

"I have to say that I'm surprised Cookie let you come out here. She's not my biggest fan."

He shifted in his chair. "She wasn't happy about it. We actually had a fight before I left. Our first one."

"You risked marital disharmony, just to see these birds?"

"Apparently so."

"Was it worth it?"

She watched him consider the question. She knew he was remembering the rise of the General's tail, the swirl and spread of bright feathers. The exploding half-moon, the color, the bird's arrogant stance.

Melvin nodded.

Years earlier, Daisy had often driven up to the house with a young Cookie pouting beside her. Before Flannery's father died, they'd had many visitors. Guests were a rare phenomenon now, with the exception of one or two of her mother's friends, and Miss Mary and Gigi. Occasionally a writer friend made the trip, but it had been over a year since anyone had come specifically to visit Flannery. She smiled to herself. She'd been thinking that this conversation was unusual, but perhaps this was a normal conversation, and she simply no longer knew what normal was.

The General stormed around the corner of the house, and Melvin lurched in his chair. Flannery leaned back into hers.

It occurred to Flannery that her mother, who was always aware of every movement at the farm, must have noticed that they had a visitor by now. That meant she was staying away on purpose, probably because she believed that it was good for Flannery to be social. *She thinks about me like I'm a child*, she thought, and shook her head. She was thirty-seven years old, but she felt eighty-seven; her joints creaked when she moved in her chair. Her crutches were propped against the wall behind her.

Melvin cleared his throat. "I'm a little embarrassed to say that I didn't know who you were when we first met. I hadn't come across your work, but that's because I'm not much of a fiction reader."

Flannery touched her jawbone. She remembered the stabbing pain of a few weeks earlier, and the tediousness of having to lie still in bed. "Or maybe," she said, "you hadn't come across my work because I'm not much of a fiction writer. I'd tell you to ask around, but there're only about six people in town who've actually read my books. Even my mother had a hard time getting through them."

Melvin studied her, apparently trying to discern if she was kidding. It was his turn to think, *This is a strange conversation.*

Flannery was aware that she was talking mostly to amuse herself. She decided to let him off the hook. She said, "Miss Mary told us that you're starting a new job."

"That's right. I've taken a position at Berenger's."

"The Realtors?"

"They do insurance too."

She tried to think what the polite response to this would be. All she could come up with was, *That sounds terribly boring.*

"Chuck's phasing into retirement, so I'll be running the office most of the time. I'll have the option to buy the company if I want, later on." He wiped a bead of sweat from his forehead. "It should be an interesting challenge."

"Really?" Flannery asked.

"I think so."

"I would think you'd want to be certain, before signing on the dotted line. After all, this is your new life. Far from the big city, far from your old career. You don't want to make a mistake."

Melvin's eyes were on the parade of birds traversing the lawn. "Do you talk to everyone like this?"

"Like what?"

"So," he hesitated, "candidly."

Flannery felt the strange restlessness inside her again. She shifted in her chair. "We're not fending off streams of visitors out here. But the answer is yes, if I find the person interesting."

He smiled, as if the answer pleased him. "You think my taking the job at Berenger's is a mistake?"

"I think you have options."

"Like what? There aren't many business openings in this area."

"Have you considered not working?"

"At all?"

"You don't need a job, do you? Aren't you extremely rich?"

Melvin laughed. "You're the first person to ask me that. People have been making veiled references to my financial state since I arrived."

"Well, most folks are more polite than I am."

"No kidding." His face became more serious. "Obviously, money's not the point. I can't exactly sit around and do nothing. I need to fill my days." He spread his hands. "I shouldn't have to explain this. Every man worth his salt is employed in some capacity."

Flannery regarded him. Cookie's husband had the appearance of a man who looked no further than ten steps ahead. She could tell that he didn't believe in God. Melvin would probably call himself agnostic if asked, unwilling to commit to there being no God at all, but also unwilling to seek him out.

She shook her head. Her mother liked to convert people, but that was not Flannery's game. Her religion was part of her bones; it was the skeleton that held her up, that allowed her to engine through the days. Her belief was personal and private. As a Catholic in a town full of Protestants, there was no point in its being anything else. Her mother was willing to waste her breath; Flannery wasn't.

"You could do anything," she said. "People would cut off their right arm to be in your position."

"Well, they should value their arms more highly."

"You don't have the measure of this town yet. There are a lot of people struggling here, and in their cases, money is always the point. How old are you? Thirty? Look at what God's given you . . . a wife, a full bank account, health." Flannery listened to herself talk, and frowned in disapproval. What was she doing, shaking a tree she had no business shaking? Still, she didn't stop. "You don't need to settle for anything," she said. "In fact, it's insulting to the rest of us if you do."

Melvin's eyes followed the General, who was bulldozing through a fat bush. "Insulting?"

"Yes."

"Isn't that a bit strong?"

"Maybe." Flannery grimaced. She realized how much she was enjoying this conversation, and the thought made her uncomfortable.

"If I could do something original, like you do, then I would. But I don't have those talents. And this job," he paused, "suits my skills, and my needs. I want my father-in-law to respect me. I want to fit into this town. I think those goals are lofty enough."

Flannery pictured her mother peering out from the second floor of the barn. Regina would be wondering how much longer Melvin Whiteson would stay, and what he and her daughter could possibly have in common. She would be wishing she were closer, so she could overhear their exchange.

Flannery shook her head. She knew that she could say anything she wanted; the freedom to speak was in the air. She also knew that the smarter choice was silence. She should ratchet herself up now, an exercise in control that she was used to. She should send this man away and retreat into her solitude.

But she was tired. Tired of self-control, tired of being watched, tired of the land beneath her feet, tired of the warm air in her lungs. She stared across the lawn, as if trying to push her view beyond the available horizon. She found herself staring at the only unfamiliar object in her line of vision.

"Nice car," she said.

"It's new. We just bought it."

A thought formed in Flannery's head. Before she had time to censor herself, or reconsider, she heard herself speak. "I haven't been allowed to drive for years. My doctor forbade it. But my medication was changed recently, and my joints have improved, so I'm ready to get behind the wheel again."

Melvin hesitated, as if trying to figure out the appropriate response to this statement. "Congratulations."

"I need lessons though, to refresh my memory." She was pleased that her voice sounded calm, and rational. "My mother would prefer that

I didn't drive at all. It makes her nervous when I move under my own locomotion, so she won't help me."

It was a hot afternoon. The birds were almost motionless now, unwilling to exert themselves any more than was necessary.

"Maybe you could help me." Flannery felt color rise in her cheeks. "Once a week. It would give you a chance to see the peacocks."

She couldn't look at his face, so she concentrated on the sweat spots on Melvin's shirt. She watched his chest rise and fall with each breath. She felt the schoolteacher frown disapprovingly from the center of her novel. She found herself wondering if she would ever publish another book. She wondered if her legacy would be worth anything at all. She wondered if she had made a mistake, centering her life on a string of words typed on a page.

"You want me to give you driving lessons?" Melvin asked.

She shrugged.

There was another pause. "I guess I could do that."

Flannery felt mortified. He was saying yes.

"When would be convenient for you?" he asked.

She said the first day that occurred to her. "Tuesday?"

"In the afternoon?"

"Sure. That's fine."

Melvin rose from his chair. He waved the wrapped picture frame in her direction, an awkward salutation. He crossed the lawn with quick strides, taking the route farthest from the birds. He climbed into his car, revved the engine—which set the peacocks in motion, slapping their tails against the ground—and pulled slowly away.

Flannery stayed on the porch while the sun fell. She had surprised herself, and it had been years since that had happened. She smiled, and then tamped the smile out. She heard her mother clatter through the back door and berate the housekeeper about dinner preparations. Flannery forced her attention to the three precious hours at her desk the next morning and what she needed to accomplish.

Adolescence had calcified Joe Treadle: it stiffened his gait and strangled his vocal cords. He grew six inches in one year and had a hard time keeping his balance. He became painfully shy at school. He quit the baseball team, and wasn't bookish enough to take part in academic clubs. He was completely incapable of speaking to girls. He found them loud and abrupt; they reminded him of the hens he fed every morning, bursting into sudden cackles of laughter. Joe walked the school corridors with his head down.

At home, he avoided his mother. He felt like he had no choice. Miss Mary liked to hug him, and he couldn't bear to be touched. Joe spent as much time as possible in the barn. When he had to be in the house, he pretended not to see her. His body reeled in the opposite direction, and his voice came out in a grunt. He headed for his bedroom and closed the door behind him. He sat on the wooden floor with his eyes shut. He could almost feel his limbs creak through another awkward inch of growth. Pinpricks dotted his chest as dark hairs pushed through tender skin. His joints burned as if they were being held to a low heat.

"It's just a growth spurt," his mother said, when he complained of the pain. "The doctor said it's perfectly normal." Joe nodded, but he knew she was wrong. There was nothing normal about what was happening to him. His voice sounded tinny and unfamiliar in his ear. While washing his hands in the school bathroom, he doubled over with abdominal pain. He spiked fevers in the middle of the night and drenched his sheets.

He wondered if instead of growing in a normal way, he was, in fact, dying. He wondered how many teenagers died each year because of massive tumors spreading throughout their bodies. Joe wondered how much time he had left. He suspected that he needed medical attention, but he couldn't bear to ask for it. The last thing he wanted, the last thing he could tolerate, was any kind of attention. So he continued to spend his free time alone in his room, his teeth gritted against the discomfort.

His parents informed him through his closed door, one night after dinner, that they had found him an after-school job. His father suffered from a bad stammer when away from the farm, but he spoke clearly now. "I don't know what you're doing in there," he said, "but it's gonna stop."

"I'm just thinking," Joe said.

"Well, it's no good. You're worrying your poor mother to death. You're gonna come out and join the rest of the world, whether you like it or not."

Joe knew his father would hit him if he didn't do as he was told, so the next afternoon he stood on the curb outside the high school and waited for Mrs. Waters.

He knew her only as Gigi's mother, someone who appeared at the front door around dinnertime. He didn't need to know any more than that; the mere fact that Mrs. Waters was a mother discouraged him. In his experience, mothers were intensely watchful creatures. They could read your thoughts, and they tried to trick you into sharing your feelings. Joe knew that maternal behavior wasn't limited to one's own children; he had watched his mother shoot pointed looks and leading questions at Gigi for years. He also knew that it wasn't out of the question for Miss Mary to have enlisted Lona Waters's assistance to try to decipher her teenage son. He sighed, and braced himself for an interrogation.

Mrs. Waters studied him for a long moment after he climbed into the car. Then she nodded and started the engine. Joe thought her pale blue eyes looked sad. They sat in silence for several blocks.

Joe began to sweat. Was she not going to say anything at all? Surely some kind of introduction, or discussion of the job, was in order. A few blocks farther, the silence was making his skin itch. Joe's manners rose up like a bout of nausea. All the courtesies his mother had drilled into him as a boy could not be ignored.

"Good afternoon, ma'am," he heard himself say.

"Good afternoon," she said softly.

Joe began to doubt that she intended to pass on information about him to his mother. Mrs. Waters looked like she had forgotten he was in the car. She wove through the town's angular streets, finally parking in front of a beaten-down house by the railroad tracks. She got out of the car, so Joe did the same. She stood very still and stared at the place, a habit Joe would become accustomed to over the coming weeks. Mrs. Waters liked to visualize how her curtains would look from both the inside and the outside.

Joe carried the heavy tool bag to the front door. The woman who answered was the cashier at the local food market. She was wearing a gray housecoat, and her hands were stained with nicotine.

"You said your curtains collapsed?" Mrs. Waters said.

"Yes." The woman fingered the door nervously. "But I can't afford new ones. And I can't pay you besides with coupons. I'm sorry, I shouldn't have called."

"Don't worry," Lona said. "I'm sure we can manage something."

The woman stepped back reluctantly and let them in. The house smelled of mayonnaise. When they turned into the living room, Joe couldn't help but let out a low whistle. There were two piles of filthy, tattered fabric sitting on the floor. They looked worse than the rags his mother used to dust furniture.

The cashier settled into an armchair, her mouth glum.

Joe watched Mrs. Waters gingerly handle the disgusting material. She took the needle, thread, and scissors out of her bag. She folded, refolded, and smoothed the fabric before she picked up the scissors. She cut with confidence, smooth slice after slice. Then she picked up the needle and thread. Within an hour she'd created a thin, sleek window covering with a scallop-cut hem that reminded Joe of tulips. Under Mrs. Waters's direction, he attached the rings and wove it onto the long rod. When she gave a small nod, he pulled the fabric across the open window, and the curtain dimmed the room. The cashier mumbled thanks and Joe blinked, soothed by the shadows.

When Mrs. Waters showed up at school the following afternoon, Joe climbed into the car and they drove to Andalusia. This farm was adjacent to his own; Joe had been there many times with his mother, though in the last year Miss Mary had taken to bringing Gigi instead of him. Miss Mary claimed that her visits were an act of charity. *Those two women need me*, she said. *Locked away out here in the middle of nowhere with only a bunch of horrible ducks and chickens for company.*

When they turned onto the property, Joe was struck, after his absence from the place, by the sheer density of birds. Peacocks sat heavily on branches above their heads. A cluster of chickens danced excitedly next to a mud puddle, and the outline of a brown quail could be discerned against a tangle of briars. A turkey cooed from the top of a shed. More peacocks appeared, a near-straight line of fowl against the stained grass. Joe knew that the local hunters talked about this place with a kind of awe. On more than one occasion men had stumbled, drunk, onto the farm in the middle of the night. Their goal was to shoot a peacock, but they were chased away by the business end of Mrs. O'Connor's rifle before they even got close.

Joe shut his eyes for a moment to block out the messy view. He had the sudden urge to speak, if only to make Mrs. Waters talk. He liked her silence, but it also confused him. In his experience, adults always generated conversation. He had, he realized, thought of it as a grown-up requirement, kind of like paying taxes or putting food on the table. Why was Mrs. Waters able to shirk that duty?

He cleared his throat. "Have you read Miss Flannery's writing?" This was the first question that came to his mind. He hadn't read any of it, himself. But he knew people in town had strong feelings about her books. He had heard his mother and her friends get all hopped up on the subject. He knew that some people had carried Flannery's novel around town in a brown bag, as if it were an open bottle of Jim Beam. Others claimed to be scared of Flannery, fearful she would put them in a story. This seemed silly to Joe—Flannery was nice, and the stories were made up—but he was interested to hear what Mrs. Waters thought. He was interested in hearing Mrs. Waters speak.

She parked next to the house. She said, "It's so loud here."

Outside the car, the birds seemed to be involved in a verbal disagreement—hisses and shouts filled the air. Joe nodded. It was an unusual farm.

Flannery met them on the front porch. She appeared to be holding her crutches, rather than leaning against them. "Come inside," she said. "Regina had to go into town, so she gave me precise instructions on what I'm allowed to say."

They followed her into a small dining room. There was a neatly folded square of fabric on the wooden table. Joe knew that this room was rarely used; Flannery and her mother ate their meals in the kitchen.

"A relation of my aunt in Savannah passed away of shingles recently," Flannery said. A small smile passed over her lips, like a tremor, and then was gone. "She left us an heirloom of a curtain. It needs repair, and it's clear from all the lacework that it requires an expert hand. That's where you come in."

"It's a rare design," Mrs. Waters said, nodding.

"Shall I leave you to it?" Flannery asked. "I'll just be out on the porch, working on a letter. Holler if I can help."

Mrs. Waters spread the curtain across the table. She ran her hand over the fabric, her gaze focused. Joe suspected she was going to be in the contemplation stage for a while, so he sat down on one of the chairs against the wall. He didn't know where to look—it seemed rude to watch Mrs. Waters work—so he kept his eyes on the window. He stared at the back of Flannery's head, a stretch of off-color lawn, and a fat magnolia tree dotted with peacocks.

They were funny-looking birds when their tails were down, he decided. Their expressions reminded him of the popular girls at school; both the girls and the birds seemed to think they were something special. But the girls were, at least, basically attractive. These peacocks had fat bodies with skinny, limp tails dangling behind them. Joe could understand why the local hunters thought of the birds when they were intoxicated; there couldn't be an easier, more ridiculous, target.

Mrs. Waters had a needle and thread out now. She was so close to the material her nose almost touched it. "This is delicate work," she said.

Joe knew he wasn't supposed to respond. Mrs. Waters had forgotten he was in the room. He kept his eyes on the window, and watched a black sedan drive up the driveway. It came to a stop beside Mrs. Waters's dented car. Joe recognized the man who climbed out as Mr. Whiteson. Everyone in town knew him; he was something of a local celebrity. *He has more money than God*, his mother liked to say, with a hand gesture that indicated nothing else could be said on the topic.

Joe looked at Mrs. Waters, who was poking the curtain lightly with her fingertip as if it were a hot stove that might burn her skin. He wondered whether he should point out Mr. Whiteson's arrival. He knew that his mother and her friends would have found this fascinating—he could hear his mother's voice saying, *Oh my, why is he here? What could he want with our Flannery? Isn't this interesting?*—but as soon as the idea came to him, Joe knew Mrs. Waters wouldn't care. If he took her attention away from her work, she would be confused, and probably annoyed. So Joe kept quiet, and just watched.

Flannery met Mr. Whiteson halfway across the lawn. They stood for a minute talking; Joe noticed that Flannery seemed to depend on her crutches even less now. She balanced them against her right hand, as if someone had asked her to watch them as a favor. When she laughed, she tipped her head back like a young girl. She followed Melvin to the driveway, where they both got into the shiny black car and drove away. Joe thought it was odd that Flannery hadn't said goodbye to him and Mrs. Waters first—had she forgotten they were there?

Joe and Mrs. Waters had been alone in the house for twenty minutes when she sighed and said, "I need to bring this home. I need a finer tool."

"Okay."

She looked around, as if perplexed by their surroundings. "Should I drive you to your house or can you walk?"

"I can walk, but don't you need to pick up Gigi?"

A fog seemed to clear from Mrs. Waters's eyes. She shook her head. "Of course," she said. "Of course. You're right."

The first few months of the job passed in one near-silent appointment after another. To his surprise, Joe found that he didn't mind the time away from his room. He liked the curtains for their promise of darkness. When he drew a new or resurrected curtain across a pane of glass, he left it closed for as long as possible. He stood facing the solid stretch of fabric and forgot the strangers behind him. The pain in his limbs dulled while he disappeared into the artificial dusk. More than once, Mrs. Waters had to call his name before he remembered to pull the curtains apart.

Even when sunlight bore through the windows and he had to interact with customers, he didn't suffer too much. He appreciated that each job had a beginning, a middle, and an end. He grew to like the fact that Mrs. Waters paid him almost no attention. She asked him to carry the tool bag or to lift the curtain rod a little higher on the right, but otherwise she never attempted to make conversation. Her watery blue eyes passed over Joe, or the client she was talking to, with the same blank disinterest. The only time he saw her focus was when she worked. It hadn't occurred to Joe that making curtains was something a person could be good at, but Mrs. Waters handled fabric like it was the most natural thing in the world.

There were moments, when his employer was engrossed in her work, that Joe allowed his mind to wander. It had been a long time since this had happened. Before, he had kept his thoughts carefully controlled. Every subject seemed dangerous, like the thorns of a barbed wire fence. It had been safer, and easier, to withdraw into a ball and focus on surviving these sixty seconds, and then the next. But now, Joe thought in small, careful clips about his future. He thought about graduating from high school in less than a year and inheriting the farm, a plan that had been in place since before he was born. He pictured himself on the tractor, one hand draped over the steering wheel, one hand on his hip. He pictured himself leading the meetings his father held each morning with the workers. He pictured his wife—she was no one he knew now, but in his mind she was a pretty brunette with freckles—waving from the kitchen door as he left for a day of hard work. These were images from a distance, with no sound. It was like flipping through postcards from a prospective life.

Joe worked for Mrs. Waters on the days she had appointments, and helped his father every other afternoon. He and Mrs. Waters developed a rhythm and rarely got in each other's way. They respected their mutual quiet. There was an unspoken agreement by which she never pointed out the cracks in his voice or the way his hands sometimes shook, and he never mentioned the joints she smoked or the fact that she often parked the car a block away from their appointment and then sat still for twenty minutes, humming along to the radio. During these occasions, he would sit in the backseat, pretending to look out the window while watching the tendrils of hair on her neck rise and fall.

"You have such nice color in your cheeks," his mother said when he returned to the farmhouse. Miss Mary beamed at him. "Isn't this working out beautifully? Aren't you feeling better, now that you're spending less time in your room? Would you like something to eat? You must be famished."

Joe had been working for Mrs. Waters for six weeks when they started the Whiteson job. Mrs. Waters warned him this would be a lengthy assignment, because she had been asked to make curtains for the entire house. On the first day, they sat in the car for an unusually long time.

She had the radio turned so low that the song wasn't discernible; the music was simply a low murmur working its way through the enclosed space. Joe liked these moments in the parked car, him in the backseat, Mrs. Waters in the front. He felt like she was alone, and yet he was somehow allowed to be with her. It was the kind of unguarded space he hadn't known was possible to share with another person.

He fought the urge to shift his weight. He worried that a breeze or even the creak of a seat might break the spell. Mrs. Waters sat behind the steering wheel, taking slow drags on a joint. He could see her profile. Her eyes were focused far away.

The air was growing warmer. He could taste the smoke. He wondered how much longer he could last before needing cool air in his lungs.

"I knew Cookie when we were young," she said. "I was surprised to hear that she came back."

Joe nodded, slow with regret, and rolled down the car window. "She must have been homesick."

"For here?"

He shrugged, not sure what to say. This was Cookie's home, after all. He stared at the wide shady street, the row of mailboxes, the neat plots of flowers. He gradually became aware that Mrs. Waters was looking at him in the rearview mirror. He returned her gaze. She narrowed her eyes, and he thought, *She's about to do something.*

Mrs. Waters stretched her arm back, over the seat.

Joe studied her arm, and the hand at the bottom of it, and the joint held by the hand. He wondered, his thoughts spinning sluggishly like warm taffy, what this might mean. Could she be offering him a smoke?

"Cookie can be a handful," Mrs. Waters said. "This might help make the next few hours a little more manageable."

When Joe took the joint, his fingertips brushed her arm, and a shock ran through him. He brought the joint slowly to his lips. He found the paper slightly damp where her lips had been.

Joe had never smoked anything, not even a cigarette. The smoke was a horrible shock to his lungs; he felt like he was choking and drowning at the same time. It took all his self-control not to cough. He was suddenly aware of how badly he wanted to not fail at this task. He didn't want to embarrass himself, or look like a stupid kid. He wanted to manage his body's response. When the warm smoke baked his lungs, he tightened the muscles in his chest. He finished his smooth inhale with a smooth exhale.

Lona took the joint back and unbuckled her seat belt. "Don't tell your mother."

"I won't."

He started to fold the curtain samples next to him. His insides felt hot now, burnt in places. He told himself to focus on the task at hand. He knew that once Lona unbuckled her seat belt, their time in the car was over. She would stub out the joint, touch her hair with her fingertips, and open the door. She would study the windows of the house, then tell him which samples to put in the bag and which to leave behind.

Joe saw this chain of events with total clarity. He waited for her to remove the joint from her own lips. He couldn't help but think that she was tasting the dampness from his mouth now. He hoped she didn't regret the offer. He hoped she would offer the joint to him again, not because he liked the taste—he hadn't—but because he liked that they had shared something tangible. It had felt, for that brief moment, like they were peers.

The air in the car, even with the windows open, felt trapped. Joe was aware that time was slowing, as if someone were fighting the small hand on the clock. He was fine with this, since he had no desire to move. He was perfectly comfortable. His lungs pumped to clear away the smoke. His heart compressed and released. Blood inched through his veins. For a moment, he was reduced to the basic mechanics of his body. A boy, respiring.

T ell me about New York," Flannery said.

"What about it?"

They were driving down Route 441. The landscape looked to Melvin like a series of postcards. A farm followed a lake, which was followed by two young boys climbing an elm tree. There was a clump of freckled horses, and a tractor. The land was flat. Nothing—neither the houses nor the trees—rose higher than two stories. Melvin had worked on the fifty-third floor at his father's bank. When he peered out the window, he watched tiny figures running across streets, anchoring their hats, clutching umbrellas. Neat avenues crossed one another with surgical precision. Birds flew at eye level. Skyscrapers shot out of the cement and tussled for height. While he stood at the window, the phone on the desk behind him rarely stopped ringing.

It was hard for Melvin to believe that Milledgeville and New York existed in the same country. It was hard for him to accept that his life had accommodated time in such different places. *What would it be like to grow up here?* he wondered. It seemed clear to him, for the first time, that a place could change, or shape, a person. If he had grown up digging in the muck of cow pastures, instead of playing in a specific quadrant of Central Park under the watchful eye of a nanny, he would be a different man. He knew this, but he didn't know *how* he would be different. He was missing the details.

His father had called himself a "big-picture man," and Melvin had been raised in the same mold. He had rarely considered the finer points, or the hypotheticals, before his arrival in Milledgeville. Now those particulars both interested and troubled him. This curiosity felt like a constant, slight stomachache. It wasn't severe enough to take all his attention, but he couldn't ignore the discomfort either.

"Tell me anything," Flannery said. "I miss the place. I just want to hear about it."

Melvin looked at her with surprise. "You lived in New York?"

"For a time." She paused. "Before this happened." She gestured down at her body.

It was actually surprisingly easy for Melvin to picture Flannery walking, free of crutches, down one of the city's main avenues. She wore an expression—was it confidence? sarcasm?—which ensured that no one would mess with her. This attitude, which his wife crucially lacked, was essential for success in New York. It was important, while walking in the city, to keep your eyes up and your expression focused. If you showed uncertainty or fear, you were bound to end up in a conversation with a homeless man or a tourist from Iowa. You might become confused, in the rush of pedestrian traffic, and turn the wrong way. You might trip and fall to your knees on the hard cement, only to find that no one stopped to help you. Melvin hardly knew Flannery, but now he recognized the toughness in her. She was, in some strange, unlikely way, a fellow New Yorker.

"Slow down on this curve," he said. "Don't be afraid to use your brake."

"Yes, sir."

"You're driving very well."

The sun came out from behind a cloud, and they both blinked hard. Flannery lowered the sun visor.

"You have to ask me something specific about the city," he said. "Otherwise I'll just give you a string of clichés."

"Oh, I don't know." She sighed. "This is my home. I can't deny that. But whereas I used to think a person had only one home, I don't believe that anymore. I was," she paused, as if searching for the right word, "*happy* there. I find it hard to believe you left there to move here voluntarily."

Melvin squinted out the window. Did he have to respond to this? He didn't think he owed Flannery any private confidences. After all, she had put him in an uncomfortable position the prior week; he basically *had* to agree to give her a driving lesson. Any other reply would have been impossibly rude. He was here out of obligation and nothing more.

He frowned while he spoke, to let her know that he disapproved of the intrusion. "Cookie didn't take to New York."

"She didn't take to it? That's a funny turn of phrase."

Melvin fixed his eyes on a rickety white fence, but remembered the pillars of steel supporting the bank building. He heard the murmur of his parents' voices in the study. He saw the glow of the town house windows when he returned home late at night. "My family was gone," he said. "There didn't seem to be anything holding me there. Besides, this may be a different kind of place, but it's not a lesser place."

Flannery turned a sharp gaze on him. "Are you sure?"

He smiled, both because the question was absurd, and because he wasn't sure.

They were quiet for a few minutes.

"I thought there would be fewer expectations here," he heard himself say. "That appealed to me."

"Expectations from whom?"

Why was he entertaining this nonsense? Why had he said this much?

"You need to take your turns a little tighter," he said. "Go that way." He was pointing away from town. He hadn't told his wife about this driving lesson; he knew she wouldn't like it.

"Well?" Flannery asked.

"Shush," he said, and was surprised both at himself for saying something so rude and at Flannery for not being offended.

She stopped the car at an empty intersection. There were worn red barns on two of the corners. She paused for a little too long; the car hiccupped, shuddered, then went dead.

"Oh, dear," Flannery said into the air, which was suddenly quiet.

Melvin was relieved to have something to do. He checked over his shoulder for traffic. "Take your time," he said. "Give it a little gas, then release the clutch. You're doing fine."

She pumped the gas pedal with her foot, and the car lurched forward.

"Gentle," he said.

"Gentle," she repeated. The car staggered forward for a few seconds like a drunk at the end of a party, then settled into a smooth speed.

They crisscrossed the country roads, which were strung like ribbons across green and gold fields. *Physical beauty*, Melvin thought at one point, as an argument for this place, but he didn't say the words aloud.

He was constantly aware that he didn't feel settled. It had been a few weeks, but he felt like he had just arrived. *I need more time* had become a recurring refrain in his mind. More and more of his life was taking place inside his head. He was careful around Cookie. He knew how relieved she was to be home, and he didn't want to cause her any concern. She liked him calm and silent, perhaps because it was what she was used to in a man; her father's entry into any conversation felt like a special occasion. When Melvin kept his thoughts to himself, Cookie bubbled happily at his side. When he spoke, her eyes looked scared.

Here, though, in the whizzing car, next to this strange woman, Melvin's thoughts opened up with the force of a barely broken horse galloping through an open gate. The sensation was disturbing, but also exhilarating. He pictured himself as a boy running through a field. He pictured himself and Cookie kissing on a park bench, beside a pond congested with toy boats. He pictured himself handing his notice to the bank board. He pictured the rose shade that painted certain buildings in New York at sunset. *Physical beauty*, he thought again.

"How's your job?" Flannery asked.

"It's working out just fine, thank you."

"Really?"

Melvin thought about the small rectangle of his office, the reception-ist who chewed her gum too loudly, the determined silence the other men pointed in his direction. He was aware of how glad he was to be here, in the noisy car, under the wide-open sky.

"Really."

"That's not what I heard." Flannery slid her hands up and down the steering wheel with the pleasure specific to new drivers. "Miss Mary men-tioned during her weekly spiel that your workers are uncomfortable with you being in charge. I'll turn left here, okay?"

"Okay." The road she was pointing to headed away from Mill-edgeville. Away from Milledgeville was good. "They'll get used to me."

Flannery shook her head.

Melvin had been quick to pick up on the nature of his new posi-tion. He found individual insurance policies simple to negotiate. He was able to inspect a house in town and come up with an appraisal that was equal to any that Tom Brown, the office expert, could submit. The farms, however, were trickier. Melvin couldn't read the mess of shaggy land, the tight-lipped houses, or the squares of crops. He had trouble separating the sections of the farm that produced from those that didn't. He had an insurance tome that detailed the types of cattle raised in the area and what a herd of Damascus was worth versus a herd of Angus. The book further outlined the general value of all cattle, sheep, swine, goats, horses, mules, asses, and burros. This morning, Melvin had found himself standing in thick mud next to a wooden fence, trying to name a cluster of grunting, shitting, two-ton animals that were giving him the evil eye. He didn't blame them. He knew he looked ridiculous with his neat suit, ruined shoes, and reference book. He felt like he was back in elementary school again as Tom Brown, looking like he had grown out of this mucky land with his hands in his pockets, murmured the answer in his ear.

Melvin would figure it out. It was only a matter of time. He had been learning his entire life. He could learn this too. "Where does Miss Mary come up with this stuff?"

Flannery smiled again. He could tell she had decided not to push the subject.

She said, "Do we need to head back?"

He looked at his watch. It was silver and heavy; it had belonged to his father, and to his father's father before him. When Cookie dragged Melvin out to buy clothes, he always found himself drawn to the watch counter. He toyed with the idea of buying a new watch, one that didn't weigh his arm down and make him think of the past, but he could never commit to the purchase.

He was relieved when Flannery didn't repeat the question, when she rolled the steering wheel to the side and turned onto a new road. They passed a lake. The scene was idyllic. Two young boys sat on a raft with fishing poles in their hands.

Melvin was struck, for the hundredth time, by the pace of life in Georgia. Here, he was aware of every tick of the clock, every breath that filled his lungs. He could be late back to the office, because none of his employees cared where he was or what he was up to. The pulse of this place was measured, and Melvin had to slow his own in accordance. Inside the car, with this company, though, life seemed to move at full speed.

He jerked in his seat, even though they were moving steadily. He had the sensation of pulling himself back from the edge of something. There was a sinking sensation in his chest that was somehow pleasant and unpleasant when he told Flannery to turn around.

The newlyweds left the Himmel house before dessert because Daisy had come down with one of her headaches. They walked slowly, in deference to the heat. It was too hot for true darkness to descend. The air was gray; Melvin and Cookie walked on hazy pavement, past dusky houses and parked cars that appeared to float. Lightning bugs flashed on and off.

Cookie held her husband's hand. She could see her own shadow, distended by the half-light. Her figure stretched across the lawn they were passing. She watched her arm and leg move forward. On one side she looked alone, but when she turned her body slightly, her shadow joined with Melvin's. He towered over her, and her inky double looked like a small, thin appendage of him. Cookie got a measure of satisfaction, seeing herself stretched out this way. With the minutest twist of her frame, she could control her appearance.

She was glad to be on this street, in this moment. She was glad to be back in a place where the smells and the weather and the voices made sense to her. She could tell that her husband was finding the same things jarring, but she knew he would adjust. He already was. Melvin was stronger than she was; he couldn't be defeated by a place. And she was doing her best to help him. She was already the president of three separate ladies' clubs. She was stringing them to the fabric of Milledgeville like a line of Christmas lights.

Cookie glimpsed the strong shape of their house at the end of the road. It rose higher than the other houses in the neighborhood. For some reason, the sight reminded her of the grand foyer in the Whiteson town house. She pictured the marble floor and the swirling staircase. The portrait of Melvin's parents in the library. The numerous powder rooms, which were also built of marble. Cookie had followed Melvin from room to room on a tour she could tell he had given many times. The house felt like New York to her: coated in hard surfaces, needlessly large and unwelcoming. Cookie couldn't have lived there. No one was meant to live there, except the Whiteson line of heirs. Cookie sighed. She was almost home.

"It's so quiet," Melvin said.

"Yes." She watched her shadow-head bob across a neighbor's driveway.

"Listen."

She listened.

"What can you hear?"

"Bugs. Cicadas."

"Apart from that."

"Nothing."

"Isn't that remarkable?"

"Yes," she said, at the same time wondering whether it was actually worthy of remark.

"We might as well be standing in the desert. I thought it would be quiet here, the way it's quiet in Central Park, but it's not. There's no noise to be blocked out. It's silence with a backdrop of silence. We can hear everything, which is nothing."

Cookie took a deep breath in. She smelled jasmine. She glanced at her husband. His profile was dignified and handsome. She could see his lineage, his pedigree. She could see that he had excellent bone structure, that he was from a tribe that could not be vanquished. No matter what happened, Melvin would go on. She remembered looking at his profile while they toured the town house and hoping that he would leave the city with her. She had prayed that he would ask for her hand. That she would take his name, and belong to him.

She heard herself say, "Promise me you won't go back there."

Melvin turned his head. "New York is over for me. You know that."

"Not New York. Andalusia."

His eyes narrowed. He was silent for a moment. "I thought we were having a nice evening."

Their initial argument, when he had told her he was going there to turn down a peacock, was terse. Cookie had been taken unawares and had a hard time expressing herself. *Just don't go*, she said, over and over. They had been in the middle of unpacking the study, surrounded by books that had belonged to Melvin's parents.

Since that day, she had been thinking about returning to the subject. It was a door he had opened, which she needed to close. Definitively. She hadn't planned to say anything tonight, though. The request had slipped out.

"It's important to me," she said, "that we start out on the right foot here. I had a life in this town before, you know. I want to do everything right this time."

"And avoiding Flannery has something to do with that?"

"Yes."

Melvin studied her.

"I don't want her to know anything about us. She writes about people and makes them ugly. That's what she does. It's who she is."

He looked surprised. "I thought she wrote fiction."

Cookie clung to Melvin's hand and wondered why words were always so inadequate. "It's not fiction. It's real. It's about us, the people in this town. There's a fat woman in her novel that *is* Miss Mary, except she's horrible. There's a character who has hair just like Mama, and she says it looks like ham gravy. That's just rude, I mean, how can hair look like gravy?"

Melvin smiled.

The smile annoyed Cookie. She watched her shadow contort, a series of sharp angles. "Isn't it enough," she said, "that the woman ruined our wedding?"

"That wasn't her fault. It was the peacocks, and they didn't ruin our wedding. Our wedding was perfect."

Cookie shook her head. She remembered her purple, swollen eye. "It wasn't perfect."

"Sweetheart," Melvin said.

"You don't know her. She'll size you up like you're made of dollars and cents. She'll count you up and reckon how much of you she can use."

"She's ill," Melvin said. "Really ill. And as far as I can tell, completely harmless."

"Illness isn't an excuse for being mean."

"Why are you talking like this?" Melvin shook his head. "I don't want you to be upset."

"Then promise me you won't go back."

"I feel like there's something you're not telling me."

"Just promise."

He paused. "If it's that important to you, then sure, I promise."

Cookie watched her husband kiss the back of her hand. He didn't want to argue with her. Melvin was a gentle man, a good man. He would never hurt her. He had followed the path his parents had set him in New York in order to make them happy. Here and now, he cared deeply about her happiness. She knew this to be true.

She followed him into the house and upstairs to the bedroom, where they made love. They had made love nearly every night since the eve of the wedding. While they touched each other in the dark, the memory of that occasion was with her. He kissed her neck and the underside of her breast and tipped her thigh to the side like he was swinging open a door. Cookie remembered the roughness of that first night, and the noise. Melvin had never touched her with that kind of force again. His hands were weightless as they traveled her skin.

Cookie hadn't expected to enjoy sex; she had always considered it something that a woman simply did with her husband. She had expected some kind of pain, and confusion. What she had not expected was the honeyed warmth that ran through her veins, the twist of an oar deep inside her, the gasps of pleasure. Her body spun out of her control, and her mind did too. She heard the peacocks cry. Melvin said, *I love you.* He held her by the shoulders, curving her back, and then her thoughts drifted away as he landed softly on top of her.

Melvin fell asleep. Cookie lay still for a minute, then put on her robe and went downstairs to check that the doors were locked. She did this every night. She knew that three blocks away her parents never locked their doors, and neither did the neighbors, but if she wasn't sure the doors were locked then she wouldn't be able to sleep. She also enjoyed this part of her nighttime routine, because it gave her a chance to visit with the house.

The rooms were only partially furnished, and boxes were stacked in several corners, but that didn't matter. The bones of the building were on display. The doorways arched, and the ceilings were high. She walked from the front door to the kitchen, trailing her fingertips against the wall. She heated a cup of milk on the stove and drank it out of a tall glass, sitting alone at the kitchen table.

Cookie had read *Wise Blood* in her senior year of high school. It was the first novel Flannery published, and it was the only book Cookie had ever read from cover to cover. She had started books, or even skimmed them, for English class, but she had learned early on that reading whole novels wasn't necessary; it was easy to bluff the questions her teacher might ask. It wasn't like math, where there was only one right answer and everything else was wrong. Books were made up and could be interpreted in seemingly endless ways.

"Cookie," her teacher had asked one afternoon, "why does Emma Bovary have so many affairs?"

"Hm?" Cookie said.

"You heard me," the teacher said.

Cookie stalled for time by looking around at the boys and girls she had grown up with. Her first kiss had been with the farm boy in the back corner. She had two ex-best friends in the room. The football player she was currently considering dating was trying to hide from the teacher behind his notebook. He shot Cookie a smile, which she ignored. She glanced at the window; raindrops smattered the glass.

"I believe the bell is about to ring," she said.

"We have time to hear what you have to say."

Cookie sighed. She had only glanced at the back cover of the book, but she was confident, when she spoke, that her answer would meet with the teacher's approval. "Emma Bovary has affairs," she said, "because life bores her."

Cookie read Flannery's book because everyone in town was talking about it, and she didn't like to feel left out. Her mother had read the novel and screamed, *Well, I never!* several times from the comfort of her armchair. People from every corner of Milledgeville complained that someone they knew was in the book. The gossipy woman with the pear-shaped calves was Miss Mary. Apparently, the black steward on the train was the spitting image of the colored man at the local gas station. The greedy landlady at the end of the book was attributed to several women in the area; no one could make up their mind whom she resembled most.

Cookie thought Flannery had some nerve, using people's lives like that. The idea burned her up, but she didn't feel right taking part in the general conversation until she'd read the truth for herself. The loudest protesters of the *Wise Blood* controversy were quite open about the fact that they hadn't read the book. They didn't have to, they said;

they could just tell how horrible it was. Cookie had similar intuitions, but felt compelled to roll up her sleeves and make sure.

She didn't tell anyone she was reading it. She started the novel one Sunday afternoon after church. Truthfully, she was a little excited to see what Flannery had to say. She expected to laugh at some of the descriptions of people in their town. Her mother, despite her squeals of horror, had enjoyed the novel, and Cookie wondered if she would have the same experience.

Almost from the first sentence, though, Cookie felt as though the book grabbed her by the shoulders and plunged her under water in a filthy bathtub. She couldn't break the surface because she couldn't stop reading, and she couldn't breathe because there was no air. The sentences made her eyes sting, and the fetid water stained her skin and traveled inside via her nose, ears, and mouth. Cookie had never felt so uncomfortable, so quickly, in her entire life.

She regretted reading the book by the end of the first paragraph, but she knew she wouldn't put it down. It was as if the pages were attached to her fingers and the only way out of the story was through it. Cookie recognized Miss Mary and she recognized the man at the gas station and she recognized the depressing town of Taulkinham as Milledgeville. The book became uglier with every sentence. Cookie hadn't known a book could be this awful.

There was a character who drank whiskey from a fruit jar, like the town librarian's lush sister. An aggressive policeman took over a traffic intersection the same way the young cop from Decatur did. A teenage boy, who just wanted a friend, wore a yellowish suit and a pea green tie. Cookie had a vague memory of her father wearing such a suit when she was a child. Was she making that up, or was it true? She wasn't sure. The book was messing with her mind, making everything seem different and somehow worse. Cookie was discomfited by how these ugly words had the ring of truth about them. Life *was* disappointing and hideous, and she had been a fool to think otherwise.

There was a grandfather who disrespected his grandson's face because it looked just like his own. There was a tale about a beautiful woman who killed her baby simply because she didn't want her. The woman had no positive attributes other than her good looks, and, as one of the characters said, *That ain't enough.*

There were sour-looking skies and familiar landscapes and people wearing ill-fitting clothes and worst of all, there was a teenage girl that quickly became Cookie's least favorite character. The girl had bottle-green eyes. She had white skin and red lips. Cookie had these things too.

From all the gossip Cookie had heard about the book, it was clear that no one in Milledgeville believed any character was based on him or herself. Each horrible creation was obviously rooted in some other poor soul. The man at the gas station rolled his eyes when asked what he thought about the book. The librarian's sister claimed that the drunken waitress resembled one of Flannery's Savannah cousins. Even Miss Mary, who by unanimous consent was the template for Mrs. Hitchcock, was in denial. She waved her hand and said, "I've known Flannery O'Connor since she was a teensy-tiny baby. She loves me too much to do something like that. Shame on you all for even thinking it."

As far as Cookie was concerned, Miss Mary and all the others were lucky not to see the truth. Cookie knew, from the first line of description, that Sabbath Lily—the base, stupid, lustful daughter of the crooked preacher—was a cruel misrepresentation of herself. Cookie knew that every searching, disdainful look Flannery had ever given her had culminated in this character, in this moment of Cookie lying shivering in bed reading about her actual, ugly soul.

Sabbath Lily was a green-eyed, white-skinned, red-lipped phony. She was pretending to be pure, when in truth, she was the opposite. She wanted Hazel Motes, but it was almost impossible to tell what she wanted him for. She was conniving, seemingly happier to tell a lie than the truth. When she wasn't lying, she had no idea what to say; Sabbath Lily was hungry for something life had no intention of handing her. She wanted, and was always disappointed. Cookie recognized the girl in a way she had never recognized anyone before. It was like Sabbath Lily was the shadow she had always known was there but never managed to see.

No one else in Milledgeville would ever guess the connection. Sabbath Lily was described as "homely," and this was the last word people would ever use to describe Cookie, who was the most popular girl in her class, and had recently been crowned homecoming queen. Both girls had green eyes, but no one would give that a second thought. Cookie had loving parents; Lily's father just wanted to get rid of her. If Cookie were to make a list of the differences between her and the character, it would be a long one, but this would simply show how well Flannery had covered her tracks with intelligence and deceit. Cookie saw through it all.

The morning after she finished the book, she went directly to the school library. Because of the early hour, it was nearly deserted. Cookie surveyed the unfamiliar room. She located the table with several copies of the novel on display. Next to the pile was a photograph of Flannery. The writer looked uncomfortable: her hair a series of stiff curls, her smile forced. Beneath the picture, the librarian had handwritten: *Believe it or not, Flannery is a Baldwin High alumna! Aim high, boys and girls!*

Cookie glanced around. No one was in sight. She picked up the stack of books and carried them to the botany section. She hid them behind a dusty tome on plant species that looked like it hadn't been touched in decades. On her way out of the library, she brushed against the photo of Flannery with her elbow. Cookie heard it skid across the floor.

She tried to stop thinking about the book after that. When she saw someone reading it, she turned in the opposite direction. She threw her mother's copy away beneath a mess of broken eggshells in the trash, and feigned ignorance when Daisy asked if she had seen it. Talk in town began to die down, so Cookie was almost able to pretend that it hadn't been written. The novel was simply a bad dream she suffered through some nights, writhing under her sheets, silently screaming inside her head.

Sunday was the only morning that Flannery didn't work. She and Regina got dressed in pressed skirts and planted large hats on their heads. The car was broken, so they climbed into the pickup truck. This was an involved endeavor. Flannery had to pass Regina her crutches and then hoist herself up. She helped her legs into place by lifting them with her hands.

"Aren't we a sight," Regina said, once they were on their way. "I've a mind to park a few blocks from church so no one sees this rattle trap."

"God doesn't care," Flannery said.

"Well, he's not going to be impressed."

Flannery crossed her arms over her chest. She knew her mother was just talking; she would park close to the church so Flannery wouldn't have far to walk. She regarded the sunny morning. It was a relief not to be at her desk. This was the only time away from her writing that she didn't consider a waste.

"Is the car repair expensive?" she asked. "I should get the check for that article in a couple weeks."

"The one about the peacocks? Hard to believe anyone would pay good money to read about those feathered fools."

"Well, someone did."

"Hm."

Flannery looked out the window. She wished she were driving; she and Melvin had only had a couple of lessons, but she already much preferred the driver's seat to the passenger's.

This is good news, her doctor had said, when he told her she could start driving. *Now you'll have a little independence.* Regina had been out of the exam room at that point, and Flannery and the doctor exchanged a knowing smile.

A little independence was the line that kept repeating in Flannery's head during her lessons. She found the idea amusing. What was the point of a little of something like that? Could a person be just a little free? A little healthy? It seemed like the sort of quality that required all or nothing.

But still, she enjoyed being behind the wheel of the car, and she enjoyed rolling the car window down and feeling the wind spray her face. She enjoyed leaving Andalusia in an unfamiliar vehicle, with unfamiliar company. When she accelerated past Miss Mary's farm, she felt her heart lighten.

"A little slower," Melvin had said at the start of their most recent lesson. "Not so loose on the turn. All right, easy now."

Flannery had been nervous at the idea of driving, but in practice, she felt completely carefree. Her lessons as a teenager came back to her, and she remembered the necessary skills. Occasionally, she confused the gas pedal with the brake, but those instances fortunately took place on deserted country roads and had the somewhat comic effect of eliciting a gasp from Melvin, who threw his arms out as if to protect them both from flying through the windshield.

She got pleasure from teasing Melvin too; he was an easy target. She sped up and then abruptly slowed down, just to call a look of concern to his face. She asked, "How's the new life going?"

"It's not a *new* life," he said. "We only get one, as far as I understand."

"Okay," she said. "So you have the same life, just a new location, family, job, and wife. Is that right?"

He squinted through the windshield as if expecting some danger: a sudden thunderstorm or a runaway truck. "That's right."

Flannery tried to imagine adopting all those changes in her own life, but the idea made her head hurt, so she stopped. She had done her moving and changing during her early twenties. She had strolled the streets of Manhattan and gone on awkward dates. She had peered hopefully around every corner, and into every new face, wondering: *Will you shape my life?*

Her life was shaped now. She was rooted, and—outside of Melvin's car—slow-moving. She was like one of the peacocks, hard to shake from his favorite perch.

Her mother pressed her foot on the brake. The truck slowed, then stopped. They were in front of the church.

"Keep moving," Flannery said. "There aren't any parking spots here."

Regina smiled. "Not yet there aren't." She laid her hand on the horn. The noise blasted the air. H O-O-O-N-K! Men and women chatting in front of the church turned and stared. An old woman standing by the curb cupped her hand over her mouth in apparent disgust.

Regina continued to press down the horn.

"Don't you think you're being a little rude?" Flannery asked in a mild voice.

"Nope."

They both watched the librarian, clearly flustered by the loud noise, pull out of the prime parking place she had just occupied, so Regina could pull in.

Regina snorted as she turned the steering wheel hard to the left. "She's lazy. You know she lives two blocks from here and still drives every Sunday. Serves her right if she has to walk a few extra steps."

They climbed out of the truck to sighs and shaking heads. Conversations quickly resumed, though; this group knew the O'Connors well, and had, therefore, been more startled than shocked by the style of their arrival.

Regina crossed the lawn like a queen, deigning to greet her subjects. Near the front door, she stopped to survey her surroundings and
frowned. Flannery knew she had done a rough head count and decided
that attendance was shamefully low. Most of the town was currently filling the Presbyterian church across town. This imbalance had been the
case Regina's entire life, and it never failed to bother her.

"We should work on recruitment again," she said. "Really, something
needs to be done, Father."

"Good morning, Regina. Flannery," Father Cole said with a smile.
He stood next to the door in his white robes, his hands clasped in front
of him. He was young. Too young, Regina would complain on the ride
home.

"Welcome," he said.

Once they were in their pew, Flannery closed her eyes. When her
mother and the other parishioners stood, and then knelt, then stood
and knelt again, she kept her seat. She gave Father Cole only half her
attention. He was talking about the dangers of pride. She figured she
had heard every possible sermon a hundred times by now. The subjects
were the stock and trade of Catholicism: pride, gluttony, sloth, jealousy,
impiety, vice, vanity, salvation, resurrection, forgiveness, and so on and
so forth.

Flannery used the time to perform her own worship. She prayed and
gave thanks silently, in her own time. When Regina nudged her in the
ribs, she opened the hymnal and sang. Her mother's voice was loud and
matter-of-fact; Regina was shouting more than singing. The librarian,
always off-key, warbled behind them. The bank manager, proud of his
loud baritone, tried to guide them through the notes like a shepherd
leading sheep through a tricky passage. When the elderly woman in the
back row broke into a coughing fit, he gave her a stern look. Father Cole
sang with his eyes shut, his face pink and sincere.

The congregation sounded terrible, Flannery thought, amused. But
just as she was having the thought, something changed. Almost certainly

by mistake, the voices fell into line. The group rode the melody up and up, the sound swelling like a wave. Flannery found herself moved by the music. There was a moment of pure, pristine song at the top, before the wave receded and each man and woman retreated to their own private shore.

When they returned to the farm, there was a tractor parked next to the house. Two figures were waiting on the porch.

"It's a good thing you baked that coffee cake this morning," Flannery said.

Regina nodded. "I must have known."

"Hello!" Miss Mary called. She stood up from the porch swing, and the structure caterwauled with relief. "Hello!"

"Calm down," Regina said, climbing out of the truck. "This isn't some great reunion. We saw you three days ago."

Gigi waved shyly from her seat on the steps.

"I took Gigi home with me from church," Miss Mary said. "And we were talking and said, why not stop by and surprise the O'Connor ladies?"

"Why not, indeed." Flannery made her way up the porch steps, her hip aching, and settled into her chair.

"You know that you're happy to see us," Miss Mary said. "What else would you have to look forward to, without a visit from us?"

"You don't fool me," Regina said. "You just wanted my lemonade."

Miss Mary's face creased into a smile. "Well, that *would* be nice. And, don't be mad, but I poked my head in the kitchen when we got here and saw a gorgeous-looking goodie on the counter. That would be a perfect companion for some lemonade."

Regina rolled her eyes and banged through the porch door. When she returned she had four glasses tucked under one arm and a pitcher in her other hand. She laid those down, went back inside, and reappeared with a cake pan.

"We had a lovely turnout at church this morning," Miss Mary said. "The building was practically bursting. Standing room only."

Flannery couldn't stop a grin; Miss Mary knew how much this type of comment bothered Regina. Regina's face darkened, but she didn't respond.

"The Whitesons were there," the large woman continued. "What a stunning couple they are. Did you notice, Gigi? Cookie shines like my best lamp, and Melvin is so solid-looking. He has wonderful shoulders. They remind me of John and Jackie."

Regina handed them each a piece of cake on a square napkin. "It's your recipe," she said to Miss Mary.

"Delicious," the woman said after taking a bite.

Something occurred to Flannery, and she gave Miss Mary a closer look. It was possible that this unexpected visit had a motive. Perhaps Miss Mary had seen or heard about Melvin and Flannery's driving lessons. Miss Mary was certainly capable of weaving her apparently innocent patter into a net to be dropped over Flannery's head. If she had heard even a hint about Melvin driving around the countryside with Flannery, she would be here to collect the facts. She would consider herself entitled to the wheres, whens, whys, and hows.

But the large woman, upon inspection, did not appear to be harboring a nefarious plan. She had finished her cake and was gazing up at the sky. She yawned and said, "That breeze is a godsend. What a glorious day."

Flannery felt her shoulders relax. She didn't want her business spread all over town, and she suspected Melvin would feel the same way.

"Now we're going to talk about the weather?" Regina said. "Spare me."

Gigi was bent over a science textbook. From what Flannery could see, she was reading a chapter about lightning. As a child, Gigi had been chatty, but adolescence had quieted her tongue. She was more likely to laugh than speak.

Flannery considered the dark-haired girl. Miss Mary followed

Flannery's gaze. She said, "It can be dull for her, with just me in the afternoons. That's part of why I like to take her visiting."

"It's not dull," Gigi said. "I love spending time with you."

"You're a saint, Mary," Flannery said. "A veritable do-gooder."

"That's the god's honest truth," Miss Mary said. "So stop rolling your eyes." She smoothed Gigi's braid with her hands. "Did I tell you how beautifully Joe has taken to his new job? He's back to his old self—smiling and talking." She sighed. "It's a wonderful thing to see."

"That boy's got a good head on his shoulders," Regina said. "I always knew he'd be fine."

"He just needed to get out in the world. I owe your mother a debt of thanks," Miss Mary said to Gigi.

The girl shrugged. She was looking down at the book. "It says here that an irrational fear of lightning is called astraphobia. I never heard that word before."

"Doesn't seem irrational to fear lightning," Flannery said. "Being struck by it will mess you up pretty good."

"I agree," Gigi said.

Miss Mary shifted her weight, and the porch swing complained. "I don't go in for science talk. The world works the way it works, and there's no point in breaking it apart to look at the pieces." Her face brightened. "Oh, did you hear that Melvin bought Cookie a new car? Guess what color it is."

"Oh, for heaven's sake," Regina said. "Who cares?"

"It's yellow. Apparently Melvin loves the color of Cookie's hair so much he wanted her car to match it. Can you imagine?"

"Miss Mary loves that." Gigi had a finger planted in the middle of a page so she wouldn't lose her place.

"I do. I think it's gloriously romantic. If Mr. Treadle even considered doing such a thing, I'd *swoon*. Swoon, I tell you."

"You'd look dashing in a brown car," Flannery said.

The woman smiled. "There's more. Cookie's talking about making donations around town. To the library, the hospital, the college. Loads of money. She's making sure people feel her weight. All the big organizations are kissing up to her."

"It's a real shame they aren't Catholic," Regina said. "Sacred Heart could use the help. I wonder if I could talk them into converting." She leaned forward, her fingers on her lips.

Miss Mary shook her head. "Regina O'Connor. Poor Cookie only just got home from that awful city, she doesn't need you bombarding her with pamphlets."

Regina rocked her chair, her eyes thoughtful.

"And don't even think about bothering that young man. Why would someone that rich bother with religion? Melvin Whiteson can buy anything he needs. He doesn't have to pray for it. You just leave them alone." She paused. "You accuse me of doing ill with all my talk, but what you don't appreciate is that I really am out to help people."

Normally, Flannery would have laughed at this, but she stayed quiet. She pictured Melvin and Cookie beaming at their wedding. How they had bent toward each other while they spoke, looking for any excuse to make contact. How the women around them had kept up a constant chorus of oohs and ahhs, their faces almost reverential, as if they were honored to simply be in the couple's presence. To be in the presence of love.

She shook her head. Miss Mary and Regina were talking about a cow that was making its way from Andalusia to the Treadle farm in the middle of the night despite the stretch of fence separating the two properties.

"I'm tired," she said, knowing that this remark would inspire sympathetic looks from everyone present. No one would question the statement, or ask her to stay; there were conveniences to being permanently ill. Flannery stood and went inside, where she shut herself in her room.

Lona sat upright in her chair. Bill sat across from his wife in his dress uniform, his hands resting on the white tablecloth. They rarely went out to dinner together. When they visited Bill's parents in Decatur, they stopped at a fast-food restaurant on the way, but that was only once a year, and Gigi was always with them. Except for special occasions, Bill did not believe in wasting money on marked-up food, and his benchmark for what constituted a special occasion was very high. They were both awkward with the gleaming plates and the selection of forks. They stole glances at the open bottle of wine. They spoke in a near-whisper.

"I'm so happy for you," Lona said. "Three days before your birthday, even. This is exactly what you wanted."

"In a few months," Bill said, "once I've deposited a few of these new paychecks, you can finally relax."

Lona smiled, but it was a polite, watery smile. "What do you mean?"

"I mean, you can stop working. The steak is good, isn't it?"

"Yes, it is."

"I'll be chief in three years. I was more than a little worried, to be honest with you, that I wouldn't get this post. I thought he might give it to one of the local boys, even though they're thick as logs. Now I know this is a meritocracy, so I can really apply myself. The sky's the limit. I'm thinking beyond chief, beyond this town."

Lona cut her meat into small bites. She took a sip of the wine and rolled it around her tongue.

"It's been killing me, watching you work all these years. I wanted you to quit after Gigi was born, but it wasn't possible." Bill looked straight at his wife. "I'm sorry for not being a better husband in that way. I'm sorry you had to work. But that time is almost over."

"I didn't mind," Lona said. "Please don't beat yourself up, Bill. I was happy to help. In fact, I'm so used to the work, I don't know what I'd do with myself without it. How would I spend my time?"

"You could join some of the ladies' clubs, play more of a role in the community. You could even, if you wanted to, have another baby."

"A baby?" Lona's eyes widened. This topic had been shelved over a decade earlier, for financial reasons. It was covered with cobwebs. The words cracked a door deep inside her, offering a glimpse of a forgotten time, of forgotten desires.

"It's just an idea." Bill's cheeks flushed. "Maybe it's the wine, and I'm saying more than I should. But what I mean, sweetheart, is that things can be different now. We've been waiting and biding our time for years, and now we're in motion."

"We're in motion," Lona repeated. She raised her glass, her own cheeks flushed.

She was nervous over the next few weeks. She felt like she was waiting for the ground to open up beneath her feet. Lona usually smoked a joint a day, but now she averaged three. She wrote to her friend asking for extra supplies. When Bill came home from work, she searched his eyes for signs of imminent change. She was often unable to stay awake until he crept into the house though, which made sustained alertness difficult. Bill was working double shifts, and volunteering to handle night surveillance in order to further impress the chief.

Her husband had more men under his command than he'd had as

sergeant, and he spent long hours figuring out how to make their operations more efficient. Bill assured her that as soon as he had his responsibilities in hand, he would have time to eat dinner with her and Gigi again. He would have more time for his family. Lona told him that she understood, and then lay awake at night, slightly stoned, not thinking about her specific possibilities, but vaguely aware that they were on the horizon like a sunrise. She wore lipstick and her most seductive nightgown (the one with no sleeves), and held out for as long as she could before crashing hard into sleep.

She had finished two sets of curtains for the Whiteson house and had five rooms left to go. Work was proceeding at a slower pace than she had first anticipated, because Cookie liked to sit with her decisions before declaring them final. She often changed her mind. She also insisted that Lona order the fabric from Atlanta or New York, instead of from the local vendor, and there were constant shipping delays.

Since the Whitesons were paying Lona enough to ensure that they were her sole client, she didn't mind. She even liked her new routine. She picked up Joe from school and drove slowly across town. She parked in the back corner of the Whitesons' driveway, under the generous shade of a mulberry bush. She pulled a joint out of the side pocket of her purse, pressed it to the tip of her lighter, then handed it to Joe. "Thank you," he said, before bringing the rolled paper to his lips. They passed the joint back and forth three or four times, usually in silence, before climbing out of the car. While she smoked, Lona thought, *This might be my last job*.

Cookie was always at meetings, so they used the key under the mat. Lona made Joe unlock the door so she could watch his slow, concentrated movements. He insisted that pot had no effect on him, but Lona liked to test this claim whenever she had the opportunity. He gave her a triumphant look when he opened the door on his first try.

They removed their shoes by the door so they wouldn't track dirt inside. Lona was becoming familiar with the details of the home—where the stair boards creaked, where the phone was located, where the cleaning supplies were tucked away. She had never given this much time to one client before.

When they were thirsty, they drank water out of the two oldest and least expensive looking glasses, which Lona found in the back of the kitchen cupboard. They used the smaller bathroom on the ground floor. Lona in her stocking feet, and Joe in his socks, padded from room to room with their tools.

She tried to imagine, walking the long halls, how it would feel to be Cookie Whiteson. To never worry about money and feel no demand on her time. Lona imagined it must be a feeling of lightness. She imagined floating from one interest to another, doing only exactly what she wanted to do, exactly when she wanted to do it. Lona pictured herself lounging on the sofa in this house, taking long baths in the master bathroom, watching the television in the living room. She even pictured herself walking out the front door, her arm hooked with Cookie's, both wearing crisp, formidable hats on their way to an important society meeting. She couldn't imagine the same things taking place in her own home. Her house had no television, the bathtub was enveloped with clotheslines and damp bras, and she would never have the courage to show up at a meeting filled with former clients on her own, hat or no hat.

Lona ran her fingers over the rich, burgundy velvet they had ordered for Melvin's study. This was the most expensive fabric she'd ever purchased for a client, and Lona had only seen it previously as a store sample. It surrounded her on the floor now, yard after decadent yard. She couldn't take her hands off it. The velvet would make a marvelous curtain, heavy but luminous. Soft yet structured.

She had suggested the fabric for the study because it was her favorite room in the house. It looked to her like a room from a movie set. After all, who else had a personal library in Milledgeville? There were long walls of shelves filled with uniform sets of books. Navy spines with gold print, green spines with silver print. The books looked valuable, and unread. There were signs of important work on the desk. There were stacks of papers and an enormous calculator. Many of the sheets were embossed with a fancy font and the lengthy title of a New York company. Beneath the title the print read: *re: accounts of Mr. William R. Whiteson, deceased.* The lower section of the page was covered with graphs and numbers.

"Should I measure the window?" Joe asked.

Lona's shoulders jerked. She had forgotten he was there. This happened fairly often because he was quiet and seemed to share her skill for disappearing.

"This velvet is amazing," she said. "You should come feel it."

The boy shook his head. "That's all right. I'm fine."

"No, really," Lona said. "Feel this."

Joe lumbered across the room as if heavy weights were wrapped around his ankles. His slowness made Lona smile, though it was a smile she hid by turning away. She had become used to the boy's constant companionship. She now counted on Joe to do nearly all her work, except for the designing and sewing. He kept her calendar, told her where to drive next, and allowed her to be as stoned as she wanted without suffering a loss in productivity.

She had even found an aspect of his personality that interested her. She had realized, after two months of working with Joe in near silence, that the boy's polite smile masked a burbling river of sadness. If she looked closely enough, she was able to see his melancholy break the surface like silver leaping fish. When Joe's voice pitched suddenly, or his eyes drifted shut in a darkened room, or his hands shook, Lona mentally took note. The moments appeared in a random pattern, like drops of rain on a window. She wasn't sure why she found these spots of weakness pleasurable, but she did. She collected them, like stamps or rare coins. Some days, if she was in a certain mood, or if she'd smoked more pot than was probably advisable, she even encouraged them, and tried to bring them about. She drew the curtains in the room, plunging Joe into sudden darkness. She surprised him, after hours of quiet, with questions.

"What kind of relationship do you have with your mother?"

"Do you have many friends at school?"

"Would you say you are a lonely person?"

The questions seemed to make the teenager suspicious. "Did my mother put you up to this?" he asked.

"No," Lona said.

His answers were vague, designed to bore the interrogator. His relationship with his mother was fine. He didn't have many friends. He didn't know if he was lonely. Still, Lona was stubborn. She craved more moments, more glimpses for her collection. She pushed him further. She made him smoke pot before and after work, with the intent of loosening his defenses. Unfortunately, this seemed to have the opposite effect. Joe visibly fought for control against the blurring nature of the drug. She watched him become hyperaware of the movement of his hands and the expression on his face. She enjoyed testing him, though, and she assumed that when he did crack, it would be worth the wait.

Joe held the velvet in his hands. He rubbed his thumbs across the fabric. At first he seemed to be going through the motions, in a sporting effort to please his boss. But then his eyes widened, and he placed his entire palm on the velvet. "Wow," he said. "Wow. It's *very* nice." He drew out the word *very*.

Lona giggled.

"What?"

"You're stoned."

"No I'm not." He frowned, but the expression didn't stick. Joe's mouth quivered and then flipped into a smile. "Well, maybe a little, but it does feel really nice."

"It's better than nice. I've never felt anything like it. We're lucky to get to handle something like this."

They both sat on the floor, running their hands over the potential curtain. It was Joe's turn to giggle. The sound was more like a snort, and it made Lona laugh too.

She said, "I've never seen you smile for this long."

He didn't even try to control his mouth now. His smile grew wider. He said, "You should make yourself a dress from it."

"Oh, no." Lona was shocked at his ignorance. Didn't everyone have a basic knowledge of the fabrics that decorated their houses or clothed their bodies? "I could never afford it. This stuff is like gold."

She heard the front door of the house click open and the rap of high heels against the wooden floor. Lona scrambled to her feet, gathering the fabric into her arms.

Joe looked lost on the floor, his hands suddenly empty.

"You can measure the window now." Lona hurried from the room. Cookie was almost never home during the day. There were decisions that needed to be made, and Lona needed the mistress of the house to make them.

She found Cookie in the living room, sitting in the corner armchair, staring out the window. A brown paper bag sat by her feet, a head of celery poking from the top. She turned her eyes when Lona appeared in the archway.

It took Lona a moment to figure out what was strange about the scene. She surveyed the room for something extra, then something missing, before hitting on the anomaly: she had never seen Cookie sit still before. She was always doing something when she spoke to Lona—rearranging a stack of books, opening the mail, or thumping new life into a cushion.

"Are you all right?" she asked.

"I'm fine," Cookie said. "Can I talk to you about something?"

Lona hesitated for only the briefest second. "Of course." There was a shift in the air that she recognized. With a simple adjustment of her posture—a relaxation of her shoulders—Cookie was temporarily promoting Lona from domestic staff to friend and confidante. Lona had seen this frequently with her mother, a silent seamstress expected to go about her work unless a client decided she could offer a convenient perspective. Lona often found herself in this position too. The postmaster had told her, while she made curtains for his den, that he'd had a crush on her oldest sister during high school. The librarian liked to tell the story of Lona's father rear-ending her empty, parked car after a drinking binge. These kinds of shared memories zigzagged across town, an endless skein of yarn binding one person to the next.

Lona had grown up with Cookie, or at least alongside her. For a few summers, they were part of the same pack of kids who played outside together. One time, when Cookie skinned her knee, Lona had carried the younger girl home by piggyback. She could still remember the sound of Cookie's gulpy sobs in her ear. Cookie's skinny arms had been wrapped so tightly around Lona's throat that she had coughed every few steps. Insects had buzzed in the shimmering air. The sun fell behind the old graveyard as they passed the rows of cold stones.

While Lona waited for her employer to speak, she wondered if Cookie remembered clinging to her shoulders, sixteen years earlier.

"Is everything all right?" she asked to break the silence.

"We had an argument," Cookie said.

Lona wondered if she had missed something. Had she drifted off for a moment and failed to absorb a crucial piece of information? She said, "Who did?"

Cookie shook her head.

"I want this house to be perfect," she said. "Melvin is used to grandeur, from his life in New York. You would find it hard to imagine, the wealth he comes from. It's almost unthinkable. He comes from this whole, intact world—" she paused. "If he misses anything, anything at all, I want him to see it here, in our home."

There was a silence then, the kind that asks to be filled. Lona said, "You want him to feel comfortable."

"I want everything to be perfect." Cookie spoke these words reluctantly, as if passing on a long-held secret. Once they were released, she readjusted her posture. Firmness returned to her shoulders. The buzzing insects from their childhood summers streamed from the room, leaving behind two women with the autumnal status of employer and employee.

"What's that you're holding?"

Lona looked down. She was hugging the velvet to her chest. She relaxed her arms. She brushed a loose strand of hair behind her ear and told Cookie about the attributes of the fabric. She had a stab of longing for the moment an hour from now, when she would be in the car, wind rushing through the open window. She remembered her husband's phrase, *We're in motion.*

She had been describing the velvet—its craftsmanship, its rarity—for almost a minute before she realized that Cookie wasn't listening.

Lona cleared her throat. "Should we continue this another time?"

Cookie turned her gaze on her. "Would you mind," she said, "if we started over with the curtains? If we took these down, and the ones in the dining room, and came up with something new? I think we could do something really striking, if we put our heads together. How does that sound?"

"You want to start over completely? In every room?"

"Yes. I think I do."

Lona shook her head. She didn't know what to say. She considered how much work she had already done, and how much longer the job would now take. She waited for a pang of disappointment to hit her chest, but it didn't come. Instead, unexpectedly, she felt a surge of electricity.

If this *was* her final job, it had just been extended indefinitely.

Lona would keep her routine; she would continue to nestle the car beneath the mulberry bush, share a joint with Joe, and then spend the rest of the afternoon at his side. Lona realized that she had been having fun in the Whiteson house. She had been having fun for perhaps the first time in her life. She didn't want this job to end, and the realization felt exhilarating.

"Okay," she said.

Her voice was a bit too loud, and Cookie stared at her for a moment.

Was this what hope felt like? Lona looked at the rejected curtains on the window in front of her. She looked at the stripe of sunlight that painted the floor between the two women. She felt her mouth stretch into an unfamiliar grin.

"Okay," she said. "Let's do it. Let's start over."

M elvin watched Flannery approach the car, using her crutches to propel herself forward. Regina trailed behind her like a kite. Through the open window, Melvin heard the older woman say, "Driving is dangerous in your condition. I don't care what Dr. Merrill thinks; it's not safe."

"I'll be back before dinner," Flannery said.

Melvin got out of the driver's seat to allow Flannery to slide in. He carried her crutches around the car and placed them in the backseat.

"Good afternoon, ma'am," he said to Regina.

She frowned, her eyes still on her daughter.

Flannery flashed her mother a grin, in response to which Regina crossed her arms over her chest. Flannery tooted the horn on the way out of the driveway.

"You enjoy riling her up," Melvin said.

"It's one of my few pleasures."

Melvin stretched out in the passenger seat, his hands clasped behind his head. He felt an unexpected pop of relief, as if he had been waiting all day for someone else to take the wheel. He said, "This is going to have to be our last lesson."

"You say that every time."

Melvin shifted his weight and batted at a fly. He had the same impression as during his first visit, that there was no room for small talk with Flannery. If he was going to speak, he felt compelled to say something honest. This was an unusual feeling. At home with Cookie, he was careful to sound loving and sweet. At work in an office of strangers, he was always sure to sound decisive and competent. In public, he made an effort to appear good-natured and nonthreatening. Ever since he had arrived in Milledgeville, he was always making tiny adjustments to his demeanor, his expression, and even his accent, in order to fit in. With Flannery, he had to drop his pretenses. She was like varnish rubbing the paint off his facade.

"This isn't a joke," he said.

She sighed. "No. But it's not deadly serious either. Men have lied to their wives about worse things than driving lessons."

"I haven't lied," Melvin said. "I've just omitted certain things."

"Well, then," she said, as if that resolved the issue.

She told a story about a drunken dispute between Andalusia's farmhand and his wife the night before, which involved a harmonica wielded as a weapon. When she described the harmonica being passed back and forth like a saltshaker between the couple, as they took turns to beat each other with it, Melvin laughed. Flannery laughed too, a buckling, infectious noise.

Melvin fiddled with the radio knob. There was a kind of giddiness in his chest that seemed linked to the speed of the car. Flannery always drove well over the speed limit, but Melvin never commented on it, because on near-empty roads, what did it matter?

"It would make things easier for me," he said, "if you would just tell me what happened between you and Cookie."

"Why would that make things easier for you?"

"Because then I'd know whether she's overreacting."

"So, if it turns out that I did something mean to Cookie when she was ten, you'll cut off my lessons in retribution?"

"Did you?"

"Not that I can recall."

Melvin wondered, not for the first time, how he had managed to acquire a secret life. He wondered how one driving lesson per week had turned into two. He had planned to give one or two lessons total, in the beginning. He had promised Flannery before he'd promised Cookie, after all. He considered it an obligation. He felt bad for this young woman trapped on her farm. He had figured he would help her gain some freedom by way of driving, and then say goodbye. Cookie would never know.

Melvin hadn't expected to enjoy himself. He hadn't expected to feel a charge in his chest every time he saw Flannery's crazy menagerie of mottled birds. He hadn't expected to think about returning the very moment he had left.

A cumulative weight was developing, though, from his trips to Andalusia. He could hear the weight in his voice when he told Cookie an edited version of his day. He could feel the pressure sitting on his chest while he told Cookie that work had been great and that business was booming. His wife smiled in response to his words. She not only believed him, she wanted to believe him. She was invested in believing him, and this added to the burden on Melvin's chest.

The heavier he felt, the lighter his wife seemed to become. When he and Cookie were in the same room, Melvin had to keep turning his head to keep her in sight. She was like a hummingbird; something inside her resisted stillness. During their courtship, Melvin had often pulled Cookie onto his lap and wrapped his arms around her. Her body tensed at first, but then, a minute into the hug, she would relax completely. Her body melted into his. They would sit that way, in silence, for up to a half hour. Cookie would sigh, and he would kiss her neck. She would press her cheek against his. When they finally separated, they would go about their business as if nothing had happened. They would exchange soft smiles, though, for the rest of the day.

Now, Melvin rarely reached for his wife when she swung past him. He missed the feeling of satisfaction he had gotten from forcing Cookie to surrender, from using his body to contain hers. He missed the intimacy—they were more connected when she was on his lap than when they made love. But that was exactly why he was afraid to hold her. She might use the closeness to ask him questions. She might turn her body so they sat nose to nose. Her eyes would look into his, and she would see that he was hiding something.

In the middle of the previous night, Melvin had promised himself that he would stop visiting Andalusia. He could feel Cookie awake beside him. When her clubs were particularly busy, she suffered from insomnia. They shifted positions in bed, passing pillows back and forth, each trying to make the other more comfortable. *Are you all right? Yes, I'm fine. Can I help you?*

This will be the last lesson, he told himself.

Flannery did a U-turn in the center of an empty road. "How was that, teacher?"

"Perfect." He shook his head clear. If this was the last time, then he should be present and enjoy it.

Flannery turned down another road, one he recognized. "Do we have to go this way again?"

"Of course."

At some point during every lesson, Flannery drove past the mental hospital. It sat just outside of town, a cement rectangle of a building on a neglected piece of land. The hospital had no air-conditioning, so the windows were always open. Melvin had read in the local newspaper that the institution was filled to capacity, but there was never any discernible noise from inside. Occasionally, a handful of nurses in crisp uniforms would be standing on the lawn, drawing hard on cigarettes. The only constant, other than the silence, was the man in the corner window on the second floor. He was always standing there, and he was always waving. There was a curve in the road just before the hospital, and he was waving when Melvin's car came into view. He continued to wave for as long as they were in sight, and then presumably beyond.

"Do you drive us this way intentionally, because you know I find it disturbing?" Melvin asked.

"Do you find it disturbing?"

"Well, of course. Those poor people." They were almost past the building now, the man waving, the monotonous quiet a thin note in the air. "They don't even know who they are."

"Do you know who you are?"

"I'm Melvin Whiteson," he said, deliberately ignoring the complexity of her question.

"It's the rich tapestry of humanity," Flannery said. "I've always liked the place."

"I'm not surprised, having read your stories."

Flannery's eyebrows arched; he'd never mentioned reading her work before.

Melvin thought about this new addition to his underground life. He spent a growing number of hours reading in the public library, or in his parked car. He had checked out Flannery's story collection after the first lesson; it had seemed rude to meet an author and to not read her work. This development resembled his initial visit to Andalusia—he had shown up to be polite, and been sucked into something else altogether. Each story felt like a rope that tugged him forward until he reached the next one. The narratives were difficult to ingest—raw and sometimes mean— but they definitely made him feel something, and he kept returning for more. He couldn't bring the book inside his house, and as a result, he was now spending so much time in his car that he felt like he lived there.

"I'm not going to tell you that they're good," he said. "You already know that. But I do find it interesting, reading the work of someone I'm friends with."

Flannery's cheeks colored.

Was it because he had said they were friends? The words made him feel uneasy too. Up until now, they had avoided any labels other than driving teacher and student.

"Interesting how?" she asked.

"I wondered what it says about you, that there are no happy endings."

He made sure his tone was teasing. "All of your characters are left in some kind of pain."

They passed a field dotted with hay bales. In the corners, the hay was stacked into hulking pyramids. Melvin thought about Hulga, in "Good Country People." She was like Flannery: crippled, living with her mother. When Hulga's wooden leg was stolen by a salesman, Melvin had to put the book down for an entire day.

"Maybe I left them on their way to a happy ending," Flannery said. "Did you ever think of that?"

He shook his head. "No. I just figured you were a glass-half-empty kind of person. Although that's unusual for a religious type."

Flannery laughed. She liked it when Melvin relaxed enough to say such injudicious things. "I'm sure you didn't consider this," she said, "but it's possible that the characters are closer to grace at the end of the stories. Grace changes a person, you know. And change is painful. It's just like you agnostic types to see the pain, but not the transformation."

Melvin gave an exaggerated sigh. "As a group, we do lack clarity."

"*You* certainly do."

Melvin flinched. They had been dancing the line between joking and serious; Flannery had just resolutely crossed it. He usually didn't mind when she criticized his life. This time, though, he felt the jab. "Well," he said. "If we're being honest, I should tell you that I read more than just your work. I asked the librarian to pull some of your press over the years."

She narrowed her eyes. "Why would you do that?"

He shrugged. "It's public record. And it was very interesting. I can't believe you never told me about your moment of crowning glory."

Flannery looked uncomfortable. "Cookie must be terribly busy with meetings, if you have that much time to kill. Is she never home anymore?"

"Don't change the subject. The moment took place when you were five, and it involved a chicken."

Flannery made a noise that was half gasp and half laugh.

As a child, Flannery had trained a pet chicken to walk backward, and the feat had drawn national media attention. A news organization had filmed her conducting the backward waddle of her bird and then shown the footage across the country. Melvin had watched the film in the basement of the library. When the five-minute reel was over, he played it again. The little girl on the screen was pudgy, with chin-length hair. She looked proud of her achievement. Her chin was lifted. Her eyes matched those of the woman next to him.

"Your research is good," Flannery said. "That *was* the most exciting thing to ever happen to me. My life's been downhill ever since."

Melvin put his hand on her shoulder. "You must have been very proud."

He felt Flannery's body stiffen under his touch. He had touched her before, of course. He had helped her out of the car, and their hands had brushed when he took her crutches. But this felt different. When he was able to move his palm back to his side, he continued to feel the warmth of her skin on his own.

They rode out the moment in silence.

When they passed Miss Mary's farm, the car slowed. They turned into the driveway, and the birds could be heard. Squawking and whooping. There was a change in Flannery's expression—her face turned cautious, and weary. Melvin thought, *I will leave this time and never come back*. But the thought fizzled; he lost his discipline. The truth was that he wanted to come back. If he was going to live in this town, and make this life work for him, he needed someplace as loud and wide open as the city he had left. He needed the mess, and the release.

"How about next Tuesday?" he heard himself say.

"Fine," she said. "I'll see you then."

Melvin drove back toward town. He decided to go straight home and tell Cookie that he'd left the office early because he missed her. She would ask about his work, and he would tell her about the successful farm appraisal and the interest in the Morgan property. He would kiss her and ask what was for dinner. They always got along best on the nights after he had been to Andalusia. His mood was exactly the one she wanted for him, all the time.

J oe was in his senior year, and for the first time in his educational career there was no one older or stronger to fear. He hurled himself down the hallways, his adolescent energy tumbling inside him like a litter of kittens in a muslin sack. His locker was across the hall from Gigi Waters's. He nodded at her every day, and she waved in return.

Joe had grown up with Gigi, but he had never paid her much attention. She was his mother's sidekick, the one who got first dibs on a batch of cookies, the girl he tripped or tickled or ignored, depending on his mood. Now he found himself watching her. At first, he wasn't sure what he was looking for. He checked the color of her eyes—green—and decided she must have inherited them from her father. Mrs. Waters's eyes were pale blue. He noticed that Gigi didn't have her mother's long neck. Her fingers were short, instead of slender. Her smile showed her teeth, whereas Mrs. Waters's lips stayed closed. Gigi kept her books arranged by subject in her locker, and her papers were neatly filed. She was clearly more organized than her mother.

Joe reasoned, though, that as a daughter, she must share something with his employer—some gesture or look—and he wanted to find it. Actually, "wanted" was too weak a word—he felt like he *needed* to find it. He didn't know why, and the force of the desire made him uncomfortable, but the fact remained that the imprint of Mrs. Waters on Gigi was a thesis he *had* to establish. Only when he managed to locate traces of the mother in the daughter, would he be able to relax. To that end, Joe sat near Gigi at lunch, and followed her to class.

He was watching Gigi through the crack in his locker door one afternoon, when he heard a group of girls start to sing. "Joe and Gigi, sitting in a tree. K-I-S-S-I-N-G. First comes love, then comes marriage . . ."

They broke off into giggles before pulling themselves together enough to provide a loud finale: "Then comes baby in the baby carriage!"

Gigi rose out of her locker, her face cherry red, her eyes panicked. She shot down the hallway, shouldering her way through the crowd.

"Shut up!" Joe shouted. "Shut up! Shut up!" The anger in his voice scared the girls silent. They scattered in the opposite direction, and he was left alone.

He avoided his locker after that. He kept his books in his bag and carried them with him all day. He maintained a careful distance from his peers. This separation had an air of permanence. Joe had been on his way out; now he was gone. Even if he hadn't approached his fellow students in the past, he had felt a certain kinship with them. He had believed that they were in the same boat. All the boys craved a specific kind of success: a smile from one of the pretty girls, the chance to hold her hand, the dream of touching her breasts. Joe no longer shared those dreams, and the absence confused him. What did he want?

He looked around from his seat in morning assembly and realized that even the pretty girls looked the same to him: wan, desperate, and overly anxious for some kind of real life to begin. They wanted to be women, they were tired of boys, and he could understand that. Adulthood blinked on the horizon like a fog light.

Joe's father had begun to tell him, in words sawed apart by his stammer, about his postgraduation duties. Joe would be expected to order supplies, keep in contact with the buyers, balance the books, repair broken machinery, quell disputes between the workers, buy a new truck every two years, and attend an annual conference on modern farming

practices in Atlanta. These responsibilities were of course in addition to
the daily toil in the mud and dirt, amid the shitting cows and frightened
chickens, coaxing produce out of tired land.

After the locker incident, Joe resolved to not even glance at passing girls. He kept his eye on the clock throughout the afternoon, counting down to dismissal. When he banged through the front doors of the
school, Mrs. Waters was waiting behind the wheel of her car. She didn't
speak when he climbed into the backseat. She just drove.

He had been working for her for six months, and he'd learned how
to be helpful. When Mrs. Whiteson mentioned the time by which she
wanted a certain room completed, he wrote it down in the pocket calendar. He followed Mrs. Waters from room to room, carrying whatever
needed carrying. When she eyed a window in a particular way, he handed
her the sketch pad. When she knelt down in the middle of a puddle of
fabric, he made sure her scissors were within reach. He stayed quiet and
out of sight when she was thinking, and stepped into view when she
stirred to motion.

When work was finished for the day, he helped her into her coat.
He followed her to the car and climbed into the backseat. He was silent
while she drove to a quiet street a few blocks away from the Whitesons'
and parked under the shade of an ancient tree. It was a chilly November,
often dipping into the forties, so she switched on the heat.

They had passed the joint back and forth a few times when Joe
noticed Mrs. Waters looking at him in the rearview mirror. She seemed
to sense when he was feeling out of sorts. Whenever his joints ached, or
beads of sweat broke out across his forehead, or his thoughts shot ahead
to the list of chores he had to complete at the farm, Mrs. Waters's eyes
flitted to his face.

He tried to stay calm beneath the spotlight of attention. He tried to
avoid her gaze. He slouched like a comma on the Naugahyde seat, and
watched strands of hair move across her neck. He was careful to keep his
head below the window. He had grown several inches over the summer,

passing six feet in height, and he was aware that if anyone in town spotted him smoking, his mother would know inside two hours.

He stole a glance at the rearview mirror. She was still watching him. He pinched the joint between two fingers like a dart he was about to throw.

"Mrs. Waters, why do you keep looking at me like that?"

"Please call me Lona."

He tried to imagine calling her Lona.

"I can see things in you that I've seen in myself." Her voice was slow. "It's interesting. I don't mean anything personal by it though. Don't be upset."

Joe had never heard anyone speak like this. Her quiet voice sliced through his center like a fishhook. "What things can you see?"

She shrugged, a graceful movement of her shoulders. "I'm not sleeping well," she said. "Don't listen to me. I don't know what I'm talking about."

"You didn't upset me," Joe said, after a minute. "You can watch me if you want."

"Thank you." Her eyes lowered, and she turned on the engine.

Miss Mary wouldn't leave him alone that night during dinner. She patted his arm and asked him questions about his day. She piled mashed potatoes onto his plate and repeatedly offered a second pork chop. She told him and his father all the news from town, a monologue littered with pauses designed to encourage some kind of reply. She told them that Flannery had just given Regina a mule as a gift, then laughed like it was the funniest thing she'd ever heard. Joe broke away as soon as possible and headed for his room.

His mother knocked on his door an hour later. She had a slice of cake in one hand and a fork in the other. She smiled shyly from the doorway. He let her in, and searched his brain for something he could discuss with her. A year earlier, he wouldn't have been able to engage. Now, at least he could try. Miss Mary beamed while he told her about his history teacher's lopsided toupee, and how no one in class made fun of him because he was so well-liked. She watched him eat and talk with a look of satisfaction.

"I don't know how you stay so skinny," she said. "All I have to do is look at food and I gain weight."

Joe rolled his eyes. "I have to do my homework."

"I'm so proud of you," she said. "I hope you know that. For coming out of your shell. I know you weren't happy when your father and I made you take the job, but—"

"But you were right, as usual." Joe stood up and closed the door while his mother sidled out.

"It's true," she said, from the other side of the wood. "I was right, as usual."

Joe's sleep was feverish that night. He slid from conscious to unconscious and back again. He banged his elbow on the bedpost while rolling over. He was hot, so he took off his pajamas. An hour later he was shivering, so he put them back on.

He woke up early, exhausted and dry mouthed. He moved slowly through his morning chores and his father snapped at him. His classes were a blur, interrupted by a lunch he barely touched. He passed Gigi in the middle of a crowded hallway and her face wrinkled, as if she might cry.

"You look terrible," Mrs. Waters said when he got in the car at three o'clock.

"That makes sense," he said, more to himself than to her.

"Cookie called. She wants to redo the guest room again. She said it was important that we get started right away."

"Why?"

"She didn't say."

"Is it okay for us to stop work in the dining room?"

Mrs. Waters lifted her shoulders, and then dropped them. "Why not?" The question drifted over her shoulder. Joe watched it approach.

"What's wrong?" she asked. "Are you all right?"

He nodded in the direction of the rectangular mirror. They were tucked under the mulberry bush. She got out of the car, and Joe followed. His legs were shaky beneath him.

Cookie met them at the door and led them upstairs. Joe dropped back and tried not to listen while she and Mrs. Waters had a whispered discussion in the corner. At one point, Cookie laid her hand on the seamstress's shoulder.

"It's not too late for you to have another," he heard her say.

Mrs. Waters gave a funny smile. "As far as fabrics, would you prefer lace, or a solid? How much sunlight do you want?"

Joe remeasured the windows in the half-empty room while the women flipped through catalogs. He tried to stand unobtrusively, with the window at his back, while Mrs. Waters placed a phone order for fabric. He heard her request that a rush be put on the shipment and then repeat the address so there wouldn't be any confusion. The clarity of her voice made him wonder if she was running low on pot. If so, it was good timing, because they were in the middle of what could qualify as a work crisis, and Joe was feeling less than capable. He was relieved when he heard the front door open and shut with the steady click that indicated Mr. Whiteson was home. That was their cue to leave for the day.

Joe rushed by Mr. Whiteson with his head down and beat Mrs. Waters to the car. Under his jacket, his shirt stretched damp across his back. He had spent the day sweating, cooling off, and then sweating again. He wiped his hands on his knees and frowned when Mrs. Waters pulled the car to a stop a few blocks from the Whitesons'.

"I've been saving this," she said, and pulled a joint out of the side pocket of her purse. She bent forward and cupped her hand over the end. The match flamed to life and whatever had been simmering in Joe's insides all day reached a boil.

Why not?

He stretched forward in his seat. He placed his hand on Mrs. Waters's shoulder. His eyes widened in shock at what he was doing, but still, he didn't stop. He pulled her toward him, firmly. Her arms were left dangling in front of her, a lit match in one hand, the joint in the other. She didn't have time to protest. Joe pressed his lips to the back of her neck, the neck he had been watching for months. He kissed her skin, her soft skin, his heart blasting in his chest.

He felt Mrs. Waters's body stiffen.

There was a pause. A horrible pause. She leaned away.

"What was that?" she asked.

"I don't know," Joe said. He didn't know. "I'm sorry."

She was quiet for a moment. "I don't think that's what your mother had in mind when she suggested we work together."

Joe had never been so embarrassed in his life. Her surprise faded away and he could see now that she was amused. A smile played around her mouth. He had amused her. And yet, he could still taste her skin on his lips, her sweet and salty skin.

He wanted to die. "It won't happen again," he heard himself say.

"We'll pretend it never happened."

"It never happened."

"Don't worry."

"Okay."

She drove him home. The radio was off, nobody spoke, and the car hit every bump in the road.

Over the course of her life, the story Cookie heard the most often was that of her own conception. Her mother loved to tell the tale; it was Daisy's smooth stone, her good-luck piece, her perfectly crafted story. She hugged it to her chest in the middle of lonely nights. She told it to every person who was important to her; she believed that she couldn't really be known without the story putting her in context. Nearly everyone in town heard the tale at least once while Cookie was in New York. Regina, after hearing it for the umpteenth time during that period, said, "Cripes, Daisy, we know you have a daughter. You don't need to keep telling us how you got her!" But it would take much more than this to stop Daisy and her incessant narrative. She continued to recount the story whenever she was bored, or nervous, or when she thought a moment needed emotional punch.

Cookie knew, when she told Daisy she was pregnant, that her mother would not know how to respond, other than by telling the story, and she was right. Daisy cried, grabbed Cookie into a hug, then wiped her face with one of Big Mike's handkerchiefs. She brushed the tears away quickly, as if she needed to start talking as soon as possible. She rested her hand on Cookie's arm and gave gentle squeezes while she recited the well-worn words.

. . .

Daisy and Big Mike had been married for almost two decades when it happened. She volunteered in local clubs, and he ran his hardware business. They ate dinner at six o'clock every night, and then read together in bed. Nothing had changed in a long time, and they held carefully to a hard-won sense of contentment. Daisy had come to dislike any unplanned changes, and was therefore dismayed to notice, one morning in front of the mirror, that she had gained some weight in her hips. That afternoon, she found herself flushed and breathless halfway up the stairs. She shook her head in self-admonishment. She tried to limit her intake of cake and other sweets, but the pounds wouldn't budge. She thought about foregoing her nightly glass of wine, but decided she wasn't ready to go that far. If she was growing fatter with age, then so be it. There would simply be more of her to love.

While brushing her teeth one evening, the facts came together in a different shape, and tears came to her eyes. *Sweet Jesus*, she thought, *it's menopause*. She remembered that her mother's insides had shut down at around the same age. Daisy spent the next few weeks walking slowly from room to room, bidding a silent farewell to her womanhood.

She made an appointment with her doctor, and when the hour arrived, she lay back on the examining table with the resignation of a woman lowering herself into a coffin.

"You're pregnant," the doctor said.

"Excuse me?"

"About four months along, from what I can tell."

Daisy sat bolt upright and yelled, "Mike!" She had never yelled in her adult life—she'd been raised to be a lady—and the desperate, rusty sound shot through the examination room wall, down the long hallway, and around the corner to the waiting room, where it yanked her husband from his chair. Big Mike looked around, disoriented and confused, ready to defend himself from possible attack by the old lady in the corner or the bored nurse behind the desk. It took a moment for him to realize that the sound was his name, and that the source was his wife. He set off at a jog down the hallway, his heart rattling his chest like a snake trapped in a tin box.

"But you said it wasn't possible," Daisy said. "We gave up hope years ago. Are you absolutely certain?"

"I was certain you wouldn't get pregnant before," the doctor said. "And I'm certain that you're pregnant now. Isn't life funny?"

Cookie was deeply relieved to hear the news from the doctor. She had feared that what was difficult for her mother might prove impossible for her: a snowball-size problem grown, over the course of a generation, into a boulder. She asked the doctor to put the information in writing, so she could show it to Melvin and read it over and over herself.

"It happened so quickly," Melvin said.

They were in the kitchen. Light streamed through the small window above the sink. Melvin had left work early; he still had mud on his trousers from an insurance meeting at a farm.

"We could name him after your father," Cookie said. She had already considered the possibility, during daydreams about this moment. She liked the idea, because it would bring Melvin's lost history to their doorstep. If William Whiteson's namesake was pushed around Milledgeville in a stroller, this town would indisputably be Melvin's home. Past and future would converge in the same spot. She thought of the grand Whiteson town house. Her own home was finally coming together. The addition of a nursery was a huge step forward.

Melvin looked startled. "No, no. There was only one William Whiteson. Besides, it might be a her."

Cookie nodded. She cupped her hands over the small swell beneath her waistband. Him. Her. She didn't really mind, for the first one. She wanted Melvin to have a boy, of course. But a girl . . . a girl would be lovely.

"You're glad?" she asked shyly.

Melvin's face creased into a smile. Cookie was still learning to distinguish between her husband's smiles; he had several that he seemed to work on. This was his sincere smile. It came easily and started in his eyes. It was the same smile he'd worn after their first kiss in New York.

"You couldn't have given me better news," he said. "But I need you to slow down. You have to start taking care of yourself."

"I do take care of myself."

"Promise me."

"I promise."

"Cookie?"

"Really. I promise."

Cookie continued with her meetings, of course, but she opted not to run for president of the Daughters of the American Revolution. She carried snacks in her handbag, and made sure she ate lunch. When it occurred to her, she chose to sit instead of stand. She took more time to talk with other mothers, a habit she found surprisingly enjoyable. She had never had much time for chitchat; Cookie usually got right to the point, which meant discussing the meeting's agenda, or suggesting changes she thought would streamline a process. Now she asked the other women how they were and listened to their answers.

Cookie laughed when Miss Mary's congratulatory hug lifted her off the ground. They were in the downstairs room at the library, waiting for a meeting to start.

"There's nothing better in the world than motherhood," Miss Mary said. "Wait 'til you see."

"It's true," Daisy said.

"Mama, please don't cry again."

"She's going to be a grandmother," Miss Mary said. "You let her cry. If I could claim any relation to this baby, I'd be crying too. It's going to be such a beautiful child, and so lucky. Heck, I wish I *was* this child, with you and Melvin for parents. He or she is in for a charmed life."

"We haven't had a baby in our circle for so long," another woman said. "Too long. I can't wait to kiss its big, fat cheeks."

"A baby," Miss Mary said. She rolled the words around her mouth, savoring them like gumdrops.

There were nods, and wet eyes, all around. "Oh, for heaven's sake," Cookie said, but her eyes were teary too. She felt full, in more ways than she would have thought possible.

She felt the baby move for the first time on the day of the mayor's party. The sensation was astonishing—it felt like a tiny sea creature was performing a somersault in her abdomen. When it happened, she sat down suddenly on the side of the bed.

"Maybe we should skip the party," Melvin said. He stretched out his hand, as if concerned that the baby might kick and therefore propel Cookie across the room.

"Absolutely not. This is your night. I wouldn't miss it for the world. Besides, I have the perfect dress. I think I almost look slim in it."

Melvin went back to fixing his tie. He had been invited, along with Bill Waters, to join a group known simply as the Mayor's Committee. The committee had been mainly social for generations, a (behind-closed-doors) drinking club for the mayor and his buddies. In the last few years, though, it had become a more overtly political gathering, where local events, policies, and even laws were determined. Each year, one or two local men were invited, via mailed correspondence, to join the committee, and then a party was held in their honor.

"Have I met Bill Waters?" he asked.

"At the wedding. You'll recognize him when you see him; he's all over town." Cookie frowned at her shoe—was her foot swollen? "This invitation means he's going to be the next police chief. That's the only explanation for the mayor asking him to join."

"Why did he ask me to join?"

"Oh, Melvin," she said. "Don't be ridiculous." Cookie stood and found that she had to concentrate on staying balanced. *Baby*, she thought, *behave yourself tonight. Your daddy needs me.* There was a swooshing sensation in her midsection, which she took for agreement.

"Hm," Melvin said.

Cookie made sure her voice was light; she wanted to manage Melvin's mood. It was darkening, and she needed him to be charming at the party. "You know Bill's wife, of course," she said. "She's doing our curtains."

"Hm."

Cookie crossed the room. She picked up Melvin's hand—he looked startled when she touched him—and laid it on her belly. She watched his eyes widen.

"Jesus," he said.

"Darling," she said, gently. "No profanity, please."

The creature under her dress rolled. There was a pulsing in one specific spot. There was palpable life.

Cookie put her hand over her mouth. "That's the biggest one yet," she whispered. "He's saying hi to his daddy."

One beat, then two. Melvin's hand moved slightly, homing in on the source of the motion.

"Christ," he said.

Cookie shook her head.

"Hi, whoever you are," Melvin said in a raw voice. "Hello."

The party started in a blur. Cookie felt so attuned to what was going on inside her body that it was difficult to absorb the dynamic of the room. When someone asked her a question, she was slow to respond. She stayed close to Melvin, or her parents. She laughed often, a trilling noise that ran a tickle up and down her spine. She overheard someone say, *They only asked him because of his money*, but she didn't let it bother her.

She found that her hand gravitated to her belly without her noticing.

She rubbed the front of her dress and smiled at how much strain the fabric was under. At one point Cookie found herself alone by the drinks cart, but instead of feeling slightly panicked, like she normally would, she was relaxed. She didn't mind having no one to talk to. *Why is that?* she wondered. Then she realized: she was no longer alone. She felt a surge of gratitude toward the baby inside her.

The party was populated with the town's most eminent citizens: doctors, lawyers, councilmen, the current police chief, the superintendent of schools. Cookie made sure Melvin stayed close to the mayor. The two men drew everyone's eyes to the center of the room. Melvin, with his somber expression, looked like he could easily take over, should the mayor need to pass on his mantle of power. Maybe someday Melvin *would* take over. Cookie could imagine her husband as the mayor, perhaps even the governor. Melvin's future career steps were the stuff of her daydreams. She hadn't shared these thoughts with her husband; she knew he didn't yet share her aspirations. Given time, though, he would. In some ways, she knew Melvin's potential better than he knew it himself. He had put that side of himself—the goal-oriented side—on hold when he left the bank. It was like his parents had held his ambition for him, and when they died, he lost that too.

"Do you have a project in mind for my husband?" Cookie asked. The mayor had been in office for most of Cookie's life; he was so popular that he always ran unopposed. He was a white-haired man with squinty eyes and a mild manner.

"Well," he said. "You know the tradition is to give the new members of the committee the most pressing project. Trial by fire and all that. Some call it hazing. But I don't want to force Melvin to do anything he doesn't want to do. So, if he's not interested . . ."

Bill Waters appeared by the mayor's elbow. "I could work on the project on my own, sir, if necessary," he said. "I'm not afraid of hard work."

Cookie considered the police officer. He would need a little fine-tuning before he became chief, she decided. He was too eager, and his appearance lacked the necessary details. There was a stain on his shirt cuff, and he could use a closer shave.

"What's the project?" Melvin asked.

The mayor started to talk about a charitable organization called the Children's Center, which was due to open in a few months. "We need someone to oversee the final push to completion," he said. "The center will help a lot of needy kids and mothers, but it has to open first, and you know how lazy folks get when there's no paycheck involved. We need to jump in and get stuff done so we can open the doors."

"Melvin will have no problem doing that," Cookie said. "He ran an international bank, he can certainly run a project like this."

"Cookie." Melvin narrowed his eyes at her.

Cookie ignored the look. She knew her husband didn't like to have the bank mentioned; he worried that people would think he thought he was better than them. The truth was though, as Cookie saw it, that he *was* better than them. If he was uncomfortable tooting his own horn, Cookie had no problem doing so on his behalf.

"I'm sure Bill and I can work together to get it done," Melvin said.

"We'll have it wrapped up in a jiffy." Bill's chest seemed to swell beneath his uniform.

Cookie exchanged a smile with Lona, who was standing slightly behind Bill. The woman was wearing a shapeless gray dress. *She could do so much more with herself*, Cookie thought. Lona was sweet, though. Earlier in the evening, she had stopped next to Cookie and whispered in her ear that she looked pretty.

Cookie put her hand on Melvin's arm. "I'm going to step outside for a second."

He raised his eyebrows to ask, *Are you okay?*

She nodded. She felt fine, but the room was crowded, and she wanted cool air in her lungs. She headed toward the door. She was halfway there when she came to an abrupt stop.

Flannery O'Connor was standing in front of the picture window.

She was in conversation with the school's superintendent, nodding in response to something he said. Because of the window at her back and the dark curtains on either side, Flannery looked like she was posed in the center of a picture frame.

It hadn't occurred to Cookie that Flannery might be at the party. She never attended events like this, even though she was always invited. Why was she here now? Cookie pressed her hand against her belly and tried to stay calm. She studied the older woman. Flannery was wearing a belted dress, and her hair looked nicer than usual. She still wore her ridiculous cat's-eye glasses, though, and she leaned into her metal crutches.

I'm fine, Cookie thought. *Things are different now. I'm married. I'm having a baby. I'm fine.* She took a step toward the door, and stopped again. Goose bumps swept her skin, and she felt her fortitude dissipate like water down a drain. Cookie glanced over reluctantly and wasn't at all surprised to see Flannery looking back.

Flannery studied Cookie, and Cookie accepted her gaze simply because she had no other choice. She felt like she'd been handed a twenty-ton bag of cement. Cookie's insides collapsed under the weight. Her heart thrashed in her chest. *Move*, she thought. *Just keep moving.* But her legs stayed still. It was her mind that was traveling, straight into the past. Flannery stared at her, and Cookie was back in her senior year of high school.

Daisy and Big Mike, beaming with pride, had accompanied her to school the morning of the prizegiving. Big Mike's jacket pocket was filled with cigars that various men had been handing him all week at the store. Daisy wore a brand-new rose-colored hat. This was the third honor their daughter had received this year—the first being homecoming queen, the second prom queen—and they believed this trifecta was richly deserved.

Cookie and her mother had spent a weekend in Atlanta shopping for her dress. It needed to be fancy, yet appropriate for school. Cookie needed to look like her beauty was effortless, because for a girl like her, effort was not supposed to be necessary. The dress they chose was light pink, with a tight waist and flared skirt. Her hair had been styled at the salon the previous afternoon, and it bounced lightly around her shoulders. Cookie had hardly slept the night before, not wanting to ruin the style by crushing it against her pillow. She didn't feel tired, though, while stepping onto the stage. She had been dreaming about this moment her entire life; she was ready.

There were two rows of seats on either side of the podium, which was where the principal stood, making the standard morning announcements. The other seats were filled with a mixture of teachers and award winners. Cookie looked out over the crowd—there were almost fifteen hundred students in the school. She had never faced this many people before. She felt her breath quicken in her throat. She clasped her hands in her lap and crossed her ankles. She found her mother's moon-shaped face in the center of the auditorium and felt calmer. Daisy blew her a kiss.

Cookie watched her mother turn to hug someone. Cookie couldn't make out who the woman was at first, but when she pointed her face toward the stage Cookie realized that it was Regina O'Connor. *How sweet*, Cookie thought. Regina had a busy farm to run, but she had come to see Cookie pick up her award.

The principal cleared his throat. "We're very lucky today to have a special guest of honor to present our awards," he said. "I had to twist her arm, but she's an alumna, so she couldn't really say no."

A cold spot appeared in the center of Cookie's stomach, as if she had swallowed an ice cube. She listened intently.

"Please give a warm welcome to Milledgeville's very own esteemed author—the writer of *Wise Blood*—Flannery O'Connor!"

The crowd clapped enthusiastically, and the ice cube in Cookie's stomach swelled into a block. She felt the cold touch every part of her abdomen; it nosed its way through her organs. Cookie shuddered, but made sure to keep her smile steady. *Show your best side*, she could hear her mother say. *No matter what.*

Flannery rose from one of the seats on the far side of the podium. She had been ill recently, and was thin. She moved slowly to the podium, shaking the principal's hand on the way.

"Principal Jones is exaggerating," she said into the microphone. "He didn't have to twist my arm. I live for this kind of opportunity. After all, how many girls get a chance to spend their morning doling out trophies and tiaras?"

The crowd laughed.

Cookie's hair had been styled specifically to look good with the tiara. Her blond locks were smooth on top, so the crown would sit nicely on her head. She touched the top of her hair, and then returned her hand to her lap.

Flannery looked down at the list she had been handed. "Let's start with a major award," she said. "This one goes to a family friend. I've known her forever, and I'm sure she worked hard for it. The Abraham Baldwin Award for the Most Popular Girl," she said, and then paused, presumably for dramatic effect.

Cookie shuddered again. She was freezing.

". . . is Cookie Himmel."

Some of the crowd clapped, like they were supposed to, but others just laughed. They seemed to find everything that came out of Flannery's mouth funny.

Cookie stood and walked carefully to the podium. Her smile was frozen now. She had lost control of it. It perched on her face like a banana she'd put on a shelf but could no longer reach.

"Congratulations," Flannery said.

"Thank you." Cookie couldn't make her voice rise above a whisper.

Flannery was holding the tiara in her hands. It should have been familiar to Cookie; she had long admired the crown in the glass case outside the principal's office. On its velvet stand it had looked glittery and majestic; Cookie had taken a circuitous route to class every day in order to see its shine. At night she lay in bed and imagined how beautiful and grown-up she would look wearing the tiara. She fantasized about its transformative powers. Wearing the crown, she would no longer be just a pretty girl; she would become a graceful, fully realized woman. She would emerge from her cocoon; the caterpillar would become a butterfly.

In Flannery's hands though, the tiara looked different. It looked like what it was: a cheap, shiny piece of metal studded with fake jewels. It looked pathetic. When Flannery reached up to place the crown on Cookie's head, she wanted to turn and run away. She wanted to cry. But she did none of that; she stood still and accepted what felt like punishment when the metal met her scalp.

Flannery studied her for a moment. *I see the real you*, her eyes seemed to say. *I will always see the real you.*

Cookie felt her lower lip start to quiver.

"Are you okay?" Flannery asked, away from the microphone.

Smile, Cookie thought. The tin crown was digging into her skin and she wanted to cry. *Just smile*. She nodded, and backed away. She remembered to wave to the crowd before taking her seat.

She sat numbly through the rest of the ceremony. She watched the usual array of jocks, nerds, and cheerleaders cross the stage to receive their awards. They seemed fine. They looked happy and proud. Cookie was just surviving the minutes. She had been taken apart.

When the awards were over, Cookie began to gather herself. She felt twenty years older, but at least it was over.

Flannery didn't seem to be done, however. She leaned toward the microphone, her face serious. "I was one of you," she said. "Not that long ago. Let me tell you, girls and boys, that life can be tricky. If I can be so presumptuous as to offer you one piece of advice—"

"Please!" the principal boomed from his seat.

"Then it would be this . . . " Flannery paused, this time not for dramatic emphasis, but as if she were trying to figure out what she wanted to say. "Take a good hard look at who you are and what you have," she said, "and then use it."

. . .

Cookie coughed in search of air, and found the strength to stumble into motion. She rushed for the door, which involved shoving past the police chief and a councilman's wife. *Poor thing, she's with child*, she heard someone say. Then she was outside, the screen door tap-tapping behind her. The air was cold; Christmas lights were on enthusiastic display across the street.

Cookie ran to the railing and vomited into a lilac-studded bush. She threw up three times in rapid succession, gasping for air in between. She was keenly aware of the window at her back, the fact that she was on display, but she was unable to move. When the spasms finished, Cookie stayed bent at the waist. She started to sob.

A second later, her mother and husband were on the porch with her.

"Are you okay?" Melvin asked.

"Is it morning sickness?" Daisy said, with panic in her eyes.

Cookie straightened her posture and took in their concern. She laid her hand on her belly, to check. There was a thump and a wiggle beneath her palm. The zipper on her dress shimmied from side to side, searching for extended space. She saw how badly her mother and husband needed everything to be okay.

"Mama," she said, "will you please find my purse for me? I'd like to go home now."

"I thought this might be too much," Melvin said. "You don't know the meaning of *take it easy*."

Daisy rushed inside. She could be heard apologizing her way across the room.

Cookie leaned against her husband's chest. She listened to his heartbeat under her cheek. The thump was steady. She was afraid to look at the picture window, so she focused on the moon. It was fat and round in the center of the sky, white as the mayor's hair.

"Sweetheart," Melvin said. "Tell me you're okay."

Cookie sighed. "The baby's fine," she said. "And that's all that matters."

elvin's visit the afternoon of the party had been off schedule, though he was beginning to realize that the schedule was a joke. He pointed his car toward Andalusia with greater frequency, especially since Cookie had told him about her pregnancy. The news had lent a certain urgency to how he spent his time. He knew that when the baby arrived his life would change—every parent he and Cookie encountered told them that, with a strange kind of glee—and he was now anxious about the time he had left. He was bored at the office. He spent his free moments sitting in the car, reading *Wise Blood* (each sentence felt like a balled-up fist, intent on knocking him out), or driving around the countryside with Flannery.

Whcrever he was, he felt like he should be somewhere clse. When he was at home, Cookie asked so many questions about insurance deals and business contacts that he felt like he should be at the office. He fielded her questions with an air of bewilderment, like an amateur tennis player who had found himself across the net from a pro. Cookie seemed to be talking about a different, more important job than the one he had, and she seemed to be referring to a more elaborate political hierarchy than this small town could possibly support.

When he was with Flannery, he felt like he should be with Cookie. His wife spent her weeks running every committee in town and her weekends shopping for baby clothes with her mother. She tried to engage Melvin in discussions about baby names. He took part in these discussions because he knew Cookie wanted him to, but the conversations felt as phony as the ones he fabricated to mask his trips to Andalusia. He made eye contact with his wife and rarely looked at her midsection. When he did catch sight of her profile, Melvin felt like he was being confronted with an uncomfortable truth. He was going to be a father, somebody's father. His own father, while he was alive, had defined Melvin's life. While he was sneaking in and out of town, Melvin didn't feel prepared to define someone else's.

That afternoon, Flannery had shifted her weight behind the steering wheel in a way that caught his attention. That was the thing, really, that he couldn't explain, even to himself. It was like Flannery always had his attention, whether he was sitting beside her, or reading one of her books, or working at his desk.

"Are you in pain?" he asked.

Flannery shook her head. She opened her mouth, and then closed it. They had been in the car for close to an hour. They had been mostly silent, letting the landscape stream past the windows.

Melvin was familiar with her mannerisms. He knew what this one meant. "Just say it."

"I want to ask you a personal question," she said.

Melvin thought, *She's going to ask me about my love for Cookie.* The sentence appeared from nowhere in his brain, and he knew it was correct. He braced himself. "Sure."

"How did your parents die?"

He blinked, surprised. "In a car accident."

Flannery took her eyes off the road to look at him.

"They were driving home from a weekend upstate. An old man fell asleep at the wheel and hit them. I was told that they died instantly." Melvin spoke slowly; he had always wondered whether this last part was true, or if it was just a kindness the police handed to victims' families, like a wreath of flowers or a condolence card.

"What happened to the old man?"

The landscape was suddenly flickering with light, as if the world had turned into a strip of overexposed film. Melvin rubbed his eyes. "His car was destroyed, but he was fine. Not a scratch on him."

"It must have been terrible." Flannery hesitated. "I don't know what I'd do without Regina."

He shrugged, and opened the window a little more. The cool air felt good. Melvin rarely thought about his parents. His mother, with her kind eyes and immaculate clothes; his father, who was always in a rush to get somewhere important. Melvin rarely thought about that day: the doorbell, the policeman at the door, the first night alone in the house.

But that's what he was thinking about when he got home, and that was what he was thinking about when Cookie discussed the importance of networking at the party, and that's what he was thinking about when his wife crossed the room and laid his hand on her belly. He was thinking about death.

Then his thoughts stopped, as if they had crashed into a wall.

There was a direct pressure beneath his palm. The baby seemed to lean into his hand. It pushed away from its home, toward him. Through Cookie's belly, Melvin felt a solid, reaching form. His hand tingled as he returned the pressure. The baby shifted then; it gave a hiccup, or a small kick. Melvin waited to see what would happen next. He felt like he could stand there all night, his hand curved across Cookie's skin, waiting for and celebrating every ripple. He understood, for the first time, that that was *his child* in there. His child was going to come out and meet him soon. The realization made it hard to breathe.

When Melvin saw Flannery at the party, he wanted to tell her this. He knew she would understand how remarkable it was. He knew she would appreciate the fleeting value of a moment like that, how difficult it was to describe and how powerful it was beneath the inadequate words, like a monster slithering beneath a glassy lake. Melvin could be inarticulate, and still Flannery would understand. He knew this from her writing, from the way she trapped tiny disappointments, tiny hopes, tiny frustrations, and pinned them down with sentences. Flannery saw everything, and was able to translate her insights into words.

Melvin liked the idea that something he told Flannery might appear in a book. His life was a messy compilation of moments that didn't fit together. If Flannery wove them into a narrative, they would have cohesion, and significance. He would be able to read about himself, and all that was inexplicable in real life would be explained. Flannery's gift made Melvin like her even more. It made him want to tell her everything.

But the truth was, he had to keep his mouth shut.

He couldn't tell her about Cookie's pregnancy, much less about the moment when he'd laid his hand on his wife's belly. He rarely mentioned Cookie to Flannery anymore. He feared that these admissions might hurt Flannery's feelings, and he couldn't risk that. He also couldn't cross the room and ask how she was. He couldn't touch Flannery's arm in public, or smile in her direction. These seemingly simple gestures would hurt his wife, and he couldn't risk that.

Instead, he had to stand beside the mayor, a friendly but permanently drunk man who sighed loudly when he thought no one was paying attention. He had to chat with his mother-in-law and wonder what his wife would look like as an old woman. Daisy bore an eerie resemblance to her daughter, but she was missing the fizz and the sharp, shooting beauty that defined Cookie. He had to wield a manly silence with his father-in-law, and discuss a dull boundary dispute with the zoning commissioner.

When there was a flurry of movement by the front door, he had to ask a waiter what was going on. He had to be told by the waiter that the flurry was caused by his wife, and then he had to run past Flannery on his way outside. He had to forget everything, even his name, when he saw his wife crumpled by the railing.

When Cookie leaned against his chest, he felt off balance, as if the ground he had read as solid was in fact a raft in the middle of the sea. He thought about the baby, and he thought about Andalusia, and he thought about his parents driving peacefully before being blindsided and crushed into a piece of cement.

Melvin blinked and rubbed his wife's back. He felt his eyes move, like magnets locating the nearest metal, to the picture window. He met Flannery's gaze, and sighed. Melvin stood under the streaming moon, his hand on Cookie's shoulder, and stared through the plate of glass. The look he and Flannery shared was long and heavy, and it somehow addressed all this—it addressed everything—without using a single word.

L ona watched Joe walk across the high school lawn with his head down. His cheeks flamed as he slid into the backseat. He avoided her gaze in the rearview mirror.

"How are you?" she asked.

"Fine."

He stared out the window. They rode in silence, a noisy silence that made Lona aware of the ragged sound of her own breath. She heard Joe sniffle and then wipe his nose with the back of his hand. She thought, *Do I always breathe this loudly?*

At the Whitesons' now, Joe never came within six feet of her. When she asked for her sewing needle, he stretched out his long arm and handed it over from the greatest possible distance. Lona stayed away from him as well, so as not to make him uncomfortable. When she sent him to the kitchen for a glass of water, she could see the relief on his face.

Later, when she crouched down to trim the fabric for the new nursery curtains, she felt him staring at her backside. He stole glances when she was talking to Cookie or flipping through the fabric catalog. Lona pretended not to notice the attention, but still, she felt a new, strange awareness of her body. She was conscious of the way her arms moved at her sides when she walked, the shape her lips took when she spoke, and the number of times she tucked her hair behind her ear. She wondered, while eating an apple, if he thought she looked attractive now. How could he? But the flame was still in Joe's cheeks, and he was carefully positioned halfway across the room, his head turned away.

She felt badly for him. She remembered teenage lust. Looking at boys in tight swimsuits and feeling the hair on her neck rise. Watching the boys towel off next to the pool and feeling butterflies beat their wings from her stomach to the crotch of her damp suit. Joe was a victim of his age. She wanted to tell him that it wasn't a big deal, that the desire would fade. That it was nothing personal, and she didn't hold it against him. On the contrary, she was flattered. No one had found her desirable for a long time. She and Bill occasionally had sex, but it had more to do with habit than libido. When her husband reached for her, it was after the bedside light had been turned out, and the act was quick, chafing, and silent.

Lona finished the apple and climbed the stairs awkwardly, aware of her hips tilting, the flesh on her thighs rising and falling, aware of Joe three steps behind her with labored breath. In the nursery, surrounded by pink lace, she tripped on the measuring tape and had to grab the crib rail to keep herself from falling.

"Are you all right?" he asked.

Lona tried to lighten the mood. "That's the first thing you've said all day. I'd forgotten what your voice sounded like."

He shrugged, and the flame consumed the rest of his face.

Dear God, Lona thought. She couldn't recall being in a situation this uncomfortable. "Is this too much for you?" she asked, in a low voice. Cookie was downstairs. "If you can't do this, I can tell your mother that I don't need an assistant anymore. You don't *have* to work with me."

Joe's eyes widened. He looked, if possible, more stricken. "Yes, I do," he said. "I have to."

"Okay," Lona said.

"I'm not going to let you make excuses for me, and I'm not going to quit. I'm fine."

"Okay," Lona said again.

. . .

That night she and Gigi ate leftover meatloaf. Gigi pushed the meat around her plate with her fork, occasionally pretending to take a bite. Lona knew that her daughter was full from the snacks Miss Mary fed her, but she felt like motherhood obliged her to provide a meal. So they sat there, forks in hand, until Lona finished eating. While she chewed, she wondered what her daughter thought of Joe Treadle. They went to the same school, after all. They walked the same hallways and saw each other at the farm most afternoons. Gigi no doubt had an opinion about him. She would, no doubt, be shocked to hear that he had a crush on her mother. Lona had a sudden urge to tell Gigi. She wanted to see her expression. She wanted to hear her response.

"It's almost Christmas," Gigi said.

Lona nodded, although she had forgotten that. She knew it was winter, of course, but she rarely kept track of the date. "We should get a tree."

"Can I be excused? I have work to do."

"Yes," Lona said. "Yes, you can."

The girl kissed her mother on the cheek and left the table.

Lona leaned back in her chair. She was in no hurry to tackle the dishes. And she was in no hurry for what came after the dishes: laundry, followed by ironing. She looked at the empty plate in front of Bill's seat, set out in case he came home in time to join them. Since being handed the charity project by the mayor, he rarely showed up for dinner anymore. He grabbed something to eat at the diner, or at the fried-chicken joint on the highway. He called before Gigi's bedtime, to ask about her homework and wish her good night.

Lona sighed and stood up. She cleared the table and washed the dishes. She moved to the laundry room, where she surveyed the piles on the floor and wondered for the hundredth time how such a small family produced so many dirty clothes. It seemed like Gigi and Bill changed outfits several times a day. Lona couldn't help but take it personally. They knew she was the one who had to clean up after them, didn't they? She worked for fifteen minutes, then went out on the back porch to smoke, then did fifteen minutes more of folding and ironing, and then returned to the porch. By the time the clothes were cleaned, ironed, and folded, her head was pleasantly hazy.

Bill arrived home when she was in bed, about to turn out the light. He strode into the room, and Lona propped herself up on a pillow. Sleep was now at least half an hour away. If she told Bill that she was tired and wanted to rest, he would apologize for being late and promise to be quiet while he changed, but it would be the loudest version of quiet imaginable, and in the end Lona would turn the light back on and listen while he talked about his day. The most efficient route, she had learned, was to give in and let his energy run its course.

"We live in a modern age," Bill said, standing in the bathroom doorway, wearing only his boxer shorts. He held a toothbrush in his hand. "This is a decade of young men and new ideas. Look at John Kennedy, for Christ's sake. It's time for the old guard to step down. I respect the chief, I do, but he's wearing out his welcome in this town. He's slowing us down. Milledgeville could be safer and better run. We could shake off the second-class reputation the city's had since the war. But the chief could care less about my suggestions. He likes his rules, and his way of doing things. His head's stuck in the sand."

"Cookie has plenty of new ideas." Lona's head still felt fuzzy. "I think I could be making curtains for them for the rest of my life."

Bill nodded. "Now that's a woman who knows what she's doing," he said. "She doesn't just let things happen. She *makes* things happen."

Lona pictured her employer and her expanding belly. Cookie's gait was a little slower now, but just as determined. Lona knew her husband was right. Cookie Whiteson had plans. Lona didn't know what those plans were, but she recognized the look of intent on the younger woman's face. It was the same look Bill wore every day. Lona wondered how it would feel to set a goal and then approach it in a calculated manner. She had never done that. She just dealt with whatever was set in front of her in the way she was supposed to. She tried to imagine making a decision and then taking action. For a moment before she fell asleep, while Bill continued to talk, she felt a glimmer of the satisfaction such an achievement would provide. A pleasant warmth blinked on and off inside Lona, and then she was unconscious.

Over the next few weeks, while she and Joe moved quietly and uncomfortably through their work, Lona toyed with the idea of taking action. She imagined telling Cookie she was quitting her job. She pictured her hand on Cookie's arm, making her announcement in a soft, certain voice. She envisioned her departure from the large house, her pause on the front porch to contemplate her new freedom.

That's where the fantasy stopped, though, because she couldn't come up with a next step. She would go home and tell Bill that they no longer had her income? She would find another, less pleasant, client? She would stay home all day with nothing to do? She would say goodbye to Joe? Gigi would join her in the afternoons, because there was no longer any reason for her to go to Miss Mary's?

Lona turned in a different direction. She imagined setting out to get pregnant and waylaying Bill every night until the deed was done. But that thought held almost no ground. She didn't particularly want to have sex with her husband. She didn't want to feel queasy and fat. She didn't want swollen ankles and sleepless nights. She already had a child.

Lona glanced up from the fabric in her hand and caught Joe looking at her.

"Do you want these?" he asked.

He was holding her shears. They were in the nursery, preparing to hang the new curtains. The teenager stood by the window. The afternoon sun lit him from behind. Lona studied Joe, as if he were someone she had just met. She noticed his wide hand, which was callused from regular farmwork. Her eyes traveled up his arm, with its lean muscles and soft brown hairs. The arm swelled into a broad, ropy shoulder, which sloped down to his collarbone. Joe was thin, but not too thin.

"Mrs. Waters?" he asked.

"Lona," she said, automatically.

"Sure," he said.

She felt the hairs rise on the back of her neck. The idea came over her slowly, a warm tide traveling from her toes to the top of her head.

She took a step toward him.

"Mrs. Waters?" he said again.

She put her hands on his chest. She felt his heart thrash beneath her palm. She was aware that she was standing on a pile of pink lace. She was aware that her employer was only fifty yards away. She was aware that she was in front of an unadorned window. She was aware, it seemed, of everything.

"Please be quiet," she said, and kissed him.

Flannery felt her mother's gaze from the other side of the porch. She looked up from her letter and pulled the shawl tighter around her shoulders. She and Regina used the porch year round, and simply added or subtracted layers as necessary.

Regina said, "Aunt Katie sent us a letter from Savannah."

"Oh?" Her mother could never simply say whom a letter or phone call was from; she also needed to name the place. *My brother wrote from Atlanta. Miss Mary called from next door.* Regina continually inventoried the small web of the people they cared about and where they were situated in the world. The O'Connors had lived next door to Aunt Katie in Savannah when Flannery was a young child. They had moved to Milledgeville when Flannery's father became ill, because Regina's entire family lived here.

Regina gave a quick nod, a sure sign that she was excited about what she had to say. "She's made what I think is a remarkable offer."

Flannery kept her voice mild. "What's that?"

"She wants to send the two of us to Europe, all expenses paid."

"Really? Why?"

"What do you mean, why? What kind of a Christian are you? Katie wants to do something nice. She's near the end of her life, after all, and she's well-off. It's a three-week pilgrimage that's being organized by the archbishop of Savannah. It's scheduled for this spring. Neither of us has ever left the country, so I don't see how we can pass this up."

Flannery shook her head. "I can't go anywhere for that long. I have too much work to do. You should go without me, though. Take one of your sisters; you'll have a wonderful time."

"No." Regina's voice tamped down. "You have to come. I can't go without you."

"Of course you can. I'll be fine on my own."

"I'm not worried about leaving you alone. Don't be dense." Regina looked frustrated. "Aunt Katie won't send just me. There's a condition."

Flannery blinked, confused. "What kind of condition?"

"We have to go to Lourdes, so you can bathe in the miracle baths."

Flannery lifted her hand in front of her eyes, as if to shade herself from the sun. She watched three peahens prance in the distance. This was a surprise, and yet it wasn't. She had felt something of this weight headed toward her for the past few months, like a snowball hurled from behind a hidden wall. She had noticed small secretive smiles in the curve of Regina's lips. She should have known she was about to be ambushed.

"You said you'd finally solved that problem with your book," her mother said. "You should be able to take the time off."

In the center of the novel, a baptism had gotten out of hand and become a drowning. A violent death had solved the problem. Gurgles of water. Suffocation. Thrashing limbs. No redemption.

"Flannery?"

The dust on the horizon shifted, the trees parted, and Melvin's shining car came into view. Regina leaned back and then forward in her chair, the wooden slats thumping the wooden floor. Flannery felt, in that moment, what an escape the drives had become. She now relied on them. She even sometimes had the thought, flashing down the road with a man sitting beside her, that she was someone else, living a normal, contented life. And the thought was a relief.

119

Regina's voice was heavy. "I think Aunt Katie's trip is a *very* good idea."

"Don't lecture me again on the dangers of driving."

"I won't."

"Good." Flannery still hadn't looked at her mother. "Because I'm a grown woman."

"I know that. And that's why I hope you know what you're doing. This is Cookie Himmel's *husband*. They're about to have a baby. Does she know he comes out here this often?"

Flannery stood and dropped her shawl on the chair. "What does it matter? No one's going to think he's having an affair with the town cripple."

While she walked to the car, she could feel her mother shaking her head behind her.

Melvin was smiling when she climbed into the driver's seat. Flannery found herself wishing that he wasn't.

He said, "How was your Christmas?"

"Fine. Thank you." Flannery knew she should ask him the same question, but she didn't want to hear the answer, so she kept her mouth shut.

She drove too fast out of the driveway. At the bottom, she hesitated for a moment, and then turned right, instead of her usual left. She pointed the car toward town and pressed down on the gas.

"What's going on?" Melvin asked.

"What do you mean?"

He was silent, his face stiff like a carefully folded sheet of paper.

Flannery sped down the highway. They always drove among nature: cows, fields, waving trees, deep lakes. Now the car was being sucked into civilization. There was a frayed political poster stapled to a telephone pole, promoting a local assemblyman. There was a billboard for a rib restaurant, and another selling soap. "Make Your Life Sparkling Clean" read the banner beneath a smiling, attractive woman cradling a bottle of detergent.

When Flannery reached the intersection by the college, she allowed the car to pause. She pumped the gas so the engine wouldn't die. She could sense Melvin's anxiety beside her. She could feel it, like a writhing electrical wire in her hands. If she drove into the center of town, if she passed the library and the supermarket and the bank, they would be seen. Someone—some lady wearing a silly hat and white gloves who was out doing her shopping—would spot them. That lady might not tell Cookie, but she would certainly tell Miss Mary, and once Miss Mary knew, it was just a matter of how quickly she could work her phone line.

Flannery pulsed the gas pedal. One, two, three times. She thought it was interesting that Melvin had chosen not to speak. He wasn't going to fight her. He was going to let her do what she needed to do. Was this courtesy on his part? Or cowardice?

A dark place inside her whispered, *Cowardice.*

The word, and the meanness that went with it, released her. She turned left, and heard Melvin sigh. She was relieved too, relieved to have gotten the anger out. She shook her shoulders to release the rest of the unwelcome emotion. She circled the outer edge of the town in silence. Past the back of the high school, Sacred Heart, the railroad tracks, and finally the graveyard—which looked like a mouthful of crooked teeth—before the car was back among nature, among the flowers and the hay bales and the rusted tractors and the peacocks calling for her to come home.

At her desk the following morning, Flannery had a hard time pinning her attention down. She was tweaking the language in the new scene. Tarwater was in a rowboat in the middle of the empty lake, with Bishop. The two figures sat opposite each other—one short and stout, the other thin and intense. Flannery sat in the quiet of the scene too, waiting for the violence to start. Her heart scampered in her chest, and she felt sweat break out on the back of her neck. She waited, her fingers quiet against the keys.

Her mind tried to escape the scene. Flannery imagined herself in the car beside Melvin, pressing the gas pedal all the way to the floor. She imagined Melvin crying out, putting his hands on her in an effort to get her to stop. She saw a wall approaching so fast that it was impossible to turn away. Flannery put her hands over her eyes. Tarwater was at least half crazy, and she had been in his head for years. During the last few weeks, she had allowed herself to go even deeper. She had to, in order to finish with him. She had to go a little mad herself, in order to get the story right, in order to pin him down like a butterfly.

The effort was wearing. She went to bed at night shaking. She did things she wouldn't normally do. She picked arguments with Regina that she would normally have ignored. She went to a party, which had been a terrible idea. Once there, she watched Melvin put his arm around his wife's swollen waist. She watched Cookie kiss his cheek. She watched the mayor laugh with reverence at every sentence that came out of their mouths. Toward the end of the night, Flannery had even given Cookie a look that was unnecessarily hard, needlessly deep, just because she knew it would upset her.

Flannery wanted to leave her desk. She wanted nothing more than to push her chair back and walk away. She wanted to wade knee-deep into her birds. She wanted the peacocks' noise to drown out her thoughts. She wanted the birds' hysterical voices to drown out Bishop's cries. A life was coming to a brutal end beneath her chattering fingertips, and she wanted to be anywhere but where she was. She wanted to be anyone but who she was. Flannery stayed still, though, and she kept typing. Word after terrible word after terrible word, until the life was over, until the body was quiet beneath the water's surface.

They kissed only at the Whitesons' house. It was too risky in the car. No matter where they parked, there was a chance they might be spotted. A joint could be quickly hidden, a kiss could not. Even if the passerby was a stranger to Lona and Joe, that person doubtlessly knew Miss Mary, and would report back to the Treadle farm. Also, the police ran regular patrols of the town's roads. A bored cop would be more than happy to pick up his radio and let Bill Waters know that his wife had been spotted in a compromising position.

For these reasons, Joe continued to sit in the backseat, and Lona in the front. After she picked him up from school each afternoon, they shared a smoke in silence. They were careful not to make eye contact. Careful not to let their fingers touch when they exchanged the rolled paper. They shifted on the stiff seats, swallowed hard, and tried to breathe evenly in the thick, foggy air. It had been twenty-one hours since they had last been together, and they were aware of every lost minute. They were grateful the breaks were no longer than that—Lona had convinced Miss Mary that she needed Joe's help five days a week now because the Whiteson job was so big.

When they stepped out of the car, their legs were unsteady. They staggered across the lawn like drunks on their way to a bar. Once inside the house, they tried to rush through pleasantries with Cookie, who was now hugely pregnant and therefore spending more time at home.

"I feel like I'm waiting for something that's not going to happen," Cookie said. She looked stranded on the couch, lampooned by the size of her belly.

Lona stayed on the far side of the room. Joe was beside her; she had to concentrate on not reaching out for his hand. She wanted to be alone with him more than anything, but Cookie was looking at her with sad eyes.

The woman asked, "Do you know what I mean?"

Lona sighed. She did know what she meant. She could easily remember the final, interminable weeks of pregnancy, when time seemed to trudge through thick mud, and there was no longer a single comfortable position, and all she could think about was getting this baby the hell out of her body. Lona's hands had swollen so badly she was unable to open a jar, and when she left the house she had to do so barefoot, because no shoes fit her feet. She had felt like a huge, lumbering animal. When people recoiled from her on the sidewalk, she sympathized with them.

She felt some of that desperation now. She wanted to be out of this room. She wanted to put her hands on Joe. She wanted to press her mouth to his. She had been an animal at nine months pregnant and she was an animal again. Everything other than her desire for this boy— her politeness, her vagueness, her weariness—was fighting to drop away. Lona had to hang on to appearances with her fingertips, from one moment to the next.

"Have you drunk cod liver oil?" she asked.

"Yuck," Joe said. "Why would she do that?"

"Yes," Cookie said.

"Spicy food?"

"I had my mother's stuffed jalapeños three times this week."

"You're going for long walks?"

Cookie nodded. She seemed to sink even deeper into the cushions. "Go do your work," she said. "Don't waste your time talking to me."

Lona was relieved that Cookie hadn't asked whether she might have another child. She had already done so twice, and Lona had dodged giving an answer. It was like pregnancy was another club that Cookie belonged to, and she was trying to recruit Lona as a member.

Lona could picture herself with a rounded belly. She could see Bill grinning beside her. She could see the two of them strolling through town, Bill's chest puffed out. Lona knew how happy a baby would make her husband. How much he'd enjoy passing out cigars at the station with the lieutenant badge shining on his chest. How young he would feel with a baby in his arms, as if he had been given the chance to start over, this time with the life he deserved. Bill had been anxious after Gigi's birth, consumed with worry about their finances, and about the chance that he may not live up to his responsibilities. But he wouldn't feel that way now. A new child would make him feel more successful, more in control. It would make him feel like *more*.

"Can we get you anything before we go?" Lona asked. "Water, or a snack?"

Cookie shook her head, her eyes down.

Lona felt a thrill when they left the room. She was grateful for her slim, uninhabited body. She was grateful that she belonged only to herself. She and Joe used the banister to pull themselves upstairs, and they fell into the nearest empty room. Lona pushed Joe up against a wall and tilted her head back, exposing her neck.

They developed a rhythm at work. When it was safe, they drew together. When Cookie was nearby, they drifted apart and worked. Lona didn't want the quality of her craftsmanship to suffer. If anything, she now paid more attention to every cut and stitch. She measured fabric when in the past she would have judged it by eye. She pored over catalogs. She told Joe to rehang a curtain several times, until it looked right to her. She was glad for Cookie's perfectionism, because it gave her something difficult to aim for. Each time Lona designed a new curtain, she thought, *This will be the one she loves. This one won't be replaced.*

After work, they returned to their places in the car.

"Can we stop somewhere?" Joe asked.

"No."

"Your house is empty, though, isn't it?" His voice was shy.

"We need to keep to the rules," Lona said. She didn't meet his eyes in the rearview mirror.

"Okay," he said. "I understand."

"You probably don't." Lona's voice was ragged in her throat; she barely paid attention while she talked. The words were just another thing she could exchange with Joe. He talked; she talked back. When she couldn't touch him, she spoke to him. "It doesn't matter whether you understand," she said. "We need to know what we're doing. There needs to be some structure."

Lona rehearsed the rules in her head; she did this often in order to remind herself of their importance. They would kiss only at the White-sons'. They would do no more than kiss; everything that lay on the far side of that line was too dangerous to consider. She would continue to drop off Joe and collect Gigi on time. Lona would keep up the pretense of being a wife, mother, and employer. She needed to be able to greet Miss Mary with the knowledge that she was keeping to the agreed-upon schedule, if nothing else.

Still, the ride to the Treadle farm got harder each afternoon. Lona could feel Joe's desire from the backseat. He was trying to figure out how he could lay his hand on her shoulder; she could feel how badly he craved that simple contact. She knew exactly how he would feel when his fingers touched her skin. There would be an opening in his chest. He would exhale loudly, like a swimmer who had been forced to hold his breath under water for a long time. Lona had never been so certain of another person's feelings before in her life. Her husband and daughter were a mystery; she had always assumed it was impossible to access another person's thoughts. The fact that she understood Joe, without him saying a word, confused and excited her.

When she parked in front of his parents' house, she wanted to grab Joe's hand and kiss it in the fading light. He paused in the backseat, wanting the same thing. Instead, Lona opened the door and forced herself to move away.

When she returned home with her daughter, she took the first steps into a tedious, lonely evening. Bill rarely came home before ten. Lona walked around her house with the sensation of a flock of birds agitating in her stomach. She felt revved up and anxious. When she had leaned in to kiss Joe the first time, she'd thought, *This will be fun*. But the kiss wasn't fun. It dove past fun; it lasted past fun. It took Lona to a place she had never been before: a deep, serious place of richness and complexity. She was in that place now, almost all the time.

When Bill called on the phone, Lona stared at the couch in the living room. She pictured herself and Joe deep in its cushions.

"Of course," she said. "I understand. Don't worry. Don't apologize again, Bill. Gigi and I will see you tomorrow."

He continued to talk. He was telling her an anecdote from the station that she couldn't understand. When he was done, she would return to the laundry room. She would imagine herself sitting on Joe's lap on top of the rumbling machine. When Bill stopped talking, Lona said good night and laid down the phone.

Melvin awoke because of a strange squeezing sensation in his foot. He sat up in the darkness, confused and half asleep, trying to see what the problem was. When his eyes adjusted to the lack of light, he saw Cookie hunched at the end of the bed, swollen in her white maternity nightgown. She was the cause of his discomfort. She was gripping his toes, her eyes shut tight.

He reached for the bedside lamp and switched it on. "Cookie?" he asked. "Honey?"

There was no answer, no signal that Cookie had even heard him. Her cheeks were shiny and swathes of blond hair were matted to the back of her neck. Melvin had never known his wife to sleepwalk, and he wondered if it was yet another strange symptom of pregnancy, like her cravings for peanut butter, or her puffy calves. It didn't occur to him that it might be labor because Cookie wasn't due for two weeks, and it was his understanding that due dates were meaningful.

Melvin's toes felt like they were caught in a vise. He had to fight the urge to shake his foot free. He raised his voice slightly. "Are you awake? Can you hear me?"

When Cookie looked up, the expression in her eyes made him flinch.

"I'm not sure I'm ready," she said.

"Oh, God." Melvin pulled his feet out of her grip. He scrambled out of bed and dragged a pair of pants over his pajamas. He found his wife's overnight bag, which had been packed and ready for over a month. He unhooked Cookie's bathrobe from the hook on the door. He laid it over her bent back.

He said, "Sweetheart, I want to move you in the best way possible. I'm going to take you to the hospital. Can you back up a little so you can ease off the bed? Can you do that? I need your help to know what's best so I don't hurt you."

Cookie mumbled something.

"What was that? I couldn't understand." Melvin leaned in closer and put his ear right next to her mouth.

Cookie's voice was barely audible. "I'm not going anywhere looking like this. You have to get my daytime lipstick off the bathroom counter. And some bobby pins. I've sweat through this gown; I'll need a new one from the drawer. Hurry."

Melvin knew better than to argue. He ran into the bathroom and found the requested items. As gently as he could, he pulled the damp gown over her head. He froze for a second at the sight of her naked belly. He had never looked directly at it before, and the view was shocking. The belly stretched away from Cookie in every direction; it had taken over her small frame. The tight orb, laced with blue veins, looked like a force to be reckoned with. *Something huge is about to happen*, it warned him. *Something huge.*

Melvin noticed the fabric in his hand and remembered his task. He slid the clean nightgown down over his wife's body. All the while, Cookie barely moved. Her body seemed consumed with a singular focus, her eyes closed, her silence sporadically interrupted with unlikely, almost canine panting. When Melvin approached her with the tube of lipstick, she pursed her mouth. He drew the line as neatly as he could, pressing the stick into her soft lips. The artificial color made her face appear even paler. Melvin clasped the bobby pins in his palm, looked at her hair, and shook his head. He had no idea where to begin.

"I'll do my hair in the car," Cookie said. "It's time to go. Call Mama and tell her to meet us there."

When they reached the hospital, Cookie was put in a wheelchair and whisked away by white-coated staff. Melvin was pointed in the opposite direction. Coursing with adrenaline, he focused on following the directions he was given, and found himself alone in a room filled with chairs. He looked at the rows of chairs, but found it impossible to even consider sitting down.

He knew what he wanted to do. He wanted to call Flannery. He had never called her before; he didn't even know her phone number, but he wanted to hear her voice. He wanted to tell her what was happening. He wanted to tell her that the baby was on its way; his child would be in his arms in a matter of minutes. The clock would tick forward—a simple, standard, familiar tick—and he would move from man to father.

Melvin wanted to tell Flannery that he knew talking to her on the pay phone in the hall while Cookie was in labor was wrong. He knew it was wrong that he needed her to comment on his life in order for his life to feel real, but it was the truth. He craved the definition that came with her words. He pictured Flannery standing in the middle of her peacocks and he pictured the straining pink globe of his wife's belly. He watched it thump, thump, thump. He walked in slow circles, his hands in his pockets, for hours. Finally a nurse came to the door and said, "Would you like to meet your daughter?"

When the Whitesons brought Rose home from the hospital, they were met at the front door by Daisy, Big Mike, Lona Waters, and Joe Treadle.

"We'll go right back to work." Lona didn't take her eyes off the baby, whom Melvin had laid down in the bassinet in the middle of the living room. "I just wanted to see her. Congratulations."

"She's so small." Joe stood close behind Lona, as if he were her shadow.

"They're more like squirrels at this age," Big Mike said.

"A beautiful squirrel," Daisy cooed.

"My goodness," Cookie said. "This baby has turned you all into idiots."

"Happy idiots," Daisy said, in the same singsong voice, her face a moon over the bassinet.

Melvin sent Lona and Joe home, and Cookie took Rose upstairs. She carried her carefully, cradled to her chest. The baby girl was asleep, her face pink and scrunched up like a piece of discarded stationery. Every once in a while a tiny tongue peeked from between her lips. Cookie laid her on the bed, and then lowered herself down to lie beside her. She was bruised and sore; even the tiniest movements hurt. She felt like she had been crowbarred in half and then hastily stitched back together. Lying still, listening to Rose breathe in quick puffs, Cookie allowed herself to close her eyes. She felt worse than she ever had in her life. In fact, she didn't feel like a person; she felt like a broken machine: rusty, overused, surrounded by busted parts.

The vessels in one of her eyes had ruptured from the effort of pushing. She had a cut on her lower lip where she'd bitten down when the baby's shoulders twisted inside her. Her swollen breasts ached, like balloons begging to be popped. Her belly was in the process of deflating. Soft and pouchy, seemingly depressed by its sudden lack of purpose, it lay beside her on the mattress. There were three gray circles on the inside of her left arm, where needles had been inserted. She was bleeding, and the doctor had warned that it would continue for up to six weeks. Cookie wondered how she could survive the loss of so much blood. She felt like a medical emergency, and yet the doctor had grinned goodbye when they pulled away from the hospital, and her mother told her that she was glowing.

"I don't feel like I'm glowing," she said to Melvin, who had appeared in the doorway. He was holding a bottle of formula and a cloth.

"How do you feel?" He was looking at the baby.

"Like I was in a car crash."

Melvin picked Rose up and held her against his shoulder. "You get some sleep," he said. "I'll take care of her until you feel better."

Cookie felt a stab of jealousy as he left the room. She winced, and thought angrily that someone should be taking care of *her*. She took care of everything, and everyone, all the time. Melvin didn't appreciate how much she had done, how hard she worked to make their life a success in this town. He went off to his job every day, but that was it. He'd made no effort to become friends with men his age. He had accepted the invitation to the Mayor's Committee only because she wanted him to. Melvin wasn't trying to do any more than the bare minimum required. Cookie had pictured herself sweeping in and out of parties on her husband's arm. Instead, he was on her arm, and he didn't even seem to notice.

Cookie had swelled up like a tick for him, for their family. She had endured a painful birth with only a bitter, childless nurse for company. She had given everything she had. She was broken now, and Melvin had the nerve to walk away. Cookie was in the middle of another thought, something blistering, something incoherent, when she fell unconscious.

Hours later, she opened her eyes to total darkness. She stood carefully and made her way downstairs. She felt foggy, but the anger was gone. She wanted to see the baby. She found Melvin sitting beside the bassinet in the living room.

"What time is it?" she asked.

"I don't know. Three, maybe. Did you see that? She makes this face where she looks angry, and then her eyes go really wide. I don't know what it means."

"I don't either," Cookie said.

She noticed that Melvin was still wearing the suit he'd left the hospital in, and then realized that she was still wearing her pregnancy skirt and top. Both were wrinkled, and the skirt had twisted backward. She had no shoes on, and her feet were cold. She wanted to cross the room and hold the baby, but she also felt a pressing need to use the bathroom.

She was scared by the discomfort this might involve. She shivered, and wondered when, if ever, her pieces would come back together.

The Whitesons hardly left the house for two weeks. Cookie slept a lot. The baby nurse, a quiet colored woman with a stern expression, held the baby with only one arm, as if to show off her competence. Cookie didn't like how pale Rose looked against the woman's dark skin; she also didn't like how the baby never cried while tucked into the crook of the nurse's arm, but often cried with Cookie. Cookie alternated between feeling meek around the woman and resentful of her presence. She often sent her home early, preferring not to have her in the house. Early, late, or on time meant very little to her, anyway. She existed in a kind of haze. There was no discernible difference between sunrise and sunset. She and Melvin might be up with the baby for three hours in the middle of the night, and then they would sleep through lunch the following day. Mealtimes, bedtimes, and any trace of a schedule were shattered by the six-pound infant in the bassinet.

Melvin and Cookie found themselves on their hands and knees in the nursery one morning, examining their freshly diapered, sleeping baby as if she were a collection of facts they were about to be tested on. Their eyes pored over her body, trying to take in and memorize even the smallest details. Rose had a dusting of hair that was so blond it was nearly white. She had round cheeks that grew pink when she cried, and that became chapped when exposed to even the slightest chill. She had a small, clear blister on her upper lip from sucking her bottle. Her lower lip quivered when she was hungry. There was an almost imperceptible dent on the side of her nose that the doctor said was from the delivery and would disappear over time. She had huge blue eyes—they were clear blue; looking into them was like looking deep into the sea and seeing the ocean floor.

"She's perfect," Melvin said.

"Yes."

Cookie was unable to keep track of her emotions. It seemed like a different mood lurked around every corner. Sometimes she cried, sometimes she was furious, and holding Rose could fill her with happiness and terror in equal measure. Cookie tried to let the feelings ride through her; she knew they were fleeting, so there was no reason to dig in her heels.

She stared at Rose's face while she fed her. The baby's features were starting to uncrumple, as if her face was an inflating balloon. She was less pink. She stared back at her mother. Daisy brought over Cookie's infant photos and held them up beside the baby.

"Look at the similarity," Daisy said. "I told you, she's the spitting image of you. She's perfect. I can't tell you how the sight of her takes your father and me back in time. I'm not sleeping, but I don't care. It's joy on top of joy."

"I feel like I've been turned to mush." Cookie looked from the black-and-white photograph to her daughter, who was wearing a pink dress and pink tights. "I don't recognize myself in the mirror. I don't like it, Mama."

"You'll feel better soon," Daisy said. "This is nature's way of keeping you close to your baby. I remember being so exhausted after you were born that I fell asleep one night with a dirty diaper in my hand. Your father walked into the room and was appalled."

Cookie's eyes teared up. She stared blankly at the half-empty bottle, the stained burp cloth, the baby who was pumping her legs as if she were trying to swim to the other side of the bassinet.

Daisy kissed her daughter on the cheek and left the room.

Five weeks later, Cookie woke up from an afternoon nap feeling different. Sharper. Clearer. More like her old self. She sat on the side of the bed, awash with relief. She stood gingerly and took a shower, smiling through the stream of water. When she was dressed, she went to find Melvin.

"I'm going to go back to my normal schedule," she said. "I have some important projects I was in the middle of when Rose was born. My mother can't wait to start watching the baby, so I'll drop her and all her stuff off at their house tomorrow morning. I'm glad I fired that nurse, aren't you? She kept looking at me like I was doing everything wrong."

"You want to do this tomorrow?" Melvin said. "This seems a bit sudden. Are you sure you're ready?"

She nodded and mentally checked her schedule. The next day was Tuesday, which meant she could go to a Library Association meeting first thing. She would move forward with her plan to have Flannery O'Connor's books removed from circulation. Cookie had been considering the idea during her pregnancy, but now she knew, with total clarity, that it was the right thing to do. She wanted her daughter to grow up in a town where she didn't have anything to fear. She didn't want Rose to censor herself out of concern that she might be forever trapped in print. Cookie wanted her daughter to be comfortable in her skin, and in her hometown, so she would never leave her mother the way Cookie had left hers. She would do whatever was necessary to make Milledgeville a town her daughter never needed to run from. If Rose ever heard mention of Flannery, it would just be an innocent story about the crazy lady who lived with all those peacocks.

She said to her husband, "You have to get back to work too."

"I've been working."

"Not full days. My mother even commented on it. It's not right, Melvin. You're here more often than you're at the office. And you have your own big event coming up. Bill Waters called last night, didn't he? I hope you didn't cancel another meeting with him."

"He said he could handle things on his own," Melvin said. "To be honest, I'd rather be here."

Cookie stared at him. "But you were invited onto the Mayor's Committee. You have to do it."

Melvin kept his eyes on the bassinet. "I'm going to resign. Someone more deserving should have my seat. After all, Rose is only going to be a baby for a short time. I don't want to miss anything."

Cookie took a deep breath. She was pleased to find her thoughts still following one another in a logical pattern. She didn't feel the urge to cry or laugh, and she was wearing one of her pre-pregnancy dresses. She knew the woman standing here. She knew she could take care of this. She had to.

"I'll meet with Officer Waters," she said.

Melvin frowned. "What do you mean? Why?"

"Three of my organizations are involved in raising money for the Children's Center. I know all about the project. I can help Bill wrap everything up. I won't miss anything here, either. I'll meet with him at night, after Rose is asleep." Cookie thought about publicity, and the favors she would call in from different businesses in town. This was the kind of charitable endeavor people loved to be involved in, but it would take someone with her charm to make them realize it.

"The mayor won't be thrilled," Melvin said.

"I don't care. He'll be impressed by the final result, and that's all that matters."

"You're taking on too much."

"I can do it."

He sounded reluctant. "Go ahead, if it makes you happy."

Cookie picked the baby up. She kissed her soft, plump cheek. She squeezed the infant hard against her chest. She said, "It makes me happy."

Melvin's teeth ached as he rattled over potholes in Andalusia's driveway. His hands slid across the steering wheel. It had been sixty-one days. On Melvin's last visit, the day before Rose's birth, he had said, *I'll see you next week.*

He had his usual thought when the farmhouse appeared from behind the shield of trees, that perhaps he would catch a peacock by surprise and its tail would be spread wide open. He had only seen a peacock in full display once, on his first visit, and he wanted to see it again. The giant birds seemed to deliberately keep their feathers down and crumpled when he was around. Today the birds hurtled forward, the General in the lead, his neck jutted out to see who was invading his turf. The peacocks' fans were shut tight.

Flannery was sitting on the porch, writing a letter. She must have been aware of Melvin's arrival, but she didn't look up. One of the peacocks shrieked, a noise like fingernails on chalkboard.

He climbed the porch stairs. He clenched and unclenched his hands.

Flannery spoke first. "I didn't think we'd see you out here again."

"How are you?"

Her voice was quiet. "How's your daughter?"

"She's wonderful. I brought pictures." He fumbled in his pocket and handed over his wallet, open to the photographs. He knew, almost immediately, that the move was a foolish one. He was trying to rush onto positive ground, but it was far too early for pictures and pleasantries.

He watched Flannery accept the wallet, and then shut it without a glance. She dropped it on her lap.

Melvin sighed. "I'm sorry it's been so long."

"You could have called. Or written."

In her voice, and in the air between them, was the weight of the strange friendship they had developed. Melvin had told himself, since his first visit, that Flannery didn't need him in her life in the way he needed her, but now he knew that he'd been wrong. And he knew that he had hurt her badly.

"I'm sorry," he said again.

He had wanted to visit since the minute Rose was born. He had day-dreamed about stopping by the farm on their way home from the hospital and introducing the screaming, pink-skinned, blue-eyed wonder in his arms to this raucous zoo of peculiar creatures. Rose with her mouth wide open, mid-shriek, reminded him of a peacock. She had the same force, the same arrogance, the same impatient, ferocious needs. Melvin had wanted to come here with her. He hadn't wanted to visit without her. He knew, however, that turning down the long driveway with Rose in her basket beside him would involve crossing a stark line in his marriage. While he could rationalize lying about his own visits to Andalusia, he couldn't jus-tify bringing Cookie's daughter here. If Cookie found out that Flannery had held Rose, that the writer's birds had shrieked in the infant's ears, she might never forgive him. Melvin tried to come up with a workable solution, but as the days and weeks passed, his moral binds proved resolute. The fact that he was standing here today was a late, miserable compromise.

The General's shiny eyes fixed on Melvin; the intensity of the gaze made him even more uncomfortable. The giant bird was perched on his usual low branch of the magnolia tree. Flannery had resumed her letter writing. She finished another sentence before laying down her pen.

"You've been busy?" she asked.

"Newborns are consuming."

"I've heard that."

He didn't want to talk about his responsibility to Cookie. They never spoke about his marriage, and he didn't want to change that now.

She said, "I've been thinking about your parents' death."

He looked at her in surprise.

Flannery's tone was detached, like a schoolteacher giving an oft-repeated lesson. "You never talk about their accident, but you must think about it all the time. After all, that single event has informed every decision you've made since, hasn't it? You left the bank because your parents died, you moved here because your parents died . . . "

Melvin studied the white boards beneath his feet. The paint was chipped in spots. There was a nail that wasn't flush with the wood. *That's dangerous*, part of his brain thought. *Someone could trip on that.*

"I don't think about them all the time," he said. "I hardly ever do." He could feel her eyes on him. He wasn't sure how to respond. To the question, to whatever it was she was getting at that lay beneath this subject, beneath her words.

She shook her head.

"You're angry with me."

"I'm frustrated." She turned the wallet in her lap. "You're wasting time."

Melvin kept his mouth shut. He was uncomfortable, but he was also glad to be here, and strangely glad she was taking him to task. After all, he deserved to be lectured. He was saturated with guilt; this comeuppance had been earned.

"I have writing to do. I have work to finish. Every day counts for me."

"I understand."

"I don't think you do. I don't think you can understand. God has given you everything," she said. "He's given you wings, but you're walking around with the rest of us."

The mention of God annoyed Melvin. When they had mentioned

religion in the past, it had been in a light, joking way. It seemed unfair to throw that on top of everything else. He said, "I didn't ask for my situation."

"I didn't ask to be sick."

There was a long pause.

He said, "You don't know what my life is now."

"Sure I do. Instead of sneaking away from work to visit me, now you sneak away to visit your daughter."

Heat coiled in Melvin's chest. For a second it was unclear whether he was going to laugh or yell. He heard himself say, "That's unfair."

"Is it?"

"It's easy for you to throw stones, Flannery. You realize that, don't you? You reign from your seat on this porch. You're safe here. No one can attack you."

Flannery's expression changed, dimmed. "You're right, I'm lucky."

"That's not what I said."

"I'm damned lucky."

No one spoke. The birds roamed the lawn. The General shifted his beady stare from man to woman. The rumble of the school bus drifted through the trees.

"I want you to answer one question for me," Flannery said. "I think you owe me that much."

Melvin nodded, but the motion took real effort. He felt like he was trapped in quicksand. Rose's birth had opened his eyes in a way he was still struggling to come to terms with. He could now identify the coursing, thumping, animate parts of his life. When he had seen his baby for the first time—a somehow familiar, inevitable face peering out from the folds of a pink blanket—Melvin had experienced a shot of adrenaline in his chest. Standing in the hospital room, shaking, his mouth dry, he had found himself tracing that sensation backward. He was on a park bench in the city, feeling the same surge as he leaned toward Cookie for a kiss. He had felt alive. Quivering, alert, his true self.

He had refused to lose Cookie after that kiss. He followed her to Georgia, and was rewarded with the same electric charge the night before his wedding, amid the peacocks' screams. He stayed awake until dawn, hoping that the sensation would hold for the ceremony. It did not. It returned, however, when he visited Andalusia. Before Rose's arrival, the farm was the only place where the feeling grabbed him like two hands on his shirtfront. Where he felt the blood traveling through his veins, where he felt doors open inside himself, where he didn't worry about what he should do or what he should say. Now when he traced the fiery dots, the line darted from his daughter to Flannery and back again.

Flannery spoke in a voice so soft Melvin had to lean forward to hear her.

"I want to know why you kept coming to my house." She stopped, then started again. "It's not for the quiet, which is why you claim to like life in this town. Why did you keep sneaking away from your perfect life to show up out here?"

"We're friends," he said. "Friends visit each other."

"I've never visited you. Cookie would turn me away at the door."

Melvin stared at the speckled birds. Their coats were sealed shut. He was aware that he and Flannery had kept a careful distance since his arrival. He usually supported her elbow while she took a seat. He held her hand while she lowered into the car. Once, when she had complained of feeling feverish, he'd pressed the back of his hand to her forehead. Today there was at least ten feet between them.

"I liked your visits," she said. "That's my fault. I apologize. You fed my vanity, and I liked the attention. But I'm running out of time. You're no longer welcome here."

A peacock stomped on the roof overhead. The porch door rattled in its frame. "Don't do this," he said.

"You're not even brave enough to bring your daughter." Her voice broke in the middle of the sentence, but her face remained stony.

Melvin reached for something and could only lay his hands on facts. "I'm married."

"I know that," she said. "I know everything."

She stood and walked into the house. The door clattered behind her. Melvin found himself staring at something dark and scaly against the white wooden planks. He squatted down and, with the slow movement of a very old man, picked up his wallet.

M iss Mary and Regina were talking loudly inside the house. Their voices traveled a regular route from Flannery's room to Regina's, and then back again.

"You should get some sleeping pills from Dr. Weber," Miss Mary said. "You'll be exhausted from the time difference. My cousin Louise went to London and got pneumonia because she couldn't sleep a wink while she was there. You'll need your strength. Extra strength, even, for you and for Flannery."

"Help me with this bag," Regina said.

There was a loud thump.

"For goodness sakes," Miss Mary said. "What do you have in here, rocks?"

"My Bible, and Flannery's medications. You think it's too heavy?"

"Lord, yes. Let me help you. Step aside, woman."

Flannery tried to retreat as deep into her rocking chair as possible. The afternoon sky was white; the brightness made her squint. "What are you reading?" she asked.

Gigi looked up from her seat on the porch steps. She held up a math textbook, and Flannery wrinkled her nose. She looked out over the lawn. She scanned the birds, the magnolia tree, the white fence. *Goodbye,* she thought.

She wished they were leaving sooner than the following morning. She wished she were already somewhere else, somewhere distracting, somewhere that had nothing to do with him. Somewhere a world away from this front porch, from the place where her heart skipped whenever his car appeared in the driveway. She felt drunk with unhappiness.

Gigi coughed, and Flannery turned her head.

"Are you excited?"

"No. Would you like to go in my place?"

The girl smiled. "I like it here. Besides, I'm scared to fly."

"So's my mother. I think I'm going to pour a bottle of scotch down her throat before she gets on the plane."

Gigi laughed with her mouth closed. She was shy; Flannery remembered her own shyness as a teenager. It was a horrible, awkward age, she thought. It was an age where you felt your failings a thousand times a day.

She sighed and angled herself away from the young girl. She was at a terrible age too; twenty years after adolescence she had pitched back into the same pool of uncertainty and melodrama. Flannery pictured Melvin standing before her, shaken and pale. The porch step had creaked and moaned beneath his weight. He looked like he hadn't shaved in days. There were circles beneath his eyes. Flannery had sensed a new honesty, or vulnerability, in him, which she assumed had emerged with the birth of his child. The change scared her, though she had been careful not to wonder why. In the face of his discomfort, in the face of her own thumping heart, she had simply pushed him away. That had been her instinct, to push. She could have paused, and exhaled, and corralled her anger at his long absence. She could certainly have waited, and exercised some judicious thought, before she spoke.

If only life could be shaped the way she shaped stories on her typewriter. A character said something provocative, and Flannery sat with the sentence. She could read it aloud and weigh its significance. If the sentence turned the story in a new, unexpected direction, one that sent her fingers flying across the typewriter keys in an attempt to keep up with what *he* said, and what *she* said in response and what that new character who'd just showed up said, then she knew it was a keeper.

But life happened in the moment. Melvin said something, and she replied. There was no time to think, no time to stare at the blank wall above her desk and wonder what was right and what was wrong, no opportunity to try out a statement, one that might change her life, and then erase it before anyone else heard what she'd said.

She had said, *Go away.*

Flannery shook her head. *Ask Gigi a question*, she thought. *Make small talk.* But she couldn't summon the energy to open her mouth. She searched the magnolia tree, looking for the General, but he wasn't there. In the afternoons he often favored the water tower, which was out of Flannery's sight.

"The bank said I would be able to change money at the airport." Regina sounded worried.

"I think you should take some traveler's checks, in case you're mugged," Miss Mary said.

"Mugged?"

There was no reply. Presumably Miss Mary was nodding, because there were no words capable of describing the depravity of foreigners.

Flannery shut her eyes, and was surprised to find herself picturing her father. She remembered the strangled silence that had emanated from his bedroom during his last months. She remembered how, each morning, she had tiptoed past his door, holding her school loafers in her hand so he wouldn't be disturbed.

She wasn't sure why this memory resurfaced. *I hardly ever think of them*, Melvin had said of his parents, and the same was true of her. She didn't allow herself to think about her father. She had convinced herself, over time, that she didn't have to. She carried him with her, like she carried her faith, like she carried this disease in her bones. Her father had taken her childhood drawings, mostly of chickens involved in silly antics, with him on business trips. When he tucked her in at night, he told her stories in a quiet voice. He wrote speeches for the American Legion, and he labored over his sentences. Flannery had read those speeches as an adult, and she told herself that his writing wasn't better only because he hadn't had enough time to devote to the task. The important thing was that he was like her, in a way no one else was. They had shared the same blood, the same bones, and they would share the same end.

Flannery opened her eyes. She looked over her shoulder at the shingled white house. They had moved here so her father could die, and he had done so, one quiet morning when she was fifteen.

She braced herself against the arms of her chair. She had lost control of her thoughts; she was skidding through doors she usually kept shut. She pictured Cookie, paralyzed in the center of the mayor's living room. Her face was horrified, as if Flannery had just stripped her naked with her gaze.

"Oh, God," she said.

Gigi looked up. "Are you okay?"

Flannery tried to arrange her face so it would appear that the answer was yes.

"Miss Mary's all worked up about you guys going away."

Flannery considered the girl, her hair a long braid running down the middle of her back. Gigi's father was the burly cop who seemed to be at every public gathering, robust and officious in his blue uniform. Flannery rarely saw Gigi with her mother and father, though; she always thought of her as belonging to Miss Mary.

Who do I belong to? she thought, without trying to come up with an answer.

"Passports?" Miss Mary asked from inside.

"In my purse."

"You're going to miss me, admit it."

"Don't be absurd."

"Gigi." Miss Mary appeared in the doorway. "Tell these two how much they're going to miss us. Europe is full of phonies; everyone knows that. We're real, you and me. Our visits are the highlight of their week."

"What will we do without you?" Flannery asked.

"You should call me if you need advice," Miss Mary said, her face sincere. "I know how to handle foreigners. I can help you out of a situation, even from here. My instincts are spot-on."

Regina appeared at her side. "Shoot me if I pick up the phone to call this woman from France. Flannery, are you sure you packed enough socks?"

"I packed all my socks because you told me to."

"It's going to be cold in the evenings, and I've heard that the bedspreads there are thin and scratchy."

Gigi reached over and poked Miss Mary in the leg. "You told me to tell you when it was five o'clock. Mom and Joe will be at the farm soon."

"Do you need more help?" Miss Mary asked. "I could easily call Lona at the Whitesons' and tell her we're running late."

"You and Regina repacked eighty times," Flannery said. "I think we're ready for anything."

"She's right," Regina said. "You should go."

Miss Mary tried to hug them, but first Regina pushed her away, and Flannery held up a forbidding hand.

"We'll be back in a few weeks."

"I know." Miss Mary's voice was tearful. "But you never know with plane journeys . . ."

Gigi took the large woman by the arm and led her to the tractor. "Have fun," she said over her shoulder. "They'll be back soon," she said to Miss Mary in a reassuring tone.

Flannery and her mother waved as the tractor chugged down the driveway. They stopped waving only when the vehicle was swallowed by trees.

"Foolish woman." Regina crossed her arms over her chest. "Always creating a mountain out of a molehill. For heaven's sake, we'll be fine.

I'm looking forward to it." She sounded like she was trying to convince herself. "Come in here and look at what I did to your bag."

Flannery followed her mother inside. She nodded when her mother seemed to need her to nod, and said yes or no when the question demanded it, but she wasn't paying attention. She was willing time away; she was placing herself twelve hours forward. She was strapped into an airplane seat, rising up, up, up.

She and Bill had been working for over an hour when there was a gentle rap on the library door.

"Cookie?" Daisy's head appeared. "May I come in?"

"Of course, Mama."

The rest of her mother appeared. Rose was clasped to her chest; the baby craned her head. She had heard her mother's voice, but couldn't see her.

"You'd best take her," Daisy said, "before she starts up." The older woman looked tired; her arms shook slightly when she handed the baby over. She would turn sixty-five in a few weeks.

"She's a screamer?" Bill asked.

Cookie hugged the little girl. The baby tipped her head back and grinned, showing a single front tooth.

"Loudest mouth in town." Cookie matched her daughter's smile. "She gets away with it because she's so cute."

Bill nodded. "As far as I remember, Gigi was a quiet baby. Hardly made a peep."

Cookie noticed that Bill looked stiff; he was standing at attention beside the desk. He had relaxed while they worked. His face softened and his voice grew excited. They were getting a tremendous amount done. Together, they had come up with a publicity plan for the center.

They had reviewed the staff positions and responsibilities and come up with a list of recommendations on how to streamline their work. They had reviewed stacks of applications from women seeking help from the shelter. Tomorrow, they would have a third meeting with the center's director to go over what needed to be done. At their first lunch, the man had literally cried because he was so moved by the scope of their work.

"Mama," she said. "Bill caught the moon. He arranged for the *Atlanta Tribune* to do a piece on the center. They want to talk to both of us later this week. We'll be mentioned by name in the article."

"The *Tribune*. Oh my," Daisy said. "That's wonderful."

"And your daughter here arranged for the Sears in Macon to match our largest donation."

"This center's going to be a huge success, thanks to you two," Daisy said.

Bill cleared his throat. "The mayor is going to look very good at the opening ceremony."

Cookie nodded. She understood what he meant. If the mayor looked good because of their work, then they looked good. She felt a little giddy. She reached over and squeezed Bill's arm.

"I should go," he said. "We'll catch up before the meeting tomorrow."

"No, no," Daisy said. "I didn't mean to break up your work. Little Miss and I are just fine. I need a minute to use the ladies', that's all."

"You go, Mama," Cookie said. "We were done, anyway."

Daisy left the room at a half jog.

"This is going to be great," Bill said.

Cookie smiled. "I know." She followed him out of the library toward the front door. Rose was playing with the top button on Cookie's blouse. Her peach-fuzz hair was standing up straight; Cookie pressed it down with her hand. She wondered when Melvin would be home from the office; he had gone back right after dinner. He hadn't said so directly, but she knew he didn't like to be in the house while Cookie and Bill were working.

"I was thinking," Bill said, "about how much we'll be able to get done when I'm police chief and Melvin is mayor."

Cookie gave a small shake of her head. "Remember, I told you that in confidence."

"Oh, I know. I won't tell a soul, swear to God. You're exactly right, though. It's the obvious next step for him. He'll be a shoo-in after the mayor retires. Everyone in town knows and likes him."

Cookie nuzzled Rose's cheek. She had told Bill her dreams for Melvin spontaneously; she had sensed that he would understand the beauty of the plan in a way no one else would. She was right—Bill got it right away—but she felt a little uncomfortable about the admission. It seemed risky, or perhaps even inappropriate. She was a married woman; she was supposed to keep her thoughts to herself.

"Say hi to Lona," she said.

"Will do."

At the front door, Cookie lifted Rose's arm and waved it back and forth. Bill raised his hand in return.

She lay in bed that night next to a sleeping Melvin. She was too keyed up to rest. She rolled from one side to the other. She reminded herself to look through Rose's drawers to see if she needed bigger clothes for the summer. Cookie could use some new clothes herself; while she was at it, she would reorganize her own closet too. She ran through the itinerary for the Library Association meeting the following morning. She was only a few weeks from calling for an official vote on banning Flannery's books. Each meeting was now critically important. She had to handle the subject delicately; it couldn't be rushed.

She had brought the matter up for casual discussion at first, in order to feel the group out. Several women had immediately agreed with Cookie, and a couple, including Miss Mary, had pushed back.

"Nobody's making anybody read the books," the big woman had said. "It's just plain wrong to make them disappear. Flannery's poured her life into those pages. Leave them where they are, and whoever doesn't like 'em can stay away."

Cookie kept her voice measured. "It's not that simple," she said. "It's not about giving people a choice. If it were, I would agree with you. What it is, is a question of what kind of world we want to live in. Those books make this town look awful. They make *us* look awful. I, for one, don't want that version of us out there, in our library, where our children can stumble across it. I want to reject that image of ourselves. I want to push it away, and I think it's important that we do." She was flushed when she finished, surprised at her eloquence. Some of the women clapped. Miss Mary looked at her with raised eyebrows, but didn't respond.

Cookie turned her body, trying to find a comfortable position. She rubbed her cheek across the pillow. She listened for Rose, but heard only silence. She tucked her hands beneath the pillow. She took deep breaths.

When her heartbeat slowed, and a space finally cleared inside her head, it was filled by a question Bill had asked her that afternoon, out of nowhere.

"Why did you leave town after high school?"

Cookie had been surprised. "Why do you ask?"

Bill shrugged. "You seem like you belong here. This is your town; the rest of us are just living in it."

Cookie had dodged the question. She changed the subject, and put it out of her thoughts, until now.

She had stayed home for the rest of the week following the prizegiving. She thought she was faking illness, but when her mother took her temperature, it turned out she had a fever. Cookie lay in bed with her eyes shut to stop her mother from initiating conversation.

She prayed each morning that she would be able to stay in her room. She couldn't bear the idea of school: the high-pitched giggles of her friends, the football player she had kissed, who was now dropping hints about wanting more. She didn't want to make small talk with her awkward homeroom teacher, who cried in the bathroom twice a day. She didn't want to speak to anyone. She couldn't think of anyone that she wanted to see.

Still, by the following Monday the fever was gone, so Daisy dropped her daughter off by the school's front door. Cookie slowly walked inside, her eyes down. She passed a few friends, but their greetings were muted, out of respect for her recent illness. Cookie found herself passing her locker, and then her homeroom. She wove through the angular halls until she was in the library. As during her last visit, it was nearly empty.

She made her way into the center of the domed room. Flannery's novels had been returned to the main table. The books looked hard and mean, lying on their sides. Cookie shuddered at the sight of them. The librarian's placard sat beside the stack. Flannery's face looked out from the cardboard. She made direct eye contact with Cookie. *I see you. I will always see you.* Cookie turned away. She wiped her sweaty palms against her skirt. She realized that she had intended to hide the books again, but she knew now that there was no point. They would simply find their way back. She left the room with a slow gait.

When a friend tried to hug Cookie, she pulled back like a turtle retreating into its shell. She pretended not to notice the football player trying to pass her a note in math class. During lunch she hid in the bathroom, two stalls down from her homeroom teacher. At the end of the day, she practically ran home. On her way, she noticed that the bakery she'd been visiting since childhood needed a new coat of paint. The Catholic priest was in front of the post office, peering into the mailbox as if he wanted to follow his letter into the dark receptacle. Cookie's skin began to crawl. She couldn't bear the sight of anyone, or anything—she realized that she had misunderstood this entire town for her entire life. What she had thought to be beautiful and meaningful had turned out to be ugly and hollow. Once home, she took the stairs two at a time, and dove beneath the bedcovers.

"Still under the weather, sweet pea?" her mother asked from the doorway.

"Yes," Cookie said, her voice muffled. She heard her mother's footsteps grow fainter; she was no doubt on her way to make Cookie her favorite tea.

Cookie lay in the tented darkness. She felt her discomfort in her bones. She tried to picture the following day, which would be just as bad as this one. She couldn't come up with a conceivable way in which it might be better. She would be equally ill at ease, equally frustrated. Something needed to change. *You need a plan*, she told herself. *Make a plan.*

At dinner that night, she fidgeted in her chair.

"What's up, peanut?" her father asked.

"After graduation," Cookie said, "I'm going to move away."

Her mother dropped her fork. Her lower lip began to tremble.

Her father coughed.

No one spoke for a moment, then her father said, "Excuse me, young lady. Did I hear you correctly?"

Cookie nodded.

"Move where?"

She felt the calmness that accompanied certitude. She knew she needed to get far away from Milledgeville. She needed to train her eyes on a different horizon, on different people. She would dispense with everything familiar. She would stride into a place that meant nothing to her, and make it her own. That was her only shot at recovery.

"New York," she said. She repeated the words, to convince them all that she was serious. "New York."

When her parents could speak, they asked for her reasons. Cookie simply shook her head, as if the justification was so obvious that it would be foolish to say it aloud. Who wouldn't want to move to the Greatest City in the World? Who wouldn't want to shed a small, sleepy town for someplace truly *alive*?

"But we were going to be in clubs together," her mother said. "We had plans."

"Clubs," Cookie heard herself say. "Clubs are a waste of time."

She apologized when her mother began to cry, but the damage was done.

"You're not going anywhere," her father said. "You've lost your good sense, girl. This is your home. You belong here."

Cookie shook her head.

Over the next few days, Big Mike tried to demonstrate that she should stay in Milledgeville; he built a case for why she belonged there. He cited the crime and murder statistics for New York. He recited the history of Milledgeville, emphasizing the days during the Civil War when it had been the state capital. He told the story of the Himmel family, who had been among the original colonists of Georgia. He pulled out photo albums and showed her how she had her mother's smile, her aunt Bertha's nose, and Nana Irene's fiery eyes. "You have roots," he said. "You can't just hack them out."

Cookie had no reply to her father's reasoned arguments, because she had no use for reasoned arguments. Each day she simply presented the raw truth of her status as an independent person with a force of will, which in itself was a blunt rebuttal to every argument her father could muster. As far as she was concerned, there was nothing more to be said. Cookie was only hanging around for her father's blessing, which she knew would come eventually.

Big Mike became so accustomed to the rhythm and content of their arguments that he became detached from them, and at times found himself listening to his own rhetoric. Cookie knew that he disliked the anger in his voice, and the hollowness. He sounded, to his own ear, like a hypocrite. One morning, Big Mike found himself unable to swallow his orange juice past the lump in his throat. He coughed, rubbed his neck, and spluttered juice into a napkin. Something inside him had sealed shut. He turned and looked at his daughter, who was eating a bowl of cereal at the table. In a voice as rough as sandpaper, Big Mike told her that she could go.

Cookie's sense of triumph was short-lived; it lasted only as long as the plane ride. Once the plane landed in New York, she had trouble catching her breath. She felt like she had arrived at a dangerously high altitude. She got lost in the myriad corridors of the airport, and found her new dress damp with sweat by the time she collected her luggage. In the taxi, she had the disturbing sense that she was racing toward the skyline of New York like water headed down a drain. *You just need some rest*, she told herself. *You're overexcited.* But she was unable to close her eyes that night. She had pictured the women's hotel as a wide, low building, but in fact it was narrow and thirteen stories high. Cookie lay awake picturing all the young women lying in single beds stacked on top of each other like sweaters in a closet.

She started work the following morning, unpacking ladies' undergarments at a huge department store. She spent the following night awake, listening to the doorman scream in Spanish beneath her window. By day four, she had to resort to makeup to conceal the circles beneath her eyes. Cookie's boss, a miserable spinster, took daily pleasure in ridiculing the girl's accent and sending her on pointless errands.

When Cookie wasn't working, she toured the city in a bath of car exhaust and cigarette smoke. The buildings and people crowded her down the sidewalks, and her face felt gritty with dirt by the end of each day. She wrote letters to her parents, even though they begged her to call. She knew she would cry if she heard their voices, which would make her mother weep and her father clear his throat.

The seasons, so much more obvious in the northeast, churned past her window. She dressed for work in a summer dress, then a light jacket, then a parka. Cookie spent her evenings alone in her room. She kept a stack of magazines by her bedside, but spent the hours with the lights off, looking out the window. Cookie was deeply aware that since her arrival in the city, no one had told her that she was beautiful, no one had asked for her phone number, no one seemed taken with her in any way. In the swirl and mill of the city, she felt plain, and forgettable. She saw this truth reflected from every mirror and every window she passed. New York City was lined with windows, like endless rows of eyes, so the message was unrelenting.

Cookie refused to admit defeat until she had been in the city for a year, and even then, she thought, *I'll give it one more. I can make this work.* She decided that part of her problem lay in her lowly position at the department store; she needed to move up in the ranks in order to gain respect, and then friends would surely follow. When she told her boss that she was interested in the position of Senior Sales Assistant, the woman silently handed her an application. Cookie spent several evenings painstakingly filling it out, making sure every word was perfect. She detailed her year of faithful service at the store, and under extra-curricular activities, she listed her three high school awards. She felt a little uncomfortable writing these down, but she didn't know what else to write, and she thought such examples of past success might help her cause.

For the next few weeks, Cookie woke up excited every morning, wondering if today would be the day. But her boss never said a word. After three months, Cookie worked up the courage to ask about the status of her application. The woman stared at her for a moment as if she had no idea what she was talking about, and then said, *Oh, sorry. You were rejected.*

Cookie woke up on the morning of her second anniversary in the city and cried. She skipped work for the first time and walked to Central Park. She wanted some semifresh air in her lungs. She wanted to look at trees instead of buildings.

Depressed and humiliated, she followed the meandering pathways and imagined moving back into her parents' house. She would become an old maid. She would take in stray cats, and possibly turn religious. She would accept as her due the patronizing stares of townspeople who thought she had been foolish to leave in the first place. Cookie just wished she could return home with a better story. Even her failure was mediocre. If something tragic had happened to her, if she had a *real* reason to abandon this place, then at least she would have an acceptable excuse.

She sat down when her legs tired. She spoke to the young man on the bench because she had lost any shred of self-respect. Appearances no longer mattered. Manners no longer mattered. Nothing mattered. She chatted with him easily, and only gradually came to the impression that he was nice. That he was nice-looking. That she was enjoying his company, and even more remarkably, that he seemed to be enjoying hers. But she was still thinking about booking her ticket, packing her things, and telling her parents of her decision, when the young man put his hand on her arm.

She looked down at his hand, then up at his face. He seemed familiar, though she couldn't have said how. Cookie found herself cemented, turned sideways on a park bench. She was no longer plain, or beautiful, or her failed New York self, or her successful Milledgeville self. She was simply Cookie Himmel, waiting to see what would happen next.

What happened next was a kiss. It was the most tender, unexpected kiss of her life. Cookie's head spun, and she wondered—kissing him in return—why she was crying. When he pulled away and she pulled away, she noticed they were holding hands. When her head stopped spinning, she noticed that her future looked different. It felt like the world had twirled on its axis, leaving her in a spot that was both exactly the same, and brand new.

They were in the guest room. Mrs. Whiteson called it the White Bedroom. She kept a bouquet of white flowers on the bedside table, even when no one was staying there. Joe always marveled at the room; no one else he knew had a room reserved for guests, yet the Whitesons had two. When his aunt or cousins visited, they slept in Joe's bed, and he slept on the couch.

The bed had a white lace coverlet that Daisy Himmel had knit. Two matching lace doilies covered the pillows. A white quilt was folded at the bottom of the bed. On the bedside table, a black leather Bible and a small Tiffany lamp kept the flowers company. At the foot of the bed sat an antique wooden trunk. When Joe lifted the lid he was amazed to find it empty. "It's for show," Lona said. Joe shook his head. A trunk was intended for storage, or luggage. What did it show, if it was empty? He made a mental note to tell his mother about the white room, and the vacant trunk, the next time she needed to hear him talk.

They were working on the second set of curtains for this room. The first attempt had been lace, to match the coverlet. Lona had created a translucent white curtain, and then sewn the delicate lace onto the back-ing. It had been the most time-consuming of their endeavors, and when Joe hung the finished product, he was terrified he would rip or somehow sully it. He washed his hands three times before slowly sliding the fabric onto the rod. Lona assured him that it was sturdy, but the curtain looked like it might blow apart if he sneezed. It was beautiful, though. When he climbed down from the stepladder, he said to Lona, "Mrs. Whiteson will definitely love these."

He was wrong. Cookie shook her head as soon as she saw them. Rose was perched on her hip—the baby looked slowly around the room, as if judging the scene alongside her mother. When her blue eyes fell on Joe, she studied him for a minute. Her mouth started to change shape. Joe watched, curious. He had almost no experience with babies. He found Rose very beautiful with her blond hair and bright eyes. She looked like a doll, although she didn't act like one. When she cried, the noise practically shook the floorboards. *When she wants something*, Melvin had said once, over the noise, *she wants it*. The corners of her mouth turned upward, and Joe realized she was smiling. It was a big smile; it took over her round face. She bounced on her mother's hip and waved her arms. She pushed the smile in his direction like she was offering a gift that would be impossible to reject or ignore.

"Hi," he said, impressed.

"Quit squawking," Cookie said in a gentle voice to her daughter. "I think it's too much lace." She wrinkled her nose.

Joe moved his gaze between the mother and baby. He enjoyed these reviews. Cookie always saw a flaw that would never have occurred to him in a million years. The moment she walked through the door, she knew whether she liked it or not. The first set of curtains in the nursery were too pink. She didn't want her daughter dominated by the color. The curtains in the living room didn't have enough heft. When they were drawn, they didn't completely obscure the view of the neighborhood. Cookie could still make out the house across the street and the shape of the horrible broken-down car in their driveway.

The criticisms were never criticisms of Lona, or her sewing. It was Cookie who ultimately approved the fabric and the color. She often sighed and said, "Well, we tried that, didn't we?" She decided that they should go for a plain white muslin curtain with a tiny strip of lace on the hem. While Joe took down the delicate curtains, he wondered whose home they would end up in. Miss Mary had already replaced all the curtains in their house with Cookie's rejects. She had given the rest to her friends in town. When Joe rode the bus to school, he spotted familiar green curtains hanging in one house, and sheer living room curtains adorning another.

Lona refused to hang any of the curtains in her own home. She said the sight would just make her think about work, and how nothing ever turned out perfectly the first time around. She often said morose things like this, now that Cookie had gone back to her meetings and they had been left to work alone. Joe was finding it difficult to track her moods. She was laughing in his arms one minute, then leaning on his shoulder, her face pensive, then she was across the room, a needle and thread poised in her hands like tiny weapons. Joe discovered that the best way to handle her was to remain calm. If he allowed her to pull away, and hugged her when she wanted to be held, and kissed her when she tipped her face up to his, everything worked out fine. This strategy seemed to come naturally to him. For the first time in recent years, against all the odds, Joe felt calm.

He felt calm in part because he never felt alone. Even when Lona was on the other side of the room with her back turned, a sea of invisible threads seemed to connect them. It was as if all the sewing of the past ten months had stitched them together. When they were apart—while Joe was at school or at home—his body ached with the pull of string after string, but the threads never broke, and he didn't worry that they would. Each afternoon when her car pulled up in front of the school, his skin relaxed. He tried to hurry across the lawn without actually breaking into a run.

The weekends were the most difficult. He worked the farm and stayed in the company of his parents, and was apart from Lona for seventy-two hours straight. He blinked while his mother spoke to him and struggled to understand what she was saying. He couldn't bear her company, and yet he couldn't bear to be alone. The calendar on the kitchen wall haunted him. It was already April. Time was passing. Days were being lost. He would both graduate from high school and turn eighteen in a couple of months. He had an agreement with his parents that he would continue to help Mrs. Waters over the summer, whether the Whiteson house was finished or not. Then, in September, he would begin his adult life, running the farm. At that point he would no longer have an excuse to see Lona for two minutes a day, let alone the two hours he now required in order to function. The prospect—and the imminence of it—made Joe sweat through his sheets at night.

Miss Mary could detect some kind of craving in him, so she plied him with food. She brought extra sandwiches out to the fields, baked his favorite cookies, and heaped seconds and thirds on his plate at dinnertime. "Are you still hungry?" she asked. "Can you fit a little more?" "No," he said, but she continued to provide, and he continued to consume. Eating was a temporary salve, and a way to avoid conversation. He could see the concern on his parents' faces, but he also knew that they wouldn't approach him like they had last time. They wouldn't try to fix his life for him. They wouldn't presume that they had the right. They could see that he had changed, that he was now more man than boy. This both pleased and saddened them. The change kept Miss Mary in the kitchen until late at night, the oven roaring with heat, water boiling on the stove.

When Lona kissed him, they were kneeling on the floor of the white room. They were between the bed and the window, on a small round rug. Lona was wearing a blue skirt and a pale top. The window was slightly open. Cookie had added a small clock to the bedside table, and it ticked with a low hum that Joe found soothing.

Lona tasted of marijuana and raspberries. The kiss continued. It stopped and then started again. It dove down and then swam back up. Lona put her hand under his tee shirt. She pressed her palm to his belly. Joe waited for the kiss to end. He waited for her body to tighten and for her to pull away. He waited for her to say *Stop*. Lona never allowed herself to completely unravel the way he did, like a loose ball of yarn.

He cupped the back of her neck. He ran his other hand down her arm, the outside of his fingers brushing along the contours of her breast. He shivered, and felt her shiver too. It occurred to him, out of nowhere, that this time she might not stop. Her hand was pressed against his stomach. He could feel how rare their connection was. He could feel the loneliness of the people outside the window, walking around this town. He could feel his pure good fortune.

He wanted to say *I love you*, but he suspected that if he did, she would tug away, shake her head, and cross the room. Joe pulled her closer, hip bone against hip bone, clothes rubbing skin. He kissed harder, and her neck craned backward. She lost her balance. Her legs folded beneath her, and then she was on the floor. Apart from her for a second, Joe's body ached. His erection scraped the inside of his jeans. He worried that the spell had been broken, the moment lost.

Lona looked pale and vulnerable against the rug. "Don't stop," she said.

Joe thought about having sex with Lona all the time, of course. Every time he was alone, he replayed their last make-out session in his mind. He imagined being allowed to unbutton her blouse. He imagined slipping the fabric off her shoulders and holding her two perfect breasts in his hands. In bed at night, he had to masturbate in order to fall asleep. If he didn't, there was no relief and no rest.

Lona pulled his shirt over his head. Joe kept his expression serious. He kept kissing her. He knew the sight of his hairless chest would remind her of his age, and he didn't want her to stop. He didn't want her to think about her marriage or where they were or the fact that he wasn't an adult. Time was running out. They loved each other even if she wouldn't admit it. They needed each other even if she wouldn't admit it.

He lifted her skirt and kissed the birthmark on the outside of her knee. This created an immediate shift in the atmosphere, as if the birthmark was a secret button Joe hadn't stumbled upon before. The temperature rose, and a sense of urgency swept the room. Lona's body curled around his. Her tongue laced his ear. They rocked back and forth.

Joe's pants were somehow on the floor beside him. Her blouse was unbuttoned. They gained momentum. Joe could hear a heartbeat—he wasn't sure if it was his or hers. There were bare stomachs and bare thighs. They became a pendulum, thumping the floor. A chant filled Joe's insides, a rising sound, a noise that would not be ignored. *Now. Now. Now. Now. Now.*

No one in the group looked at Flannery. Not even Regina. It was very early, just after dawn, and there were more than a hundred people ahead of them. As the line moved, they passed signs asking for donations. The giant gray basilica, a twist of spires and steeples, loomed on the rocks overhead.

There was a stiffness in Flannery's bones. She moved awkwardly on her crutches, as though they had just been handed to her for the first time. She spotted another sign claiming that sixty-eight confirmed miracles had taken place here. Flannery mouthed the phrase *confirmed miracles*. She pictured a cabal of elite priests and doctors gathered around a conference table with a checklist. They nodded their graying heads, as if weighed down by great responsibility.

All around Flannery, men and women leaned on crutches. Scores were in wheelchairs. There was a string of men lying on stretchers, being pushed by volunteers. Young women supported grandparents. Mothers held babies. Nuns accompanied lepers. There were moans from those too sick to contain themselves.

Even the dying hushed, though, as they approached the grotto where the fourteen-year-old Saint Bernadette claimed to have seen the Blessed Virgin in 1858. Flannery glanced over at her mother, who looked nervous.

"Stop making that face," Regina said.

Flannery tried.

She didn't want to be here. She kept her head down. She hated the idea that people were looking at her, thinking: *That cripple's here for a miracle.*

Bernadette had visited the Virgin Mother in the grotto for two weeks. Mary had talked to the girl about belief, conversion, and a change of heart. She had promised that Bernadette would be happy in the next world. They talked about how the teenager could help others. One evening Mary instructed Bernadette to walk deeper into the grotto and wash herself. The girl protested that there was no water within a mile of where they stood. Mary shook her head, as if to say, *You must believe.* At that very moment, water began to burble through the mud.

News of Bernadette's visits with the Virgin Mary spread through the village of Lourdes and beyond. At first, the word *miracle* was merely whispered, then spoken in church, then shouted on the town green. Men and women walked into the woods to visit the grotto. They too washed themselves in the brand-new spring. They murmured prayers and requests. They shared wishes they had been hiding their entire lives.

Flannery had dragged herself through the first two weeks of the trip. She was glad to be away from Milledgeville, but no place felt comfortable. She tolerated the daily itinerary of one cathedral visit after another. She watched her mother cross herself, over and over. She watched the zealous fall to their knees. She watched the days tick by, with the specter of this day drawing closer. She turned so far inward that her mother accused her of being mute.

If Flannery had felt able to speak, she could have said, I disagree with you. I disagree with where we're going and why we're here. She could have said, I believe that God is present everywhere—in every tree, person, and pebble—whereas you and the other ladies on this tour believe that God tends to spend his time in churches, especially the nicer, older churches with Renaissance art. She could have said, I put no stock in solicited miracles. The idea that someone can line up to bathe in a particular bathtub and expect God's healing seems a bit like putting a quarter in a pinball machine and expecting the same. God is not here to be demanded of, begged from, or criticized. He hands out burdens to those who are strong enough to carry them, and I feel profoundly uncomfortable with the idea of lining up with the other invalids and asking for mine to be alleviated.

She said nothing, though. She simmered, like a pot about to boil. She had kept her deeper feelings to herself for years. She was keenly aware that she specialized in containment. The present moment, when her thoughts were particularly dangerous, and particularly unwelcome, was not the time to let go.

They were beside the grotto now. Women kissed the gray rock, their expressions sincere. They rubbed their cheeks against the smooth surface. They pushed the inhabitants of the wheelchairs as close to the stone as possible. "Touch it," they said. "Touch it right now. What do you feel?"

More people pushed forward, their mouths puckered. Kiss. Kiss. Kiss. The rock was smooth from the pressure of millions of lips. Flannery wanted to look away, but she couldn't.

"I keep thinking I see people I know," Regina said. "It's funny how everyone looks like someone else. I could have sworn I saw old Father Graham back there. And that woman looks like my sister. Don't you think so?"

"I'm not going to chitchat."

Regina looked offended. "I never *chitchat*. Who do you think I am?"

They paused to look at Our Lady of Lourdes. The stone woman was wearing a blue dress and a white cape. Her hands were clasped in front of her. A long rosary circled her arm and draped down the statue's front. The statue seemed to gaze both skyward and down at the people waiting in line. "Oh, sweet mother," the woman next to them cried. "Save me!"

Flannery closed her eyes. She tried to redirect her thoughts. Her editor had liked her novel. At least, he said he did. She knew that he preferred her stories and was glad she had returned to them. She would never admit this to him, but she was glad too. Wrestling with the unwieldy shape and size of the novel had been like trying to envelop her mother's favorite stallion with wrapping paper and a bow. The novel had stomped its hooves and snorted hot air and bared its teeth and kicked her. Flannery had walked away exhausted and bruised, unsure whether she had done the job she'd set out to accomplish.

Writing short stories was a better match for her strength. She could mete out the endeavor over months, instead of years. When she returned from this trip, Flannery would step back into a doctor's seamy waiting room. She would watch a young girl glare at a woman who was making polite conversation with her mother. Flannery would shudder at the words this girl hurled at the older woman, and because of the shudder, she would know the dialogue was right.

If there had been a typewriter in sight, Flannery would have headed for it. She wished there was a door she could close, a piece of smooth, blank paper she could crank into a machine. She wished she could enter someone else's mind, someone else's life. She had a clear preference for fiction over reality, but reality wouldn't leave her alone. She could feel Melvin hovering nearby. He had followed her across the cobblestone streets of Europe. She watched him study the long, winding line. She heard his voice in her ear. *This is interesting*, he said. *It's interesting that so many people have believed in this place for so long. There must be something in it to sustain that kind of interest.*

Hope, she answered him. *They are sustained by hope. Hope may have a positive reputation, but it has a vicious downside. If you have hope, you can be crushed.*

It was clear to Flannery that this line teetered at the rim of a cliff. Miracles were rare, as per their reputation, which meant that she was part of a terminal procession. Ahead of her, men and women fell, one by one, onto the sharp rocks and crashing waves below.

They shuffled past carts piled high with burning candles. When the line shifted, they saw a stretch of rock lined with faucets. People pressed water bottles, flasks, and cups against the silver nozzles. Their hands shook as they passed the water to the ailing person in their life.

The rising sun cut into Flannery's eyes.

The line stretched behind her and Regina as far as they could see. A nun made her way down the stretch with a stone cup. Every patient was asked to drink a sample of the bathwater for *les malades*. Flannery forced herself to take a sip. The water tasted warm, and slightly metallic. It reminded her of the wine she sipped each week at church. That wine represented the blood of Christ. This water represented a young girl's faith, and how that faith had been rewarded. The reward was supposedly a generous one, still flowing hundreds of years later through the springs beneath their feet.

Flannery said, "Do you know how many germs there must be in this air? Everyone around us is sick. We're all sick."

Regina narrowed her eyes at her daughter. "I'm not."

Flannery had lain in bed earlier that morning, ignoring her mother's repeated entreaties to rise. She had watched her mother rush between the hotel bathroom and the bedroom. Regina had changed her outfit three times. She had remade her bed twice. Flannery said, "You'll probably have lupus by the time we leave."

"I expected you to be unpleasant today," her mother said. "I hope God's not listening."

This was what she had always said to Flannery whenever she talked back as a child. Flannery found the phrase oddly comforting. She studied the light blue sky. She listened to the myriad languages being spoken; their direct neighbor was German, the man behind them was praying in French. The procession came to a sudden stop. Flannery shifted from foot to foot. She jiggled her crutches, looking for a more comfortable spot on which to rest her weight.

She had been sick for twelve years. She had known the disease was hereditary ever since her father had fallen ill. He told her, in his last days, "You won't get this. I promise you won't." Flannery had chosen to believe him. She had moved to the middle of the country for graduate school. She shifted her focus from drawing cartoons to writing fiction. She followed the brightest of her peers to New York City. She made friends and went on dates and rewrote her sentences over and over, trying to make each one lash like a whip. When she ran out of money, she lived with friends in Connecticut. She joked around with their kids and helped with household chores. When her wrists began to ache that first winter, she attributed the pain to the cold weather. The ache spread to her shoulders, and she thought, *It must be arthritis*. She planned a trip home to visit her mother. By the time the train crossed the Georgia border, Flannery's body was curled and twisted like parentheses.

She accepted the diagnosis. She made her choices. She returned to her sentences. She fought to make each word count. When her body struck out, she clung to her desk and bent over the typewriter keys. She did this every day until Melvin Whiteson showed up on her porch. Now she was standing on a rocky path in the south of France with the taste of tin in her mouth.

"Just try to keep your mind open," Regina said, as though she were following her daughter's thoughts.

They drew closer to the dressing rooms. Flannery tried to push her mind ajar. She put her weight into it, tackling a heavy door that hadn't budged in years. Since she believed that God was everywhere, she had to believe that he was also present in these brown rocks and cold water, despite her principled objection to officially sanctioned sites of godliness. It was therefore reasonable to suppose that God *might* elect to avail her of a miraculous healing.

The thought broke off; the effort hurt. Flannery's eyes stung behind her glasses. The crutches rubbed at her armpits. Life was composed of small annoyances. She was surrounded by rocks, being assaulted by pebbles.

"You're almost there," a nun murmured.

A space cleared inside Flannery's chest. *Fine*, she thought. She was here; she needed to stop wishing herself away. Of course she would like to walk out of these baths in perfect health. If that happened, life's swollen potential would unfurl before her like a long red carpet. She would open up her life. She would incinerate these damned crutches. If this worked, everything would change.

Flannery hesitated, then pushed forward again. She pictured Melvin's face, felt his breath in her ear, sensed his hand reaching out.

Regina touched her arm, then stopped walking. Flannery realized she was meant to continue on without her. She shuffled a few more steps. She ached now; she craved relief. She approached the entrance to the baths. The pain was acute. She had shelved her cynicism, and opened herself up for disappointment. She could feel the risk in her bones.

A re you nervous?" Melvin asked.

"No," Cookie said. "I'm excited. It's going to be a great success. I just know it."

They were in the dining room. She gripped her coffee cup with both hands; she was desperate for the caffeine. Rose was teething and had woken up several times in the night seeking comfort. Cookie hated those abrupt midnight screams; they sucked her out of sleep with a kind of violence that left her disoriented and slightly frightened. Each time the baby erupted, she ran to the nursery in her nightgown, her heart in her throat. She sat in the rocking chair by the window and sang lullabies in Rose's ear, trying to calm them both down.

Melvin was eating a grapefruit with a spoon. Rose lay on a blanket by the window, burbling. The child looked insultingly well slept, Cookie thought, whereas she had needed two coats of concealer to disguise the dark circles under her eyes.

"We should get there at five?" Melvin asked.

She nodded. "Oh, I forgot to tell you that I ran into the mayor during yesterday's run-through. He told me to pass on his personal apology."

"What for?"

"He said he knew this project wasn't right for you from the beginning, and that he has something much more interesting in the works that he'll discuss with you at the next meeting. He thanked me for doing such a good job on your behalf, by the way."

Melvin gave her a level look. "Cookie."

"What?"

"You know I sent him a letter, resigning from the committee."

She waved her hand. "He understands that was just because you weren't interested in working on the center. He knows you need to be challenged. So it's all been sorted out. He'll tell you about it himself at the meeting."

Cookie waited a second to see if he would argue further. She was relieved when he sighed and looked down at the newspaper. She turned in her chair and made a face at the baby. Rose grinned, revealing the nub of a new tooth. Cookie ran through the day's schedule in her head. She checked off the tasks she needed to complete and the people she needed to talk to. She knew she was organized, and she knew she hadn't forgotten anything, but it made her feel better to be sure.

"Bah bah," Rose said, in an urgent tone, as if she were passing on critical information.

When Melvin looked up again, his face had taken on a steely expression. He said, "I think I'm going to take the afternoon off."

"Today?"

"Today."

Cookie tried to sound unbothered. "You just decided that right now? Why?"

"I want to spend some time with my daughter. Your mother won't mind, she's still getting over that migraine."

Rose rolled in their direction, as if she understood that the conversation now concerned her. She waved her hands and gave a tiny burp.

Cookie shifted in her chair. "Can you just decide to do that at the last minute? It seems a bit unfair to Tom and the others. Don't you have appointments scheduled?"

"Nope."

"None?"

"Cookie, I could take a week off and not miss anything."

"What do you mean?" She stared at him. "You were just telling me about the complications in the Roylston closing, and that other new deal."

He leaned back in his chair and stretched his arms over his head. He was quiet for a long moment. Then he said, "You need to leave soon, don't you? I know you don't want to be late."

Cookie looked down at the brown liquid in her cup. Her conversations with Melvin felt like increasingly difficult tightrope walks. If she slipped in one direction or the other, they ended up tangled in a briar patch. They scratched at each other, trying to claw their way out of small misunderstandings and serpentine discussions. She had always thought it strange, growing up, how little her parents said to each other over the course of a day. But perhaps silence was the key to a happy marriage. Cookie vowed to do better. She could be quiet. She could become even more selective over which battles to pick.

She pushed her chair back. She put on a smile. "I do have to be there soon. What are you going to do with Rose?"

"I'm not sure."

"You're in a strange mood this morning, Melvin."

He appeared to consider this. "Maybe I am." He stood and walked around the table. He kissed her on the cheek. "Good luck today."

As she drove to the center, Cookie felt the nerves Melvin had asked about. She wished she had skipped breakfast and just picked up coffee in town. She didn't want to be distracted by thoughts of Melvin. It wasn't only this morning that he'd been in a strange mood; it had been weeks of glum looks and peculiar comments. She had asked him several times if something was wrong, and he had said no. She wondered if the business was failing. She decided she would ask around, tomorrow, to see if she could gather any news. Tomorrow she would make sense of what was going on.

Right now, though, she needed to focus on the task at hand. She was fully aware of today's importance. She had reached a peak she'd only loosely dreamed about upon her return to Milledgeville. She had never worked on a project this large. Her speech this afternoon would be in front of the mayor, councilmen, local press, and the most important businesspeople in Macon and Milledgeville. Her previous work had been limited to women's clubs. The Children's Center had taken her into the public sphere.

She knew she was ready for the challenge. She knew she would ace her speech and impress everyone in attendance. She was ready to speak to these people. She wouldn't have felt this prepared before the birth of her daughter. The pregnancy had filled her up, literally and figuratively. As her figure swelled—not just her belly, but her breasts, her behind, and, by the end, her face—she had felt grounded by the new weight.

Cookie also felt a fresh attachment to the community. Her little family was tethered to this place by a birth, by a brand-new history, and by the turning wheel of her own industry. Melvin was connected to Milledgeville in a way he could never deny. This period in his life could no longer be described as a visit, or an experiment. He lived here; his wife and daughter had been born here. The Whiteson family had laid down roots.

With her own family in place, she could help others to find their feet. She was proud to be a mother helping other mothers and children in need. The center would give underprivileged women a temporary home. Children would be given clothes and be enrolled in school. Women would be assisted with job searches. During the initial meetings Cookie had conducted with Bill Waters, they had spent hours reviewing the applicants' cases. There had been photos of disheveled women, children with wide-eyed stares. Some of the women looked embarrassed, others looked vacant, as if they didn't notice the camera pointed in their direction. They all looked beaten down and lost. The little girls made Cookie think of Rose in her crib, clean from her nightly bath, cherubic in her white nightgown. Her arms flung over her head in her favorite sleeping position.

Cookie reminded herself to find Bill as soon as she reached the center. She had offered to lend him one of Melvin's suits for the occasion. He had a dress uniform, but it was shabby, and she'd convinced him that a suit was more appropriate. He had refused the offer at first, but Cookie insisted. He would come with her when she ran home to change that afternoon.

She peered through the windshield at the sky. It was overcast. She hoped the rain would hold off until after the opening ceremony. She had laid her dress out on the bed before leaving, to save time later. The blue silk would not stand up well to raindrops. She had chosen the dress partly for the color, and partly because it belted at the waist and therefore accentuated her figure. Her mother had told her that with every child born, a woman's dress size increased by one. Cookie had been appalled by this idea, and was deeply relieved to have proved it untrue. She knew that when she climbed onto the podium, several women in the crowd would think jealously, *I cannot believe she had a baby.*

She pictured herself onstage, her posture erect. She imagined the look of surprise on the mayor's face as he took note of her eloquence. She saw the women from her various committees and clubs clapping. Her parents beaming from the center of the crowd. She found Rose's towhead, her little girl wrapped tight in her husband's arms. She listened to the applause, and told herself that she deserved it.

You love me."

"No, I don't." Lona's eyes were closed.

"You say that, but you don't mean it." Joe kissed her elbow, her wrist, then her shoulder.

Lona shook her head. She realized that the white sheet had drifted down to her waist, but she didn't reach to cover herself up. She was comfortable. She didn't want to move.

"I love you," he whispered, as his lips inched over her skin. "I love you. I love you. I love you."

The sunlight hit Lona's eyelids. It traveled as if through a stained-glass window and turned her insides the color of honey. She inhaled sunlight, warmth, happiness.

She heard her voice say, "I love you too."

Joe stopped mid-kiss.

Lona opened her eyes.

She knew it was the truth. She was being honest; she knew what honesty was, perhaps for the first time in her life. She wasn't trying to please someone, she wasn't trying to do what she thought she was supposed to, she wasn't trying to disappear so she wouldn't have to feel anything. She was naked, in the Whitesons' guest bed, with a young man. She was staring straight into his eyes, and he was staring straight into hers. She quivered with life, like an arrow about to be released from a bow.

"I don't want to work on the farm," Joe said.

"What?"

"I never wanted to. I didn't want to admit it to myself, because I didn't want to disappoint my parents, but I don't want to muck out horses every morning and run the plow with my father. I don't want to do it."

"I just said that I love you."

He smiled. "I know."

"And your response is that you don't want to muck out horses anymore?"

"I already knew you loved me."

Her own smile opened like an umbrella.

He tapped her thigh with his finger. "I'm glad you said it. But we need to talk about other things."

"Like how you don't want to be a farmer?"

"We only have a month left."

She pulled the pillow over her face, a petulant gesture. She saw the irony in the movement. She knew that in some ways Joe was more adult than her. He was brave and honest in a way she wasn't. He had given the first kiss, in the face of almost certain rejection. He had admitted his feelings first. When Lona met his eyes, he never glanced away. She'd had to work very hard, over the past few months, to muzzle him.

A ripple went through her stomach. An electric cord of terror and excitement. Another ripple followed. She lowered the pillow. "Okay," she said, quietly.

"Okay."

They intertwined fingers. The light shone boldly through the window, streaking the floor yellow. The white curtain was pushed to the sides. The top of the brick wall that surrounded Melvin and Cookie's backyard, the branches of the elm tree, and a gray sky were visible. Lona had become very familiar, over the past few months, with this view. She had memorized it. She used the image to calm herself whenever she was away from Joe.

"What you're talking about," she said, "giving up on the farm . . . you can do that because you haven't started yet. You're at the beginning, you can afford to change your mind. But I can't. I'm already midstream. I'm *in* my life."

"No, you're not."

Her voice came out thick with sarcasm. "I'm not?"

He shook his head. He looked so serious, his heavy brown eyes trained on her. "This is your life, right here with me. You've just been spending time 'til now."

Lona swallowed and rolled her head on the pillow. The soft cotton cooled her skin. This was why she had been avoiding this conversation.

"I want to spend the rest of my life with you."

Lona felt the blood leave her face.

She had said *I love you* to this boy. She had meant it, more than she'd ever meant anything that had come out of her mouth. He was right; he *was* her life. The years before he had worked for her were smoky, pale, and gray. Only now did she feel alive and alert every minute of the day. Only now did she feel like she belonged in her body. She knew her own shape, and the feel of her skin, for the first time. It was almost as if, in falling in love with Joe, she had been forced to discover herself. She'd had to learn where she stopped, in order to know where he began.

When she considered what he had said, she realized that the idea had been in her mind all along. It seemed inevitable, like a road she'd been aware of but had gone out of her way to avoid. She had to do this because there was no acceptable alternative. She couldn't live in this town without seeing Joe, without talking to him, without kissing him. And because of the circumstances, she couldn't live here with him for much longer. Her options had narrowed to one, and, as usual, Joe had gotten there ahead of her. But Lona, now that she had arrived, was completely present.

She said, "I want to go somewhere very different from here." Lona tightened her grip on Joe's hand. She suddenly felt as light as a balloon; she was afraid that if she let go, she would take off. "I want to go to a big city."

"Atlanta?"

She shook her head. "Too close." Bill's relatives lived near Atlanta. They were a family of cops; someone would find her. She needed to leave the South, leave everything familiar. She hesitated. "New York."

Joe lifted his head off her stomach.

Lona pictured them walking hand in hand down a city block. Their heads were tilted back, taking in the tall buildings, the long sheets of glass. They would rent a small, cozy apartment. Joe would get a job, and go to college at night. Lona would work too, but not with her hands. She was done sewing. That was a real gift her husband had given her. Bill had told her that she could have a different life, and she had begun to believe him. Perhaps she would work in a skyscraper, answering phones and making coffee. Or a copy shop, or a clothing store. She didn't care what the job entailed, so long as she got to be with Joe.

"We won't tell anyone anything," she said. "We'll slip away when everyone's asleep." As far as Lona was concerned, this was the only way to leave a place. Her entire family had left between midnight and sunrise.

Joe hesitated. "We could bring Gigi," he said.

Lona was overwhelmed, for a moment, at how far he was willing to go to make her happy. Of course he didn't want her to bring her sixteen-year-old daughter; he was offering because he thought it was what she wanted.

"Gigi wouldn't come," she said. "Bill will be a better father without me here. And your mother will look after her, of course. I'll contact her when you let your mother know that you're fine. And when she's done with high school, she can come north if she wants to." Lona tried to imagine Gigi as a grown woman sitting on an ottoman in their love nest. She had to blink hard to clear the image of her daughter glaring at her. "Everyone will understand, if we give them enough time."

"I don't care if they understand." Joe kissed her hip bone. "I don't care what they think. You and me are going to have an amazing life."

Lona felt a grin spread across her face. "Come here," she said. "I like to look at you when you're making bold statements."

He climbed her body as if it were a ladder. "You don't believe me?"

The sky was so bright, their faces were dispelled of all shadows. "I believe you," Lona said. "I definitely believe you."

Joe closed his eyes, and a few minutes later fell asleep. Lona lay still and looked at him. He was, she considered, beautiful. Joe had pale, soft skin everywhere but his palms, which were rough. His brown curls slid over his forehead and the back of his neck. When awake, he was always brushing stray curls away with his hand, but in sleep they flopped wherever they pleased. His lips were pink and slightly open.

He had told her, when she picked him up at school, that he now missed her so much at night that he couldn't sleep. He paced the floor of his room, or tossed and turned beneath his sheets. He needed her, he said, to function as himself. Lona gave a small shiver of pleasure. She envisaged the skyscrapers of New York bending the sky. She pictured herself at their feet.

Flannery pushed open the porch door. There was a book in her hand, but she had no interest in reading. Her brain was foggy with jet lag. She sat down and looked at her birds. Several were crossing the lawn. Her appearance had raised the overall volume—there were coos, cries, and squawks coming from all corners. If she didn't know better, she would have thought that they had missed her while she was away.

The General had been lurking near the steps since she'd woken up that morning. He stared at her now, his eyes two black pellets. The remaining peacocks were traveling around the side of the house, from the water tower, the barn, and the low ditch they favored beside the fence. One after another, they lined up behind the General like soldiers called to sudden duty.

Flannery smiled, wondering what they were up to. She was deeply glad to be home, glad to be among these noisy, unpredictable creatures. She listened to the General's low, guttural wail. She watched him take a step forward. The giant bird's movements were slow and deliberate, as if they had been planned in advance. He straightened to his full height, then lifted his tail. He spread the feathers unhurriedly, like a true show-man, a circus ringmaster, the P. T. Barnum of birds. Golden suns and orange teardrops zinged and popped against his six-foot, royal blue fan. The effect was breathtaking, and he knew it.

Behind the General, not to be outdone, another peacock unfurled his fan. His tail was only half the width, its colors more tightly packed. The skinny peacock beside him opened his feathers in a rush, like an umbrella in an unexpected rainstorm. A shaggy male unlocked his beak, then bellowed as he cast his tail wide. Within moments two-dozen birds stood before Flannery on full display, while still others rushed to join the parade. Jade and cerulean moons rose from the earth. Bright yellow feathers shot upward. Bronze halos looped across gray skies. Tangerine striped bright chartreuse. Fuchsia dots speckled across ivory leaves.

Every presentation seemed more beautiful than the rest. The peacocks competed for the tallest, the widest, the most resplendent display. The General—his size immense, his coat glistening, his colors deep and true—was the clear standout, but the rest vied for second place. The birds lined up across the yard, their heads tilted back. Defiant and proud, they showed themselves. A thousand eyes stared out from their feathers, the collective gaze so powerful it seemed to rake across Flannery's soul.

She held her breath. The peacocks had never put on this kind of show before. She was aware of feeling more devout in this moment than she had at any point in the miracle baths. She moved her eyes from one bird to the next. When she had acknowledged the group, she gave a measured nod of appreciation. The General, apparently satisfied by her response, was the first to put his tail down. The rest followed suit.

When the horizon cleared, Flannery noticed a figure standing behind the birds. It was Melvin Whiteson, holding a baby in his arms.

His face was slack with amazement.

Flannery's heart thumped in her chest.

"That's Rose?" she heard herself ask.

"I had to come back," Melvin said.

The birds were in the process of scattering, their gait casual, as if nothing unusual had taken place.

"I'll get us something to drink." Flannery was already turning away, reaching for the door. She needed a moment alone, in the dim house.

She leaned against the wall in the front hallway. She pressed her hands to her face.

"Flannery? Are you all right?"

She looked up and saw her mother standing at the top of the stairs. There was panic in Regina's voice. She knew her mother was thinking: *She's in pain, I'll call Dr. Merrill, which route should I take to the hospital?*

"I'm fine," she said.

Her mother descended two steps and looked at her more closely. "Are you sure?"

She nodded.

"Well, something's wrong," Regina said. "I can tell."

"Melvin's here. He brought his baby girl."

Regina squinted through the front screen. Her expression mellowed.

Flannery thought, *You're a mother. You know what having a child feels like. I'll never know that feeling.* There was a gnawing ache in her middle. She had hoped to never see the baby. She had deliberately avoided the photographs Melvin brought on his last visit. She hadn't wanted to meet her, hadn't wanted to see what she looked like, hadn't wanted to watch Melvin care for her. Flannery didn't care whether this made her a terrible person; she wasn't interested in the value judgment. She simply knew who she was, and what she could handle.

"She's cute," Regina said. "Blond towhead, just like Cookie."

"I came to get lemonade."

Regina traveled down the rest of the steps. "I'll get it." As she passed Flannery on the way to the kitchen, she laid her hand on her arm.

Alone again, Flannery's mouth twisted into a smile. Mixed in with the pain was pleasure. He was here. He had come back.

Outside, Melvin scanned the lawn. The peacocks had scattered. Perched in the tree, on the fence, in a sporadic pattern across the lawn, they pecked and squawked and ignored him.

He turned Rose to face the scene. He pressed his stubbly cheek to her smooth face, and felt her squirm at the sensation. Rose smelled of baby powder and formula and whatever sweetness babies carry in their skin. He breathed her in, deeply.

"Look," he said. "Chicken. Peacock. Rooster. Duck."

Rose's head swiveled back and forth. When one of the chickens flapped its wings, she giggled. Melvin watched the house and wondered if he would be able to summon the right words.

He caught a glimpse of Regina walking past the screen door, and lifted his free hand to wave. Melvin had developed an appreciation for the cranky older woman. He had heard about the O'Connors' trip to Lourdes by eavesdropping on Miss Mary at the library. Upon his return to the office, he had phoned Andalusia and asked the housekeeper when Flannery was due to return. He hadn't planned to do anything with the information, at least at first. He had been summarily dismissed by Flannery; he knew she didn't want to see him again.

But as the days passed, he found himself increasingly trapped in his daily routine. Any time he spent at work, shuffling papers and answering needless questions, now felt painfully ridiculous. He couldn't retreat to his car and read, because he had finished all of Flannery's work and had no desire to move on to another writer. He also wasn't comfortable visiting Rose at his mother-in-law's. Daisy wore a faintly alarmed expression whenever he showed up in the middle of the day, as if she expected to hear terrible news. Big Mike left his store only in cases of dire emergency, and it had been twenty years since there had been one of those. Daisy considered Melvin's casual visits somehow inappropriate, and unmanly.

At night, he had lain awake and pictured Flannery in Lourdes. He had been there once as a teenager, on a trip to Europe with his parents. They had toured the town and the area of the grotto. He remembered a discussion between his parents about whether they should take a bath. His mother had grown upset at the idea. "We're perfectly healthy. We're fine, William. We can't take a miracle away from someone else who needs it."

"If we're fine," his father had said, "then there's no miracle we could receive. It would just be a bath."

Melvin's father had wanted to try the baths for the experience. He and his wife had ended up turning to Melvin to decide the issue. The boy had opted to leave. He disliked walking through the crowded streets wondering if everyone he touched was contagious with some horrible disease. The long line of invalids, attended by solicitous nuns, depressed him. He couldn't escape the town fast enough.

Twenty years later, Melvin had a different perspective. He felt comforted, night after night, picturing Flannery on that serpentine line. He respected Regina for taking her there. If Rose ever needed help, or healing, he too would travel to the ends of the earth. He would never give up. He could imagine dragging his daughter onto a plane, coercing her to undergo a desperate attempt even if he knew the chances of success were slim at best. Flannery had reached for her crutches on her way into the house, which obviously meant the baths hadn't worked. *Still*, Melvin thought, *Regina did the right thing.*

Flannery opened the screen door with her hip.

He said, "I can't live in this town without your friendship."

She set his glass of lemonade on the floor and sank into her chair.

Melvin sat down on the porch step. He took a small blanket out from under his arm and spread it on the grass. He laid Rose down by his feet. She gurgled and stretched her arms above her head. Several chickens cast her a skeptical glance as they marched past, but the rest of the birds ignored her.

Flannery said, "Would this be a real friendship? The kind where friends can be seen in public speaking to each other?"

"A real friendship."

She was quiet for a moment. "Even if I were to agree, Cookie won't like it."

"She's in a good place right now. I think I might be able to make her understand."

Flannery pursed her lips.

Melvin noticed that when she looked at him, she kept her eyes up. She ignored the baby by his feet. "Cookie's mistaken about you," he said. "After all, why shouldn't I be here? What's wrong with this?" He waved his hand at the scene. At the birds, the grass, the child on the blanket.

"That's in the eye of the beholder."

"Well, I'm beholding it, and it looks fine. I stayed away for months because I thought it was the right thing to do. But that was stupid, and a waste of time." He paused. "I missed you."

The silence that followed felt intentional. It was accompanied by the distant murmur of a tractor engine, the chatter of various birds, and the occasional burbles of an infant.

"I went away . . ." Flannery stopped. She stretched her hands out in front of her and studied them. "Sometimes I think I'm the worst kind of fool."

"What do you mean?"

She shook her head.

Melvin wanted to help her. He said, "I've been thinking about what you asked me the first time I came out here, about what I want to do with my life."

Flannery rolled her eyes. There was relief in her expression. "That sounds interesting."

"And I realized, I want to do this. I don't want to do anything more than I want to do this."

"This?"

"This."

A peacock hammered the porch roof with his feet. Flannery shook her head. She still looked shaky, holding on to the arms of her chair. "What are we doing, exactly?"

"I'm not joking."

"Who said you were joking? I'm listening. I'm interested in your answer."

"I want to sit here with you and watch my daughter lie on the green grass."

Her voice was quiet. "That doesn't sound terribly ambitious."

"Ambition is overrated." Melvin took a moment to briefly survey his surroundings. "This is what I want to do; it's perfect. Why do I need anything more?"

She laughed.

He realized that he hadn't heard her laugh in a long time. She had a deep, croaky, infectious laugh that he had tried to provoke during their driving lessons. It was gratifying to hear it now.

"I like to take baths," she said. "But that doesn't mean I should spend my life in a tub of hot water."

"Why not?" Melvin felt giddy. "Maybe you should."

"Well, it might be nice, but there's more to life than being comfortable."

"It's not about comfort," he said, "it's about pleasure. It's about feeling alive. I've come to realize that you have to take these moments whenever you can find them."

This was definitely a moment, as far as Melvin was concerned. Rose breathing, one hand on her belly, her face tilted up. The sun orange and low, massive in the dimming sky. Flannery, her lips sealed shut, eyes thinking.

"I'm glad you're happy," she said. "I can see that you are, and I don't mean to belittle that." She looked away from him, and said in a low voice, "Right now, I'm happy too."

"Good," Melvin said. "Then let's freeze this moment. Let's stay right here, right now, forever."

"I don't think that's how it works," she replied.

L ona was staring at her face in the bathroom mirror. She rarely gave time to her reflection; she glanced in the mirror first thing in the morning while brushing her teeth, but that was it. The woman who stared back at her was familiar, but only vaguely so. She was younger than Lona remembered. Her face was softer; the corners of her mouth curved up slightly.

Lona turned her face to one side and then the other. She noticed the unusual quiet—even the sparrows outside had ceased their tweeting. She was thinking about how the silence seemed dense—it was solid like the countertop beneath her hands—when she heard the first sound.

Clump.

Again. *Clump.*

Lona watched her face freeze. Her blue eyes were alert, awake. The woman in the reflection appeared more curious than scared. She looked, Lona thought, like someone who could handle herself.

She heard Cookie's voice. "The suits are in the closet in there. Melvin's and his father's, so you should definitely be able to find one that fits. I need at least twenty minutes to make myself presentable, so don't hurry."

A man's voice. "Thank you again."

"It's nothing."

The voice made something inside Lona stop. She turned away from the mirror and opened the bathroom door.

At the same moment, the door to the bedroom opened.

Her husband was framed in the new space.

Lona thought, as though the phrase was as unexpected as anything else: *my husband.*

Bill's eyes widened. "Lona?"

Something about his tone made her look down at herself. She was naked. Bare arms, bare legs, bare flat belly, and bare pink breasts. When was the last time Bill had seen her completely naked? She was always covered, at least by a blanket, and more often, even in their moments of intimacy, by at least one piece of clothing. She could not remember ever standing before him like this, like a soldier stepped forward for review.

His breath slowed and grew labored. Lona watched his gaze turn to the side. Bill looked at Joe, asleep on top of the bedspread. The boy's white skin was almost blinding. Brown curls fell over his forehead. His penis lay like a rope against his thigh.

Bill put his hands on his belt as if he needed something to hold on to.

Lona thought of the rules she had abandoned. They had drifted away quickly and completely—like smoke from a car window. She was without rules now. She was standing naked before her husband and her boyfriend. She had goose bumps, and her throat was dry.

She thought about how important rules had always been to Bill; they were his skeleton. They kept him upright and allowed him to power through his days. This is right, *check*. This is wrong, *check*. Lona thought about the quiet that had preceded this scene. She longed for it to return; her chest ached for it. A new type of silence swung now, like a hammer, between the naked woman and the policeman.

"Bill," she said.

His eyes, which were already wide, went further, as if the mention of his name, or the utterance of any sound from Lona, was some fresh kind of scandal. His hands were shaking against his belt. His billy club tapped against a metal snap on his pants, and the noise filled the room. Tap, tap, tap.

Joe was smiling in his sleep, his lips slightly parted. The sheets were tangled at his feet.

"Bill," she said again. She didn't know what to say next.

Sweat fell down Bill's forehead like a curtain. He blinked. His hands smoothed his belt, traced the edge of the holster, the top of the club.

The boy on the bed moved. His leg twitched, and then his eyes were open.

Lona swallowed. The air in the room beat like a heart.

"Officer Waters," Joe said. He sounded polite, as if they were being introduced at a party.

Bill's hand jerked. He pulled out the gun.

"No," Lona said. "No. No. No." She spoke the word as if it had power, as if the word was a weapon she had pulled from her own invisible belt. Like the word could change what was about to become her history.

Joe gasped and sat bolt upright.

Bill's finger, slick with sweat, slipped down on the trigger, and the gun made the worst noise Lona had ever heard in her life.

The gunshot was too far away for Flannery or Melvin to hear, but it wasn't too far for the birds. The crack of the pistol sent the General straight up in the air, and every bird at Andalusia followed. Ducks quacked, geese honked, and peacocks screamed. The smaller birds scurried under the porch. Others leapt on the roof, thumping the wooden shingles with their weight. The water tower behind the house swayed beneath the force of so many birds landing on it at once. The air heaved with flapping wings, jutted beaks, and falling feathers.

From her seat on the porch, Flannery looked around for the source of the panic. Melvin put his hands on the railing to brace himself. "What kind of hell on earth is this?" Regina asked from somewhere nearby. Melvin couldn't see her; he couldn't see anything. He lost track not only of distance, but of time. The chaos seemed eternal. The peacocks were screaming to break eardrums. The chickens were beating the air with wings that couldn't fly. Other birds flew in jagged circles. They descended on the porch like nails drawn to a magnet.

Melvin tried to see Rose on the blanket, but his vision was obscured by the rain of feathers. The General's blue body powered past him. His large mass streaked in front of Melvin's face, momentarily blocking out the light. He heard a tiny noise, almost a squeak. The mass lifted and flew away.

C ookie ran down the hall.

At first, she thought the noise was a car backfiring on the street, but the crack was too sharp and piercing for that. She had heard a gunshot once before, in New York City, walking home from work. There was a loud noise, as loud as the one she had just heard, and a man grabbed her shoulder and forced her to her knees. He pointed across the street, and she saw a young man sprint out of a storefront holding a gun in his hand. Two skinny men her father's age burst out of the door behind him, waving their arms and shouting. She watched the youth tuck the gun into his belt and disappear around the corner. Ten minutes later, when the cops gave the all clear, Cookie climbed to her feet and found her stockings ripped, gravel embedded in her skin.

This sound had come not from the street, but from within her own house. The floor beneath her had jolted. There must have been an accident. Bill must have dropped his gun. She pictured a puncture hole in her perfect white wall.

"Bill?" She reached the guest room door and pushed it open.

Her first impression was that the room was crowded. It was crowded and everything she laid eyes on looked wrong. Bill was standing in front of her. He held a transistor radio in his hand. He was crying.

Lona was there too. She was naked. She was on all fours on the white bed. Her hair hung across her face. She was leaning over Joe Treadle, who was also not wearing any clothes.

Joe's eyes were open; he was staring at the ceiling. His curly hair fell over his forehead, and Cookie thought, *That boy needs a haircut.* There was a red circle on his chest. As Cookie watched, red liquid poured out of the hole.

She took a step backward.

Bill said nothing.

Lona said nothing.

Joe said nothing.

"I'm supposed to give a speech," Cookie heard herself say.

There was a pounding noise. It came from downstairs. It came from the front door. There was a man's voice. "WE'RE IN THE HOUSE!" he shouted. "I REPEAT, WE ARE IN THE HOUSE!"

"Lona," Cookie said, "you're not wearing any clothes." She looked around for clothes to hand her, but didn't see any.

Feet thumped up the stairs.

"Back here," Bill said. He was still holding the radio. He was still crying. "I'm back here."

Sometime later—twenty minutes? an hour?—Cookie was standing in her living room. Policemen walked in and out of the front door as if they owned the house. No one looked at her. Joe floated past on a stretcher. A white sheet covered his body.

"Has someone called Miss Mary?" she asked, but she was alone in the room. She wrapped her arms around herself. She had a sudden physical urge for her own child.

The phone rang.

Cookie picked up the receiver. "Hello?"

"Cookie?"

She dropped into the nearest chair. With the sound of his voice, she felt energy flee her body. She felt boneless, strengthless. "Oh, Melvin," she said. "You won't believe what's happened. I can't believe what's happened. Did someone tell you? I called the center; they're going ahead without me." Her voice broke again. "I think we're going to have to throw away the mattress."

"Cookie," Melvin said.

"Come home," she said. "Please come home right now. Where are you?"

"At the hospital."

She felt a flash of exasperation. "Why? I need you here."

The phone line was silent.

Cookie listened to the silence. "Melvin?" she said, after a moment. "You're scaring me. This is no time for jokes."

"Do you feel strong enough to drive? You should come here now, if you can."

"Why? What's wrong?" Cookie didn't recognize her own voice. "Is it Mama?"

"No." She didn't recognize his voice either. "It's Rose."

Hard

The plot was directly across the street from the church where Melvin and Cookie had been married. While the minister— who'd presided over their wedding—did his best to attach words to the wretched occasion, Melvin watched his father-in-law run a handkerchief over his forehead. Big Mike wiped the same stretch of skin fourteen times, undoubtedly beating the sweat to the punch.

Melvin was unable to look directly at Cookie. He knew that she couldn't look at him either. She had been sleeping at her parents' house. She'd sent Daisy over to gather some of her things. When Melvin opened the door for his mother-in-law, the woman standing before him was unrecognizable. Daisy was bent over, with faded eyes and shaky hands. Melvin had to carry the box of clothes and toiletries to her car.

Big Mike pocketed the handkerchief. He shook the minister's hand. Melvin realized that they were done. The Himmels took their spots on either side of Cookie, and began to make their way across the uneven ground. Melvin followed. He tried to keep his eyes moving; he didn't want to linger on the sad trio in front of him. He watched a large bird skid across the sky. A line of blue pickup trucks steered down the street. He noticed a thin figure dart into the graveyard through the side entrance. The woman moved with a directness that caught Melvin's attention. He stopped and squinted, and realized it was Lona Waters.

Cookie and her parents passed beyond the cemetery gates; in a moment they would be out of sight. Melvin stayed where he was. He had read about Joe's murder in the local paper. He knew that Joe had been just a few weeks shy of his eighteenth birthday. He knew the caliber of gun Bill Waters had used to shoot the boy. He knew that the mayor had pronounced the day of Joe Treadle's death as a day of singular sadness in the long history of the town. He knew the coroner had said that the gunshot had been perfect and that Joe had died instantly. Melvin thought that was a peculiar turn of phrase, to say that the shot was "perfect." It seemed to him that however you looked at it, the shot was far from perfect.

He watched Lona come to a stop in front of the teenager's grave. Melvin looked at it too. He had been unable to look at his daughter's plot. He noticed that the fresh dirt, which rose in a neat mound over the opening in the earth, had a light, fluffy appearance. On closer inspection, the dirt appeared insubstantial, almost gossamer. It looked like an inadequate covering for what lay below. Melvin found it hard to believe that this particular pile of dirt would be able to harden and pack down like the ground that covered the rest of the graves. He wondered if the gravediggers had made a mistake and covered the new coffins with some unorthodox, insufficient material. He wondered if Lona was also scrutinizing the fresh dirt, and whether she too found it lacking.

Lona kneeled down and patted the ground. There was no tombstone to touch or read. Both graves had temporary wooden markers that would remain until enough time had passed for words to be chosen and carved into stone. Lona picked up a handful of dirt. She climbed to her feet, her fist tight. Melvin was too far away to read her expression. He wondered if she regretted loving the boy. He wondered if she blamed herself for what had happened.

He didn't worry that Lona might notice him; he could tell she had no interest in anything other than Joe. If she did happen to look up, he knew what would happen. He would nod, and she would nod in return. They would mimic their first, silent exchange, which had taken place a lifetime ago behind the church across the street, within sight of these two graves.

Lona didn't move. She stood with her head lowered, the dirt closed in her hand. When the sun began to drop behind the trees, Melvin turned away. He made the walk home last as long as it could, although three blocks didn't afford much latitude. Once he reached the house, he took his seat behind his desk.

His study was the safest location. He kept the velvet curtains drawn, and was only able to tell whether it was day or night by the presence or absence of a strip of sunlight beneath the fabric. A week before the accident, Melvin had made himself a list of things to do, and he decided to work his way down it. He looked over a financial document that needed to be returned to his New York accountant. He reviewed the numbers on his stock accounts and saw that his father's investments were turning their usual profit. The monthly dividend alone was more than triple what Melvin needed to pay his bills. He initialed the sheet of paper so that he would know the information had been read. There were pauses in his work, seemingly timeless pauses where he caught himself staring at his hands or at the sheen on the curtain. He coughed or rubbed his eyes to bring himself back to order, but a few minutes later he would lapse again. He kept this up, late into the night.

Once, he heard a rustling noise—from the curtain? or a cat rubbing through the bushes?—and was reminded of the sound of the peacocks' beating tails. The sound of pronged feet slapping the porch roof. The sound of a door hinge squeaking. Melvin didn't want to remember, but he did. He remembered plunging his arm through the beating tails and slapping feet. He remembered reaching for Rose. He remembered how his arm had been blocked, and how he had misjudged the distance, and how it was another long moment before he was able to pick her up. He remembered the doctor saying, *crushed organs.*

He cupped his hands over his ears until the noise abated. He studied the list and watched the words swim on the page. He drank two scotches and then had an urge to read his parents' obituaries. He wondered where the articles were. Probably at the storage facility in Queens, where the contents of the town house had been deposited after the house was sold. The envelope was no doubt buried in a box, in a dark room, lumped together with old receipts, correspondence, and photo albums. Melvin was annoyed with himself for not taking it with him. He should have filed those words about his parents in a drawer here, so that one day he could show Rose who her New York grandparents had been. *They died before their time*, people had repeated in sorrowful voices at their funeral. If that was true, if his parents had died before their time, what did that mean for Joe Treadle and Rose? What did that mean for time?

Melvin sat with his head cradled in his hands. He took a nap on the leather sofa. When he woke up, he circled the room. One, two, three laps. He could feel himself warming up. On the fifth lap he headed out the study door. As if from a distance, he watched himself walk upstairs. He kept his eyes straight ahead while he passed the nursery and then the bedroom he'd shared with Cookie. Apart from one quick trip to gather some clothes, he had not been upstairs since he'd returned home from the hospital.

He reached the end of the hall and pushed open the door to the guest room. He flipped the light switch. He blinked for a moment at the brightness. When his eyes adjusted, he looked at the white bed and the red stain in the center. There was also blood on the floor, tracked across the wood by a pair of shoes. The bathroom door was open. The curtains were open. Melvin had asked the police's cleaning crew to stay away until he gave the word. The scene looked exactly like the newspaper had described. It looked like a murder scene. Melvin drew a strange satisfaction from how closely the view matched his expectations. At a time when nothing was making sense—people were walking down the street as if nothing had happened—this made sense. There was no denying that something had happened here. Blood had been lost. The man-made walls had a shocked appearance, as if they were unable to forget what they had seen.

Cookie slept in her childhood bed, in her childhood room, which Big Mike and Daisy had left untouched. The same pink roses climbed the wallpaper, the same high school notices were pinned to the bulletin board, and the same wooden crucifix hung over the door. Cookie lay beneath the same pink coverlet, and drank the soup and tea her mother brought her. She was too tired to chew, but drank everything so her mother wouldn't worry. Cookie had noticed, while Daisy sat by her bedside with her hands fidgeting in her lap, that her mother looked old. Her father's head, poking through the doorway to say good night, was covered with white hair. His face was speckled with age spots. The room and the house might look the same, but the people inside had changed. Cookie slept for as many hours of the day as she could.

The sight of her horizontal with her eyes closed became so customary that her parents allowed themselves to have conversations beside her bed. They assumed she was asleep.

"I didn't even know he was friends with Flannery," Daisy said one evening.

"That bastard," Big Mike said.

There was a long silence.

"It was an accident," Daisy said in a weak voice.

"We don't even know what really happened. But she does. It was her marriage. The little girl I raised knew how to raise hell. I wish she would fight back."

"Against who?"

There was a pause. "She's too calm."

"She's broken," Daisy said. "Broken."

Cookie tried to lie perfectly still. She tried to keep her breathing perfectly even. She tried not to feel a thing.

Her father came into the bedroom one afternoon and sat in the chair Daisy usually occupied. He cleared his throat. Cookie pulled herself into a seated position, propped up by pillows. She knew her father didn't like to see her looking vulnerable.

"He signed the divorce papers without a fuss," Big Mike said, and then paused. "Chuck Berenger told me he's returned the business to him. He's moving back to New York. You'll get half the house, I imagine."

"Melvin will give me the whole thing."

Big Mike looked down at his hands. "You might be right."

They sat in silence for a few minutes. Cookie had the sense that her father wanted her to say something, but she had nothing to say. She gave him a small smile, in apology, and watched him leave the room.

That night, she was unable to sleep. She lay still with her eyes closed, but couldn't find the sweet spot where unconsciousness lurked. She spent hours trolling the darkness behind her eyelids, thinking, *I'm almost there. Almost there.* When she did finally locate the spot, when she finally dropped to the other side and felt sleep drape across her body, the relief was wonderful.

In the nights that followed, however, such moments of relief became harder to come by. Cookie awoke early, before the first streaks of light separated the sky outside her window. She found herself awake during odd pockets of time. She would open her eyes suddenly at 2 A.M. and then, just as suddenly, pass out again at 4. There was no discernible pattern. She couldn't keep track of the time she spent asleep; she felt like she was simply swallowed whole and then, without ceremony, spat out. There were no interrupted dreams for her to keep track of, because she had stopped dreaming. She'd always had a vivid subconscious life in the past. She used to come up with ideas for meetings, and make household decisions while she slept. Now when she was asleep she disappeared, and when she awoke she was confused. The night became a long, distorted stretch of time, which Cookie spent alone in her room. She clicked the bedside lamp on and off.

She decided to sort through her closet. Her mother had asked her to do so years earlier, before her wedding, but she had never found the time. Cookie opened the closet door and looked at the rack of clothes and the rows of shoes. She'd worn very few of them since moving back in with her parents. She was partial to one or two dresses, the most comfortable ones. She generally wore sneakers now instead of shoes. On the floor of the closet, to one side, she noticed a stack of boxes. Cookie picked one up. It was a child's puzzle, with a picture of a seascape on the cover. She carried the box over to her desk, emptied the contents, and turned the pieces face up.

Cookie moved the pieces slowly across the desktop, as if shifting handfuls of sand. She separated the sections by color, and then by shape. She fit together a corner, and moved inward, locking together piece after piece. When her eyelids began to droop, she returned to her bed. An hour or two later, she was back at the desk.

The next morning, her mother told her that the puzzles had been birthday gifts for her eighth birthday. "You never liked them. You found them boring," Daisy said. "I kept them, though, for a rainy day."

"I finished two," Cookie said. "I'm working on the third now."

When Big Mike came home from work that night, he brought a stack of brand-new puzzles with him. Cookie thanked him and took them upstairs to her room. As she made her way up the steps, she heard her parents' voices behind her.

"She's finally showing an interest in something," Big Mike said.

"Puzzles?"

"I don't care what it is. If she'd taken an interest in Japanese dogs, I'd have brought one of them home with me."

"You drove all the way to Atlanta?"

"I wanted to get good ones."

"Oh, honey," Daisy said in a sad voice.

Cookie quietly clicked the door to her room shut. She brought the prettiest of the new puzzles—a picture of a sunlit field—to her desk and set to work. She finished the entire batch in three days. Cookie watched the sun rise and fall outside her window, and linked together piece after piece until she'd created something whole. She amassed a collection of mountains, seascapes, and meadows. She realized that her father had deliberately chosen puzzles without children or scenes of domestic life. She spread a special glue across the back of each one so her work would remain intact. Once a puzzle was finished, she didn't like the idea of it breaking apart again.

As the weeks passed, Cookie began to dread her father's visits to her bedroom. He always brought a new puzzle, which she then felt compelled to complete. She didn't have the heart to tell him that she didn't want any more. The puzzles had held her attention at first, but now she didn't like the look of the broken pieces. She fixed the knobs and holes together as quickly as possible, because she knew she wouldn't be able to sleep with a half-finished puzzle in the room. Sleep was her paramount concern. Her days and nights were organized around the possibility of rest. She felt like a bookmaker, constantly weighing the odds of whether a specific activity at a particular time would be likely to result in eventual sleep.

When Big Mike arrived in her doorway empty-handed one evening, Cookie felt her shoulders relax.

"Your mother," he said, "would like it if you got back on your feet." His eyes were focused beyond her, as if something of interest was happening just outside the window. "You have to eventually, you know. You could attend a meeting, or go out to lunch with some friends. Get some fresh air. Start slow." He grimaced. "You can't stay in this room forever, baby."

Fresh air, Cookie thought. *Fresh air might make me tired. It might help me sleep.* She said, "Okay, Daddy."

"Okay?"

"I'll get up in the morning and go out with Mama."

Big Mike's face sagged with relief.

Cookie went to a meeting and sat in the back row beside Daisy. She was pleased to find that the window nearest her was wide open. She filled her lungs completely, then emptied them. The Library Association was being chaired by the same elderly woman who had covered for Cookie when she gave birth to Rose. Cookie tried to calculate how many weeks of meetings she'd missed then. Maybe five? She tried to figure out how many weeks it had been since her last meeting now. Six, or eight? Ten? Cookie realized that she wasn't sure. Her mind slipped across the calendar like it was a sheet of ice.

The temporary leader, a retired schoolteacher, started the meeting by saying how wonderful it was to see Cookie out and about, and how they all looked forward to her taking her position back, whenever she was ready. Everyone in the room clapped loudly, including Daisy. Cookie, still caught up in calculations—trying to figure out what the date might be—nodded distractedly.

A woman sitting near her raised her hand. "I missed last week. What was the vote on Flannery's books?"

Cookie was aware of her mother's body stiffening beside hers. "Not now," Daisy said under her breath.

A voice responded from the opposite side of the room. "There weren't enough votes. We're not going to ban them—"

The leader interrupted, her voice stern. "Ladies, I don't think we should discuss that today. Let's move on to the budget."

Cookie concentrated on gathering more air in her lungs. She pictured her chest as a steel trap, dragging open and snapping shut. She tried to take in more, more, more, until she was light-headed from the effort. When she started listening again, the women were talking about the annual book fair at the high school. Several questions were raised, and at one point there was a heated discussion about the state of the tires on the bookmobile. Cookie tried to arrange her face so that she appeared to be paying attention. She was aware of the furtive glances being thrown in her direction. At the end of the meeting, on their way out of the room, women pressed against her as if trying to pass on their warmth.

"I thought that went fairly well," Daisy said in a bright voice when they were back in the car. "Didn't you think it went well?"

"I guess so."

"You handled yourself marvelously."

Cookie stared out the window, noting what passed. The scenery looked like pieces from a jigsaw puzzle: house, yard, church, traffic light, dog on leash, two tan cars in a row. "It didn't make any sense to me."

"What didn't?"

"What they were talking about during the meeting . . . it didn't make any sense. But I know I've missed some time. I just need to catch up."

"You can take a nap after lunch." Daisy reached over and rubbed her daughter's arm.

Cookie wondered why everyone felt the need to touch her. She looked down. Her body looked the same to her. Thinner than usual, perhaps, but otherwise normal. She studied her arms. They were hanging limply at her sides, like cured meats in a butcher's window. She regarded them with curiosity, as if she'd never seen them before. They looked ridiculous. She reflected to herself how something so familiar could become so strange if you just considered it long enough.

She squinted her eyes and tried to pretend that these were not her arms but someone else's, and they had just been pinned to her temporarily, like a tail on the donkey. While she watched, her right arm twitched, as if she'd been dealt an electric shock. After a short pause, it twitched a second time, and then her entire arm was shuddering. The force of the movement took the rest of her frame with it. Cookie's body started shaking from head to toe.

"Cookie?" Daisy cried. "Sweetheart? What's wrong?"

The quake was over before Daisy could pull the car to the side of the road. It was over as quickly as it had started, and Cookie was still once more. The mother and daughter stared at each other, and Cookie gave a careful shrug. Two days later, during dinner with her parents, the shaking returned. She trembled so hard that her silverware and plate spilled to the floor. When she started to twitch during a Sewing Collective meeting, Daisy tried to hide the attack by covering Cookie with her coat. But Cookie knew better. She knew, with her teeth rattling in her head like a bag of marbles, that nothing could be hidden anymore.

Gigi's last class that day was about the Civil War. It was a month-long project in which the class focused on a different battle each time they met. Today had covered the quickest and bloodiest of the various encounters: the Battle of Antietam, when twenty-three thousand men were killed in twenty-four hours. That horrifying number and the pictures in her textbook made Gigi's stomach turn. The soldiers looked like the boys in her class. Gigi imagined every boy in her school splayed out on the football field, bleeding to death. She scanned the scene, pools of blood collecting like puddles after a storm. Her eyes stopped when she noticed a young boy who looked like Joe Treadle. She couldn't see his wound; it must have been covered by his clothes. Gigi stared at his brown curly hair, his long eyelashes, his pale, draining skin.

When the bell rang, she leapt out of her seat and threw her books into her bag. She speed-walked through the halls and pushed open the front door. She stopped in the middle of the lawn. She briefly considered her options. She didn't have many. She couldn't bear to stay at school. She also couldn't go home; that felt impossible right now. She and her mother had gotten the news last night. Her father had been sentenced to seven years at Georgia State Prison. Gigi watched her mother while the lawyer told them the verdict. Lona's blue eyes stayed distant and unfocused. There was no change in her expression.

Gigi climbed onto the country bus, her face turned away so she wouldn't have to see the driver's questioning look. She found a seat and lowered the window. She wanted the air to blow directly into her lungs. She felt like a deflated balloon; she felt like she was draining away the way Joe had, dressed in an antique uniform in the middle of a lake of blood.

The bus left the smooth streets of town and jounced down the highway. Houses were replaced by farms. Neat front lawns were replaced by wide swathes of yellow and green crops.

"Please stop here," Gigi said.

"Here? You sure?"

"Yes."

The old yellow bus, which had been driving the country route for fifty years, mewled to a stop, then slid slowly to the edge of the highway.

The students and the driver avoided Gigi's eyes as she traveled down the aisle and the steps. She stood by the mailbox and watched the bus pull away. She felt her stomach clench and unclench, like an angry fist. She was acutely aware that she hadn't thought this through.

Andalusia had been the only place where she imagined she *might* be welcome. Miss Mary had made it clear that she wanted nothing to do with her. Her mother seemed to have lost her voice, and her father was gone. Her schoolmates seemed frightened of her, as if she was no longer their peer, no longer a girl they had known their entire lives.

Gigi rubbed her hands on her shirt and opened the mailbox. There were three thin letters inside; she pulled them out and held them to her chest. The highway was now empty of traffic; the only sounds were whipping leaves and the distant hum of a tractor. Gigi glanced in the direction of the Treadles' driveway. What would she do if Miss Mary suddenly pulled out in her pickup truck? Would she wave her arms and throw herself at the vehicle, or dive into the bushes so she wouldn't be seen? Either seemed plausible, and both were humiliating. Gigi shuddered. She had abased herself enough. She'd called the Treadle farm every night since the funeral.

Twice, Mr. Treadle had answered and said that Miss Mary couldn't come to the phone. The remaining times, the line had been blocked by a busy signal.

She sighed and started to walk. She was pleased to have the mail in her hand. At least she had a task. She knew Mrs. O'Connor was always busy on the farm, and it must be difficult for Flannery to walk the long driveway with her crutches. She could tell herself that she was doing the O'Connors a favor.

She emerged from the bed of trees and came face-to-face with the white farmhouse. Flannery was sitting on the porch, bent over a piece of paper. She hadn't noticed Gigi yet. The girl hesitated. Flannery looked intensely occupied with whatever she was writing. Gigi told herself that she should have called ahead; she should have considered staying away. But still, she walked forward. She moved in slow jerks, as if someone were pushing her from behind.

Flannery glanced up and squinted. For a moment it appeared to be no more than a shift of focus; she was staring at the letter, then she was staring at the girl making her way across the lawn. Her face was inscrutable. Slowly, gradually, it relaxed into a smile.

Gigi had the fleeting thought that Flannery must not have smiled for some time; the expression seemed to have to fight its way to the surface.

"I have this," Gigi said nervously.

"What is it?"

"Your mail."

Flannery took the letters from her. "Sit down, child. Please. Make yourself comfortable."

Gigi sank down on the nearest step. Her heart was thudding, and her thoughts flitted in circles like birds trapped in a small room. She knew her cheeks were flushed. Her seemingly bottomless anger flared up, like a flower forging its way through Andalusia's stained grass. It was her mother's fault that she was here. It was her mother's fault that no one talked to her at school. Her mother should have kept her hands to herself. She should have known better. She should have acted more like a mother.

"Would you like something to drink?" Flannery asked.

"No, thank you." She shifted her weight; she felt acutely uncomfortable and wondered if it would be rude to stand up and pace. She said, "Can I ask you a question?"

Flannery regarded her. "Sure."

"It's about the funeral." Gigi frowned, surprised at herself. It had been bothering her since it happened, but she'd had no intention of confronting Flannery. She had planned to never mention that awful occasion ever again.

She had known, as she approached the church with her mother, that Joe's funeral would be terrible, but it ended up being a kind of terrible she had never imagined existed. When she and Lona sat down in the church pew, everyone already in the row stood up and filed out. The townspeople apparently preferred standing three deep against the back wall to making contact with the Waters family. Disgusted looks punctured Gigi's skin like arrows. She found it difficult to breathe, as she realized for the first time that she was going to be blamed for her parents' transgressions.

When the wide church doors opened, and a gust of wind rustled the stiff black dresses of the women present, Gigi spun around in her seat. She hadn't spoken to Miss Mary since the murder. Gigi had come to the funeral because she wanted to help her friend, give her a hug, and at least be near her. Along with the rest of the congregation, she pinned her gaze on the Treadles; they were standing at the top of the aisle like a miserable bride and groom. Miss Mary was wearing a dark gray dress. She had used her overnight curlers but clearly forgotten to brush the curls out, so they sat on her head like arched waves about to crash. Mr. Treadle held her arm as if it was the only thing keeping him upright. His suit was baggy on his frame.

Miss Mary did not look to her right or left. She ignored the few friends who reached out to touch her arm. There was no sign that she'd even noticed the back row, much less the woman and teenager stranded on the long wooden seat. She kept her eyes straight ahead. There was nothing in them. No warmth, no pain, no anything. Gigi watched, along with everyone else in the church, as the husband and wife walked to the front pew.

The girl was keenly aware that Miss Mary was now seated as far away from her as was physically possible within the small confines of the church. She knew, with total certainty, that Miss Mary would not turn around, look for her, or even acknowledge her. She wouldn't take her home with her. The older woman had locked herself away in an icy box.

Gigi began to panic, but she didn't allow her expression to change or her body to move. She would suffer this alone, inside herself. She could see that her life would never be the same again. This was an understanding that would become more specific over the following weeks and months; for now it descended and settled like ash onto the girl's skin.

A few minutes later, Gigi felt a weight lower down on the pew beside her, and she looked over blankly. The weight belonged to Flannery. The woman gave her a nod, but otherwise said nothing. She stayed at Gigi's side for the duration of the service. It was the only act of kindness Gigi had experienced in weeks. Otherwise, her life had been a vacuum.

She said, "Why did you sit next to me?"

"You looked like you could use the company."

"You should have sat with Miss Mary."

Flannery studied the girl, her brow almost furrowed. "Why?"

"Everyone else did. Your mother did. And Miss Mary's your friend."

Flannery was quiet for a moment. "There were very few guiltless people that day, Gigi, but you were one of them. I didn't think you deserved to be on your own."

There was a burning sensation inside Gigi's chest. She decided not to mention that she had been sitting beside her mother at the time. Flannery was right; for all intents and purposes, she had been on her own.

"It doesn't matter what I *deserve*," she said. "What I deserve, or what you deserve, has nothing to do with anything."

"Why do you say that?"

Gigi shrugged, an almost violent motion of her shoulders. She had no idea how to explain herself. She had no idea where to begin.

Flannery tried again. "Do you really believe that?"

This she could answer. "Yes."

Flannery paused. "Well, even if that's true in a larger sense, on an individual level we can still try to even things up. Those fools weren't treating you fairly."

Gigi looked around at the strange grass and the clusters of birds. She eyed the peacocks and wondered which one had trampled Rose Whiteson. She wondered how any creature could be capable of such a crime. She imagined lying helpless on the grass, and feeling sharp claws slam—one, two, three times—against her chest. Gigi coughed now, beneath the impact.

She liked picturing herself bruised or bleeding. It made her feel calmer somehow. At random points during the day, she stared down the barrel of an imaginary gun. Every night Gigi dreamed she had a perfect hole in her chest. She felt her blood stampede toward the exit. She became light-headed, dizzy. She stuck her finger inside the cavity and touched her insides. Her tissue, her organs. Her finger bright red and warm.

She was pleased to be at a murder scene now. She appreciated that she could lay eyes on the crusty grass, the guilty birds, and Flannery, who had seen everything. It occurred to her that maybe that was why she'd come. She wanted to see where the baby died. She wanted to see the birds who'd done the deed. Gigi, for her part, had seen nothing. She had believed that her father was the consummate cop, the person who knew more about the difference between right and wrong than anyone else. She had believed that her mother was a grown-up, whose life was settled, dull, and predictable. She had seen no signs, no hints, no warnings that her parents were capable of lighting a match and torching their lives, all three of them atop a raging pyre.

Flannery cleared her throat. "Gigi?"

The girl turned around.

"The only person Miss Mary has allowed through her front door since the funeral is my mother. Please don't take it personally."

Gigi almost smiled. Flannery assumed that she had gone to the Treadle farm first, and then come here once she was rejected. That was an understandable assumption. The Treadle farm was where she belonged, or at least used to. Now Gigi was being forced to make room for herself somewhere new.

"I need to earn some money," she heard herself say. "No one in town will hire my mom."

Gigi didn't know that this was true until the words were out of her mouth. She had seen her mother bent over bank statements in the middle of the night, a stack of bills held in place by the half-full coffee pot, but she hadn't spoken to Lona or heard her complain.

"I thought maybe . . ." She hesitated, and the hesitation surprised her by turning into a sob. She was only just able to stop the gulping cry from escaping her throat.

Flannery studied her. She had a deep, piercing look that made Gigi squirm. It felt like Flannery could see everything about her. She could see the bruised chest, the hole in her skin, the bright red splatters of fear.

"Regina was just talking about how we could use some help around here, a few hours a week." Flannery leaned back in her chair. "She can't do everything, even though she likes to claim otherwise. Maybe you could come by after school, some days."

"I'm free on the weekends too." Gigi blurted this out; her cheeks burned.

"That's fine. We can't pay much, but I'm sure we can work something out."

"Thank you." The girl bent her head. She studied her shoes and listened to the birds call and squawk. She felt devout, as if her gratitude was a form of prayer.

She shucked corn and tore the ends off beans. She scattered seed for the chickens, ducks, quail, pheasants, and peacocks. She polished the silverware in the dining room and sanded down an old family chest Regina

wanted to repaint. She walked out to the back field to deliver instructions to the farmhands. She ate apples off the tree behind the barn when
she was hungry, and sometimes, while waiting for another chore, she did
her homework on the front porch.

One afternoon, Regina asked her to climb the huge tree behind the
water tower and detangle an old boot from one of the middle branches.

"That does my soul good," she said when Gigi was back on the
ground. "That boot's been up there for over a year. It's the little things
that tie your insides up in knots."

The older woman was looking at her, so Gigi, slightly out of breath,
trying to wipe sticky sap off her palms, said, "I guess."

"Don't guess," Regina said. "That kind of talk makes a person look
weak. You're a strong girl. I can see it in your face. When someone asks
for your opinion, give it."

Gigi nodded, pleased that a strong woman thought she was strong
too, and watched Regina march back to the barn.

When Gigi was at the farm on weekend mornings, she only caught
glimpses of Flannery through her bedroom window. The writer sat erect
at her desk, her fingers on the typewriter keys. Sometimes she sat perfectly still; sometimes she pounded the keys without interruption for
what seemed like hours. Gigi liked to watch her work. She envied the
woman's concentration. Flannery's focus reminded her of a magnifying
glass burning a hole through a sheet of paper. Gigi envied her ability to
disappear into an entirely different world. She wished she were able to do
the same, but she knew that if she sat down at a typewriter, she wouldn't
be able to create a thing. Make-believe seemed inconceivable to her now.
When she used her imagination, it was to worry about what might happen next. She was consumed, during every waking moment, with reality.

She wasn't the only one who spied on Flannery. She noticed that
Regina too went out of her way to walk by the front windows. When she

thought no one was looking, she paused and studied her daughter, an austere expression on her face.

On Gigi's first Sunday at the farm, Regina didn't stop to stare, but climbed the porch steps and slammed open the two doors that separated herself and her daughter.

"So, you're really not going to go?"

"I thought I was perfectly clear."

"You've never missed mass except when you were sick."

"Well, I'm sick."

"No, you're not. What are you not telling me?"

There was a silence. Gigi was standing to the side of the house; the mother and daughter were in Flannery's bedroom. A few chickens gathered by Gigi's foot, as if they wanted to eavesdrop as well.

"This is *church*, Flannery. God's service. You need to rise beyond yourself."

A chair was pushed back. The porch door slapped open, making Gigi and the chickens jump. Flannery led the way onto the porch; Regina followed.

"Mother, I literally don't know what to tell you other than that I'm not going. I *can't* go. Please don't push me."

"You *can't* go? Don't be ridiculous."

Gigi was raking leaves, trying to appear as though she couldn't hear a word even though the mother and daughter were standing only fifteen feet away. Gigi noticed that Flannery's voice sounded bunched up, the way her own did right before she cried. Gigi held tight to the rake, and felt tears rise in her throat. *Please leave her alone*, she thought at Regina. *Please leave her alone.*

But Regina wasn't done. "Whatever's bothering you, come to church and speak to Father Cole about it."

Flannery didn't reply.

"Is it about the child? Or that man?"

Gigi listened with all her might, but heard nothing.

Regina gave a short, choppy sigh. "I refuse to be left in the dark."

"Dark, light, what's the difference?" Flannery said, in a tired voice. "You're still standing in the exact same spot. Go to church, Regina. I have work to do."

"You're dismissing me?"

"You can take it however you like."

Gigi was gathering dead leaves into a pile when Regina roared by in the truck, her face stony, her hat large and lavender.

Flannery sank down into one of the porch chairs. She waved to Gigi, and Gigi waved back.

"I'm sorry you had to hear that."

Gigi searched her brain for an eloquent response, but couldn't find one. "That's okay."

She continued to rake leaves. She concentrated on building perfect pile after perfect pile. She could feel the writer's eyes on her. She hoped that her repetitive action had the same soothing effect on Flannery that the writer's typing had on her. Gigi made an effort to pull, lift, and drop at the same pace each time. She took slow breaths, and moved her muscles to a steady rhythm.

She had gone to church only sporadically throughout her childhood. She had found the experience boring and the sermons irrelevant. From the yawns that surrounded her in the church pew, and her own parents' halfhearted attendance, she had assumed that most people agreed. She could tell, though, from Regina and Flannery's expressions and the strain in their voices, that church meant something more to them. Flannery's face looked drawn now; her hands rested limply on the arms of the chair.

Gigi continued to pull and grab with the rake. There was something she wanted to speak to Flannery about, but she didn't know how. She was also afraid that saying the words out loud, bringing what she had realized to someone else's attention, would be dangerous. The thought paralyzed her in the middle of the night; it made her stuff her sheet in her mouth to keep from crying out. Still, she had the urge to make confession.

Gigi turned her back on the writer. She knew that if she caught Flannery's eye she would talk. She looked, instead, at the peacocks. She noticed one with frayed feathers, an older bird with gray beside his beak and knowing eyes. He was less colorful than the others. He blended in with the mud. He looked tired.

Gigi glanced over her shoulder. Flannery's eyes were closed.

She looked back at the aged peacock. His feathers were every shade of green; he reminded Gigi of an ancient tree. He was studying her, his expression understanding. It seemed possible, to the girl, that he had been standing there for hours, simply waiting for her to turn to him.

She whispered, "I'm the only one who survived."

The peacock tilted his head to the side. *What do you mean?*

Gigi held on to the rake. She was still now. She was filled with the knowledge that no adult had bothered to notice. She had been waiting to read about it in the newspaper, or hear it in the school corridors, but it had become clear that no one else had done the math. No one else had noticed that there were three children involved in that tragic afternoon. People had counted up to two, and stopped.

Cookie and Melvin had one child, Rose.

Miss Mary had one child, Joe.

Lona and Bill had one child. Gigi.

She crouched down in the crinkly leaves. She had the weight of Joe and Rose on her back. Flannery had said she was innocent, but that wasn't true. She was involved. She was the only child to survive, but why? What for? Why her?

She looked at the old peacock, hoping for an answer. He shook his head and gave a soft, marbled cry. He sounded at first like an infant—squalling and hungry. Then his voice deepened. The descent wasn't smooth; it broke awkwardly at points. He reminded Gigi of an adolescent boy stumbling through an important plea. Finally, his call gained strength. Discordant and hoarse, but louder now, it commanded more ground. It reached right through Gigi's skin and into the bright sky overhead.

Flannery was deep in the story, inhaling exhaust fumes, simmering alongside the terrified-angry mother and the terrified-angry son. The bus jerked, and she jerked with it. There was a sharp noise—the bus's tailpipe spat out black smoke. *Could it break down?* Flannery wondered. *What would happen then?* The driver swore under his breath and the mother gripped her seat, her mouth sealed shut with concern. She was always expecting something terrible to happen. The bus backfired again.

Something made Flannery glance up from her desk. She looked out the window and saw Gigi Waters staring back at her. The girl's fist was raised, as if she were about to knock on the pane of glass. Flannery shook her head. She looked at the clock on her desk. She was still on the bus. She wanted to be on the bus. It was the middle of the morning. Everyone knew not to disturb her before noon.

"Please?" Gigi asked. Her voice was faint.

Flannery had to think for a moment about how to organize her muscles to push back her chair. She had to think about standing up. Once she was standing, she gave her head a small shake, to clear it. By the time she reached the porch, she was present, and annoyed.

"I told you about my schedule," she said. "This couldn't have waited ninety minutes?"

Gigi looked scared, and small, standing in front of her. Flannery reminded herself what the girl had been through, how much she had lost. "Wait a second," she said. "It's Monday. Why aren't you at school?"

There were smudges beneath Gigi's eyes and cuts beside her fingernails. She stuffed her hands in her pockets, and then took them out again. She glanced to her right, toward the line of trees that separated Andalusia from the Treadle farm.

"I have to ask you a question."

Flannery waited.

"Could I please live here? With you and Mrs. O'Connor?"

A gust of wind swept the yard, shifting the leaves Gigi had missed with her rake the day before. Flannery sat down in the nearest chair. She stared at the girl.

"My mother told me that she's leaving town. No one will hire her and we have no money. She says I have to go with her, but I don't want to." The words came in a rush. "It would only be for another year, until I graduate high school. I wouldn't be any trouble. I'll keep working on the farm. I'm quiet. I don't eat much. I promise I won't get in your way."

Flannery looked at her hands. She looked at the floorboards. She looked at the birds stalking the grass. She missed the General. She missed him fiercely.

The day after Rose's death, Regina had rounded the house carrying a shotgun. Flannery was sitting on the front porch, and she didn't think to question the sight. Her mother often carried a gun. She used it to scare off foxes and snakes. She used it to put sick cows out of their misery. It was one of her daily tools.

Flannery had rocked in her chair—the motion seemed to be the only thing holding her together—and watched Regina cross the speckled grass with a relaxed stride. Her mother came to a stop ten paces from the magnolia tree. She raised the gun to her shoulder.

Flannery stopped rocking.

The General, even with the bull's-eye pointed directly at him, remained perfectly still on his perch. He didn't shift a feather. He stared her down. Flannery could tell he didn't believe that she would follow through. He thought Regina was bluffing. The giant peacock puffed his chest out, his eyes as black and sure as stones.

The shotgun cracked. Regina took a step backward. The General's head dipped forward, and then slowly, slowly, he dropped off the limb. Flannery's mind and heart beat like a hollow drum as the peacock hit the ground.

She knew that she should blame him for what had happened, but she couldn't. Flannery was his keeper, and she absorbed his culpability as her own. His crime was hers. Flannery told herself that if she hadn't been so selfish, so wrapped up in her own pointless, petty emotions that terrible afternoon, she would have seen trouble approaching. As it was, the flurry that had arisen on the ground and in the air had matched the tornado inside her so exactly, so perfectly, that for a second or two she didn't recognize that anything was wrong. She wished she could re-create that moment. She wished she could go back to the beginning. If she had been alert, if she had been prepared, she would have commanded the birds' attention. She would have calmed them down. She would have called out directions to Melvin. She would have made sure that no one was hurt.

It was impossible for Flannery to lay blame at the peacock's feet. And since she was steeped in guilt either way, she wished the General was here. She'd had enough of absences, enough of things tearing apart. She was down in the mud with her characters now, scrapping around, climbing from one hour of the clock to the next with nothing to believe in. If God did exist, he was not the figure she had long depended upon. He was clearly immoral, or at least amoral. A baby had died on this lawn—*a baby*—while Flannery, riddled with disease, looked on. It wasn't the lack of fairness that bothered her; she had never expected, or even hoped for, an even hand in life. It was the needless, unwarranted pain inflicted on everyone involved, even herself.

223

Her sense of God had evaporated that afternoon, like drops of water under a hot sun. And now, with her faith gone, very little held her days together. Very little held her thoughts in focus. All she had was her work.

She allowed herself to think about Gigi moving in. There was a spare bedroom upstairs. It might be pleasant to have a young person banging up and down the stairs, waxing dramatic to her friends over the telephone, coaxing sweets out of the housekeeper. It might be pleasant. *I don't deserve pleasant*, she thought, but this too was just a fleeting, disconnected thought.

"You told me that a person can try to even things up." Gigi touched her hair in a nervous, quick gesture, as if worried she'd forgotten to brush it that morning. "They can try to take something wrong, and make it right."

Flannery considered that this was the second morning in a row she had been disturbed at her desk. First by her own mother, and now by this child looking for a new one. *Interruptions are like pressure on the space key*, she thought. *Or starting a new paragraph. Space after space after space.*

"Please say something," Gigi said.

"I have my work," Flannery said. "I can't be distracted."

"I'm sorry. I should have waited until lunchtime to talk to you. I thought, I mean, it seemed—"

Flannery felt a gavel fall inside her. She felt the hard part of herself—which was always there, always pushing, always ready to slam the door—rise to the surface. "You don't want to live here," she said. "A young person doesn't belong in a place like this. All I do is work, and all Regina does is work. We don't live. You need to stay out there, in the world. You'll shrivel up and disappear on this farm."

Gigi's cheeks were wet. "I do want to live here," she said.

The girl looked like she was about to say more; Flannery cut her off. "Besides, you're still a minor, and you have a living parent who wants you with her. I could never step in the way of that. It wouldn't be right."

"My mother doesn't really *want* me. She just feels responsible . . ." Gigi stopped, as if she didn't know what else to say.

"I'm sorry," Flannery said.

"No, I'm sorry," Gigi said. She turned and ran down the driveway. She disappeared into the dark cave of trees.

Regina was the one to find out, two weeks later, that Lona and Gigi Waters had driven out of town in the middle of the night. Melvin, it turned out, was gone too. There was a "For Sale" sign in front of his house. A moving truck had emptied the contents of the rooms and driven away.

Flannery had to force herself to stay at her desk upon hearing the news. She felt like an overinflated balloon; she had lost any sense of gravity. She dug her fingers into her typewriter keys and tried to generate sentences by the sheer strength of her knuckles. A few letters made up a word, and a few words made up a sentence, and a piece of punctuation moved her forward. The quality did not matter, just the motion.

"This is not your fault," Regina told her. "You're not that child's mother. She has a mother. If anyone should have showed her a little heart, it's Miss Mary. That girl didn't do a darn thing to make Miss Mary give her up like this. I've told her so. I know she's grieving, and she's a friend, of course, but for heaven's sake, Gigi didn't sleep with Joe. She didn't walk into that room with a gun. She didn't do a darn thing. Not a darn thing."

Flannery listened to this without filters. She usually passed her mother's words through a sieve of humor, or an appreciation of the absurd, or her own sense of how God meant the world to work. She needed those filters, and she depended on them, but she'd lost them now. All she heard was the truth. She heard what her mother *meant*, as well as what she said.

"Not a darn thing?" she asked.

Regina looked at her suspiciously.

"You're not *this* upset about Gigi, Mother."

"Who are you to say what I'm upset about? Of course I'm upset about the girl. You are too."

Flannery shook her head. "You're upset about me. You're upset about what *I* did."

"Believe it or not, my every thought does not revolve around you, Flannery."

"There are two things that you always liked about my illness. One, that it kept me close to you, and two, that it kept me good."

"Oh, for heaven's sake."

"If I never had a life, I couldn't mess one up, could I? I was almost like a saint, until Melvin showed up here. Then I went and ruined everything. I disappointed you. Now I'm sick and I'm human. We're both disappointed."

Regina's face was dark. "Don't be absurd. This is sacrilegious talk."

"You wanted me to turn Melvin away because he was married. You think what happened to Rose was my fault. You think God was punishing me."

A peacock honked outside the window. It was a low, lonely sound, followed by silence.

"What I think," Regina said, "is that you should go to church and give confession to Father Cole."

"No," Flannery said. "No."

That night, she was unable to sleep. Usually, when this happened, she lay very still with her eyes closed and tried to bore herself into unconsciousness. This time, she pushed back the sheets, got dressed, and found the car keys on top of the bureau in the front hall. She used as little gas as possible to maneuver down the driveway. She was pleased when the birds hardly rustled on their perches and her mother's bedroom stayed shrouded in darkness. She had no desire to be seen or heard.

She drove toward town, her thoughts twisting like sheets in the wind. It was impossible for her to be behind the wheel and not think about Melvin. She missed the wry glance he delivered whenever she said something provocative. She missed the way he smelled: like mouthwash and chewing gum. The way he pushed his hair back with his hand when he was tired. The way he listened, with his whole body leaning forward, as if her words were the most interesting he had ever heard.

Flannery closed her eyes, then opened them. There was no one else on the road. She moved into the wrong lane for a minute, just to see what it felt like, and then moved back. The town was asleep. She passed the college, the library, the post office. She drove by Sacred Heart. She drove toward the red light on Wayne Street and considered driving right through it. What was the risk? That a cop would come out of nowhere and give her a ticket? That another car would suddenly appear on a course perpendicular to hers and they would crash?

Flannery could imagine the sick crunch of metal meeting metal; she could hear the screech of brakes; she could see the smoke and sparks pricking the air and her own head slamming the steering wheel. The vision held some appeal. She regarded her slumped body, and the blood trickling down her forehead, without the sense of any particular sadness. It was almost satisfying. Death by car crash was an unexpected ending, and she liked unexpected endings. *We all thought she would die from that disease*, people would murmur at her funeral.

She savored this idea for a moment before shaking it away. A crash would involve another car, and therefore another person. She couldn't allow that. She couldn't tolerate having another person's life on her hands.

Flannery pulled over to the curb. She sat behind the wheel, her breath heavy in her throat. Her publisher had sent a copy of her new novel, *The Violent Bear It Away*, which would come out officially in a few days' time. She had removed the book from the envelope and stared at the cover, then flipped through the pages. The professional part of her brain had immediately assessed it as a product. She had thought: *nice font, good layout, I don't like my author photo.* She pictured the book being distributed to stores around the country. The Milledgeville librarian would order eight, of which only two or three would ever be checked out. The novel would appear in bookstore windows in Atlanta, and it would be stacked on tables in New York. The book would be everywhere, at least for a short time. Newspapers and magazines would give it review space. There might be a couple of radio spots, and the novel might eventually make it onto the curriculum at a couple of universities where the professors were Flannery's friends. The book would flow away from her, beyond her, like blood from her veins. Melvin might see it, walking by a big glass window on a busy street. She tried to imagine his reaction, but failed. He felt so far away from her now.

Flannery studied the empty street. She knew this town inside and out. She knew who lived in nearly every house. She could list their relatives, their pets, their shortcomings. She knew every stack in the library; where the teenage boys hid their dirty magazines, and where the mayor liked to sit and snooze behind his newspaper. She knew the nicks and wobbles of every pew in her church. She knew which hymnals were missing which pages. She knew a lot. Her brain was crammed with regional data.

What good was the information, though? What use was it? All it did was make her heart feel like it was breaking. The details were nothing but tools for her writing and her writing was barely propping her up, barely keeping her recognizable to herself. She could stare down every person in this town and still feel herself fade away. God had been more than a support to her; he had been her greatest challenger. He had demanded, every day, that she live to her potential. She had both savored that pressure and struggled under it. She had depended on it; she had used it to shape her life.

God had provided a portal, a path to greater understanding, a way to see the world as a richer, more meaningful place. She didn't feel so much like she had stopped believing in God; she felt like the portal had been slammed shut in her face. She no longer had access; she had lost her invitation; she was outside a door with no obvious knob to grab hold of and twist.

Flannery was staring out the windshield, down an empty street, when she spotted a blur of motion in her peripheral vision.

She turned her head and found herself looking directly at a woman. She was wearing sneakers and a flowered robe. It was, Flannery realized, Cookie Whiteson.

Cookie was standing beside the car.

Flannery's heart smacked unevenly in her chest. She recalled Gigi standing at her bedroom window, and felt sick. She slowly opened the door and climbed out of the car.

"Hello," she said cautiously.

Cookie didn't reply. Her face was expressionless. She appeared thinner than Flannery remembered, and her blond hair was unkempt. There were gray smudges directly above her cheekbones.

At her wedding, Cookie had been beautiful, despite a black eye. Clinging to her new husband's arm, she smiled with the force and steadiness of a fog light. Now she looked so different, so lightless, that the reality standing in front of Flannery was hard to accept.

She wondered if perhaps they were both dreaming. This was such an unlikely scene. Maybe this wasn't happening in the real world, in real time. The town was dim around them. Black sky, dark buildings, the occasional streetlight glowing yellow.

"It's cold out," Flannery heard herself say.

Cookie scrunched up her nose, as if considering the verity of the statement. "Yes," she said, finally. "I've found that it's always colder after midnight."

"There are reasons for that, I suppose." Flannery hid her hands in her skirt, a nervous habit from her childhood. What was she talking about? The temperature?

Cookie tapped the tip of one of her sneakers against the pavement, like a runner looking for a good spot to take off from. Flannery became worried, suddenly, that she would leave. She could imagine her sprinting down the street, her bathrobe flapping behind her. Flannery didn't want her to go, though she couldn't have said why.

"Why are you out at this hour?" she asked.

"Why are you?"

Flannery looked up at the night sky, which looked exactly the same as it did from her front porch. A scattering of faraway stars against a black canvas. She felt like she was standing in the depths of everything dark: her guilt, her heartbreak, her breaking body. Melvin was far away. Regina was far away. Her typewriter was far away.

Flannery tried to brace herself. She tried to summon strength she wasn't sure she possessed. She had never particularly liked Cookie; she had always considered her a silly woman, more concerned with appearances than substance, but she found it painful to look at her now, for new reasons. Cookie had obviously changed; circumstances had changed. It felt as though Rose lay between the two women, burbling in her baby language on a blanket. She was right there, but also out of reach.

"I moved to New York after high school because of you," Cookie said. "Did you know that?"

It took a lot of effort for Flannery to shake her head.

"Of course you didn't. How could you? I went to New York because when you left Milledgeville, that's where you went."

Flannery could only stare.

"You wrote such terrible things about this town, but my mother said you loved New York. And I thought, well, if she likes New York, then it must be good. It must be the place where nothing gets spoiled, where things make sense."

"There is no place like that," Flannery said.

Cookie was quiet for a second. "I know that now. I couldn't fit in there at all. No one even noticed me. Melvin was the only one in that whole time who stopped and looked at me. The only one. I don't even know why he stopped. I don't know what he saw. I never asked him."

The air wrapped icy fingers around Flannery's skin.

"I wrote a letter to him," Cookie said. "Yesterday, I think."

"Oh?"

"I told him that I blame him for what happened, not you."

A dog barked, his chain rattled, in the distance.

At the beginning of Melvin's last visit, Flannery had watched from the corner of her eye as Rose grabbed at grass and offered her father a wide-eyed, trusting gaze. It had been difficult for her to look directly at the baby. She was Melvin's child with another woman, and she was glaringly new. The baby was pink-toned and healthy. Her skin looked like it would be impossibly soft to the touch. Rose had an entire, privileged life ahead of her, and Flannery felt like looking at her was akin to staring directly into the sun. She felt—she forced herself to admit this now—jealous. In the storm cloud of feathers that followed, Flannery lost sight of Rose, and everything else. Afterward, she got only a sense of the child's stillness—her terrible stillness—before her father gathered her in his arms.

"Did you mean it?" she asked.

Cookie shrugged. "I did at the time. He's the one who lied to me. He's the one who married me and took vows. Now that I see you, though, something bothers me."

"What's that?"

"You were the last one to see her alive."

Oh, God, Flannery thought, out of habit. Then, *oh God*.

"You were the last one." Cookie emphasized every word this time, as if she were trying to make herself clear to someone who had only a loose grasp of the language. Her eyes were big in her face.

"You're right."

"I'm not myself anymore. I don't even want to be myself anymore."

Flannery wanted to ask what she meant by this, but she didn't dare. She hesitated, then said, "I never touched Rose. I was never within a few feet of her. I never held her in my arms. She was always with Melvin."

Cookie seemed to take this as it was intended, as a small gift. She put her hands up to her face.

"I'm very sorry, Cookie."

Flannery was sorry. She was sorry for Rose. She was sorry for the loss of what might have been. She was tremendously sorry.

Neither woman spoke for a moment. Flannery was aware of feeling strangely comfortable, in the middle of the night, in the middle of the street, talking to a woman with whom she'd shared a mutual dislike for many years.

"I've been sleepwalking," Cookie said finally.

"Would you like me to drive you home?"

Cookie rounded the car and slid into the passenger seat. Only when she had clicked the door shut did Flannery feel capable of movement. She lowered herself onto the seat and started the engine. She pulled into the road and then stopped immediately. The traffic light was red.

"Just run it," Cookie said.

Flannery did as she was told.

Melvin awoke before the alarm. He lay in bed for a few minutes, blinking his way into consciousness. For a brief, blurry moment, he thought he was in Milledgeville. He listened to the baby chirp in her crib, and felt the warm weight of Cookie asleep by his side. He smelled cut grass through the open window.

Reality rolled over him and squeezed his breath out with a slow, relentless force. Noises began to separate and distinguish themselves. The radiator hissed from the corner of the room. He heard a car horn bleat in the distance. The burbling sound resumed, this time as the building's pipes clearing their throats. The bed was cold around Melvin, and he was alone.

He pushed his face into his pillow. He had to make himself roll over, and then sit up. He walked into the kitchen and turned on the coffee maker. His day in New York had officially begun.

He drank a cup of coffee and got dressed. He looked for his watch for a moment, before remembering that it had been lost in the move. He pocketed his keys and wallet, and left the apartment. On his way out of the building, the morning doorman handed him his copy of the newspaper. Melvin tucked the paper under his arm and walked three blocks to a café, hidden on a quiet side street beneath a red and yellow awning.

The waiter knew Melvin didn't like to chat, so he simply nodded and gestured to the table by the window. Melvin sat down and started to read the front page. He was on the fourth page when his coffee arrived, and in the business section by the time his oatmeal and orange juice were delivered. By the time he'd capped his breakfast with another cup of coffee, he'd read the paper from front to back. He didn't have a favorite section, or a part he lingered over. Melvin liked the paper for its length. On Mondays and Tuesdays, when the news was a little thinner, he had to bring a magazine to the café, in order to fill the same amount of time. After paying the bill, he carefully tore out the crossword puzzle, folded it into his pocket, and headed back to his building.

He sat at his desk and completed as much of the puzzle as possible. He reviewed his mail, which usually involved requests from his lawyer or accountant. He had a metal filing cabinet for financial documents. He finished his work around noon, and then, if the weather was agreeable, he left the apartment again. He purchased a sandwich and soda at the deli, and walked east.

He moved quickly. He knew that these wide cross streets created most of the noise the city was famous for. Buses grumbled, taxis screeched to a stop, and drivers clambered out of cars and swore at one another. Babies complained from the depths of their prams, dogs whinnied, newspaper salesmen waved their product and announced the stories of the day. There was always at least one siren that could be heard. Fire trucks, police cars, and ambulances streamed through the city, attending to one emergency after another.

The noise made Melvin sweat. It felt personal, like a megaphone pointed at his ear. It was impossible to avoid, but he did his best not to involve himself in the cacophony. He walked purposefully, and avoided meeting anyone's eye. If a tourist asked for directions, he pretended not to hear. He shuddered with relief when he turned into the park, and sank down on an unoccupied bench.

He read a mystery novel while he ate. Melvin had never been a fan of detective fiction in the past, so the genre was wide open to him. He wasn't picky about the quality of the writing. What he appreciated was its remarkable capacity to keep him engaged. Once a month, he took the subway down to the West Village to visit a bookshop that specialized in mysteries. He bought ten at a time, all volumes recommended by the friendly owner. Melvin found that he could easily lose an hour or two in each plot, whose formula somehow contained both predictability and surprise. He never allowed himself to pause between books. He read like a chain-smoker, putting a paperback down after the final sentence and immediately picking up another.

When he was finished with his sandwich, he walked back to the main avenue and decided what to do next. This was the only block of time that varied from day to day. If he'd read about an interesting movie or art exhibit in the paper, he went to see that. If he needed to meet with his lawyer or accountant, he did so in the afternoon. Generally, Melvin's rule was to keep himself out of his apartment until dinner. Fresh air, distractions, and the proximity of strangers were key elements in keeping his spirits level.

Dinner was delivered by a local restaurant, and Melvin ate in front of the television. He watched the news, or whatever show was on that night. *The Andy Griffith Show*, *Gunsmoke*, or *The Dick Van Dyke Show*. He and Cookie had never watched television, so the programs were all unknown to him. They also gave him something to discuss with the elevator attendant and doormen. He was careful to store one or two reflections about the night's shows to discuss the following morning. He went to bed early, and read until he fell asleep.

There were a few interruptions to Melvin's careful routine. His Realtor, a nosy woman who had been dealing in high-end Manhattan real estate for twenty years, spread the word among his parents' friends that Melvin had returned to town. When the first rash of party invitations and "Welcome Back" notes arrived, Melvin was annoyed at himself for not asking her to be discreet, but also thankful that he hadn't told her about his daughter. He filed the correspondence in the bottom drawer of his desk and stopped answering the phone. His accountant and lawyer knew to set appointments with him, and there was no one else he needed to speak to.

It was during one of these scheduled phone conversations that his accountant paused, and said, "Mr. Thompson called again."

"I'm not interested."

"They just want you to stop by and say hello."

"I don't see any reason for it."

"Look at it as a professional courtesy. These men worked with your father—and you—for years. You turn a nice profit every quarter from their stock. There's no benefit to putting their noses out of joint. I can arrange it so you're in and out in under an hour, and then you won't have to go back."

Melvin sighed. "Okay, fine."

He had his hair cut on the morning of the appointment and wore a suit. He was greeted in the lobby by half the board and led through the floors of the bank. The secretaries all wore aggressive smiles, and former employees strode forward with their shaking hand outstretched. The phones never stopped ringing as they navigated the labyrinthine halls. Melvin found that although the surroundings looked familiar, they seemed only vaguely so, as if his time there had been a dream, or had taken place so long ago that the details now escaped him.

While they waited for the elevator, one of the board members leaned in and said, "You know we'd all be pleased as punch if you came back to work here, right? You had a talent for the job, and of course your name means everything in this building. You'd be welcomed back at the top. We realize you might have other plans, but we hope you'll keep us in mind."

Melvin knew this wasn't a casual statement. He'd been asked here to be felt out. The board was curious about why he'd returned to town. They wondered if he intended to start his own bank, or another competitive business. It was the kind of thing his father might have done, and if nothing else, Melvin had his father's bankroll. These men, who had been trained to focus on the bottom line, couldn't help but see both the possibilities and the threat of Melvin Whiteson.

He smiled at an innocuous painting hanging by the elevator. The style was abstract; he knew the piece of art had been chosen to look bold and modern, but not too much so. He also knew that no one would understand if he explained that his current plan covered only the next ten minutes, at which point he would devise a plan for the following ten minutes, and so on, until bedtime. No one would understand if he said he had no ambition at all, other than to be left alone. The man standing before him might even be offended by such an explanation, or suspect he was being mocked.

"I'm flattered," Melvin said. "And of course I'll keep you in mind. I don't see how I couldn't."

"Excellent," the man said, though he still looked anxious. The answer hadn't been concrete enough for his liking. The elevator doors parted, and he gestured with his hand. "After you."

The tour ended in his father's office, where Melvin gripped Mr. Thompson's wide palm, and exchanged pleasantries about summering in Palm Beach, the golf season, and William Whiteson's fondness for single-malt scotch. Melvin was pleased by his ability to handle the conversation. He knew how to make this kind of small talk and could do it well. Still, he escaped as soon as was politely possible. He took the express elevator down and burst onto the street like a swimmer breaking the water's surface, in desperate need of air.

It took a few weeks following the visit to feel anonymous again. He received several notes from board members saying how nice it had been to see him, and how he was welcome back anytime. He found himself more conscious of faces on the street. He didn't want to bump into anyone, or be caught unawares. He hurried to the park at lunchtime, and then hurried home again.

He felt less comforted by his routine. He had trouble staying at his desk, and his mystery novels were less effective at holding his attention. At night, he flipped through the seven available television channels without finding anything interesting to watch. He went for walks after dusk because the darkness offered the invisibility he craved.

At all hours of the day, he found himself thinking about the two slips of paper in his top desk drawer. The first was a letter from Cookie. He had read it several times, and the experience was always excruciating. It was more akin to tearing open a recent wound than reading correspondence. Cookie had reached from inside her chest into his. She threw Rose at him; she threw the cubic ton of their loss at him; she accused him of betraying her with Flannery; she pinned everything on him.

Melvin's chest tightened every time he opened the top drawer. The letter seemed like a physical presence in the apartment, a sheet of words that revealed the worst of him. The letter stated, clearly: that she did not want to see him or hear from him ever again, that any monies from the house sale should be delivered to her parents, and that she would be changing her last name back to Himmel with immediate effect. Melvin had no intention of disrespecting her demands, but the letter still grabbed his throat like a pair of hands whenever he laid eyes on it.

When he had walked himself to exhaustion, and there was nothing on television, and he couldn't sleep, he turned to the second sheet of paper. This one was also complicated, but much more manageable. It was a bill he had found on his desk shortly after Rose's burial. The invoice was handwritten by Lona Waters, and dated before his daughter's death. Melvin had studied it carefully, and then, when it came time to pack, he placed it in one of the moving boxes.

He had changed his mind several times about what to do. At first he had been inclined to ignore the request. After all, the woman had brought murder and scandal to his house. She had conducted an illicit affair in one of his bedrooms, for months. She had shown, by nearly anyone's estimation, no respect for the Whitesons as people or employers. She didn't deserve to be paid for what she'd done. She didn't deserve to be punished—surely what she'd lost was punishment enough—but she also didn't deserve to profit from her behavior. On the other hand, she had done excellent work, despite her indiscretions. Shouldn't that be valued, apart from everything else?

Melvin had decided not to pay her, until one of his Milledgeville movers mentioned that they were also packing up the Waters's house, and that Lona and her daughter were moving to New York too. Melvin found himself removing Lona's invoice from the box and putting it in his inside suit pocket. It traveled on the plane with him, toured prospective apartments with him, and stayed in his pocket until he found a new place to live. It had been the sole document in the top drawer until Cookie's letter arrived.

A few weeks after the bank visit, Melvin asked his lawyer to track down Lona Waters. Within an hour, he had her phone number and address. He found the speed of the exchange strangely disturbing. He reviewed the information: she lived in a low-income neighborhood downtown. He could picture the block; he'd had a college friend with an apartment near there. He tried to imagine Lona and her daughter walking around the city, but the image made no sense. They belonged in Milledgeville. Why would Lona come here?

He wasn't comfortable with her proximity. He wanted to be the only person in the city who had lived through those days in Georgia. He wanted to be the only one who knew, the only one who had suffered, the only one who remembered. Why couldn't she have gone somewhere else? What right did she have to this skyscraping island? This was his town, his retreat, his finish line.

He remembered Lona smoking a joint behind the church on his wedding day. He recalled glimpses of her in his house, studying a new curtain with a sewing needle pursed between her lips. He saw her crouched over a teenager's grave while trucks shot down the street and birds circled overhead. He remembered the crunching pain of that afternoon, and the look of the fresh dirt over the two new plots.

His eyes drifted and fell on Cookie's letter. He remained perfectly still in his chair, and perfectly silent, but inside he uttered a cry so loud and piercing he could not help but think of the peacocks.

L   ona slept on the pullout couch. This piece of furniture was included in the rent, which was why she kept it, but it was in rough shape. She often wondered about its past. It looked like it had been involved in several vicious brawls. The couch's color was indeterminate—it could most accurately be called dark. Its legs were dented, as if they had been kicked with steel-toe boots. A bite seemed to have been taken out of the center of one of the cushions.

The furniture's appearance was most intimidating, though, when it was opened up. The first time it was unfolded, both Lona and Gigi unconsciously took a few steps back. They found themselves pressed against the wall, wishing the room were larger so they could put more distance between themselves and the mattress.

The thin bed was a snarl of gray lumps that seemed to shift, under the dark of night, to locate and mangle Lona's spine. They had an unerring sense of direction. Lona tossed and turned and tried sleeping in every possible position, but she was never able to successfully evade them. It took five minutes for her to climb to her feet in the morning, and the bathroom mirror revealed a woman who had lost a fight.

That's what her life in New York felt like: a series of lost fights. The tiny apartment was only two rooms: one bedroom, occupied by Gigi, a desk, and a bed, and the living room, where Lona lived. A small counter, stovetop, and refrigerator hugged the side wall. There was a constant smell of coffee in the air, even though neither Lona nor Gigi drank coffee. The mother and daughter constantly bumped into each other in the restricted space. Or, more precisely, Gigi bumped into Lona. She seemed to have taken it upon herself to make her mother's life miserable.

"Moving here was a ridiculous idea," she said one morning. They were standing near the kitchen counter, eating bowls of cereal. The only available seat in the room was the unfurled couch, which neither of them went near.

"It will get better," Lona said. "We have to be patient."

"You don't believe that."

"Of course I do."

"I heard you crying last night," Gigi said. "I hear everything through these stupid walls. You're as unhappy as I am. You just feel like you have to lie because this was your idea." She paused. "I heard you talking too."

Lona pushed her spoon through the bowl of milk.

"It sounded like you were having a conversation with someone."

Lona looked at her daughter. Gigi's jaw was set; Bill adopted the same expression whenever he was stressed. She felt a stab of guilt for dragging the girl to this loud, unfamiliar city. "It must have been the neighbors. It wasn't me."

"Bullshit."

Lona considered reprimanding Gigi for her language, but only for a second.

"If you're going crazy, I need to know. I need to make plans. I don't know *anyone* here."

Lona tried to sound convincing. "I'm not going crazy."

Gigi shook her head, then picked up her backpack and left the apartment.

Lona was deeply relieved at her departure. She never knew when her daughter was going to attend class and when she was going to stay home. "School holiday," Gigi would announce on a random Wednesday morning, and then go back to her room. Sometimes Gigi's "school holidays," which had no affiliation with any public holidays, lasted almost a week. "What are you doing in there?" Lona would ask through the bedroom door. "My life is none of your business," Gigi would answer.

The girl flashed between anger and silence. She would devote several days to tearing her mother apart verbally, and then spend a week pretending Lona didn't exist. Lona found both unsettling. She thought it was unfair that she was the one bearing the brunt of her daughter's emotions. Surely Bill deserved some of the shouting, some of the rage. After all, he was the one who had pulled out a gun and killed a boy. He was the one who had destroyed everything. Gigi should be writing him letters, and Bill should be begging them both for forgiveness. Instead, he had told his lawyer that he wouldn't be in touch with anyone; he had apparently decided to let his precious justice system swallow him whole.

Lona got ready for work; the process didn't take long. She had purchased two white blouses as well as one navy and one tan skirt for her professional wardrobe. She wore a pair of sturdy black pumps. She forced herself to concentrate for a moment in front of the mirror, to make sure she successfully applied her lipstick and pinned back her hair. She had received strange looks at work once or twice when she looked less than presentable. "Make an effort," she told herself, but it was an effort to even say the words.

She traveled to midtown via two subway lines. Every day she marveled at the sheer number of people underground. She had never been with this many people at one time in her life. The true New Yorkers were apparent in the subway cars because they took no notice of the crowd. They read their newspaper or dozed in the middle of the teeming mass. Lona was unable to do anything but stare. She felt like she was in a movie theater, or pinned up against a hundred household windows.

She watched an elderly woman, magnificently dressed, cry neatly into a handkerchief. A child sucked a lollipop, then threw it on the floor. A couple argued over a dinner invitation. A young woman on the other side of the car held a mascara wand in one hand and a small compact mirror in the other. Two men wearing hard hats spoke to each other almost exclusively in swearwords. A teenage girl folded and then unfolded the hem of her jeans, presumably trying to decide which looked best, as unself-consciously as if she were at home in her bedroom. A foul-smelling man in a huge overcoat lay across three seats at the end of the car, snoring. People wrinkled their noses and gave him a wide berth.

Every day there was someone Lona could identify with. Today it was the old woman crying into her handkerchief. Lona felt as wrinkled and finished as this other woman appeared to be. They were both surrounded by couples, and parents with young children, and old friends, and people at the beginning of a day they hoped would be exciting and fulfilling. These people held on to each other, or their seats, or the straps suspended from the ceiling. The old woman looked like she had nothing to hold on to. This train tunnel was just one more river for her grief. She was swept along with the current.

Lona missed Joe.

She imagined him sitting beside her on the train, holding her arm while she rode the steep escalator to the street, whispering something funny in her ear as they crossed the wide avenue. Gigi was right. She had been wrong to come here. In Milledgeville, reality was set. What happened, happened. The signs were everywhere—a freshly dug grave, Miss Mary's ice-pick eyes at the funeral, the constant stories about the murder in the local paper. There was no argument about what had occurred, or who was left behind to survive.

Here was different. Here hurt. Every breath Lona drew in New York City scraped like a razor in her lungs. The future she had wanted was staring her in the face, taunting her. Here, she and Joe would have been together, happy and free. Even if she had done the exact same things: rented the depressing apartment, rode the subway to work, and shopped for groceries with coupons on the way home, she would have done them with Joe, for Joe, and every second would have sung with joy.

Lona could feel the schism between what was and what should have been, and this gap was abysmal, a black hole invisible to everyone but her. Only the hard facts of existence—the need to pay rent, eat, clean herself—and her daughter's belligerent stare kept her present. She was only here loosely, though. She held on to her routine, she tried to show up where and when she was supposed to, she tried not to crumble under Gigi's offense. But all the time, through every hour, every minute, she was thinking about Joe. There was a cozy restaurant across the street from Lona's office building, and each time she passed it she had the same inevitable thought: *Joe and I would have definitely eaten there.*

Lona was a secretary in a large law firm. After being hired, she was trained to take dictation, and she spent her days walking from one lawyer's office to another, transcribing letters, memos, and contracts. She didn't mind the work. Shorthand was its own language, constructed, she had been told in the training seminar, "to serve efficiency." The demands of the fake language, and the clatter of the stenotype machine, helped keep her thoughts at bay. She knew that if she let herself drift in this mechanical environment, she would be fired immediately, and that couldn't happen because she needed the money. She was barely making ends meet in New York, and she had hopes of paying off her debts in Milledgeville.

Her focus on the job left her exhausted by the end of the day. She did the reverse commute home, then stopped at the cheap bodega on the corner to buy a packet of hamburger meat and toothpaste. She prayed, as she climbed the five flights to her apartment, that Gigi wouldn't be home. She wanted a few minutes of peace, a few minutes alone with her thoughts. A few minutes with Joe. She had resolved, after this morning's encounter, to be more disciplined with her grief. She would restrict her thoughts to periods of true solitude. She couldn't risk being overheard by Gigi, even in the middle of the night. Which meant that from now on she would be truly alone with the snarled, lumpy mattress. The nights would promise nothing more than long, gray stretches of discomfort.

When she reached her floor, she was out of breath and near tears. The hall light had either gone out again, or one of the other tenants had stolen the bulb. This was far from inconceivable; the general population of the building appeared either down-and-out or somehow menacing. Lona was almost convinced, because of the late-night traffic, that her next-door neighbor was a drug dealer. She had considered, once or twice, asking him how much he charged for pot, but the prospect of speaking to him terrified her, and no matter how cheap it was, she still couldn't afford it.

She thought the hallway actually looked better in the dim light, less dirty and depressing, and that they should leave it this way. She pushed her hand through the contents of her purse, searching for her keys.

"I don't want to startle you," a voice said.

Her head snapped up, and she saw a man standing in front of her door. *Joe?* some small part of her brain thought, hopefully. But his voice was nothing like Joe's, and his shape was nothing like Joe's, and, as she drew closer, his face was nothing like Joe's either.

"Mr. Whiteson?"

"You look startled," he said apologetically.

Lona's mouth was suddenly too dry to talk.

"Hello," he said.

The last time Lona had seen him, he was leaving the Milledgeville cemetery. She was there to visit Joe's grave. She'd watched Melvin exit the grounds and make his way down the street. She stared at him to keep from looking down, to keep from throwing herself on top of the soft, warm dirt. She had used Melvin's presence to remind herself that she still belonged in the corporeal world. When he turned a corner and was out of sight, Lona left the cemetery too.

She had thought of him several times during the days of packing and moving that followed. She told herself that if Melvin could manage to walk across the grass and down the street after what he'd been through, then she could load up a car, and remember to check the tank for gas, and feed her daughter at regular intervals. She had used his image to keep her moving forward.

When Lona spoke, her voice shook. "I don't understand how you're here."

"I have something for you. Do you mind if I come inside for a moment?"

She mentally scanned her apartment. She had closed up the couch before she left this morning; she didn't think she'd left her bra or underwear looped over the oven handle to dry, but she couldn't be certain. She moved past Melvin and inserted her key in the lock. She noticed that her hands were shaking. She wondered if Gigi had been right and she was going crazy. Maybe she had moved beyond imagining Joe and was now imagining other people as well. But why Melvin Whiteson? Why would he be the one to follow on the heels of her beloved?

The silence was thick while she pushed the door open. Lona felt a wave of embarrassment. The apartment looked dingy and small. "Gigi?" she called.

No answer. *Thank God.*

Melvin seemed to tower next to the door. His clothes looked impossibly clean and well made against these surroundings. Lona found herself admiring the stitchwork in his coat. *I'm hopeless*, she thought. *This is hopeless.*

"Would you like something to drink?" she asked. "We have water, and milk, I think." She doubted that either of their two drinking glasses were clean.

"No, thank you."

She gestured at the couch. "Please, have a seat." She looked away, unable to watch him lower himself onto the monstrosity. She thought of all the exquisite furniture in the Whiteson house, but she could only allow herself to remember that house for a second. She couldn't afford to bring up those memories right now. They were dangerous. They had the power to suck her away from this room, drench her with sweat, and pummel her to the floor.

"Can I help you?" she asked.

He gave a smile so small it was barely a smile. "Please forgive me for the unexpected visit."

Lona nodded.

"I moved to the city when you did. I'm from here, so it made sense to come back." He shifted on the couch and reached into his coat pocket. He asked, in a businesslike tone, "How long are you planning to stay here?"

I should have offered to take his coat when he arrived, Lona thought, miserably. *He'd be more relaxed if he wasn't wearing his coat.* "I don't know," she said. "Awhile, at least. I have a job, and Gigi's in school."

He nodded. "I brought your check."

She stared at the envelope he had taken out of his pocket.

Melvin pulled himself up from the couch. "This is the full payment for your invoice." He glanced around the room. "You did the work, so it's only right for you to be paid."

"Thank you," Lona said, because she knew that was what she was supposed to say.

"Fair is fair," he said, and held out the envelope.

When she took it from him, their fingers touched for an instant. Lona remembered the line of Melvin's shoulders leaving the cemetery. She wondered what he was remembering. They both took a step away from each other. The silence was suddenly dense. Lona wondered which of them would break it, and what they might say. Anything seemed possible.

At that moment the front door swung open, and Gigi appeared. She was almost crouched under the weight of her book bag, and the hem of her blue jeans was ragged. Her eyes took in the scene, and flashed. Lona couldn't tell whether the look was one of fear, or anger.

"What the hell is this?" she asked.

Anger, Lona decided.

"This is Melvin Whiteson," she started. She felt flustered, and strangely guilty.

"I know *who* he is," Gigi said. "What's he doing here?"

Neither adult answered right away.

Gigi shook her head. "Are you going to sleep with him too?"

Lona's face burned. She didn't dare look at Melvin. "Go to your room," she said.

"Don't tell me what to do."

"Go to your room," she repeated.

"I was already on my way." The girl brushed past them, then slammed the flimsy piece of wood behind her.

The door to the hall was still open, and Melvin was moving through it. "I have to go," he murmured.

"I'm so sorry." Lona followed him into the hall.

Melvin's face looked drawn. "Don't worry about it."

Lona felt an unusual urge to talk, to keep him there a few seconds longer. "You didn't have to pay me," she said. "I didn't expect it."

"I could have put the check in the mail."

"Yes."

"I don't know why I thought it would be a good idea to come here."

Lona wanted to say something helpful, but she didn't know what that would be.

Melvin shook his head and turned away.

The tears were in her eyes again, but she wouldn't allow them to drop. Lona watched through a haze the line of Melvin Whiteson's back while he traveled down the hallway and disappeared into the dark cavity of the stairwell.

Cookie's mother was wearing her good white gloves. Her father was wearing a blazer. They stood framed in Cookie's doorway as if posing for a portrait.

"Take a shower and get changed, kitten," Big Mike said in a tone that barred any argument or compromise. "The three of us are going out."

Cookie noticed the deep lines beside her father's mouth and nodded.

During the drive, the scenery again imitated her puzzles. Fields, barns, horses, stretches of blue sky, puffy white clouds, and lakes passed her. Big Mike pressed down on the accelerator as they approached Andalusia. Cookie watched the driveway appear and disappear. The farmhouse wasn't visible from the road. Miss Mary's house was next.

"Lona and Joe worked in my house nearly every day," she said. "I saw them all the time, but I had no idea they were having an affair."

Daisy squinted over her shoulder. "No one did, baby. No one." She sighed. "What a terrible mess."

Cookie felt like she should have noticed. Her obliviousness bothered her. Surely she should have picked up on something? A furtive glance, an innuendo. A blushing cheek, or smudged lipstick. She had seen none of those things. She had never felt even the slightest twinge of discomfort or alarm around the couple. In fact, she had actively enjoyed their presence in the house; she'd liked coming home after a string of meetings and hearing soft voices in the study. She realized now that she had changed her mind on the curtains so many times partly just to keep them there. They had made the house feel full before Rose was born. It hadn't just been her and Melvin; it had been her and Melvin and their life, which burbled with kind voices and the possibilities of expensive fabric.

She had rarely connected Bill and Lona Waters in her mind. Bill was part of her work life, and Lona was part of her home. They were one of those couples that seemed to exist in separate states, perfectly respectable, but not joined at the hip. Still, they'd had a marriage and a house and a child, just like her.

Cookie watched a blank field pass by, a stretch of low grass and sky. Her father turned on the car radio. She tried to picture Bill in jail, locked behind bars. It was a difficult image to accept. Bill was so robust and strong, it seemed possible that he could pry the bars apart with his bare hands. Cookie watched him do so in her mind. His muscles strained the seams of his shirt, like a character from a comic book. His teeth were gritted and sweat swam out of his forehead.

Cookie laughed.

"What's so funny?" Daisy asked.

She shook her head.

Her father parked on the main street in Macon, and she followed her parents into a nondescript office building. Cookie decided that it must be a weekday, because several men on the sidewalk were wearing suits. This meant that her father had closed the store, which meant in turn that they were here to do something important, because Big Mike never closed his store. Cookie felt a twinge of concern. She checked her reflection in a storefront window. Her mother had straightened her collar and picked out her shoes before they left the house.

She was told to sit in a light gray waiting room while her parents went behind a dark door. Cookie tried to hear what they were saying, but their voices were only occasionally distinguishable.

"She was fine in the car," Daisy said. "You heard her, Mike. She sounded like her old self. We can't do this."

"Shaking," her father said. "A total recluse. She doesn't sleep. She wanders around in the dark."

"She's naturally thin . . ."

"Doctor, how long would she have to be there for?"

Their voices faded. Cookie leaned forward, trying to make out more words, but it was like trying to catch swimming fish with nothing more than cupped hands. Her mother's voice was tearful, her father's voice hard and low. Cookie told herself not to worry. She told herself to simply enjoy the familiarity of her parents' voices being lobbed back and forth, like tennis balls over a net. But the worry was inside her now, nibbling away at her ribs.

When Big Mike and Daisy appeared in the doorway, they were accompanied by a man in a white coat.

Cookie stood up. "Do you need to speak to me?"

The man raised his eyebrows. "No, I don't think that's necessary."

His deep voice was a surprise. How had Cookie not heard him through the door? She looked at her parents, but they avoided her eyes.

Cookie felt her hands begin to shake, so she hid them behind her back. "I know things haven't been ideal for a while," she said. "But there's no need for drastic steps. I think that after what happened, I deserve a little more time to pull things together."

The man paused before he spoke. "Your parents are understandably concerned about the path you're on."

Cookie looked at Big Mike and Daisy.

"You're a lucky girl to have them to take care of you."

This felt like an unnecessary insult, a blow out of nowhere. Did he not know her history? Did he not know what she'd lost?

"I'm not a girl," Cookie said.

"Now, now," the man said, and smiled.

Butterflies flocked through her middle, wings beating, another scene from another puzzle. She felt disoriented. She would never have believed that getting in a car with her parents could take her here.

"I'm sorry we wasted your time," Big Mike said to the doctor.

"Don't worry. It's a difficult decision to make."

"I'm just not convinced it's necessary," Daisy said.

The doctor looked at Big Mike. "Give me a call when you're ready to take the next step."

Cookie turned and stared out the window. They were on the fifth floor. Below was a busy street. People streamed by, talking and laughing. A car honked, the driver impatient with traffic. Cookie considered, for a moment, opening the window and sliding out. She wondered what kind of sound she would make when she hit the pavement.

Cookie left the house that night at the earliest possible opportunity. She knew her only hope of feeling safe was to be outside, surrounded by darkness. She savored the black, fragrant air, and soaked in the animal sounds: the cicadas, the owls, the insomniac dogs. Most of all, she appreciated the absence of people. Except for her encounter with Flannery, she was always alone at night. Her father was snoring by nine thirty, and her mother, if she was unable to sleep, did a good job of faking it. Cookie was free to leave by the front door, without fear of being stopped.

It seemed that everyone in Milledgeville was asleep by eleven. Every light was off, every car was neatly parked in its driveway. A few steps into the dimness—secure in the knowledge that no one was looking at her, no one was worrying about her, and no one was judging her—Cookie felt her body relax. Her gait changed. During the day she crept from room to room like an old woman; at night she strode down the streets.

She set about exploring the town with a thoroughness she hadn't brought to the task since childhood. She noticed the new juniper bushes a neighbor had planted, the fancy shutters at City Hall, the way the moon lit the graveyard tombstones. They looked like rows of street signs.

Under the warm light, it looked like each stone was inscribed with some kind of specific direction. *Turn right on Wilshire for good ribs. Wear socks to bed. Tell your children you love them every single day.*

Cookie never went close enough to the graveyard to inspect the fine print. She avoided that block, as well as the few stretches of forest that dotted the town. She preferred the tidy lawns to the clusters of trees that pressed together like adolescents up to no good. She spent a lot of time walking up and down the main street. It occurred to her, more than once, that she was hoping Flannery would reappear. She hadn't enjoyed their conversation, but it had offered a certain satisfaction. It had scratched at an itch deep inside her. She had appreciated how Flannery spoke to her, as if she were an equal. Her parents looked at her with fear and worry, and during her few trips out during the day, most townspeople chose not to meet her eyes. Flannery had looked straight at Cookie. She seemed, oddly, to *respect* her, in the way one weary soldier respects another, regardless of whether they fought on the same side.

That night, Cookie allowed herself to walk past her old house for the first time. She hadn't been there since the afternoon Rose died. She made her way slowly, aware of her heart doing heavy backflips in her chest. She counted her way down the block; the house was four driveways and three hundred steps from the corner. Cookie noticed the familiar visage of the broken-down Chevy across the street. The car's condition had always annoyed her. She remembered calling a contact at City Hall to complain about the eyesore, and telling the man that the decaying convertible brought down the value of the entire neighborhood. Now, though, in the moonlight, the dented metal looked almost pretty. It seemed amazing that recurring thoughts about having the car towed had kept her awake at night.

She stared at the car for a long time. When she finally mustered the courage to turn around, she found a different version of the house she had left months earlier. It looked dark and empty, like a pumpkin that had been hollowed out and allowed to rot. Not surprisingly, there had been little interest from buyers in a house that had been witness to a teenager's murder.

Cookie studied the structure, and had the sense that it was studying her in return. She felt like it had been waiting for her visit. She sighed, and the house—an amalgam of shadows—sighed too. She stepped onto the lawn. She took her sneakers off and stood on the ground in her bare feet. It had rained the day before, so the earth was soft. Mud squished between Cookie's toes. She felt herself sink slightly, as if she were taking root.

She picked up a smooth stone and passed it from one hand to the other. She liked the weight against her palm. Her eyes traced the outline of the house—the shingled roof, the ornate trim. She couldn't help but think of Melvin. She tried to picture him, standing on the front porch. She put his image together slowly, as if dictating his features to a sketch artist. His hair, which always looked mussed from driving with the car window down. His pale, serious face. His dark eyes.

When the picture of Melvin was complete, he looked like he belonged to the house. He was hollowed out, an abandoned human being. She wondered, had he always looked like that? If so, why hadn't she noticed?

Cookie shuddered and pulled back her right arm. The muscles in her shoulder stretched, creating an immediate ache. She was surprised, though, when her arm sprang forward. Cookie felt a strange, wonderful sense of release, and only then realized that the rock she'd been holding was flying through the air. She watched it arc and smash through Melvin's study window. The accompanying chime of shattering glass was incredibly loud.

Cookie stared at what she'd done, at the gaping hole she'd created. Was it possible that she had actually thrown a rock through a window? Wasn't that behavior reserved for delinquents?

After the initial shock, she scanned the lawn for another rock. She collected one and took aim. This time, the sweet release and clattering sound warmed her insides. Cookie ran across the walkway to a small pile of stones. She picked one up and threw it. Then another, and one more. God, this felt good. She laughed out loud, but the noise was swallowed by the breaking of windows. She tried to calculate how many windows the house had, and how long it might take her to smash them all.

Cookie was winded when she first heard a low growl enter the air. She headed for a large stone beneath one of the bushes. She weighed it on her palm. She sized up the remaining panes of glass and decided on her old bedroom. She lifted the rock and swiveled her body into the optimal position.

The growling grew louder, and stopped. Cookie was suddenly aware that she was no longer alone. A car door clicked open and shut behind her.

"Ma'am?" a voice asked. "What do you think you're doing?"

Cookie's arm was in full rotation. She released at the highest point and watched the rock somersault through the air. It rose up, then started to fall. It followed the natural path of any cannonball or rainbow. It was the rock's finishing place that set it apart. The stone thudded—creating the exact sound of disappointment—against the wooden shingles of the house. It missed the window by inches.

"No!" Cookie cried.

She was reaching down for another rock when the cop grabbed her arm.

"Let me go. I'm not done."

"Ma'am, you've got to stop. Do you even know what you're doing?"

Cookie turned to look at him. The cop looked very young, with pimples spread like a rash across his cheeks. Why would he ask such a stupid question?

She wriggled her body. "Let me go!"

"I can't allow you to do that."

"Yes, you can. This is my house. This is *my* house!" Cookie was aware that she was yelling. She missed the crackle of shattering glass. She wanted noise; she felt like she needed it, so she would provide it.

"You're disturbing the peace. Neighbors are calling the station. You have to come with me, right now."

Cookie pulled against his grip, but he was too strong. She had her eye on a perfect rock beside the front steps. She knew how to correct her aim; this time she would not miss.

The cop grunted with the effort of holding her back. "Stop it! Show some respect!"

This caught Cookie's attention. She thought it was interesting that he chose that word, since she had been thinking about respect, and soldiers, and Flannery. Or were those thoughts from another night? The darkness eddied through her mind like black water; nothing could be pinned down. She looked at the cop's speckled face again, and suddenly felt not old, but ageless, like a mountain. She felt like she had been alive so long that she was now possibly on her second or even third life. Those too ran together, like the nights.

She sought out the young man's eyes, which were green and uncertain. She thought: *You have no idea what's going to happen in your life. You're scared that you might end up like me, and you're right to be scared.*

"Let me throw one more," she said in what she hoped was a calm, persuasive voice. "Just one more. Then I'll go wherever you want."

The cop looked at the house. Cookie watched him note broken window after broken window. She watched him study each black, jagged hole in the black glass. She watched his face harden. His fingers dug into her skin. Cookie knew, as he half dragged her to the police car, that her arm would be lined with bruises by the time the sun rose.

"I'll come back!" she cried. "I'll come back and finish the job!"

"I doubt that, ma'am," said the cop. "I doubt that very much."

Gigi walked into the public library and asked for a part-time job. She did the same thing at the bodega on the corner, the record store down the street, and the local vegetarian restaurant. *I love to read*, she said. *I live for music. I'm a vegetarian.* She gave each establishment her phone number and went away. As soon as she got home, the vegetarian restaurant called. "Can you peel potatoes?"

"Yes."

"Because that would be your job, peeling potatoes. You want it?"

"Yes, sir."

During her first shift, her hand cramped, and her thumb developed an angry blister, but she went back the following afternoon, and the next. She worked with a double Band-Aid on her thumb and her long hair pulled back. She made a dollar fifty an hour, which she hid in her sock drawer. She had to do extra loads of washing in her building's creepy communal laundry room because she sweat through whatever she wore to the restaurant. The inconvenience was worth it, though. Every dollar she earned gave a small, unfamiliar thrill.

The degree to which she enjoyed the job surprised Gigi. She had sought it out as part of a muddled whim. She hated the hours spent in the apartment with her mother between school and bedtime, and she had come to the conclusion that she needed money, in case something happened. What that *something* might be, she wasn't sure, but she was aware that at the moment she would be helpless in the face of a catastrophe. And since she knew that catastrophes had a way of showing up out of nowhere, she decided to seek employment.

The fact that the job was the highlight of her day shouldn't have been too much of a surprise, considering the competition. From her first shift onward, Gigi spent her class time looking forward to the swampy air of the kitchen. School was nothing more than a place to be survived. She might have the courage to fight at home, but she wasn't dumb enough to try that tack at school. Instead, she tried to blend in to the point of invisibility, which in an institution that contained nearly a thousand teenagers, wasn't terribly difficult.

She wore her hair over her face, and stuck close to the walls as she made her way from room to room. The entire school smelled of cigarettes and grape soda. The floors were always sticky, despite being regularly mopped. Gigi's English class had forty-five kids in it, which meant the teacher was lucky if she got through roll call and announcing which page of *Romeo and Juliet* to turn to before the dismissal bell rang. The smokers raised their hands to use the bathroom at least three times per lesson, and in most cases, the teachers didn't say no. In Gigi's math class, half the students chatted to each other in Spanish while the teacher screeched chalk across the blackboard. There was a group of long-haired boys who never left the bench by the school's front door; despite being enrolled students, they appeared not to attend class at all.

In the days following President Kennedy's assassination that November, everyone showed up at school, but almost no one was where they were supposed to be. A group of senior boys commandeered the auditorium and reenacted the shooting, over and over. Girls packed the school's bathrooms, whispering and crying and fixing their makeup. Teachers smoked in the faculty lounge and didn't show up for their own classes.

One afternoon, Gigi was shoved out of the way by teachers who descended like a swarm of bees on two girls in a fistfight. When they were pulled apart, one girl had a bloody lip and the other a patch of raw pink scalp where hair had been torn from her head.

Gigi nearly ran to the restaurant when the final bell rang.

She scrambled onto her assigned stool in the back corner of the kitchen and picked up the dented, ancient peeler. The stool in front of her held an enormous pot for cleaned potatoes. Gigi dropped the peelings on the floor, and every few minutes an eight-year-old boy, the son of a cook, swept them away with a broom. When the pot was filled, it was immediately replaced with an empty one. Gigi moved her arm back and forth as quickly as possible, so that the peelings fell away like froth. Her shoulder ached, and her arm began to shake after a while, but there was peace in the motion; it allowed her to forget school, and her mother. It allowed her to forget about everything but the rote mechanics of her body.

The cooks in the kitchen seemed to speak every language except English, and though they frequently smiled at her, no one spoke to Gigi. She didn't mind this; in fact she appreciated it. She didn't want to talk. She was alone, but not lonely. She took a five-minute break every hour to use the tiny bathroom and drink a glass of water.

She wriggled her fingers when her hand cramped. She felt pearls of sweat pop out across her forehead as she chose another potato. She sweat continuously in the balmy air, and had to stop often to wipe her face with a dish towel. The temperature in the kitchen was a real force to be reckoned with; it leaned on her like a grizzly bear, big and heavy, occasionally swatting her with a giant paw. The heat loosened her muscles and her thoughts. The combination of physical fatigue and warmth led her to visit people and ideas and memories that she was usually careful to stay away from.

She daydreamed about her time at Miss Mary's farm. She remembered driving the tractor, or kicking her heels against the kitchen chair while Miss Mary stirred pots on the stove. She recalled the sensation of her hours there, the way she had always felt warm and safe and understood. She remembered the rainfall of Miss Mary's words: part gossip, part nonsense, part loving advice.

She wondered why she hadn't heard from her father since she left Milledgeville. He had sent her one note before his trial, which she'd ripped up without reading. Was he only willing to reach out once, before giving up on her for good? Was the tie between them that easily broken? Gigi rarely thought about him since moving to New York. Had she given up on him as well?

Gigi's output grew steadily. At first, she could only peel sixty potatoes an hour; soon, she was up to a hundred and fifty.

"Good job," the head cook said, in broken English. "You attack those potatoes real good."

"Thank you."

Gigi had canceled three appointments with the school guidance counselor. She had no idea how to talk about her future, which would officially start in a few short months when she graduated. She had always imagined spending her life in Milledgeville. After high school she would marry or get a job—whichever option seemed more appealing at the time—and she would attend club meetings with Miss Mary. She would eat dinner with her once or twice a week. When Gigi had children, Miss Mary would love them as if they were her own flesh and blood. In some of her daydreams, Gigi and her baby lived in the Treadle farmhouse.

She didn't know how to picture a different path. She literally didn't know how. Gigi sat with drenched hair and clothes on a rickety stool, wiping her vision clear with a towel, measuring her self-worth by how many potatoes she was able to peel. Still, this felt okay. It felt better than anything had for a while. She was on her own, and she was taking care of herself. She didn't need to figure out the future yet. It was enough to just get by.

When she left the kitchen, it was dark, or as close to dark as the city could ever manage with its streetlights and neon signs. It was raining, and while Gigi crossed the street, the rain turned to hail. Tiny shards of ice bounced off her shoulders and crunched under her feet.

Since starting her job, she always arrived home after her mother. Still, every night when Gigi entered the apartment, Lona looked startled.

There was a flustered expression on her face as if she'd forgotten, during the ten hours they spent apart, that she had a daughter.

With her first step inside, Gigi wished she were back at the restaurant, back on her stool. It didn't help to know that her mother felt the same way.

"Good night?" Lona said.

"Yes." She walked past Lona and closed herself in her room.

Gigi had just been paid; she took the worn bills out of her pocket and tucked them in her top dresser drawer. She dropped her heavy coat on the floor, creating small puddles of melted hailstones on the carpet. She climbed onto the bed, and did the same thing she did every night. She swept the stack of books and magazines from the side table onto the mattress. She liked to feel their weight beside her own.

She liked being surrounded by everything that Flannery had written. Gigi had read none of it before her arrival in New York. She had seen Flannery's new novel in a bookstore window and bought it with her first wages. The rest she had checked out of the school library, with the help of a kind librarian. The reading was not enjoyable—the librarian said, *You wouldn't want to take these to the beach*—but it felt important.

It also felt personal; she couldn't read the sharp, clean sentences without hearing them in Flannery's voice. Some of the characters made Gigi cringe, and she knew there were meanings and symbols that she wasn't grasping completely, but she pushed ahead regardless. Gigi read not only the books, but all the reviews and essays about Flannery that she could get her hands on. She felt like she was looking for something in particular; she read quickly, as if she were under a deadline.

The night before, she had finally found it. There was an essay in *Holiday* magazine that the librarian had ordered from another school. It was called "Living with a Peacock," and it was about Flannery's collection of birds. Gigi had already reread the piece to the point of memorization; the words made her feel like she was back at Andalusia. They re-created a world that felt more real than the one she lived in.

Gigi looked at Flannery's photograph now; it was printed beside the essay title. The image was the author from the shoulders up. She was smiling, but the expression in her eyes was skeptical. Flannery looked like she wanted to say to the photographer: *Please point that thing away from me*.

Gigi had just started to read when an unusual noise permeated the air. It took Gigi a minute to realize it was the phone; she couldn't recall it having rung before.

"Hello?" she heard her mother say, on the other side of the door.

Silence pulsed through the plaster and wood.

When Lona spoke again, her voice was lower. "Of course, Mr. Whiteson . . . Okay, Melvin, sure. I'll see you then."

Gigi felt a familiar kick of panic against her chest. She shivered in her damp clothes. What was her mother up to now? Gigi's eyes stayed on the essay. She didn't know where else to look, but her vision began to blur, threatening tears. She dragged her eyes from one word to the next. Flannery's writing was so strong that it made the birds come alive.

She described their haughtiness, their stiff gait, their penchant for eating her mother's flowers. She painted their feathers—green-bronze, clay-colored, and royal blue. She re-created their cries, which ranged from brays to heart-stopping screams to infants' howls. Gigi was glad to hear the birds again; she found the ruckus comforting. She listened to one bird bark in annoyance at another, and watched them bump chests, a physical warning to *back off*.

Gigi rolled over onto her side to watch. The peacocks gave a nod, pleased with the attention, and went back to their argument. Another bird hopped up on her desk and brushed her schoolbooks to the floor. The old, mud-colored peacock appeared in the corner. Gigi smiled in recognition; she had missed him. He looked at Gigi with kind eyes and matched her sigh with his own. He shook his head as more peacocks and peahens spilled into the cramped room. They pressed against Gigi's bed and rustled their feathers against the walls. They cooed and clacked and swayed their fat bodies. They rocked her mattress, gently, until the girl fell asleep.

Y ou're coming with me," Regina said. "I don't want any back talk."
Flannery laid down the book she was reading. She squinted
into the sun and her mother's flinty expression. She didn't want
to vacate her seat, much less the farm, but she also didn't want to antago-
nize her mother unless absolutely necessary.

She followed Regina across the lawn and climbed into the pickup
truck, an awkward maneuver that made her hips click with pain. She
pulled her crutches in behind her, and shut the door. "Where are we
going?"

"We have a few stops." Regina drove to the end of the driveway
and turned left. Then she turned left again. The Treadle farm appeared
before them.

Oh no, Flannery thought.

It was the first time she had laid eyes on the place since Joe's death,
and if she had been driven there blindfolded, she wouldn't have recognized it. The house appeared to be uninhabited. No lights were on; no
smoke rose from the chimney. The painted shutters were peeling. The
cast-iron pot beside the front door held nothing but weeds. The surroundings were quiet too; there was surprisingly little animal or tractor
noise coming from the fields.

They knocked and waited on the front stoop. Miss Mary was slow to appear, and slow to lead them inside. The three women sat together in the living room, a previously unused area of the house that Miss Mary had always claimed to dislike. The furniture had belonged to Miss Mary's parents; it was stiff and faded, scuffed in places. The air in the room was musty, like the inside of a coat closet. In the past, visiting had always taken place in the kitchen, but now the kitchen was dark and the oven turned off. The phone hung quietly on the wall.

Regina chatted about farmwork, and the weather, and the health of people they all knew. Flannery sat beside her mother, keenly aware of the sadness oozing from Miss Mary's pores. A cool, gray fog crossed the room and soaked Flannery's skin. She knew her mother wanted help sustaining the one-sided conversation, but Flannery felt unable to step in. She knew what it was to have a life, and then lose it. She wished she could tell Miss Mary that everything would be okay, but she didn't want to lie. Flannery, after her diagnosis, was still able to write. Miss Mary, after her loss, could no longer mother.

"You're going to waste away if you don't eat more," Regina said.

Miss Mary snorted. "Not likely." She had lost weight, though; her massive dress was no longer tight.

"You need to keep your strength up," Flannery said.

"What for?"

"Well, for one thing, Mr. Treadle needs you."

Miss Mary acceded this, with a small shrug. She looked past the fussy curtains on the windows, at the overcast sky. "He needs me . . . " she said, "to a degree."

The weather suddenly picked up, and a strong wind shook the house. The three women sat quietly, listening to the storm. Flannery thought about degrees of need. She thought of Melvin, and wondered to what degree he had needed her, if any. Had she needed him? There was a steady ache in her chest. She hadn't seen or spoken to him since he'd left the farm in the ambulance. Rose's funeral, to the relief of nearly every-one in town, had been a private, family-only affair. Flannery had wanted

Melvin's friendship, but had she needed it? Without food and water, you die, but to what degree do people need each other?

She gave a small shudder as rain pelted the window. The wet fog emanating from Miss Mary had soaked through her skin, into her bones. She didn't like to think about Melvin. Her thoughts slid again toward her own life ending. She was aware that such thoughts sat very close to her these days.

Regina's voice roused her. She was shocked to hear her mother's words, which seemed risky in the best of moments, and downright dangerous now.

"Did you hear that Gigi and Lona left town? Apparently, they drove away in the middle of the night."

Was this why her mother had brought her here today? Had she been afraid to bring up the subject alone? Perhaps Regina had been trying to find a way to mention Gigi for weeks, but chickened out every time.

Miss Mary touched her lips with her finger. Her eyes flattened. It was clear that she hadn't heard. News no longer stretched from town to the Treadle farmhouse, because when it did, it was turned away at the door.

"You could send her a letter, you know." Regina leaned forward. "She didn't do anything wrong in all this. She was like a child to you."

The skin on Miss Mary's face turned pale and doughy, and her eyes looked like they belonged to someone else. They might have belonged to one of the unhappiest, and meanest, of Flannery's characters. The large woman waited a moment for the noise of the storm to abate.

"I only had one child," she said. "And he's dead."

Regina and Flannery were silent as they left the house, and silent during the drive to town. They stopped at the supermarket, library, and post office. Flannery was accustomed to receiving looks and inspiring whispers behind cupped hands, but Rose's death had upped the ante. Everyone wanted more information about the accident at the farm. They wanted to know the nature of the relationship between Flannery and Melvin Whiteson. They wanted to know why Regina hadn't stepped in.

They wanted to know why no one had kept a closer eye on that sweet baby girl.

The increased attention made Regina bullish. "What are you looking at?" she said to an old couple at the bakery. "If you have something to say, then say it." The couple hurried away, shaking their heads.

At the post office, they shipped a package to Aunt Katie in Savannah. As they were driving away, they got stuck at the traffic light in front of the bank. Regina touched the horn in the middle of the steering wheel, but didn't apply pressure.

Flannery had stood with Cookie in the middle of the night on this same stretch of road. She wished it were dark now; she wished she didn't have to keep squinting into the sun, which after the brief thunderstorm, seemed to be chasing her across the sky.

"That's enough," she said in a sharp voice, when Regina took a turn away from the direction of the farm. "I need to go home."

"One more stop."

Flannery pursed her lips while her mother parked in front of the church.

Regina opened her door. "Come on."

"I'll wait here."

"Father Cole is expecting us."

Flannery looked at her. "For what?"

Regina returned her stare. "Confession."

Flannery felt despair roll like a snowball through her insides. The ball gained weight and mass until it was a freezing white boulder that blocked up her throat and made it hard to breathe. A few days later, she would look back at this moment and recognize it as a medical symptom.

She coughed, and considered trying to explain herself to her mother. She could say that walking inside this church and kneeling in the confession booth would change nothing. She could explain that God was no more here than he was in any other place. She could tell Regina that the only presence in this small, picturesque church was Father Cole: a kind, slightly myopic man who missed his twin sister in Missouri so badly he put a letter to her in the noon post every single day.

She knew, however, that offering these explanations was futile, as pointless as dumping freshly made soup down the drain. In Regina's black-and-white world, there were only two options: she could say no, or she could get out of the car.

Instead, she asked a question. "Why does this bother you so much?"

"What?"

"The fact that I don't want to go to church."

"Because." Regina's heart-shaped face—which had been considered beautiful in her youth—tightened. "Because . . . it doesn't just concern you."

"What do you mean?"

"You're a strong personality, Flannery. You ought to be, you're my daughter, after all. But you're being selfish, letting yourself get caught up in this . . . this whirlpool of negative stuff. I was there that day too. I live with you, young lady. We're together day and night, seven days a week. I might be strong, but I'm older now." She stopped. "I can't live with you this way for much longer."

Flannery looked away, out the window. "You're afraid you'll get sucked into my whirlpool? That you'll stop believing?"

She felt her mother's nod, rather than saw it.

The pressure on Flannery's chest deepened. This made sense to her. She could see the risk to Regina, and she could feel the extent of her own selfishness. Her ego was large; she knew that to be successful as a writer this needed to be the case, but that didn't mean she liked it. And right now, she felt very clearly that she didn't like herself.

She climbed out of the truck. She could talk to a nice man for a few minutes and then go home. She could play the game, to make her mother happy. She wasn't going back on her principles, or compromising her beliefs. She no longer had any.

She favored her right hip as she made her way to the door. She had taken this walk hundreds of times before. She had run up the path as a child. She had slid down the front banister once and been yelled at by an elderly aunt. She sat in these pews beside her father during his last year. She had loved those moments. During mass, she held her father's hand and rested her head against his shoulder. She pretended that he wasn't sick, that he wasn't going to die. She told herself that she would hold his hand every Sunday until she grew up, moved away, and started a family of her own. These foggy daydreams, mixed with the priest's booming voice and the feel of her father's hand wrapped around hers, had made her love church long before she understood the stories or anything about God. She had always felt safe, loved, and even hopeful, here.

She sighed as she climbed the steps, good hip followed by bad hip, crutches tucked beneath her arms. She could tell her slowness irritated Regina, who was holding the door open.

"I'm so glad to see you, Flannery," she heard Father Cole say. "I've missed your face on Sunday mornings."

She was in the church now. The sun was finally out of sight, which meant she could stop squinting. She was overcome by a powerful yearning for her father. She wanted him to walk out of the shadows and take her hand.

"Are you all right?" Father Cole asked.

She tried to keep her voice steady. "My mother can go first. I'd like to sit down for a minute."

He looked confused. "Go first?"

"For confession. Isn't that what we're here for?"

"I gave confession on Saturday," Regina said.

Flannery was hit by an unexpected flash of rage; a roaring noise filled her ears. She spoke through gritted teeth. "What, and you haven't sinned since then?"

Her mother stared at her.

"How about tricking your daughter into going places against her will? Isn't that worth a Hail Mary?"

"Mary Flannery O'Connor, not inside the church!" Regina looked shocked. The apostles, lined up on the stained-glass windows behind her, looked shocked.

"I'm sorry," she said. "I'm sorry." She lowered her head, waved a crutch at the priest, and followed him behind the red velvet curtain.

Once there, settled in the cloaked darkness, she was quiet. She felt strangely emotional. She felt like she had taken on Miss Mary's sadness, and the morbid curiosity of the couple at the bakery, and the dipping blood pressure of her father.

She said, "This is a waste of your time."

Father Cole's voice came from behind the wooden panel. "If you don't mind, I'll be the judge of that."

Flannery wished she could leave, just climb behind the wheel of the truck and drive. She thought about her encounter with Cookie. She remembered not the substance of the conversation, but the pin-drop quiet of the air around them.

"How's your sister?" she asked, thinking, *Let's get this over with*.

She could hear the smile in the priest's voice. "Very well, thank you. She had a bumper crop of strawberries this year. When she sends me a case of jam, I'll give you a couple jars."

"That sounds nice." Flannery made a face at the red curtain. She felt adolescent suddenly; as a fifteen-year-old she had spent confession making scuff marks on the floor with her shoes while fabricating a string of innocent lies. *I didn't take out the garbage even though my mother told me to. I thought a mean thought about my math teacher. I fibbed about brushing my teeth last night.* She had enjoyed the lies, and the long streaks that stretched across the cement floor when she left the booth.

"Flannery?"

"Yes?"

"Do you want to tell me why you haven't been to church since the accident?"

Alone in the curtained box, she gave a wry smile. "The accident?"

269

"Wasn't it an accident?"

"I don't know. I don't think of it that way." She waved her hand. "I shouldn't be here now."

"Why not?"

"I should be at home, writing."

There was a silence. "It was kind of you to come here for Regina."

Flannery shrugged and looked down at her weak legs. She had fainted a few days earlier while throwing seeds to a pocket of squalling peacocks in the backyard. She had opened her eyes to see a pale sky and the looming silhouette of the water tower. A chicken twittered next to her head. She heard her birds tapping across the earth she was lying on. She tried to sit up and found that she could. Flannery had climbed to her feet, grateful there were no witnesses, grateful that her mother had been spared the sight of her crumbling to the ground.

Father Cole said, "I hear you've been doing a lot of things for other people lately."

"Excuse me?"

"You gave Gigi Waters somewhere to go, in the weeks before she left town."

"Yes, but when she came to me asking for more, I said no."

"You drove Cookie Whiteson home in the middle of the night, when she was out wandering the streets."

"How did you hear about that?"

"You visited Miss Mary today. And came here for your mother."

"Gracious," Flannery said. "You missed your calling. You should have been a spy, Father."

There was a light chuckle through the wooden panel. "A priest hears many things, and I've had years to observe you, child. I want to tell you something. May I?"

"Go ahead."

"It's not your fault that Rose Whiteson died. Accidents just happen. And, Flannery, even if you do hold some small parcel of responsibility, as all of us do from time to time, God will forgive you if you ask him."

"That's not saying much."

"Pardon me?"

Her mouth twisted; she tried to keep her voice polite. "God will forgive any fool as long as he asks nicely."

She closed her eyes, and tried to conceive of the event on her lawn as an accident. An accident was when you spilled milk. An accident was when you confused two relatives' birthdays and forgot to send a card. An accident was when you lost control of the steering wheel and drove into a tree. As far as Flannery was concerned, an accident was something you walked away from. Words mattered to her, as did accurate definitions, and what happened on her lawn had not been an accident.

"You need to stop punishing yourself," the man said.

She felt another surge of anger. Another yearning for her father. Another wish to be behind the wheel of the truck, driving fast. "If I were punishing myself, I would have stopped writing. I tried to do that, but I couldn't." She paused. "So please don't pretend that I'm martyring myself somehow. I may be unhappy, I may be behaving a little differently, but I'm just fine. Don't feel sorry for me."

She shifted her weight on the thin seat. She was supposed to kneel, but that wasn't possible for her. She'd always figured that the kneeling was intended to keep you just uncomfortable enough that you had to pay attention, and since she was uncomfortable all the time, she was already fulfilling the requirement. "Really," she said, "I'm the last person you should feel sorry for."

"Is that so? Who is it that *you* feel sorry for?"

Flannery shrugged. She was done talking. She knew this as surely as if a switch had been flipped inside her. She had no more words.

"If you won't forgive yourself, and you won't allow yourself to ask for God's forgiveness, then maybe you should seek forgiveness from that person."

271

That person, Flannery repeated dully, in her head.

In her past experience, confession always ended with an assignment of Hail Mary or the Lord's Prayer. *Make your way through the rosary beads*, Flannery had often been told. She had never argued, or ignored the task. After all, it was no trouble. Reciting the prayers was as easy as brushing her teeth or waking up in the morning. The words were as familiar to her as drawing breath. She could literally deliver them in her sleep.

She had always secretly considered confession to be a lazy affair. Sin, be forgiven, then perform an incredibly simple task in penance. It was another flaw, as far as she was concerned, in an ancient practice. Flannery waited now for the priest to fall back on his training. For him to reduce their meeting to the usual narrative arc and tell her that her problems could be solved by a bout of tired worship. But the black-clad man was quiet too, so after a few minutes Flannery struggled to her feet and shoved the curtain aside.

Melvin arranged to meet Lona at a bar in midtown. The bar was one of those New York establishments that seemed to have existed forever. Its dark and quiet met the needs of every generation; there was no call for it to transform into something new, no reason for it to try to reflect the times. It was a place for hushed tones and privacy, a place to hide without being alone. Melvin had been there as a young man, and it was the first place that came to mind when Lona asked for an address.

She was standing just inside the door, looking unsure, when he arrived.

"Thank you for meeting me," he said, and led the way to a small booth in the back corner.

"Of course."

"I thought you might have plans, at such short notice."

She settled in across from him. "No," she said. "No plans."

A waitress appeared and asked for their order.

"Scotch," Melvin said.

"I'll have the same," Lona said.

They didn't speak until the drinks arrived. Melvin didn't think the silence was awkward; he hoped it wasn't. He knew it was his responsibility to talk, but he didn't feel up to it yet. He looked around the dim room and considered how sometimes shadows are exactly what a person wants. Swathes of darkness are generally given a bad reputation, but in truth, a well-placed shadow can be a gift.

He took a large sip of the dark drink and let it burn down his throat. He felt relieved to be here, glad he wasn't alone.

"How's your daughter?" he asked. He knew immediately he should have chosen a different word. "Daughter" hurt.

Lona held her glass with both hands. "She's fine, I think. She got a job at a restaurant, in the kitchen." She paused. "She hates me."

Melvin wasn't sure what to say to this. He tried to imagine Rose, grown up and angry, but it was impossible. All he could picture was Cookie. He took another drink to clear the image.

"I'm sorry," Lona said. "I shouldn't have said that. Pretend I didn't."

"You could talk to her," Melvin said. He wanted to be helpful. "Try to explain yourself."

She sighed heavily. "I have."

Melvin lifted and then dropped his shoulders. He hoped the gesture conveyed that if he had another, better suggestion, he would offer it. He had none, and truly, he was in no position to offer advice. Surely she realized that.

"I've never had one of these." Lona touched the rim of her glass with her finger.

"Never?"

"Bill didn't drink, so we never had anything in the house." She looked around the dark room. "I used to go to bars with my father when I was a kid, but that was just to make sure he got home all right."

Melvin considered the woman across from him. He realized that he didn't know anything about her, beyond the information that had been made public about her affair with Joe. He knew about the most dramatic period in her life, but nothing else. He decided that he was fine with this. He didn't particularly want to hear about her childhood, her family, or her marriage. As far as he was concerned, she had only one story. He figured that everyone had, at best, only one big story in his or her life; a story that rendered everything else a footnote. Melvin's story—maybe even just that one afternoon with Rose at Andalusia—overshadowed the rest of *his* life.

He realized Lona was talking again, and struggled to listen.

She said, "I made some beautiful curtains for your house."

"Excuse me?"

"The curtains? The ones I made?" She looked embarrassed. "I'm sorry," she said. "I'm no good at small talk."

He shook his head. "No, no, I was just distracted. I liked the curtains in my study very much."

She appreciated the compliment. "Those were my favorite."

Melvin remembered hiding behind the dark velvet curtains in the days following Rose's death. He tried to remember which curtains had hung in the upstairs guest room, where Joe had been shot. They must have been white. The entire room was white until the boy's blood stained the bed, and more of his blood was tracked across the floor. That room had been the last place Melvin visited before leaving the house, but still, he couldn't picture the curtains.

"I was surprised to hear from you," Lona said. "I thought after what happened when you stopped by, I'd never see you again."

Melvin heard himself ask, "Did you want to?"

"Yes."

"Why?"

Now it was Lona's turn to shrug. She didn't look embarrassed; she looked like she simply didn't know the answer.

He took another long sip of his drink. What was he doing? Why was he here? He hadn't had a drink since leaving Milledgeville, and his head was beginning to feel funny. *What do you know?* he asked himself. *Make sense of this.* He knew what had spurred him to call Lona. He did know that. The answer was folded in his inside pocket. He took it out now and looked at it.

She asked, "Is that a letter?"

He nodded.

She looked at him politely, waiting for more information. He noticed that her drink was nearly finished. He gestured to the waitress for another round. He fingered the yellow stationery. The paper was smooth; it felt worn to the touch, even though he had received it in the mail that afternoon and read it only once.

"Do you want to show me?" Lona's voice was gentle.

Melvin felt a pulse of relief in his chest. *Yes.* He didn't want to talk about it. He pushed the letter across the tabletop.

He closed his eyes. It wouldn't take her long to read the words. His ex-wife's second letter was only three lines long.

"Is this true?" Lona asked, after a pause.

He nodded, and reached his hand back out. It seemed wrong to leave Lona with the letter. He should hold it; it was his; it was directed at him. He had needed that moment of relief, but he didn't deserve anything more. The letter belonged in his chest pocket as a burning, painful reminder of everything he had done wrong.

Lona didn't seem to notice the outstretched hand. "Cookie sounds angry," she said, studying the text.

"She is."

Melvin remembered driving past the mental hospital with Flannery and thinking that it looked like a huge tombstone. He had asked her not to take that route anymore, and she ignored him. They had circled past the quiet building with its untidy lawn time and time again. The image was seared into his memory, tied to Flannery and the relief of those drives, and the guilt that had dribbled up and down inside him.

"This is terrible. What are you going to do?"

"What do you mean?"

"Are you going to go see her?"

An unpleasant taste materialized in Melvin's mouth. He tried to imagine visiting Cookie in a mental hospital. He pictured inmates lunging at him in the halls, and his ex-wife in a straitjacket, shrieking that it was all his fault.

He put his forehead in his hand. "You should give me the letter now," he said.

"Are you all right?" Lona touched his arm.

"Usually," he said.

They both took sips of their drinks. Melvin was trying to clear the rotten taste out of his mouth, and the scotch seemed to be helping. His mind traveled from Cookie's place of residence to his own. His New York apartment was a string of dark, well-decorated rooms. With the exception of the Realtor, no one had set foot in the apartment since he had moved in. His neighbor—a stocky, elderly woman—had tried to step inside as she welcomed him to the building, but Melvin had physically blocked her path. He had searched his brain for polite phrases that would send her away. When she finally left, his heart knocked with relief, and he triple-locked the door.

He cleared his throat and looked at the woman across from him. She was fingering the yellow stationery now, a pained expression on her face. Melvin felt a surge of gratitude toward her. For meeting him here. For holding the letter like that. For wearing that expression.

"I have to be at work early in the morning," she said.

"I'll ask for the check."

She nodded.

They struggled into their coats and stumbled into the dark night. The sidewalk was empty of people; it was late. Melvin held up his hand and a taxi stopped in front of them.

They both stared at the yellow car as if they didn't know what to make of it. "Thank you for meeting me," Melvin said.

"Sure." Lona turned toward him.

She reached her arms out, and again Melvin found himself confused. He stepped into the space she'd created. He embraced her, and felt a hard pressure behind his eyes. *Am I going to cry?* he wondered, in surprise. He hadn't cried in years. He hadn't cried for Rose. Was he really going to cry now?

He breathed in the smell of her hair. "I didn't have an affair with Flannery," he said. "I know people thought I did, but I never touched her."

Lona pulled back and looked at him. "Do you wish you did?"

He shook his head, his thoughts muddied by the scotch and the icy air and the threat of gulping sobs taking him over and drowning him. "It would have been more honest, maybe. I don't know."

The taxi driver honked his horn, and Lona hurried into the backseat. Melvin shut the door, and, just like that, she was gone.

At lunchtime, the hospital reminded Cookie of high school. When the bell rang, the patients made their way through linoleum hallways to the cafeteria. They took trays and stood in line. They chose between meatloaf and chicken, between mashed potatoes and collard greens. Dessert was always red Jell-O or a slice of dry yellow cake. Once their trays were full, the men and women chose seats at long rectangular tables. As in high school, where the cool kids, athletes, and nerds claim their own designated spaces, here the most competent patients sought each other out and sat side by side.

Lunch was the only time of day when Cookie felt remotely like herself. She had thoughts, even if they were as mundane as whether the meatloaf was as good as the week before. In fact, all her thoughts were mundane. They seemed stapled to the here and now. Cookie was in a fog before lunch, and she would descend back into one after the meal. Merely having the thought that the cafeteria lady's hair was a pleasing shade of blue felt like a cool breeze on her face. She felt conscious and alive.

She picked at her food, and eyed the small paper cup filled with pills in the corner of her tray. A nurse had placed them there, and a nurse would make sure she had swallowed each one when the lunch period ended. Some of the pills were the size of Cookie's thumbnail; she felt that she had to save room in her stomach for them. Ingesting these hard nuggets every few hours felt unnatural, as if she were swallowing screws and bolts from her father's hardware store.

She was turning as hard and brittle as her tablets. She had caught a glimpse of her reflection in a bathroom mirror, and her face was composed solely of sharp edges. Her body was a rattle bag of collarbones and elbows. When her mother visited on Sundays, Cookie could see the horror in her eyes. Daisy had stopped hugging her. She spoke to her daughter from across the room, as if she feared Cookie might break if she came any closer. Her father couldn't even bear to come inside; he waited in the car.

Cookie didn't think about her parents during lunch. Nor did she think about her fragile frame. She thought about the pills because they were right in front of her. She thought about how many more bites she could manage of the meatloaf. She looked up when the nurse said, *It's time*. She tipped her head back and swallowed. She was led back to her room, where she sat on a metal chair by the window. She didn't remember, or even think, after that. Late in the afternoon, the doctor with the low voice appeared and talked to her. Cookie didn't respond to his questions, and he left. Dinner was delivered, with another cup of pills. She didn't eat any of the food. There were more pills before bedtime, and then she slept. Waking up felt like stepping from one foggy shore to another. The morning involved a bath, supervised by a nurse. Cookie dressed and then sat by the window until the lunch bell rang.

During the walk down the plain hallway, her head began to clear. She looked at the patients who were not permitted to eat in the cafeteria. They were the faces pressed against small, square windows. They were the ones screaming and thumping behind locked doors and cement walls. They were the ones whose whimpering stopped Cookie in her tracks, her hands clutched to her chest.

These sounds caused Cookie to regret her moments of clarity. The whimpering cut through the insulating fog. It was the sound of Rose crying herself to sleep. Rose in her position of resistance, her small bottom pushed up in the air, her fists dug into the mattress. Tears leaking across flushed cheeks, hoping that her mother or father would come running. Cookie wanted to run to her now. She wanted to rip these walls down with her bare hands and find her daughter. She wanted, yearned, and ached to hold her, to shush her, to wipe away her tears. She wanted to tell her that everything would be all right, that Mama was here.

Cookie stood in the hallway, wearing slippers and an oversize pink gown. She radiated pain. Sometimes the pain was so extreme that she felt she would rather submit herself to physical torture than endure it any longer; at least the torture would occupy her mind. She was surprised when her body started to move, as if of its own accord. *Get out of here*, her bones, muscles, and tendons seemed to say. *Just get out of here.* She walked forward, until the sound was gone, until she was in a large room that clattered with silverware and was bused by women in crisp white dresses and hats.

She was in her seat, holding the small cup in her hand, peering down at the nuts and bolts the doctor said were making her well—*She'll get worse before she gets better*, she had heard him warn her parents—when the nurse beside her spoke.

"Those ain't going to turn into no chocolate milkshake no matter how hard you stare. You might as well just swallow and be done with it."

Cookie turned her head. The nurse's hair was gray in spots, as if she'd been splashed with paint. She had a thin, long nose that reminded Cookie of a horse she used to ride as a child.

"I won't be *done* with it," she said. "I'll have more pills in a few hours."

The nurse's voice hardened. Her eyes looked tired. "Don't overthink it, child. Just swallow."

Cookie emptied the contents of the small paper cup into her mouth, and returned her tray to the kitchen. During her walk through the long halls, her thoughts skittered toward and then away from Rose like nervous mice. The patients were quiet now; no more cries could be heard..

When she pushed open the door to her room, she sensed the room wasn't empty. She looked around the white space. Her eyes passed the window twice before she realized that there was a woman standing next to it.

Flannery gave a nod. Her crutches were propped against the wall. "I hope you don't mind," she said. "I wanted to see you again."

Cookie studied the woman: her tilted frame, her glasses, her lips that were pressed together in such a way that had to involve constant effort.

"Are you real?" Cookie said.

"As far as I know."

"You don't look well."

Flannery's face appeared slightly swollen, and her skin was an off color. Her mouth twisted. "Thanks."

Cookie sat down on the chair by the door, the chair the nurse occupied when she decided the patient needed company, or perhaps surveillance. She was aware that she was glad to see Flannery. This was the visit she had been waiting for, ever since their midnight encounter on the street. Further conversation with the writer felt inevitable, even necessary, though she couldn't have explained why.

"I only just heard about you . . . about this." Flannery waved her hand at the room. "I had to have an operation, and my mother was apparently trying to protect me. Or spare me, I'm not sure which. In any case I was . . ." Flannery hesitated, "I was very sorry to hear what happened."

"Me too," Cookie said.

There were footsteps in the hall and the crackling of a fluorescent light. Flannery looked uncomfortable, propped up against the wall.

"Why don't you sit down," Cookie said.

"I don't want to waste your time."

Cookie thought this was funny, so she laughed. The noise rattled and disappeared in the air.

Flannery opened her mouth, then closed it. She shook her head.

"What?"

"This is difficult for me." Flannery spoke quickly. "Not that that matters, in the scheme of things. I'm stubborn and set in my ways and I prefer to work things out on my own. But there's something I should have said to you months ago." She touched her crutches lightly, as if to check that they were still there. She shook her head again. "I never thought I'd get so tied up with other people," she said in a different tone. "I thought I'd given that up years ago, when I was first diagnosed."

Cookie thought about her own diagnosis, which was listed on her entrance form as "mentally unstable." She wondered how long she would be sick. She wondered what wellness would feel like, if and when it returned to her. She imagined it being delivered in a garment bag, like a brand-new dress. She would unzip it and ooh and ahh before trying it on for size.

"I should have sent Melvin away," Flannery said. "I knew it was wrong for him to visit without your knowledge. I just didn't believe that any harm would come of it."

A light in the hall buzzed and zapped. The noise made both women jump.

"But it did," Cookie said.

"It did."

No one said anything for a few minutes. Cookie didn't feel strong enough to speak, and Flannery looked even weaker than her. Cookie had been angry for months, but she couldn't find any anger now. She thought of Rose, and how these thoughts were a new development. In the period following her daughter's death, Cookie had never allowed herself to picture her baby. Now it was as if the thought of Rose was always with her. She wasn't sure if this was a good change, or a bad one.

"You're dying," she heard herself say. "Aren't you?"

Flannery shrugged.

Cookie kept her eyes on the woman's face. In the past, she remembered being uncomfortable making extended eye contact. She had always looked over a room while speaking to someone: at the couch, out the window, at a tiny stain in the carpet. Now, her gaze was still; it felt rooted She said, "I always envied you. Even when I was a child, I envied you."

Flannery made a small noise in the back of her throat. "Why would you do that?"

The fog was beginning to creep across Cookie's brain. With concentration, she held it off, but the effort was wearing. "Because of your certainty." She paused. "You seemed to know what you were doing. And you didn't care what anyone thought."

A nurse's face appeared in the small square window in the door, then disappeared.

"That's in the past tense," Flannery said.

"You're not better than me." Cookie issued this as a fact, not an accusation.

"I know."

Cookie closed her eyes. She took a deep breath, and her body shuddered. When she opened her eyes, she met Flannery's gaze. The two women looked at each other for a long moment.

"Can I ask you a question?" Cookie asked.

Flannery nodded.

"I need to know if you're going to write about what happened at your house." Cookie paused, and wondered if she needed to say more. She needed to know if her lost life—her loss—was going to be typed onto a page. She felt that she deserved to know. She wanted, somehow, to be part of the decision.

Flannery was quiet. Her face twitched a couple of times. "No," she said finally. "No, I won't." Her voice was quiet. She looked like she could say more, but had decided against it.

"Good."

There was quiet again while both women recovered.

Flannery stood up straighter; she tried to reach for composure. "I thought I would be the one who ended up here." She paused, then said in a low voice, "If I could, I would switch places with you. You don't deserve this."

There was a growl in Cookie's chest. She almost rose out of her chair. "Don't say that," she said. "You don't owe me anything. You certainly don't owe me that."

"I should go," Flannery said, but she didn't move from her place by the window.

It came to Cookie slowly, what Flannery wanted, but wouldn't, or couldn't, ask for. Strangely, the knowledge felt like she was being thrown a rope. If she grabbed hold, would she be able to save herself?

"I forgive you," she said. "Okay? I forgive you for everything. Is that what you want?"

She was surprised when Flannery started to cry. It was like seeing a mountain cry, or a street sign. Flannery and tears did not go together. The eruption was rough and messy and hard to watch. Cookie felt all the cracks and bumps and bruises within herself as she made her way across the room. She didn't know what else to do, so she held the woman's hand until the moment passed.

Flannery was sitting in the doctor's waiting room after another round of blood tests when the image of a shoeless man filled her head. He was lying on his stomach on a table. She thought at first that it was an exam table, and that the man was in the hospital, but then a bearded fellow, who was clearly not a doctor, leaned over him and pressed a silver pen into his skin. The man grunted and let out a sigh of what sounded like relief. He gripped the table with both hands. His eyes were hard and desperate. He looked like he wanted to find a way out of his own body.

Flannery ached for her typewriter. Sitting here was a waste of time. She rubbed her hands against her skirt. "Have you got any paper?"

"Certainly not," her mother said. "Why would I have paper?"

"I don't know. To write a note, or a list."

Regina shook her head. "Don't be ridiculous."

"I wasn't aware I was being ridiculous."

"Well, you are."

The nurse waved at them from behind her desk. "He's ready for you now, ladies."

The doctor gave them the bad news as soon as they walked through the door. He spoke through nearly closed lips. The lupus was back.

"It's like a sleeping volcano," he said. "You don't want to do anything to piss it off. And the operation pissed it off."

"She's beaten it back before," Regina said quickly.

"Yes, she has."

"She'll do it again."

Flannery felt her mother's eyes drill into her. She nodded in a show of agreement. She had beaten it back before.

The days peeled back to reveal a scorched earth and blanched sky. The peacocks whinnied and cackled complaints about the heat. There were constant warnings of drought on the radio. *Restrict water use*, the black box in the kitchen told them. *Take showers, not baths. Do not water your lawn. Give the livestock only as much to drink as they absolutely need. Unless you are planning to sell your animals, do not wash them.*

"If you want to take a bath," Regina said, "you take a bath."

Flannery almost smiled. This comment furthered her suspicion that she and her mother were trying to protect each other. *I'll be fine*, she told Regina, whenever her mother seemed uneasy. *You'll be fine*, Regina told her, her eyes like anvils, every single day. But for Regina to suggest something as hedonistic and impractical as a bath during a drought, things must be bad.

Most of the time, Flannery felt like she was treading water, trying to keep her head above the surface. The effort required was almost too much. She was exhausted, and needed up to fifteen hours of sleep every night. She started a new medication, which affected her appetite. Her favorite meals suddenly tasted metallic. Her hands were always clammy, despite the heat. Her face became even more swollen. What Miss Mary referred to as "life lines" were smoothed from her skin, and when Flannery looked in the mirror, a younger version of herself stared back. *How ironic*, she thought.

Her fingers pummeled the typewriter keys. If she had the strength to leave her bed, she was at her desk. The story was almost done. The man on the table was receiving a huge tattoo, large enough to cover his entire back. He was enthralled and disgusted by his wife, whose sharp words dug into him like scalpels. Flannery followed the story backward to uncover how they'd first met, then further back, to when the man was a boy and he had seen his first tattoo at a circus. It took her a while to realize that his new tattoo was of Christ. *Idolatry!* his wife cried.

Flannery spent her afternoons motionless in her porch chair, watching the peacocks stalk the lawn. The birds soothed her; their bright colors and disdainful expressions were precisely what she wished to see. Flannery held her breath when a peacock opened his feathers into a blistering rainbow. She exhaled only when he shut it back down. A fierce blue fan was revealed, then an auburn one. The long feathers were decorated with moons and suns and peering eyes. These displays were more frequent than usual. The birds were generous with Flannery, seeming to sense her need for beauty. She dreamed about them at night—they crowed and bullied and flaunted their coats across her consciousness.

One Sunday morning, she found herself getting dressed to leave the farm. She stood in front of her closet and tried to steel herself to face people. She had let herself grow soft and vulnerable lately—surrounded by her birds and pills, filled with her stories—but she was capable of resurrecting her tough exterior. She surveyed her hats, and chose one that would cover as much of her swollen face as possible.

She met her mother by the car.

Regina beamed with approval. "Just out of curiosity," she said. "Why now?"

"I couldn't say," Flannery replied.

It was true; she couldn't. Perhaps she was returning to the church simply because she no longer had the energy to fight her upbringing and a lifetime of belief. Perhaps it was because she had finished the story about the tattooed man, but the image on his back remained in her thoughts. She didn't give the reasons much thought, though; she just returned, like a duck returns to water.

Flannery didn't pay attention to Father Cole's sermon that morning. Instead, she spent the mass praying for the people she cared about. She had done this in the past, but only occasionally, and out of a sense of duty. Now each name counted, each name meant something, each name beat inside her like a heart.

In late June, she fainted in the kitchen. She hit her head on the table, and the resulting cut splattered blood across the linoleum floor. Her mother's shouts competed with the loud hum of the refrigerator. Flannery looked at the pattern of blood—it reminded her of a peacock's outstretched fan—and felt a pressure inside her release. Her words, and her tenacious resolve, seeped like water down an internal drain. She was still herself; she was still Flannery, but she knew, and finally accepted, that her situation was changing.

She lay on the backseat of her mother's car. She suffered through the bumps in the driveway, and then the road.

"Keep talking!" her mother yelled from the front seat. "I want to hear your voice!"

"I'm here, Mama."

"What else?"

Regina was speeding. Flannery watched a red traffic light approach and disappear. She allowed herself to remember her drives with Melvin. How much she had loved driving. How much she'd loved the speed. The freedom. The company. The occasional touches of his hand on her arm. Wind blustered through a crack in a window.

"I mean it!" Regina yelled. "Say something. Anything."

"Take care of my birds," Flannery said. "I don't care how much you hate them. I want you to take care of the peacocks. Promise me."

There was a beat of silence from the front seat. The car swiveled right, then accelerated. White sky, hot wind, blurred tree branches.

"I promise." The words were issued through gritted teeth.

"Good."

At the hospital, tucked beneath a tight white sheet, with tubes running from her arms and nose, Flannery thought of Lourdes. She remembered feeling like a swinging door: open to her real life, and open to the one she might have had. She remembered the hope, and the desire. She felt those emotions flicker in her chest now, and thought she might cry.

More of her had seeped away, possibly through the clear tubes and protruding needles, by the time she returned to the farm.

She approached her mother on the porch one afternoon. "The book is done," she said. "I'd like you to send it to my editor, if you don't mind."

"You sure you're done? It's not like you to be satisfied."

Regina's face had aged in the past few months. She felt like she was dying too, but she would, in fact, live for another thirty-one years. Time had found a different way to torture her. Her daughter had been given too little, Regina far too much. It would be impossible for her to appreciate that she might gain some relief, if not joy, from no longer having to care for Flannery. She would deny that, even to herself. She loved her daughter with every fiber of her being.

Flannery met her mother's eyes. After a few seconds, they both had to look away.

Over the following weeks, Flannery rallied, and then declined. Her health became a terrifying, unpredictable roller coaster. Flannery's greatest worry was that she would die suddenly, without having time to receive a final sacrament. So, on an evening when she was feeling neither less nor more unwell than usual, Father Cole stood beside her bed.

He took her confession, then dipped his thumb in oil. He made the sign of the cross on her forehead. He made the sign of the cross on both her hands. When he spoke, it was in a voice so low that Regina couldn't make out the words from her spot in the doorway. She didn't lean forward, or ask him to speak up. She knew what he was saying. She had heard him on another occasion, in a bedroom upstairs.

She knew he was offering her daughter the companionship of God during this final journey. She knew he was giving Flannery permission to set down her heavy burden. He was giving her permission to take leave of her ravaged body. He was giving her permission—he was even encouraging her—to fly away. Regina had to buckle her hands to her sides, and clamp her mouth shut, to keep from objecting at the top of her lungs.

Summer in New York was hot in a different way than summer in Milledgeville. It was more humid; Lona had never sweat much in the past, but while she climbed in and out of subway stations, the perspiration poured out of her. She was aware of the body odor of strangers, and struggled to avoid pressing up against a particularly damp man on the train. She noticed that New Yorkers were less modest than Southerners (at least the ones in Milledgeville). Women wore short skirts and halter tops. Young men walked the streets topless. It wasn't uncommon to see children head to and from the local park wearing only underpants.

Gigi seemed to adapt to this new culture without effort. She wore her hair pulled off her face for the first time in her life, and her basic uniform was a tank top, short shorts, and sandals. While she read over her morning bowl of cereal, she repeatedly tugged at the bra strap that was falling down her arm. Lona felt almost embarrassed, as if she were seeing her daughter in a state of undress. She hadn't seen quite so much of her since she was a baby.

Lona tried to eat her grapefruit, but she was too hot to eat. Gigi didn't seem to have the same problem; her cereal was almost gone.

"I'm not a movie you can just watch," the girl said.

"I know."

Lona had recently become aware that Gigi was now the same age

Joe had been when he died. She would graduate in a few weeks. When Lona asked her about her plans, Gigi said she was going to get a full-time job and move out of the apartment. She offered no details, though, and something about her tone made Lona wonder if her daughter had any plans. She sounded like she might be bluffing. Lona didn't feel she had the right to ask more questions. Gigi attacked her less and less as time went on, but they hardly spoke, either; the silence made it feel like Gigi was already gone.

"Why do you keep doing that?"

"Doing what?" Lona was startled.

"Putting your hand on your side. Are you in pain?"

"No. I'm fine." Why did all of their conversations sound so confused? It seemed as if they spoke different languages and lacked an interpreter. Lona pressed through the fabric of her work skirt to make sure the piece of paper was still there.

"I'll be home late," Gigi said, and bustled out of the apartment, her book under her arm.

Lona slid Cookie's letter from her pocket. She had been carrying it for almost three months. She hadn't intended to leave the bar with it, but between the drinking and the curbside hug, the piece of paper had somehow ended up in her purse. She knew she had to return it to Melvin, but she felt like she needed more time. Twice the phone rang in the evenings while Gigi was at work, and Lona chose not to answer it.

Instead, she read the words over and over. The letter was so short it reminded her of a poem—there was emotion and tumult in every phrase. The bottom line was that Cookie was locked up, just like Bill. What bothered Lona was that she couldn't see what Cookie had done wrong. She hadn't pulled out a gun, or slept with a minor, or even paid secret visits to a friend. She must have erred somehow—Lona could sense the presence of an error, like a squeaky floorboard beneath her foot—but she couldn't name it. Cookie seemed to have done everything right, and in return lost her daughter, her husband, and her sanity.

Lona hadn't really considered the other victims before. She had been unable to move her eyes from Joe's face. But now she thought about Cookie, Miss Mary, and Melvin. She pictured Bill behind bars—for the first time she considered him without anger—and her daughter, bent over a pile of gnarled potatoes.

Lona caught herself crying on the way to work. She realized that the letter had made her feel guilty. She didn't like the emotion, but it was, in a way, satisfying. It was the first time she had felt anything other than grief in as long as she could remember. Even Gigi's best efforts—Lona could see now that her daughter had tried to reach her, to shake something out of her stupor—had failed to puncture her pain.

But the image of Cookie locked in a padded room, day after day, also reminded Lona that she was free. She was no longer tethered to Bill, or Milledgeville, or even Joe. If she chose to look in the rearview mirror, it was by choice, not obligation. Lona was walking down a crowded sidewalk, hundreds of miles from her old life, with her hands in her pockets. She had gotten away.

At the office that morning, she found it easier to focus on her typing. On her way home, she considered pulling out her sewing machine and making herself a new outfit. The thought was so unusual, so frivolous, that she smiled.

When she called Melvin, they arranged to meet in Central Park during her lunch hour.

"Do you have it?" he asked, after pleasantries. He had brought sandwiches, chips, and sodas.

She handed him the letter. "This is too much."

"Nonsense. It's lunch." He folded the paper carefully, as if the yellow card was hot to the touch, and slid it in his pocket.

With their business complete, they leaned back against the bench, sandwiches on their laps. They watched men in business suits stride past.

Women pushed strollers occupied by sleeping children. A black man on roller skates, sporting fat headphones, floated by.

"I come here every day," Melvin said. "It's part of my routine."

"What's your routine?"

Melvin told her about his schedule, and his detective novels.

Lona couldn't help but look surprised. She had never heard anything like it. "You have a lot of free time."

He shrugged. "It's not *free* time."

She offered him an expression of sympathy. She wouldn't want to have her time empty of requirements. She needed a job to get up for, and a daughter to feed. Without those buttresses in place, she might collapse.

"Maybe you should look for work," she said.

He looked down at his hands. His face contorted, as if he were coming up with one answer after another, but none of them were right.

Lona picked up her sandwich. Her appetite showed up suddenly, like a late guest flying through the door, and she ate with satisfied bites. Her eyes moved around the scenery. She was curious about the world—this was another recent change.

Melvin said, "I keep having the same dream at night."

"Oh?"

He kept his eyes down. There was a little girl giggling at the far end of the walkway; Lona knew that he was avoiding the sight of her. She avoided the sight of young, brown-haired men all the time.

"Cookie is following me around the city." He paused. "She's a few steps behind me, and she's talking, but I can't make out the words. She's not yelling. It seems like she's telling me something important." He shook his head. "Every night, before I go to sleep, I tell myself that tonight I'm going to stop walking and listen, but I never do."

Lona didn't know what to say, so she kept quiet.

"She has this expression on her face. I don't know how to describe it." His voice dropped.

Lona put her hand on his arm. She wished she still had the letter in her possession. She had derived some strength and clarity from the correspondence, but it was clearly a source of pain for Melvin. She wanted to help him.

He was silent, his face a closed door.

Lona recognized his expression, and the desperation behind it. She said, "Maybe we should do this once a week. Meet here for lunch. It might be good for us."

Melvin was already still; now he seemed to freeze. "I can't remember the last time I ate a meal with another person."

Lona nodded. She kept her eyes on the yellow paper jutting out of Melvin's pocket. It looked like a sail, floating against the blue of his pants. This seemed appropriate to Lona, because—in an effort to make sense of things—she had begun to picture her life as an ocean.

She had been submerged until Joe, and then her head burst through the surface and she gulped air and saw the shining blue sky and the crowing birds and smelled the salty, spectacular air. When Joe died, she simply sank below the water's surface again. She was under water, but not drowning. She knew, thanks in part to the letter, that there were people worse off than her. She, at least, had memories of when she had truly loved, and truly lived. She knew what that felt like; she knew, intellectually anyway, that it could happen again.

"The dream has gotten so bad that I don't want to sleep," Melvin said. "I want to stay awake, day after day."

Lona considered this. She scanned the horizon for blond girls and curly-haired farm boys and at the same time tried to come up with a response that would offer Melvin some relief.

Finally, she said, "Stay awake, then."

He looked at her.

Lona met his eyes and gave a firm nod. She tried to convince him with her face that she was serious. After all, she no longer believed in physical laws; she no longer believed in anything. Which meant that anything was possible.

The noise saturated the air around the hospital. It pushed through the closed front door and gassed open the windows. It pulled strips of paint from the already peeling walls.

"Do you hear that?" a nurse shouted.

"Do I *hear* that?" another nurse asked, incredulous.

"What is it?"

"Whatever it is, it's bad news."

"What can we do?"

The attendants, nurses, and doctors waved their arms in the air, as if they might be able to fight off the sound.

A few patients moaned. One pounded on his door. There were confused voices and garbled sobs. The inmates were accustomed to strange sounds and unexpected discomforts, though, so on the whole, they took it better than the staff.

Cookie sat beside her window. She didn't hear anything unusual. A hum occupied her mind. She pictured images from the puzzles she had done at her parents' house. She saw ships and meadows and mountains. These were live shots, though; moving pictures instead of still photos. The white sailboat bobbled in the ocean, a young man at the helm. The meadow rippled with golden wheat, baked by warm and constant sunlight. Snow-capped mountains, peppered with skiers, reared up into the sky. The winter sportsmen zigged and zagged across the white powder, wide smiles on their faces.

While the nurses shouted in the hall and the attendants ran around closing windows, Cookie's images took a turn for the worse. In the seascape, the horizon darkened and lightning frazzled the sky. The man tipped his head back, his eyes anxious.

A giant harvester moved across the sunlit field, systematically mowing down the wheat. One yellow stalk after another disappeared from view and was pulped to a fine dust.

The face of the largest mountain took on a strange complexion. Under a bright sky, the snow acquired shadows. The packed powder crumpled, then sagged. Chunks broke free. The pieces rolled and gathered speed. They quickly became boulders, and the boulders swelled to the size of houses. The skiers weren't yet aware of the approaching avalanche. They played below, in their final seconds.

The screams stopped as abruptly as they had started.

There was peace, and the scent of a calm summer day.

The staff shrugged, and went back to work. The doctors issued orders to double the afternoon medication, in order to calm any frayed nerves. Cookie, slick with sweat, fell asleep sitting upright in her chair.

An ambulance sped past the hospital, its siren barely noticeable after the din. The vehicle was headed in the direction of Andalusia.

Look

Melvin was halfway through a cup of coffee, and hadn't yet touched his oatmeal. The waiter had just set the steaming bowl down. When he took a breath, the air smelled of cinnamon.

He scanned the newspaper, trying to decide which article to start with. The picture caught his eye first. He saw curled hair, cat's-eye glasses, her chin.

Flannery.

He gave himself a second on the image, then lowered his eyes. He expected the headline to say something about a literary prize, or a new book. He had to read the words several times for them to make sense. His eyes swept the line like a broom. The content didn't change, though, no matter how hard he stared.

"Southern Writer Dies at Her Peak."

He folded the paper in half and set it down.

The next thing he knew, he was standing on the sidewalk.

It was rush hour. Taxi drivers leaned on their horns. Pedestrians swarmed across the nearest intersection. There was a determined shine to people's faces. Coffee cups jutted out in front of them, like flashlights necessary for them to find their way in the dark.

Melvin realized that he was holding his breath. He released it and coughed. The cough made his entire body shudder, like an engine igniting after a long rest. He started to walk. He left the side street and turned onto the avenue. He wasn't sure where he was headed. He walked faster. Not satisfied by the pace, the walk became a jog, and then a run. Relief warmed his lungs.

This was what he wanted to do. He wanted to run.

He crossed the avenue and headed east. He hadn't exercised since high school, and he was wearing expensive leather loafers, but the speed felt good. It felt right. His arms pumped at his sides. His knees rose and fell. People got out of the way.

There was a hum in his ears that he struggled to identify; it wasn't a single noise, but the blur of many sounds. He crossed the final avenue before the park. He weaved through a group of tourists pointing cameras at the sky. He was trapped, for a brief moment, between a heavyset man and three little boys holding balloons. Melvin could feel his heart beating in his ears. It thudded, like a bass drum.

He panicked, shimmied sideways, and broke free. He thrashed his feet against the sidewalk, scuffing his shoes, his knees pumping up and down. He strayed onto the grass and found another gear, thrusting his arms like pistons on a steam train. He sped past trees and fountains and a pond dotted with rowboats. Melvin gasped for air. His throat began to burn. Sweat ran into his eyes and down his cheeks.

The muscles in his thighs smoldered and blazed. There was a tugging sensation in his joints. His mouth tasted of blood. He must have bitten his tongue somehow. He soared past actual runners, lean young men in sweatpants and sneakers. He passed a boy resting against a lamppost with his hands in his pockets. Heads turned in Melvin's direction; people wondering, *What's wrong with that man?*

He bore down on the reservoir. A pool of deep water, a high fence, trees with skyscrapers peering over the top. Melvin had never felt like this before. His heart had taken over his body, the thumps so rapid they blurred into a single reverberation. It was one continuous spasm, keeping him alive. His breath squeaked like air leaving a tire.

He lapped the reservoir. Two laps. Three. Melvin's body was failing beneath him, his being now composed entirely of pain. Every inch of his skin, every organ, every cell screamed for mercy. He had the sudden insight, as he started lap four, that his heart was going to explode. Any second now. If he continued to run—and he would continue to run—he would die.

The idea, instead of alarming him, excited him. His brain, which was now overwhelmed with oxygen, seemed to find the prospect of death more tolerable than usual. Melvin ached and burned and sweated his way toward an invisible finish line. He was grinning. He was crying.

He was suddenly in the air.

A few seconds of weightlessness, spinning, and he landed on his back. Hard. The air, which had become so difficult to come by, was knocked clean out of him. His body made a horrible sound, like a donkey braying. He watched his chest lurch upward, then fall back down, and repeat, spasmodically, of its own volition.

He had tripped on something, and tumbled down a slope beside the running track. He was lying on a pile of moss. His breathing began to sound more like breathing. His body twitched, the muscles and nerves wondering what had happened to them, wondering what would happen next. Melvin closed his eyes, turned his head to the side, and vomited.

Spasms ripped vertically through his throat. He retched and heaved. He was still vomiting when he became aware of a warmth spreading across his thighs. It took a moment for him to realize that he was urinating on himself. Melvin shook again, this time with a convulsion of laughter. He was too far gone to be embarrassed. Instead, this seemed hilarious. The contents of his body were jumping ship, no longer confident that he was a trustworthy captain.

Only now did Melvin allow himself to think of Flannery. Lying at the foot of a mossy hill, entirely spent, he felt strangely connected to her. He thought of their car rides. He thought of their conversations, their arguments, their silences. He remembered the sound of her laughter, and the surge of pleasure he always felt in response. He thought of his final afternoon at the farm. The moments of peace, before the eruption. The sunlight, the smell of grass and dirt, the joy in Rose's blue eyes. The softening in Flannery's voice.

He was able to see a few things clearly.

Flannery had been right. He had wasted his life. He'd had a few chances to truly live, and he had screwed up each and every one of them. He'd lost the people that mattered. He had done what he thought he was supposed to do, and not what he wanted to do. He had simply filled thousands of days: woken up, passed the hours, and gone to bed. He had loved—of that there was no doubt—but he had been a coward. It was his fault that his daughter was gone. It was his fault that his wife was in a mental hospital. It was his fault that Flannery had died without knowing what she meant to him.

All of this felt true, and all of this was unforgivable. Melvin couldn't change anything that had happened, but he could change things that were yet to happen. These realizations came at him in a sudden rush, one concrete block falling from his chest after another. Sitting in his apartment hadn't helped anyone. His routine, his quiet, his solitude—none of this had made a damned thing better. He could see that now.

He sat up; the world tipped from side to side like elephants on a seesaw. He waited until his vision steadied and then climbed to his knees. His legs jabbered beneath him. They begged him to lie back down, to stay still, and yet, he rose to his feet. He looked down at himself. His shirt was soaked with sweat. There were splotches of blood in a diagonal line across his chest. His pants were grass-stained, ripped at the knees, and damp. He took a careful step, to test his joints. Nothing appeared to be broken. In fact, all things considered, he felt surprisingly fine.

He headed out of the park with a long stride.

An idea was emerging. A shiver threaded down his spine.

He smiled at the audacity of the notion and ignored the stares of pass-ersby. His heart was thumping in his chest again, this time with excite-ment. He devoured the blocks, the landscape reduced to a blur around him. He approached his building and bounded up the curb. With sweat, vomit, and urine on full display, Melvin flashed a wide smile, and the startled doorman doffed his hat.

R egina was in the kitchen when the phone rang. She had moved into town after the funeral, and was still getting used to the house. This new phone was shrill and always made her jump.

She resolved not to answer. After the tenth ring, though, the sound was driving her crazy, so she grabbed the receiver. She didn't say hello; she just listened. The man on the other end of the line was a stranger, and difficult to understand.

"You're calling about my daughter's words?" she yelled. Regina didn't mind crazy people, but she wasn't going to give them her time. This caller had another thirty seconds to make sense before she would hang up and go back to preparing her lunch of two slices of roast beef on white bread with mayonnaise.

"Your daughter's *birds*, Mrs. O'Connor. Flannery's peacocks, her pets, the birds."

Regina pursed her lips. "They're bothering you too? Where do you live exactly? If you're over two miles away, then you're wasting my time." She had recently fielded a call from an old woman in Macon who claimed to have been disturbed by the peacocks, even though she lived thirty-five miles from Andalusia.

"No, ma'am. They're not bothering me."

"Where do you live?"

"Nashville, ma'am. Please don't hang up. I'm with *Southern Communities Magazine*, and we ran a piece about Flannery and her peacocks. Anyway, folks are broken up about her passing, they really are. Some are readers, some aren't. They just felt like they knew her. We've been swamped with calls and letters from folks who just wanted to do something. We got eighteen offers from individuals and institutions offering to give the peacocks a happy home. To take them off your hands, as it were. And I've got a college kid who's willing to liaise the whole project. You won't have to do a thing."

There was silence.

"Mrs. O'Connor?"

Regina was thinking: *Home, happy home, the birds had a happy home, I had a happy home, this is not a happy home.* She looked at the roast beef and the white bread. She had no appetite.

"Is this a joke?"

"No, ma'am."

"Eighteen people want those awful birds?" Her voice had lost its bluster. She had the sound of a punctured balloon.

That afternoon, Regina lay down for a nap. She told herself: *You are an old woman. You should rest.* She couldn't sleep, though. She lay on her side and watched light shine through the bare window. The day seemed very long. She was accustomed to constant activity. She wondered how she was going to get used to this kind of quiet.

There was a knock at the front door, and she sat up. She perched on the edge of the bed and listened to the door frame rattle. She considered ignoring the sound and lying back down.

"Regina O'Connor, I know you're in there!"

She sighed and traveled down the stairs. She swung the door open and blinked into the direct sunlight.

"You asked for time," Miss Mary said. "So I gave you time."

"Not enough. I need more."

Miss Mary crossed her arms over her chest. The large woman had changed physically in the prior eighteen months. There were more lines on her face, and she was thinner. She was slow to smile.

"I want to be here for you," she said. "I know what you're going through. I *understand*."

Regina sighed. She wondered how many times she had sighed since Flannery's death. Hundreds, probably. "Your understanding doesn't help."

"Well, nothing helps. But you don't have to be alone. You don't have to cook or clean. I can help you with those things."

Regina remembered showing up at Miss Mary's door, trying to introduce some fresh air and conversation into that musty house. She wondered if her house smelled. She took a step back and turned toward the kitchen. She listened to the thump of Miss Mary's footsteps behind her.

Regina put the kettle on the stove. Miss Mary opened the refrigerator door and leaned in. "I need to do some shopping," she said. "That's abundantly clear. You need everything. Mr. Treadle said he was hoping I would cook for you so he could at least get some leftovers."

Regina stood by the back door. She wondered why she had wanted to stay inside ever since the funeral, yet was drawn to windows and doors.

"I think he might be in luck. You need soup. You're always cold, right?"

Regina nodded. She couldn't pile enough blankets on top of her at night. Right now, her fingers were like icicles. She was wearing a turtleneck sweater and a cardigan.

"Soup and casseroles will do the job." Miss Mary sounded like she was thinking out loud. "You need warm food that doesn't require much chewing. I couldn't bite my way through a steak for a year. It was too much work."

She was in the cupboard now. She pulled out a box of cookies. "At least we have something to nibble on with our tea. When we're finished I'll head to the market. Would you like to come? It might make you feel better to leave the house for a few minutes."

Regina wasn't listening. She let her old friend's words run over her. She stared at the colors outside. Green, yellow, red, blue. Grass, hyacinths, roses, sky. She pictured her daughter standing in the back corner of the yard. Leaning into her crutches, smelling the flowers. Flannery had always liked flowers. She had pretended not to care when the birds ate everything but the stems, but in truth she always derived great pleasure from Regina's garden. She weighed in, every spring, on what should be planted.

The kettle whistled.

Regina left the window reluctantly. She positioned herself behind the steaming cup and watched wisps disappear into the air.

Miss Mary considered her friend. She said, "We'll just take this one day at a time, okay?"

"Okay."

The clock on the wall made its rounds. The pilot light on the stove clicked on and off. Miss Mary tipped teaspoons of sugar into her mug.

"Oh, I forgot," she said. "Your farmhand asked me to pass on a message. He said he couldn't get through to you on the phone."

"He's complaining about the peacocks again?"

"He said they've spread out, away from the house. They're sleeping in the tractor, and one of them knocked over an oil drum. They're driving him crazy." Miss Mary paused. "I can attest to the noise. They're screaming for Flannery, day and night, loud as I ever heard."

Regina took a sip of tea, even though she knew the liquid was still too hot. It scalded the back of her throat, but she drank it anyway. When the mug was empty, she said, "They're getting picked up in a few weeks."

"The peacocks? Really? You found homes for them?"

She nodded.

Miss Mary was quiet for a minute. "I know that's what you wanted, but still, it's sad."

Regina struggled to speak past the lump in her throat. "Is it?"

Melvin appeared in the doorway, a vision from one of her dreams.

Cookie regarded him from her seat by the window. He looked tired; his hair was graying around the edges.

Warm air brushed one side of her face. She had just been remembering how, as a child, she spent hot summer days like this one almost entirely outside. That seemed remarkable to her. How had she given so many hours to climbing trees, squinting at the sun, pumping her legs on the swing set, and chasing other children? How had she maintained that level of energy?

She noticed the way Melvin was staring at her, and turned her face away. Maybe he wasn't a vision, after all. His expression was the one people pointed at her these days: a mixture of horror and pity.

She listened to him cross the room. He dropped to his knees beside her chair.

"Oh, God," he said. "Cookie." There was a pause. "I'm so sorry."

It had been weeks since she'd spoken aloud. The effort involved was far too great. Cookie hoped one of the nurses had told him that this was the case so he wouldn't take her silence personally.

"How could this be allowed to happen?"

She wondered what, exactly, he was referring to.

He made a noise in his throat, a strangled sound.

Cookie felt her mind drift. She was ten years old, scaling the big tree behind her house. She looked for one foothold, then another. She held her breath in concentration; she refused to fall.

Melvin's touch drew her back. First he held her hand, then he reached up to stroke her hair. The contact made Cookie uncomfortable, although she thought it was very brave of him. The only person who touched her anymore was the nurse assigned to help her bathe.

"I just came from your parents' house," he said. "They didn't tell me . . ." He shook his head. "I want to make things right."

For a moment, the only sound was both of them breathing. They seemed to take turns. First Cookie, then Melvin. Cookie, then Melvin.

He said, "I used to think that wasn't possible, but I don't anymore." Cookie continued to breathe, as if it was her job.

His hand cradled the side of her face. He whispered her name.

Melvin sounded like he might cry. Cookie wondered whether it was her, or this place, that cracked people wide open. She was too tired to know the answer, and too tired to really care. She was sorry, though, when Melvin pulled his hand away and stood up to leave.

She was assigned a new doctor. He was beardless and much younger than her previous physician. He shook her hand vigorously, as if he were truly happy to meet her. On her first day under his care, she was given six pills instead of sixteen. During her bath that night, Cookie was surprised to find herself actually listening to the nurse's story about her mischievous new puppy. The following morning, she opened her eyes of her own accord for the first time in as long as she could remember, instead of waiting to feel a hand shake her shoulder.

When Melvin came to visit, he brought a book for himself and a magazine for her. They sat together in silence for the duration of his stay. He methodically turned pages while Cookie studied the pictures in the magazine.

Within a week, the daily total was three small pills that she had no problem swallowing. She dressed herself, and even did her hair. She was able to form thoughts and hold on to them, instead of having to release each one like a balloon. When the doctor and nurses spoke to her, she gave clear, reasoned replies. Before meals, she felt a strange cramping in her midsection that she couldn't make sense of until the food arrived. It turned out that she was hungry. She cleaned the tray, and asked for more.

When Melvin showed up, she felt her face break into a smile. "What's that?" she asked.

He looked down at the box in his arms, as if he'd forgotten it was there. "I don't want you to feel like you have to talk," he said, "unless you want to. This gives us something to do."

He unpacked the backgammon board, and they each chose a color piece. Neither of them had played the game since childhood, so they had to review the rules several times.

When they made the same mistake three times in a row, Cookie laughed.

Melvin looked startled. He put down the rules manual and rubbed his hand across his eyes.

"What's wrong?" she asked.

"Nothing," he said. "I had something in my eye. I think I figured out what we're doing wrong."

They soon developed a rhythm, and found themselves evenly matched. They played several games per visit, and Melvin visited every day. He appeared to have special hospital privileges, and was permitted to come and go as he pleased.

Cookie's attention sometimes wandered. The visits sapped her energy, but her strength and focus steadily improved. Her fog dissipated, as if she'd driven through a dense storm into a clear, sunny afternoon.

"What will you do, when you go back to New York?" she asked during a particularly long match.

Melvin shrugged, his concentration on the board.

"You should go back and slay dragons."

He looked up. "Excuse me?"

"You don't belong here."

"*You* don't belong here."

"I didn't mean in the hospital." She surveyed the board and shifted a few pieces to the right. She wanted to win the game, and she could see a path to that conclusion. She sighed and stretched her arms over her head. Cookie felt restless in her seat. She found that her moods shifted rapidly since her change in medication. She liked her new clarity, but she also found it unsettling.

Melvin cleared his throat. "What will you do, when you leave here?"

This answer was easy; she knew it by heart. "Take care of my parents. They're starting to need help, and God knows they've spent enough of their lives taking care of me."

He gave a slow nod. "Your parents are angry with me."

"I know."

"Why aren't you?"

She picked over her thoughts, as if trying to find a small, particular item in a crowded handbag. "We're on the other side of it," she said.

Melvin's mouth worked. He looked like he was about to say something.

There was a knock at the door; a nurse leaned in. "Can I get you two anything?"

"No, thank you." The door shut, and Cookie smiled. "They're so nice to me when you're here."

"Are they not nice to you in general? You'd tell me if there was a problem, right?"

Cookie's gaze returned to the black-and-white circles on the board. She didn't like it when Melvin stared directly at her. She knew that she was too thin, that her face had aged, that she was no longer pretty, and she didn't know what to do with that information. She didn't know who she was. "Everyone is nice to me," she said. "All the time."

They buckled down, and completed the game in silence. Cookie won, which took their running tally to twenty-seven games in her favor, with twenty-five for Melvin.

"I could use a soda," he said. "Would you like one?"

"Yes, please."

When he left the room, she walked to the window. It was a hot day, and even with the window open, the air in the room hardly moved. There was a noise in the distance, a cutting scream. It was one of the peacocks. Cookie had begun to hear them only recently, although she realized the noise must have been there all along.

She allowed herself to picture Andalusia, and Flannery. She had heard about her death from one of the nurses, although the news had come as no surprise. Cookie felt like she had already known. The announcement made her think, though, about how she and Flannery had been young together. About how they had sat side by side at the beginning of their lives. Both healthy, smooth-skinned, and hopeful. She could remember the feel of the sun on her arms, the sound of Flannery's girlish laugh, the taste of the cookies that Regina brought them during visits to the farm.

Cookie thought of her own sweet baby girl, of Lona and Joe kissing in her house, and Bill Waters trapped behind bars. She thought of all the mothers in town who had lost their children: Miss Mary, Regina, and herself. Even her own mother had suffered a loss; every Sunday when she visited, Daisy was a woman in mourning. Cookie thought about how there were expected deaths, and unexpected ones, but that the result was the same either way.

Flannery's death had nudged a tectonic plate deep inside Cookie. Beneath her fog, she felt her perspective slowly shift. She became aware, for the first time in a long time, that she wanted to live. She was sorry that Flannery hadn't been so lucky.

When she turned around, Melvin was there. He put a chilled bottle into her hand. "Do you feel up to another game?"

"You don't usually stay this long."

"Would you rather be alone?"

She answered honestly. "No."

She watched while he set up the board. The soda tasted good: sticky, sweet, and cold.

He said, "I'm flying back to New York at the end of the week."

"Really?" Cookie was aware of a stab of disappointment in her stomach.

"I didn't expect to be here this long."

Her turn, his turn, her turn. He was ahead, but it was still early in the game.

Cookie fingered one of the smooth round pieces. It felt like sea glass, or one of the worn rocks she used to throw into Lake Sinclair as a child. The piece had a satisfying weight in her palm. "I'll enjoy reading about your future achievements in the newspaper," she said. "You put the black piece in the wrong row."

"What? Oh, I see." He moved it to the correct place.

She slid her piece across the board.

"Cookie?" Melvin said.

"Yes?"

He looked at her.

She looked at him.

"Do you want to come with me?"

She frowned. "Where?"

"To New York." His voice sounded strange, as if his heartbeat was interfering with the words, throwing off the rhythm of his speech. "We could have a second try at everything. We could start over. We could even . . ." His voice trailed off.

"Are you sure you should be saying this?" The words came out quickly. She held on to the arms of her chair as if he were going to drag her away right now.

"Yes." He paused; he seemed to struggle for words again. "Yes, I am."

She shook her head.

"I feel like I could say anything to you now. I can be myself with you.

You can be yourself with me. And we had moments together even then, didn't we?" He rubbed his hands across his knees, as if his palms were sweating. "We could take care of your parents. We could set them up here and you could visit, or they could move to the city. The adventure might make them feel young again. I think your dad would like it."

"Melvin." Cookie felt flattened into her seat, as if she were already on an airplane and it was throttling skyward.

"Think about it. Don't answer right now. Just think about it." He pointed at the board. He took a shaky breath, and released it. "It's your move."

Cookie thought about it that night. She thought about everything. The doctor had recently told her that she was ready to be released. She had disagreed. She told him that she needed more time. He looked at her from a place of great stillness and calm. He said, *You can have whatever you need, but the truth is that you're ready to go out there again.*

Melvin had said, *We could even . . .*

Her window was wide open. Warm air laced the room. She smelled magnolia blossoms, wet grass, gardenias. The full moon draped the bed in pale light. Cookie was aware of a feeling of fullness as she breathed in the dappled air.

A peacock squealed, shattering the peace. The shrill cry brought back the night before her wedding. She remembered pitching off her bed in the darkness. She remembered the shock and surprise and ferocious pleasure of Melvin's hands traveling her body.

Cookie was full from dinner, full from three little pills, full from weeks of talk after months of silence. She looked out the gaping window, and allowed herself to consider a future.

Gigi read at the gate, and kept reading when they allowed her onto the airplane. She tried to keep her attention pinned on the book even as the behemoth lurched into the sky. She failed, and tried again. Her eyes skidded across the page.

"First flight?" the man beside her asked.

She nodded.

"Piece of cake," he said, and then, as if to prove his point, tipped his head back and fell asleep.

Gigi told herself not to look out the window. The stewardess arrived with the drinks cart, and Gigi gratefully accepted a glass of water. She used the paper napkin to blot her face. When the plane gave a frightening bump, like a rodeo horse trying to buck his rider, she pressed her hand to her mouth. She looked around and saw that none of the other passengers had even noticed.

She reached into her bag and pulled out the material the magazine editor had sent. She kept his letter in a green folder, along with the original article, which was now food-stained and torn. She took those words in, trying to keep her focus on something she *could* control.

She had called the editor the same day the librarian found the article, and asked if there was any way she could help with the relocation of

Flannery's peacocks. She said that she was a fan of the author's work and would like to be involved.

"Well," he had said, in a thick drawl. "The mother is grieving, so maybe you could help with logistics. Make sure the peacocks get where they're going. Supervise the first couple of days. You could even act as the contact person for the recipients."

"Absolutely," Gigi said.

"You can get yourself there? We don't have the funds . . ."

"Absolutely."

She didn't tell him that she was from Milledgeville. She didn't tell him that she knew the grieving mother. She didn't tell him that she had known Flannery. She didn't tell him that the peacocks meant something to her, and that following them to their new homes sounded a lot like salvation.

To be fair, the editor didn't ask any questions. He simply told her he would put the details in the mail, and hung up the phone.

Gigi had bought a one-way ticket with her saved wages, and packed all her belongings into two suitcases. She told Lona she would call her when she reached her destination, wherever that turned out to be. Her mother had just nodded, but that night Gigi heard her crying through the thin wall.

The plane twisted left, and Gigi's stomach tightened. She leafed through the information about the separate destinations for the peacocks. In making her decision, Regina had tried to honor Flannery's Catholicism, and her fondness for the state of Georgia. A third of the peacocks would be given to Stone Mountain Park outside of Atlanta, where they would live in the semiwilderness beneath carved heads of the three Confederate heroes: Davis, Jackson, and Lee. Another third would be taken in by Our Lady of Perpetual Help Cancer Home, and the final slice would live with the Benedictine monks at Our Lady of the Holy Spirit Monastery.

Gigi had done research into the three locations, and she had concerns. Her grandparents lived near Stone Mountain Park, and had taken her there as a child. She knew the grounds were filled with foxes, bears, and other wild animals. How would the domesticated peacocks survive such lethal cohabitants? She pictured the fat birds hiding in the highest branches, calling out to one another in alarm.

Our Lady was a home for terminally ill cancer patients. Men and women spent their final weeks there, dozing in bed or meditating beside the rose garden. Such serenity would be rudely derailed if a peacock were to strut along, bite the head off a rose, and then scream in their faces. These patients were attached to oxygen machines; many could eat only through tubes. How would they survive the obnoxious volume of the peacocks? How could anyone die in peace with one of those birds in their ear?

The monastery seemed like it had more potential. The monks who lived, prayed, and labored on the grounds were members of the Order of Cistercians of the Strict Observance, and they followed the Rule of Saint Benedict. They walked the grounds in black-and-white habits and broke into prayer and song at all hours. Two in the morning, six in the morning, three in the afternoon, their voices pierced the air. Gigi could imagine the peacocks happily joining in, offering their own kind of holy ruckus. Of course, that would only work if their noise was welcomed and embraced.

The plane's nose dropped abruptly, and Gigi forgot about the birds. She held her breath. She didn't fully release it until the wheels slapped the runway. She was glad to take part when the passengers around her broke into polite applause. The safe flight seemed to her a kind of miracle.

She gathered her bags. She knew a taxi was picking her up. She knew she was going to Milledgeville, but chose not to dwell on that fact. She would be there for only a few hours. The editor had told her that she would be the sole person at the farm when the trucks arrived for the birds. Gigi would be in charge, and as soon as the peacocks were packed up and ready to leave, she would leave with them.

Miss Mary stood by the baggage carousel holding a sign. She had terrible handwriting, so Mr. Treadle had written the name of the magazine on a piece of poster board before she left for the airport. Normally, she would have refused outright to drive as far as Atlanta on her own to pick up a stranger, but she knew Regina was more anxious about this day than she was letting on, and she wanted to help out in any way she could.

Miss Mary could also feel the significance of the day. She recognized the hills and mountains that marked the terrain of loss; she was experiencing them all over again through her friend. After Joe's death, there had been the funeral, and then two months later, circled in red on the kitchen calendar, was the day he was supposed to start working full-time on the farm. That day was harder than the one in church and on the uneven dirt of the graveyard. The numbness had worn off, and Miss Mary spent that day imagining life as it had been planned, life as it should have been. Joe eating bacon and eggs at the kitchen table, then pulling his boots on by the back door. The sight of him through the small window above the sink while he drove the tractor to the cornfield. The sunburn on his cheeks when he came inside for lunch. His shout of laughter at the dinner table while he teased his mother and she teased him back.

Thanksgiving was awful, and she and Mr. Treadle tried to ignore Christmas completely. There were still days when she didn't see the point in getting out of bed, but overall, the pain had diminished to a manageable ache. Miss Mary wanted to help Regina through the worst of her grief, and she knew that involved surviving days like today. Days that meant something, days that stabbed your heart. Regina loved Flannery, and Flannery had loved these peacocks. Saying goodbye to the birds would be like saying goodbye to her daughter all over again, and Miss Mary could sob just thinking about it.

She did let out a small sob, then. It seemed safe, in the anonymity and hustle of the airport. She wept for her friend, she wept for herself, she wept for Joe, for Flannery, for the unsuspecting birds who were about to lose their home for good.

When she was finished, she put the poster board under her arm and fished a tissue from her purse. She felt a small sizzle of relief, as if air had been let out of an overfull tire. She put the tissue up to her face and blew her nose.

"Miss Mary?"

The voice was familiar. The voice made her heart thump in her chest. She lowered her hand.

A terrified girl was standing in front of her. She was holding a suitcase in each hand. She was laden down and shaking. Her hair was pulled back in a ponytail. She was too thin. She looked like the loneliest child in the universe.

Miss Mary, her heart gunning inside her now like an engine warming up for a race, did the only thing she could think to do. The only thing she knew how to do. The only thing, the very thing, she wanted to do more than anything else. She threw her arms open wide and caught Gigi as she fell forward.

R egina watched the car drive up the long driveway and park beside the three white trucks. She shook her head.

"I should have known," she said, when Melvin stepped out of the car. "You were almost as obsessed with these birds as my daughter was."

"I read about it in the paper," he said. "Do you mind?"

She looked over the lawn. The truck drivers and their associates were in a huddle by the porch steps, presumably working out a strategy. The birds were unusually quiet, dotted across the grass and studded throughout the bushes like Christmas ornaments. They seemed to sense that something was about to happen.

She said, "I heard you were back in town, trying to be helpful."

Melvin gave a wry smile. "I'm trying."

Regina turned to study him. It was the same look she gave a cow she wanted to sell, before deciding on the animal's price. The stare lasted several long seconds before her face relaxed. "I have no ill feelings toward you," she said. "You should know that. My daughter considered you a real friend, and she had less of those over the course of her life than I would have liked. She judged you to be worth her time, and I have no interest in second-guessing her judgment."

"Nor do I."

Regina tilted her head to the side, a gesture Flannery had shared.

Melvin's chest ached, but he also felt stronger, like he had passed a test. He wasn't sure whether the test was Regina's, or his own. He figured it didn't really matter.

There was a loud shout, and the men sprang into action. Regina and Melvin stood side by side and watched as six burly men chased, lunged for, wrestled, and lassoed forty peacocks. This was not an easy process. The birds gave all they were worth. They dodged, weaved, jumped, screamed, and spat at their captors. They leapt from limb to limb of the magnolia tree. One man stood at the bottom, his hands wrapped around the thick trunk as though he hoped to shake them free. Several peahens quivered on the porch roof. Others scaled the water tower. A pack zig-zagged across the lawn, darting away from a sweaty pursuer.

From every nook, cranny, and hiding place on the grounds, the peacocks screamed.

Bellowed.

Wailed.

The din was directed at Regina and Melvin. It was directed at the empty farmhouse. It was directed at the empty bedroom, the vacant desk, and the deserted bed. It was directed at the invisible veil between life and death. The peacocks were arrogant enough to think that their screams could raise Flannery from the earth. They thought they could turn back time. They thought they could get exactly what they wanted, if only they could make enough noise.

The sound blasted the sky.

It rattled the farmhouse windows.

It was the sound of desperation and desire.

The burly men clamped their hands over their ears. Regina and Melvin dug their heels into the dirt. Three miles away, in town, the corridors of the empty high school reverberated. The police chief looked up from his midafternoon flask and shuddered. The mayor picked up the phone, certain there was someone he should call in response to the disturbance, but unsure who that was. Big Mike paused over the cash register in his store. Bill Waters, trapped in a distant cell, mistook the birds' cries for the clink of metal doors closing, one after the other.

Cookie stood at the window and let the birds' voices wash over her. She stared at the straight trees and the road that twisted past the massive, square hospital. She could smell the sun-soaked lawn and taste the dirt beneath it. She pressed her hands against the sides of the window, not out of need for support, but in order to feel the smooth paint against her palms. Cookie was due to be released the following morning. The peacocks' cacophony didn't surprise her. It sounded right. She'd been bathed in this sound upon her return to Milledgeville; it was only fitting that it should trumpet her next step, whatever that might be.

Miss Mary and Gigi, still ten miles away in the car, stared at one another. They were late because Miss Mary had felt too shaky to drive right away; they had sat over cups of coffee in an airport café for an hour. They spent the journey talking and laughing and reaching out to touch the other's hand. They had been giddy, almost hysterical, at their reunion. They were silent now. The noise felt like the past to one, and the future to the other.

Lona was walking down a busy avenue in New York. She had finally agreed to go out for a drink with the secretary who shared her desk, and the young woman was chatting at her side. Lona was loosely tracing her words—something about a wink she had received from a man on the subway that morning—when above, below, and through the story, Lona heard the birds. She felt her stride grow longer, and a smile crossed her face. A gust of air filled her lungs, as if they were balloons preparing for takeoff.

Regina understood the peacocks' outrage. She almost appreciated it, standing with her arms crossed over her chest. Their cries made sense. She felt the same way much of the time these days. She woke up in the morning wanting to scream and curse and kick up dust. At least the birds were doing something. They were able to do something. There was nothing Regina could do. She walked around her life straitjacketed, her audience and her responsibility and her heart gone.

Melvin stared at the white farmhouse, the chairs on the porch, the spot where he had laid down his daughter's blanket. It was hard to accept that Flannery was dead; hard to believe that a light that bright could be extinguished. She had been so fiercely alive. She had spoken honestly, and lived with an honesty that few could claim to match. She had made the most of every minute she was given. She bargained and rationed and managed the seconds. She burned up the days. Melvin had simply been drawn to her, like a moth to a flame.

He felt like he was standing in her presence now. He felt like she was issuing a challenge with this wall of sound. She was demanding the best of him, once and for all. Melvin watched a red-haired man throw a net over the biggest of the peacocks. The bird puffed out his chest and stared the flame-haired man in the eye. The man gaped for a moment, and then, in a seemingly animal response, pushed out his own chest. He flexed the muscles in his arms and growled an obscenity. He tugged the net tighter, crumpling the peacock's feathers.

The peacock was unperturbed. He seemed not to notice, or believe, that he had been contained. Slowly, deliberately, the bird shook his tail. It waved back and forth, a thin pointed reed at first, then a dark triangle, then a swell of motion. Melvin watched the tail shake free and the feathers spread. Sea green, inky sapphire, specks of yellow—the shimmering colors cascaded up into the air, pushing the loose weave of the net aside.

Acknowledgments

I want to thank my parents, Cathy and Jim Napolitano, for their unflagging love and support. They are wonderful parents, and people. I have been very fortunate in the parental department.

My agent, Elaine Koster, sadly passed away before this book became a book. She was one of my best readers, and I appreciated and depended on her constant faith in my ability. I'll miss her.

I have been blessed with two great editors. Janie Fleming loved this book and pushed me to make it the best it could be. She went beyond the call of duty and was a huge help to me. Ginny Smith took over the novel with grace and generosity, and guided it to the finish line. Her input has been invaluable and has helped to make the book what it is.

Julie Barer is wonderful, and I'm very pleased to have her in my life. The same goes for Brettne Bloom, who led me through a tricky period with her inimitable poise and style. I am thankful for her friendship.

It is because of Blanche McCrary Boyd that Flannery O'Connor showed up in this novel at all. It makes perfect sense to me that Blanche, who had the greatest influence on my start as a writer, would introduce me to my subject.

Most of all, I need to thank my husband. No one challenges me or expects more from me than he does. It took six years to write this book, and he was at my side—questioning, cajoling, and cheering—the entire time. Everything is better because of him.